She was born Gina Rossi, daughter of an Italian restaurant owner executed by Mussolini's Fascists. At seventeen, orphaned and penniless, and with a young brother and sister to support, she had landed in New York, determined to survive.

And survive she did. Now, twenty years later, Gina Cornell is a media darling, a beautiful, talented and above all successful entrepreneur in booming 50's America. Owner of New York's most fashionable restaurant, of Las Vegas's swankiest night-club, of a phenomenally successful chain of franchised eateries, and married into the Cornell family whose hotel floors she had once scrubbed, Gina has it made. Her empire is growing, expanding into hotels – and into the movie business.

THE LAST SUMMER was Robert Fallon's masterpiece, a war novel to rank with THE NAKED AND THE DEAD. Now the company filming it is in trouble. Gina, trapped in a loveless marriage, and dreaming still of her wartime romance with Fallon, decides on a rescue bid. Only one woman stands in her way: Barbara Graham, a mysterious ex-movie star with a scandalous past. Without her say-so no deal can be done. But as Gina moves into deeper waters, the sharks begin to gather. For Gina has enemies, big and small, who will do anything to bring her down. Physically and financially, in secret and in broad daylight, Gina is under attack. As she struggles to protect her empire and her family, to win back the man she loves, she begins to see everything she has fought for slipping away from her. And when the grim shadow of McCarthyism falls over her lover and her brother, Gina finds herself facing a cruel and agonizing dilemma.

Continuing the story told in THE LADY, Alan Stratton has created in Gina Rossi a memorable heroine with an overwhelming passion for life: GINA is a rich, absorbing saga of life, love and danger at the top.

Also by Alan Stratton 1988

THE EMPIRE BUILDERS
THE PEDDLERS
THE HUNTERS
THE LADY

ALAN STRATTON

Macdonald

A *Macdonald* Book

Copyright © Alan Stratton 1988

First published in Great Britain in 1988 by
Macdonald & Co (Publishers) Ltd,
London & Sydney

All characters in this publication are fictitious and any resemblance to real persons, living or dead, is purely coincidental.

No part of this publication may be reproduced, stored in a retrieval system, or transmitted, in any form or by any means without the prior permission in writing of the publisher, nor be otherwise circulated in any form of binding or cover other than that in which it is published and without a similar condition including this condition being imposed on the subsequent purchaser.

British Library Cataloguing in Publication Data

Stratton, Alan
  Gina.
  I. Title
823'.914[F]

ISBN 0-356-12292-1

Photoset in North Wales by
Derek Doyle & Associates, Mold, Clwyd
Printed and bound in Great Britain by
Richard Clay Ltd, Bungay, Suffolk

Macdonald & Co (Publishers) Ltd
Greater London House
Hampstead Road
London NW1 7QX

A Member of Pergamon MCC Publishing Corporation plc

Chapter One

A million dollars.

Whistling enthusiastically, Gina strode along Fifth Avenue figuring what to do with a million dollars. Thirty minutes ago, Wheldon Hoyt had been advising caution, secure investment against a rainy day. Gina might have pointed out she couldn't see a cloud on the horizon; the money should be working for them not lying around growing old. But that would only have prompted the banker's set lecture on the folly of 'speculative commercial intercourse', and Gina was too full of this sunlit April morning to draw the shades of financial prudence.

With a smile to the corner news vendor which lit up the rest of his day, she skipped from the sidewalk, dodging traffic across the hectic intersection, her brain buzzing with schemes for her forthcoming funds.

Heads turned to watch the tall, striking figure. For even in a city teeming with cosmopolitan faces, Gina Cornell was exceptional. Few would have thought her Italian from her height and thick halo of tawny golden hair flouncing on the collar of her cinch-waisted, blue cashmere suit, though her strong, finely sculpted features and wide, upcurving lips clearly distinguished the Roman half of her ancestry. And while her aura of vivacity and self-confidence identified her as a woman of this New World, there was a dark depth in her eyes, a restrained sensuality which was unmistakably Latin.

At the corner she swung into Forty-seventh Street. Ahead, a marquee canopied the lunchtime throng, its silver-grey scripted with one of the half-dozen most famous restaurant logos in Manhattan: in elegant pink – The Lady.

Gina greeted the busy blue-uniformed doorman, 'Hi, Joe,' and entered the lobby.

It could have been Times Square on New Year's Eve. Convivial lines crocodiled to the hatcheck booth, reservation desk and pink-robed archway to the dining-room and bar. Chatter and laughter clattered against the background melody of a debonair piano. The air was exotic with the aromas of wine, cigars, expensive perfume and rich cuisine.

Briefly scanning the crowd, Gina recognized all the regulars, the usual complement of celebrities, several newcomers. She stepped forward, negotiating with practised ease the handshakes and kisses, pausing to exchange a joke, to accept a compliment, to gather a tidbit of gossip. It took fifteen minutes to cross the room – par for the course. And she loved every second of it. For wherever Gina travelled throughout the West-Rossi restaurant-hotel empire of which she was president, her heart remained here. Whomever she met, her special joy was in chatting with The Lady's guests. Whatever pleasures she indulged, nothing held the satisfaction of being in this place which once had been the realization of a dream.

Between urns of overflowing camellias at the rear of the lobby Gina went through a door marked PRIVATE into a narrow corridor. A staircase to the right, another door to the left. She chose the latter; entered the kitchen.

Steel and ceramics, white fluorescent light. An apparent havoc of din and activity. Waiters sweeping out with silver trays of completed orders; busboys rushing in with armloads of dirty crockery; over by the servery, the aboyeur swiftly receiving the written chits, yelling instructions to the preparation stations; assistant cooks hurrying from storage cupboards to tables and ovens; through an archway the scullery, dishwashers at the bank of sinks enveloped in loud camaraderie and steam.

An outsider witnessing this scene could have been forgiven for thinking chaos was reigning. Gina, however, knew better. 'If a kitchen looks and sounds like a factory at full blast,' she'd once explained to a magazine interviewer, 'you can be sure it's running as smoothly as a well-oiled machine.'

At the centre of the ruction, marshalling his troops with consummate efficiency and inscrutable calm, the restaurant's maître chef de cuisine. Chang beamed widely and waved to Gina.

'A Chinese chef, in an Italian restaurant!' Max Barzini, Gina's godfather, had exclaimed with chauvinistic dismay on hearing of her appointment of the Oriental. To which Gina had riposted good-humouredly, 'Chang's credentials are impeccable. And there's no reason why he shouldn't prepare *gnocchi alla romana* as well as he does *subgum chow mein*. Besides, according to New York's Board of Health, his countrymen in Chinatown run the cleanest kitchens in the city, and, remember, what Poppa used to say, you judge a good cook not only by what he puts on his plates, but also by what he keeps off his floor.'

Gina strolled down the side of the kitchen, observing, exchanging a friendly word with each man and woman, greeting all of them by their first name. At the rear of the room, about to turn and retrace her route she glanced through the porthole in the door to the yard. What she saw made her stride swiftly outside. 'Don't do that,' she called.

The swarthy, squat character in overalls jerked around from where he was about to dump a bunch of old newspapers into a five-foot high metal drum.

'That's the swill bin,' Gina admonished, crossing the yard. 'You know better than to throw anything but food waste in there. Please put those papers in the trash, where they belong.'

The cropped-haired man glowered, hesitating, the sheaf raised in his fist as if he might hurl it at Gina. Then, as she halted within a few feet, he swung around, tramped to the bins in the corner and disposed of the papers. As he sullenly returned, he stared down at his purposely scuffing boots.

Gina, smoothing her vexation, asked without rancour, 'Have you dropped any other rubbish in the swill?'

'No,' the man rejoined churlishly, not pausing or looking up when he passed, and growling under his breath, 'Who cares about goddamn hogs?' as he yanked open the kitchen door to disappear inside.

Stung by the unwarranted aggression Gina was about to pursue the malefactor. But she took a deep breath, deliberately silently counted to ten, remaining planted to the spot. She didn't know the man, guessed he was new, conceded he might not have been instructed about the bins. Further, it wasn't up to her to upbraid anyone; the authority was Chang's and she wouldn't impinge upon it. Still, she made a mental note to tell the chef what she'd seen.

Stepping to the swill bin she peered down into the morass of raw vegetable scraps and cooked left-overs. As far as she could see nothing was in there that shouldn't be. Satisfied, she walked back and re-entered the kitchen. The swarthy man was hefting a bucket of potato peelings toward her. Gina nodded to him with an offer of amicability and headed toward the exit, mouthing, 'See you later', to Chang as she made her way out to the corridor and the staircase.

By the time she reached her office on the next floor, the episode had been supplanted by renewed plans for the future of a million dollars.

Gina still preferred this room, where she'd planned The Lady's first menu fourteen years ago, to her suite at West-Rossi headquarters down the street; just as she loved her old apartment here on the top floor, and only used her Fifth Avenue duplex when entertaining important business guests.

Checking her watch – fifteen minutes before she was scheduled to meet Howard – she walked between the time-worn but deeply-patinaed hide sofas, and switched on the television. Twelve months the mahogany-cabineted, four-foot high, fourteen-inch screen console had resided in the corner. Gina tolerated it with scarcely less disenchantment than she had the day it was installed. For years she'd resisted the purchase of a receiver ('Who wants to see a beer commercial every three minutes?') until Harry Dix, one of her directors and oldest friends, finally had persuaded her to rescind her ban.

'Television is the entertainment medium of the future,' Harry had insisted. 'I guarantee it's where a great many of our Rossi Entertainment Management clients will be earning their living. Plus,' he'd emphasized, 'it's going to become the most powerful advertising showcase in history. We can't afford to ignore it.' A few months later he'd advised a try-out television commercials campaign for the company's Rossi Taverns Christmas Special Menu throughout New England, Texas and the northwest states. Business for the two hundred Taverns of these regions had subsequently outstripped that of all one thousand others across the country.

Gina at last had yielded to Harry's counsel on the power of the small screen. Nevertheless, she still rarely watched anything but the news.

The set flickered into life.

The one pm bulletin. The main story, as it had been for over twenty months, was Korea. Gina shook her head at the continuing serial of madness. Fifteen minutes on and she'd been no more encouraged by the ensuing pictorials: Eisenhower waving from the rear of his Presidential campaign train; Senator Joseph McCarthy ranting; Marilyn Monroe being harried to admit she'd posed nude; a gang of demonstrators brandishing AMERICAN FRIENDS OF FREEDOM placards; scientists celebrating the perfection of a bigger and better atomic bomb.

Gina pushed out from behind the desk, advanced to silence the set, pulled up in mid-stride as the commentary to the aerial shot of a movie studio said, '... possible liquidation of Monument Pictures Corporation. No decision has yet been reached by financial backers, but sources within the long-troubled company report sweeping economies in all divisions as well as rumours of extensive upcoming layoffs.'

The scene cut to an outdoor fieldscape, with a battle-scarred tank beside a farmhouse; a ruddy-faced man in short-sleeved white shirt, panama hat pushed to the back of his head, striding away from a gaggle of reporters and photographers. The voice-over explained:

'Producer Felix Gilbert, whose current war drama is being shot on the famous Monument backlot near Anaheim, California, refused to comment on the present crisis but stated that filming of *The Last Summer* would continue.

'Also on the Hollywood front, Elia Kazan, director of *A Streetcar Named Desire* and *Death of a Salesman*, has been called before the House UnAmerican Activities ...'

Gina snapped off the broadcast.

She returned to her desk, sat staring at the papers before

her. But she didn't see them. For several seconds she saw only kaleidoscopic images of the past as her head was stormed by a legion of memories, and it took a positive effort to wrench her mind back to the present.

Drawing deep, steadying breaths, she remained absolutely still for a long moment. That was the first time in four years she'd recalled Robert Fallon so clearly. She'd known, of course, the Englishman was presently in Anaheim acting as consultant during Monument's filming of his novel *The Last Summer*, but she'd not permitted herself to dwell on the fact, had kept his image – and thus the emotion it might ignite – at bay, as she had since that night in 1947 when she'd sliced him from her life, cauterized the wound with burning activity. The vivid mental picture she'd just seen, had flared, she rationalized, in response to the unexpected television report. There were no deeper reasons.

She mentally shook herself, re-arranging her disrupted emotions. This was no time to be dallying in the past; the future was far more important. And most important of all was the soon-to-be finalized agreement whereby North State Roadhouses would have all their three hundred restaurants franchised as Rossi Taverns – the deal which would give West-Rossi a cash injection of one million dollars.

Not that a million was a fortune these days, but it did mean the company could expand; and expansion, Gina always had been convinced, was the key to survival. The bigger you grew, the stronger you became. Thus she'd never kept a spare cent in her coffers. From the day she'd opened The Lady, everything had been ploughed back into the business. Of course, Weldon Hoyt the banker had constantly fretted over such financial venturing, delivering his rainy-day speech, deploring Gina's risking her personal capital to back her schemes. But, 'Don't worry,' she'd always assured him, 'everything will work out fine.'

And it had. Since her arrival in America, as a penniless refugee from Mussolini's Italy, Gina had built a company – a nationwide chain of franchised restaurants – of which her poppa would have been proud. Above all she'd secured the future of her younger sister and brother: Paola was now a wife and mother, a respected and committed member of her church and community in Phoenix, Arizona; Filipo was a student at Harvard Law in Boston, due to graduate in two years' time and be admitted to the bar.

Wasn't that a thought? It thrilled Gina whenever it entered her mind – as it did frequently. Imagine, her brother, an attorney, a professional man; this would be the crowning achievement which made all the years of sacrifice and struggle worthwhile.

Gina glanced from the file on North State Roadhouses to her watch, remembering she was supposed to be meeting her husband here – five minutes ago.

She went quickly out of the office, along the hallway toward the small reception area used by business visitors to the restaurant.

He was sitting, alone, on an ivory chesterfield, legs casually crossed. His navy, double-breasted blazer, paisley silk tie and pocket handkerchief were worn with easy elegance. He glanced up from a copy of *Colliers*, smiled, 'Hi.'

At forty-eight Howard Cornell had a physique sculpted by a virtual lifetime of riding, skiing, sailing, posed in a relaxed confidence born of the wealth which financed those pursuits. His hair was black, a colour seemingly reflected in his deep eyes beneath which his features and wide mouth were sharply defined. For an instant the light behind his greeting was that of a child before a parent. The impression passed in a blink, however, and Gina was looking into a face of extraordinary strength and maturity.

She said pleasantly, 'Howard, what are you doing out here? Why didn't you come into the office?'

'The last time I stuck my head around the door,' he replied jokily, 'your secretary said I didn't have an appointment.'

'That's not true,' Gina rejoined. Then: 'Well, maybe I was especially busy that day.' She kept her tone light. 'How was your trip to – where've you just been – Kentucky for the races? Will you be here in Manhattan long?'

'The trip was fine, thanks. No, that's why I wanted to see you today, to let you know there's a yachting party going down to Chesapeake Bay. I'll be leaving this afternoon.' He scanned her face. 'You're looking good. Radiant. Are you hatching a plot to make a few more millions?'

He really knows me rather well, thought Gina, despite the fact we haven't spent seven consecutive days together since our honeymoon. Or had he learned to recognize the look he'd seen in his mother's eyes? She answered, 'Something like that.' She wanted to say more, to tell him about North State Roadhouses, but to have talked corporate expansion with Howard would have been as futile as discussing it with a twelve-year-old.

He said openly, 'I know whatever it is, Gina, you'll make it a success. You always were the best. At everything.'

The suggestive hint was delivered with a genuine smile, and Gina's eyelids almost automatically dropped in response. She forced them open. Yet even as she denied the physical reflex she couldn't help but glance over his long legs, his muscular thighs, thence to the width of his chest and shoulders. As her eyes once more met his she felt a vague embarrassment, mingled with a sexual need she hadn't experienced in many months. A voice in her head reminded, You have a business appointment in thirty minutes. With a flush of unsettling distraction and self-reproach she watched him idly turn the pages of the magazine. She asked briskly, 'Howard, what were you doing with Oliver Randolph?'

His eyes jumped from the society pictures. 'Who?'

Gina inwardly sighed. The boyish side of Howard; caught with his hand in the candy jar, denying, 'I didn't do it,' even before he'd been challenged. She briefly felt sorry for him, vexed at herself for jolting him. Nevertheless, she added with measured calm, 'I heard you and he had lunch together yesterday. Did he mention me?'

Her husband's hesitation lasted only a moment more, then the mask of his maturity was back in place. Setting the magazine at his side, though not releasing it, he replied casually, 'Yes. We happened to meet in the lobby of the Plaza. He passed the time of day, asked how you were. Then he suggested lunch. I know you don't like him, Gina, but, frankly, I find him quite charming. We had a long and interesting chat.'

Gina noted that Howard was once more in control, his

eyes signalling self-assurance. She wondered, for the thousandth time, how many people could see beyond the facade – and whether Oliver Randolph was one of them. 'I never said I disliked him, Howard. I've only met him once, fleetingly. Not long enough to form much of an opinion. However, I admit I don't care for the style of his hotels and restaurants, or his methods of running them.'

'The Randolph Corporation is very successful. *Nations Business* named it as the fastest growing company in the country. Its share value has doubled in the past eighteen months. I think Oliver must know a thing or two about the hospitality business.'

Which was an expression Howard, off his own bat, never would have used. It had been coined, and much broadcast, by Randolph's public relations department, and, Gina guessed, her husband had been fed it over lunch, along with the share information and magazine quote – the only literature Howard ever read was of the type presently resting under his hand, or that with cover pictures of sailing boats.

Had this not been the case Gina would have had one or two observations to make about Mister Oliver Randolph; the self-proclaimed 'modernizer of America's hotel and catering industry' wasn't yet a thorn in her flesh, but his burgeoning empire of garish hostelries and eateries was undeniably a very sore point.

Six years ago nobody east of the Rockies had even heard of the ex-Army-corporal-turned-insurance-peddler who had launched Global Security & Trust, a Seattle-based mortgage and credit brokerage whose exorbitant interest rates were exceeded only by the extremes of its sales techniques. That, however, was before Randolph magnanimously had agreed to accept, in lieu of outstanding loan repayments from their septuagenarian owner, half-a-dozen timber-and-tarpaper diners plus a run-down Palm Springs motel-saloon. Within twelve months the dingy old identities of these seven buildings had disappeared beneath glittery new chrome and plastic veneers, and a hard-hitting series of small-town newspaper advertisements carrying the tag, 'Enjoy the best – you've won the right', whet precisely the desired appetites amid the army of discharged G.I.s and their families impatiently seeking their slice of post war pie in the sky.

The Randolph Hotel & Leisure Corporation had been born.

'You have to agree,' persisted Howard, 'Oliver is one of the most successful businessmen in the country.'

Resisting the urge to refute the point Gina enquired, 'Did he ask any questions about West-Rossi?'

'No.' Rising suddenly, 'I have to be going.'

'Howard. What did Randolph want to know?'

'Nothing. It was everyday conversation. Business in general. About the growth of his company. All the offers he's had to sell out. He said he imagined West-Rossi received the same sort of approaches. I said of course we – you – did. He wondered what your reaction was. I told him you'd always vowed you'd never part with the company. He asked if you could be overruled. I said that since mother's death you held the majority of the controlling votes. It was all right to say that, wasn't it, Gina?'

Reassuringly: 'Yes, Howard, it was fine.'

'I did say that I wouldn't mind, though, if the corporation was sold. Maybe then you and I could spend more time together.' He reached out and touched the back of his hand to Gina's cheek. 'You're always so busy.'

Gina stepped back a pace. 'I have to be.' She offered a small, bright laugh. 'So we can continue to eat at fancy restaurants like The Lady.'

But Howard didn't return the humour. A slight frown knitted his brow. 'If West-Rossi was sold you wouldn't need to work. We've discussed this before, Gina. Perhaps …'

She moved forward and kissed his cheek, parried with sincere fondness, 'You know I'd only be seasick on your boats. I'm hopeless at golf. I can't keep up with you on a horse. If I retired I'd be getting on your nerves inside a week. We'd quarrel. And that's something we've never done. How many of your friends could make a similar claim?' She squeezed his arm, adding briskly, 'Now, better hurry, or you'll be late for your getaway to Chesapeake.'

Howard hesitated, his cloud lingering, until he eventually said, 'I guess you're right.' Thereupon his smile returned and he declared abruptly, 'I'll bring you the winner's pennant.' He swiftly kissed her on the mouth, turned and strode away.

Gina, watching his back, sighed. Another small upheaval avoided. She felt mildly fatigued. Had Howard's attitude toward her involvement with the business seemed more resentful than usual? She re-ran the encounter. Perhaps she shouldn't have pushed him about Randolph; there was no reason to suppose their meeting had been anything other than accidental. Maybe it was she who was becoming somewhat paranoid, imagining threats from competitors around every corner.

She sank onto the settee, listened to the pulse of The Lady: a steady rhythm of distant laughter, conversation, music; all the intimate activity which had been the background of her life since the day she was born.

It always had been the most pleasurable time of her day, during the heat of the afternoon when Ristorante Rossi was shuttered and she sat with her father on the tiny, third storey balcony looking across the tangled red and ochre rooftops toward the ruins of a Rome two thousand years past, planning the family's future.

Throughout her formative years Gina had been particularly close to Alfredo Rossi, sharing his love of life and literature, eagerly absorbing all he taught about running their restaurant on Via Condotti, never tiring of listening to his tales of their heritage. Wide-eyed she'd urge, 'Please, tell me some more, Poppa. Tell about great-grandpa selling basins of *anguille carpionate* in the Porta Portese market; about your father opening his trattoria; about your visit to America, meeting Momma there, bringing her home and marrying her in Trinita dei Monti.'

Following her mother's death, in her later teenage years Gina had shared deeper, late-night conversations with Alfredo, her godfather Max Barzini, and the English Reuters correspondent Robert Fallon. After the restaurant was closed, the quartet would sit at a corner table with a bottle of Barolo discussing the dark brutalities of Fascism which were taking place behind the glittering facade of Gina's beloved Eternal City.

It had been the week of her twentieth birthday when that brutality had erupted into the Rossis' lives. Alfredo had been arrested, falsely accused of anti-government activity, condemned and sentenced to internal exile.

In the space of a few weeks Gina's ivory tower had been shattered. Her entire previous existence, and that of her family, all its joys, its plans, its loves had been snuffed out, for ever. She had felt an almost physical agony, as if a part of her had been torn away. How in God's name, she asked over and over, could this have happened in the country she had held so dear? She'd wanted to lash out at something or somebody, not only to inflict pain in retaliation against the savage wrong being done, but also to punish herself; for she felt she was somehow responsible, that she had known what was happening throughout her homeland but had chosen to put a veil over the truth, had not allowed the shadows to darken her carefree and elegant lifestyle.

Perhaps this was why she chose to accompany her father into exile. Robert Fallon had exclaimed, 'Gina, you cannot. You don't understand what exile is like. Banishment to a village or island where none of the inhabitants is permitted to communicate with you. I've seen what it can do to people, to strong intelligent men and women. It's a punishment designed to break the soul.'

'Which is why I must go with Poppa,' Gina had replied. 'To cook for him, care for him. To do whatever I can to make his existence bearable. It isn't in return for all he has given me – that is unrepayable – it's simply the way it has to be.'

In a settlement called Baremo, in the blistering wilderness of southern Italy, it had taken all Gina's determination to uphold her pledge as she watched the reality of Fallon's words crush her father. For six long months she was witness to the man who once had lighted her life with his wit and wisdom, his strength and honour, being reduced to the wreckage of a human being. But as Alfredo Rossi's spirit died, so Gina's achieved a reborn endurance. Each day she willed herself to survive. She vowed that one day there would be a new Ristorante Rossi; that her family – her younger sister Paola, their baby brother Filipo, their godfather Max Barzini – would be reunited; that they never again would be separated. Not once did she permit herself to believe this would not come to pass. She expunged all images of defeat. And within her soul formed a hard core of stubborness, a kernal from which would spring the all-enveloping vine of her future resolve.

Gina and Alfredo Rossi's banishment ended as it had begun – cruelly and suddenly.

When at last Max Barzini and Robert Fallon discovered the exiles' whereabouts and arrived to snatch them to safety, Alfredo, broken by his ordeal, could summon the strength only to order his daughter, 'Go. Forget me. You must think of Paola and Filipo. You must be more than their sister now.'

In the decrepit hut she and her father had shared throughout the punishing months, Gina had hesitated. In that instant the door had burst open and their Blackshirt captor had lurched drunkenly into the room. Wrenching at his belt buckle he had lunged for Gina. She had sought to flee, but he was too big, too strong. He had rammed her against the wall, his hands tearing into her blouse. 'No!' Gina had screamed.

The cry woke her. She sat suddenly upright, disorientated, misplaced in time and space. Pink wall lights bathed her vision; music and laughter clattered distantly; the aromas of wine and food drifted on the air.

On the settee in the reception area above The Lady, Gina stilled her trembling hands, strove to drive away the harsh images of the past. It was some moments before she regained her composure. And yet even then she remained troubled, shadowed by a sense of unease.

'Foolishness,' she declared aloud, glancing at her watch, discovering she'd been asleep for five minutes. That was the first time in her life she'd nodded off during the day. Must be getting old, she joshed herself in an effort to rekindle her earlier good humour.

She returned to her office and sat behind her desk to check over the papers she was scheduled to discuss with Irving Prentiss, the company's chief accountant. A knock came at the door and to Gina's call of, 'Come in,' Irving entered. 'You're early,' Gina remarked pleasantly.

Irving strode across the room. 'I thought you'd want to hear right away,' he said. 'I just received the news. North State Roadhouses have sold out to Oliver Randolph.'

Chapter Two

Gina cracked down the telephone receiver, 'It's confirmed,' she snapped. 'The deal's signed and sealed. Damn. Damn Oliver Randolph.'

It was the afternoon following Irving Prentiss's delivery of the news. During the intervening hours Gina had done everything possible to track down the owner of North State Roadhouses and prevent him from reneging on the agreement he'd been about to conclude with West-Rossi. Her efforts had failed.

'Bribery,' she declared, rapping an angry fist on her desktop. 'That's how Randolph persuades people to sell to him. Offers them under-the-counter payoffs into Swiss bank accounts. Money the IRS never hears about. Damn,' she said again.

Irving agreed, 'It's how he operates. But,' he added, 'nothing we can do about it, unless we're prepared to play the same game.'

Gina remained tensely silent for a moment; then she declared, 'No, we won't. We may have cut a few corners in our time, but we've never stooped to Randolph's level – and I don't intend we should start now.'

Irving nodded. He was a calmly elegant man in his late forties, his pale grey suit and his dark hair as immaculate as the balance sheets and profit forecasts he produced. The straight lines and planes of his features rarely displayed emotion during a business discussion. Now, however, there was a measure of sympathy in his expression as he said, 'The loss of North State Roadhouses isn't the end of the world.'

'It would have been a million dollars,' returned Gina, 'to help finance West-Rossi's expansion.'

'Actually,' said Irving, 'I'd been going to advise we hold onto the money for a few months, to help offset some of our liabilities.'

Gina was about to respond, to press her belief in the need for corporate growth, but she bit back the words. She'd had little sleep in the past twenty-four hours and knew her overtired nerves might cause her tongue to run away with itself. She said, 'If you don't mind, Irving, I'd rather talk about liabilities after a good night's rest.'

The accountant accepted the decision with a smile of understanding, and after a few more minutes he left the office.

Gina stared down at the North State Roadhouses file. The loss still rankled. Losing to someone as underhand as Oliver Randolph was doubly galling. One of these days, she thought to herself, the devious wheeler-dealer would get a taste of his own medicine. One of these days ... 'Forget it,' she said aloud, and in a gesture of finality dropped the file in her OUT tray.

She spent the remainder of the afternoon doing her best to catch up on a pile of business chores. She managed to clear much of the backlog, but by six o'clock, with fatigue a cloud in her head, she decided to call it a day. One final task: deliver to Chang her suggestions for the new summer menu.

Gina went down to the restaurant kitchen.

Entering the hubbub she scanned the activity. Unable to spot the maître chef, she enquired of a nearby assistant cook, 'Chang?'

The young man glanced around, shook his head. 'Shall I check the washroom, Mrs Cornell?'

'No, that's okay, thanks,' returned Gina. 'I'll catch him later.' Beginning to turn, struck by an afterthought that Chang might have stepped out for a moment, she headed toward the rear exit. Opening the door she looked into the yard, and saw the back of a stocky figure facing the far corner of the encompassing walls.

The man's head jerked around.

Gina stared at the swarthy features beneath the close-cropped skull. Where had she seen him before? Abruptly, yesterday's encounter jumped into her head: the man she'd caught dumping newspapers in the swill bin. Now he was fumbling down in front of himself. With what? Gina peered. The buttons of his pants? For a second she didn't understand, but then she saw the wetness glistening on the ground at the man's feet. 'What on earth do you think you're doing?' she shouted.

The man glowered but offered no reply as he walked sullenly toward her.

'Just a moment,' Gina challenged, advancing to bar the man's path. Her anger was rising, and she was unable to keep it from her voice as she demanded, 'Aren't you aware our food deliveries come into this yard? Don't you realize you could spread disease?'

The man halted before her, glanced from side to side as if seeking some other way out. He muttered under his breath.

Gina recalled his previous churlishness, and her patience began to crack. Count to ten, her inner voice warned. 'If you can't use the toilets like everybody …'

The man growled and started past Gina, bumping her with his shoulder.

Gina's taut nerves snapped. 'If that's the way you want it,' she threw, 'collect your belongings. Now.' As the man glared around at her, she ordered, 'Get off these premises. And don't come anywhere near here, ever again.' Not waiting for an argument she strode back into the building.

The man, Chang said, had been one of those characters who carry a permanent chip on their shoulder. He'd been employed at The Lady less than a week, during which time he'd ignored all cautions about his slovenliness and disregard for hygiene. Chang had been on the point of handing him his dismissal. Nevertheless, Gina apologized to the maître chef for her hasty action, and remained annoyed with herself for having allowed bad temper to rule her conduct.

Later, alone in her apartment, she tried to recapture a happier spirit. Was it only yesterday she'd been swinging up Fifth Avenue planning what to do with a million dollars? It seemed an age.

Untypically she was in bed by ten, expecting to sleep like a log. But she suffered a fitful slumber. Her fragmented dreams were of her husband Howard, sailing on a boat; the Englishman Robert Fallon in a movie studio; a swarthy character confronting her in the restaurant yard, his features distorting to metamorphose into the face of Oliver Randolph.

It wasn't until two days later that Gina's optimism returned. It was delivered along the telephone line.

'Hi, Sis,' her brother's voice called. 'Just letting you know I'll be home for the weekend.'

The dress Gina chose was beige wool, cinched at the waist by a slim natural suede belt. No decolletage to speak of, but a V-neck deep enough to reveal the swell of her full bust, to accentuate the line of her strong throat. She added a triple choker of pearls after a touch of rouge, whisper of eye shadow, lick of lipstick. Her halo of blonde hair shone. Her good spirits rose as she regarded herself in the full-length mirror. Filipo would say, 'Very chick,' pronouncing it tongue-in-cheek that way, as he had at ten years old, on scrutinizing her satin purple sheath the first evening she'd gone to dance, for ten cents a ticket, at the Starlight Room.

Gina smiled at the memory as she descended the curving staircase to the elegant bustle which was lunchtime at The Lady. Filipo was beyond the crowded tables at the bar.

She never failed to get a charge of pleasure from seeing her young brother. During the past few years Filipo's looks had matured dramatically. His deep hazel eyes seemed intensified by their thick lashes. His nose was Roman straight with flared nostrils above a wide permanently tilted mouth which appeared always to wear a roguish smile. The jaw was square, dark with shadow which shaving twice-daily could barely keep at bay. Topping all this was a mass of tumbling black curls barbers rarely got a shot at.

You're far too attractive, my lad, Gina thought affectionately as her brother arose to her approach. And so much like Poppa. Yet inches taller. The long legs you get, like me, from Momma. No wonder all the girls in the West-Rossi Building go doe-eyed whenever you walk by.

They'd make you top of the box-office if you were a movie star.

Gina winced fractionally at that suggestion. For it was what he had wanted to be.

Since Filipo was old enough to pin pictures on his bedroom walls, his childhood privacy had been overlooked by one small painting of the Madonna plus umpteen photographs of Hollywood personalities. Far into his teenage years he'd harboured the ambition to see his own portrait on the covers of those silver screen magazines. Gina, however, had hoped fervently he'd change his mind. She'd said to her friend Felix Gilbert – presently producing *The Last Summer* for the troubled Monument Pictures – 'Our family does not need a shooting star, no matter how bright. What it needs is the strong, steady light of endurance. I'm sure one day Filipo will realize that.'

Happy to say, he had – more or less. Filipo hadn't been cured entirely of the movie itch, but at least he'd acceded to Gina's request to keep the bug under control to permit the continuance of his commercial law studies.

Now, as she walked toward him, he gave her a quick once-over and grinned, 'Hi, Sis. Very chick.' He squeezed her, kissed her and in an excellent Humphrey Bogart asked, 'What're you drinking, Blue Eyes?'

Gina requested the smiling barman, 'Club soda, please, Sam.' Returning her brother's sartorial scrutiny, she took in his jeans, white sloppy-joe sweater, and those new-style blue suede loafers. Did that look like an attorney? Still, she said, 'It's lovely to see you,' and automatically pushed a stubborn lock from his brow.

They sat, and for the next fifteen minutes shared the news and gossip.

At last, Gina remarked, 'You said on the telephone you had something to tell me.' She prompted expectantly, 'So, go ahead.'

Filipo moved his rangy shoulders inside his sweater, his previous chipperness apparently cooled by his sister's breezy, unheralded question. He looked around, watched Sam place fresh drinks on the bar, then with a sudden breath declared, 'There's someone I want you to meet.'

Gina waited in the ensuing silence. 'Yes?'

'A girl.'

'Oh?' Gina's eyes widened with surprise; for it was the first time in his life Filipo had presented such a statement.

Since she'd returned from her London Red Cross unit in 1946 to discover a brother who, during the three years she'd been away, had grown taller than she to stand on the brink of manhood, Gina had been aware of a permanent parade of females beating a path to his door like besotted sheep who couldn't wait to throw themselves into the den of the big, bad wolf. Not once, however, had she met a single member of this fervent fan club. Nor had she ever seen the same one twice.

And for three or four years it hadn't bothered her – too much. Recently, however, she'd set to thinking it perhaps was time her twenty-four-year-old-soon-to-be-an-attorney brother began to consider settling down. In her more speculative moments she went beyond that to calculate how old she would be before Filipo's son (despite her ardent support of women's rights she still thought in traditionally Italian terms of male continuance of the family name) followed in his father's professional footsteps.

Filipo married? The prospect produced a mixed reaction as she faced him beside the bar. On the one hand it thrilled her. On the other she suddenly saw a piece of her life breaking away.

He said, 'She's a good friend. We've known each other a while. Six months. Her name's Mickey.'

'Mickey?'

'Michelle, actually. Michelle Rooney. Hence ...' His smile returned. 'She's a very pleasant person. Bright. And caring. Everybody likes her. You will too, Gina. I know it.'

Gina thought, Six months. Her brother had been dating the same girl for an entire half year. Holding all her conflicting emotions under rein she asked casually, 'Where did you meet? Is Mickey a law student?'

'No,' replied Filipo, hesitating, glancing amid the bottles behind the bar as if he might find some further response there. He returned to face his sister. 'We met at a meeting. I mean, a public meeting. Well, not exactly. More a lecture, really. Sort of political. But not very. Nothing important.' He wiped his palms on his knees. 'Mickey doesn't attend our school. She trained at the WPA Federal Theatre Project. She's going to be an actress. That's her great ambition. Right now she's a dancer.'

Gina's conviviality slipped several rungs as she thought of the Project Theatre workshop in the old Tenth Avenue Bethany Church; characters in rummage sale clothes presenting plays without plots, poetry without rhyme. Her mind jumped to a vision of the beautiful females who'd flitted in and out of Filipo's life. Dancers? Is that what they'd been? Why had she fondly imagined they all were history or science or law students? Scrabbling to re-arrange her dishevelled thoughts, she enquired with cautious optimism, 'A ballet dancer?'

Filipo cleared his throat. 'Not exactly. That is, she did some classical training. But her routines are modern. She choreographs them herself. Tap. Soft-shoe. High kick ...'

'She's a hoofer!'

'But a very good one,' Filipo returned quickly. 'Really, she's extremely talented. I know, I've seen her work. She's dedicated, too, to making it to the big time.' He gave an emphatic nod.

Gina, for the moment, couldn't find a response. He looks so serious, she thought. And, remember, he's been seeing this Mickey for six months. Obviously he's got more than a fleeting crush on a pair of long legs. The girl must be special. So, does he have to marry a bluestocking? Would it be so bad to have a dancer as a sister-in-law? Momma was a dancer. A second in the family ...

'Gina.'

'Pardon?' She pulled back from her reverie. 'Sorry, just musing,' she said, then added brightly, 'So?'

Filipo began slowly, 'Well ...'

'Go on.'

'I've fixed Mickey an audition with Rossi Entertainment.'

The silence was opaque.

Filipo hurried on, 'I know we've always had a rule never to use family influence to arrange jobs for friends. I appreciate the talent agency is Harry's domain. All decisions are his. But it's only an audition. A chance for Mickey to show what she can do. If, after seeing her routine, Harry says she hasn't got what it takes, okay, I'll abide by his opinion. No arguments. I won't push for a special favour. Mickey knows that. Besides, she wouldn't want me to. She can stand on her own two feet.' He smiled faintly at his small, unintentional witticism, then added quietly, 'I'm sorry, Sis, for breaking our rule, but Mickey's a good friend. As I said, I'm sure you'll like her.'

Gina stared. Was that all her brother had to tell? Her expectations went spinning into the void. After a long moment she responded, 'I'm sure I shall.'

Filipo beamed. 'I'm so glad you understand. Thanks, Gina.' Then, 'By the way,' he added, 'I arranged Mickey's audition simply because I reckoned she deserved a break. No ulterior motives. We get along fine, but that's all. Please don't start imagining you hear wedding bells.'

'What?' Gina produced surprise. 'I never thought …'

'Sis, you've been thinking it for the past six months. Every time I've been home you've had the isn't-it-time-he-was-settling-down glint in your eye. No point in denying it. I know it's the old Italian matchmaking rising in your blood. Propagation of the clan.' He laughed. 'Well, no need to fret. I assure you you'll get to dangle a whole bunch of bambini on your knee when the time comes. But, for now, you'll have to be patient. Okay?'

Gina regarded him through slitted eyes, trying hard to manufacture her steely look; but in the face of his knowing grin her pretence was hopeless. She gave way to a full smile, prodded him in the ribs and enquired, 'Since when were you so tall?'

Filipo winked.

Gina, with a touch more seriousness, said, 'You know, by canvassing for Mickey, you might have put Harry on the spot. I hope you'll make your peace with him.'

'I already did,' assured Filipo. 'We're still buddies. He's set up the audition for next Friday morning. I'll be there. I hope you'll be able to make it too, Sis, so's you can meet Mickey.'

Gina replied, 'I wouldn't miss it for the world'.

*

That night Gina's thoughts were filled with her brother's girlfriend. 'Dedicated to her career' was how Filipo had described Mickey. But that didn't mean she couldn't raise a family as well, did it? The question kept returning to unsettle Gina.

Despite having spent so many years in America, there were still old conventions of her homeland which she found difficult to oppose. One such fundamental lore decreed a married woman must be dedicated wholly to caring for her husband and children. Youngsters needed a mother – not a neighbour or nanny – to greet them from school. Why? Gina mentally argued. So long as children are fed, clothed, above all loved, will they suffer one jot if their mother isn't on hand every second. After all, when Filipo and Paola were in their teens you weren't able to watch out for them twenty-four hours a day. Still they've grown into pretty good adults. So, must I insist my brother's wife be chained to her home?

You haven't even met Mickey yet, she reminded herself; and at last fell asleep once more, unsure whether the girl's arrival in her life made her happy or sad.

What did make her happy – always – was clinching deals.

This Wednesday following Filipo's weekend visit, Gina was in her office studying Irving Prentiss's financial proposals for the purchase of a parcel of land in Las Vegas. The West-Rossi Corporation already owned the largest casino-hotel, The Silver Lady, in the gambling city, but the additional acreage, Gina was sure, would be a sound investment. The present owner of the land had agreed his willingness to sell earlier in the year, and now was awaiting West-Rossi's terms. Gina had decided to pay him a personal call when she visited The Silver Lady next month.

Satisfied with Irving's proposals she was about to phone the accountant when a sharp rap sounded at the door and Mabel, Gina's secretary, entered and said hurriedly, 'I'm sorry. This person insisted on seeing you. I told him you were busy. He said ...' Mabel broke off as a large figure filled the doorway.

Gina, taken off guard, stared at the man, and with a chill of surprise recognized Oliver Randolph.

He said, 'Mrs Cornell, please forgive my calling without

notice. I had intended to telephone you. However, having just lunched at your splendid restaurant downstairs, I saw no reason to delay matters. If you will permit me to claim fifteen minutes of your time, I assure you it will be to your advantage.'

Gina's surprise had flickered toward anger at the abrupt intrusion, but before she could produce a response Randolph was advancing into the room. She hesitated, then said, 'Thank you, Mabel, I'll take care of this,' and after a moment the secretary, with an acid glance toward the gross man, went out, closing the door.

With cool courtesy, Gina said, 'Mister Randolph,' and gestured to the chair in front of her desk.

He strode forward, smiling confidently, extending his fat fist. 'Please, call me Oliver.'

Gina fleetingly considered ignoring the proffered hand, but incivility wasn't second nature and her arm instinctively rose in response. Though the man's grip was powerful, there was a clamminess in his sausage fingers, so that Gina was glad to be released from them; and as she watched him sit, the rancour she'd previously experienced whenever hearing of his devious deals, now assumed a tangible distaste. She'd never been given to snap judgments, but from the instant Randolph had touched her she'd been convinced that all her speculations about him had been thoroughly founded.

She regarded his big face with its contrived tan, the red-lipped smiling mouth, eyes almost violet beneath carefully plucked brows, thick hair combed back, too perfectly black on top, too perfectly silver at the temples. The archetypal image of the successful tycoon, as precisely tailored as the dark grey mohair suit, cream silk shirt and New York Athletic Club tie.

Gina's dislike swelled. She asked, 'What was it you wished to see me about, Mister Randolph?'

'That's what I like,' he said self-importantly, 'someone who comes straight to the point.' He leaned forward and declared, 'I'm prepared to offer twenty-five million dollars for the West-Rossi Corporation.'

Shock leapt upon Gina.

'I appreciate your surprise,' said Randolph. 'However, I do

not believe in long overtures. The old-fashioned ways of doing business might once have had their place in our country, but not any more. Times have changed. Too rapidly for some. But it is they who will be left behind. Those who move ahead, seizing opportunities rather than ceaselessly prattling about them, will be the winners. I'm sure you're such a person, Mrs Cornell. I'm sure you'll see the benefit of accepting my offer.'

Still too startled to collect her spinning thoughts, Gina merely stared at the man.

He said, 'You're aware, I'm sure, of the rapidly expanding interests of the Randolph Corporation. In the past five years we have grown to become a major force within the hotel and leisure industry. It is my intention, Mrs Cornell, to accelerate that growth tenfold. Before the end of this decade my company will be the biggest organization of its kind in the country. Already, several business owners have recognized the advantage of being part of such an organization. They have appreciated the wisdom of being my allies rather than my competitors. And, of course,' his vulpine lips curved redly, 'they have profited handsomely into the bargain.'

Gina at last found her voice. 'That's as may be,' she said. 'Everyone is entitled to do with their companies as they see fit. As far as West-Rossi is concerned, however, we are not for sale.'

Randolph countered, 'But I think you will be, my dear, once you have had time to think over the proposition. After all, with your current liabilities ...' He smirked, 'Oh yes, I make it my business to know such things. With your current liabilities, I believe twenty-five million is more than a fair price for your ...'

'It's absurd,' shot Gina.

Randolph's fat smile retreated.

The rejoinder had been all Gina could snatch from her mental whirl. Though her dislike of the man had swelled toward repugnance, she had not intended to allow her emotion to surface. But, she inwardly fumed, the gall of the man, barging in here uninvited. If I was down to my last ten cents, hell would be frozen over before I sold so much as a teaspoon to this bloated wheeler-dealer. Impetuous words, her rationality cautioned. Count to ten. Don't let the man's huckstering or his patronizing attitude unbalance your objectivity.

Taking a calming breath, she said, 'Mister Randolph, there really is no point in continuing this conversation. I reiterate, I have no intention of selling the West-Rossi Corporation, to you or anybody else.'

'That isn't what your husband led me to believe.'

'Howard?' Gina exclaimed.

'We lunched together last week. We discussed corporate expansion and business takeovers. Howard expressed a marked interest in ...'

'Whatever my husband might have said,' cut in Gina, 'was in no way representative of my opinion.'

Randolph paused, and then he nodded, a slow, knowing movement of his head. 'Yes, I understand, Mrs Cornell. I had heard that you and he didn't, shall we say, share certain interests.'

Gina burned, clearly seeing the sexual implication in the man's eyes. Before she could retaliate, however, he went on:

'Therefore, let me assure you, any financial arrangements, over and above the official sale figure for West-Rossi, will remain strictly between the two of us. I guarantee neither your husband nor your fellow directors will learn anything of our personal transactions.'

Gina's anger rose.

'After all,' Randolph said slyly, 'we – leaders such as you and I – are entitled to our perquisites, are we not? So, what is your price? Ten per cent? I think you'll agree that it is a fair sales commission. Ten per cent of twenty-five million. Two and a half million dollars. And, of course,' he moved closer to the desk, 'to be paid into any bank in whatever country you choose.'

Gina jumped to her feet, banging her chair back against the wall. Her impulse was to slap the man's arrogant face, and it was with difficulty she held her arms at her sides, fists bunched. Her cheeks felt livid, and it must have showed, for Randolph's smugness paled. Through taut lips Gina ordered, 'Get out of my office.'

The gross man returned her gaze; then he pushed his bulk

away from the desk and slowly stood. He said, 'You're making a mistake, Mrs Cornell.'

'I already made it,' rejoined Gina, 'by even thinking you might have anything to say fit to hear.'

Randolph's features became ashen as his eyes darkened. For a second Gina thought he was going to erupt, but she stood her ground, fierce in her aversion, until at last Randolph sucked in air through his flaring nostrils and with a parting venomous glare strode to wrench open the door and disappear from the room.

Gina remained staring at the vacant doorway, almost wondering if the encounter had been an illusion. Reality, however, was proven by the heaving of her lungs. She felt as if she had endured a physical contest. She sensed too a chill of apprehension, imagining there'd been an aura of menace about Randolph. 'Nonsense,' she said aloud, shaking off the irrational unease. 'He's simply an obnoxious lout.'

'An obnoxious lout,' she asserted to Irving an hour later.

The accountant nodded understandingly. When he'd come over to Gina's office for one of their regular meetings, he'd been unaware of the encounter she'd had with Oliver Randolph. However, he'd learned about it soon enough. Gina had related the entire episode almost word for word, emphasizing her indignation with small thumps of her fist on the desktop, never pausing long enough for Irving to get a comment in edgewise.

Now, at last, she had reached the end of her tale. She took a gulp of air and blew it out; and with it went much of her pent-up emotion. With a wry smile she said, 'Sorry, Irving. I didn't mean to bend your ear quite so hard. It's just that that overbearing creature really got my goat. Can you believe the nerve of the man?'

'No need to apologize,' returned the accountant. 'Sounds like Randolph's typical approach. It's only a pity a few more people don't show him the door. But, it's always been the case, when companies or individuals need money, they'll entertain even the Randolph's of this world.'

'I'd rather go bankrupt,' said Gina, 'than see West-Rossi

fall into his greasy hands. The very thought of the man makes my hackles rise.'

'I know how you feel,' agreed Irving. 'But, I'm afraid, he's a fact we have to live with. And he isn't going to disappear yet awhile. He's astute and he's aggressive; and his claim to you about accelerating the Randolph Corporation's growth was no idle boast. West-Rossi isn't the only major company he's approached recently. I even heard a rumour this lunchtime that he's offered a salvage deal to Monument Pictures.'

Gina said, 'Oh?' and her mind jumped back across several days to the television report on the financial difficulties of the studio where her old friend Felix Gilbert was currently producing *The Last Summer*. She thought too of the Englishman, Robert Fallon, from whose novel the movie had been taken. Swiftly obliterating his image, she asked, 'Do you think Randolph's serious about buying Monument?'

'It would be a logical step. He already owns a string of movie houses and has various showbusiness connections. Most importantly, though, Monument's the sort of company he's looking for at the moment – prestigious. The studio's produced some distinguished pictures in its time. It may be broke but it has esteem. That's what Randolph wants – something to give his corporation a cachet of respectability.'

Gina murmured, 'I see.' For several moments she remained pensive; then she said briskly, 'Well, we've far more important things to discuss. Are these the cash flow reports? Thanks,' and she opened the grey folder the accountant had brought to the meeting.

For the next three hours her concentration was given wholly to the concerns of West-Rossi.

Later, however, when she was once more alone, Gina was unable to prevent her attention returning to her earlier conversation with Irving. She thought of what he'd said about Randolph and the movie company. She recalled too all she'd experienced of the unscrupulous hustler during the past week – especially his capturing of North State Roadhouses.

The following morning she called Irving and asked him to prepare a preliminary report on the financial position of Monument Pictures. She added, 'Confidentially, of course.'

Chapter Three

Harry Dix was tall and thin, greying hair widow's peaked above gentle blue eyes in a glowing lantern face. Fourteen years ago Harry had owned the Starlight Room where Gina had danced in her purple satin sheath for ten cents a ticket. Gina had not worked long at the Starlight, however, before she'd discovered her desperate need for a job had been almost equalled by Harry's want of someone to straighten out the shambles of his account books. Thus had begun a commercial relationship which had developed into an abiding friendship; and when Gina had required a guarantor for the loan she took to open The Lady, it was Harry who signed his name to the bank's papers.

Later, after Gina's business had expanded, she'd asked Harry to join her. Today he took care of all West-Rossi's showbusiness interests; most especially he was in charge of Rossi Entertainment Management, the company's talent agency, as well as the running of The First Floor, the night club above The Lady which he and Gina had opened in 1942 and established as one of Manhattan's most popular rendezvous.

The club was shades of mauve and pink, antique mirrored walls multiplying the Tiffany-lamped tables which semi-circled the intimate dance floor and, beyond, the orchestra platform. Tonight the room would be packed with music and conversation amid a hectic glow. Suzy the cigarette girl in silver fishnets would be passing to and fro with her tray as waiters swiftly threaded the throng and pressmen popped their flashes at the famous faces who'd wake up in tomorrow's social columns.

Right now, however, The First Floor was still in its

dressing gown. Bright overhead tungsten yellow lit Suzy and the band's drummer at the bar munching breakfast hotdogs as a pair of male cleaners hefted chairs onto tables and Clara, the building's housekeeper, gathered linen into her wheeled hamper.

Gina walked slowly toward the dance floor's edge, surveying the girl there.

Michelle Rooney – Mickey, as Filipo had called her – was small, maybe only five-three, a shortness accentuated in the presence of Filipo and Harry, and also by her choice of footwear, white tennis shoes, the latest fad, along with her tiered skirt puffed out with layers of crinkly paper-nylon petticoats, and a check workshirt, sleeves pushed to her elbows. 'The Country and Western look,' Filipo had said to Gina a couple of months ago. 'You should try it, Sis. Got to keep with it, you know.' She had tried it. And she'd left it where she found it, in the store. Maybe it didn't appear too bad on some filmic female warbling by the light of the silvery moon with Gordon MacRae, but on her, she'd decided, it looked ridiculous, plus, she'd told her secretary, Mabel, 'In those petticoats it feels like there's chicken wire stuffed up your skirt.'

Michelle Rooney said, 'I'm very pleased to meet you, Mrs Cornell.'

Freckles. Wouldn't you have known it, thought Gina, seeing them on the tip-tilted nose and sprinkled beneath the wide blue eyes. A shiny pink mouth. Short blonde hair. And dimples! They appeared as she smiled brightly, extending her hand.

Gina took the proffered fingers – and received a surprise. The girl's grip was firm and positive. So too was the look in her Wedgwood saucer eyes. It met Gina's gaze, not over-confidently, but certainly without the naivety the face superficially signalled. Gina held the grip and the look. And she liked both; liked, instantly, her brother's friend. 'Hello, Michelle,' she greeted. 'Welcome to The First Floor.'

As they released hands the girl said, 'I'd be happy for you to call me Mickey. Everybody does – I guess Filipo told you – because of you know who.'

'Well,' smiled Gina, 'if you're going to be someone's

namesake, you couldn't have chosen a more successful person. I hope you'll be as famous as he is one day.'

Mickey's eyes responded with pleasure.

And in that split second Gina saw the eager young would-be Broadway dancer Filipo had described. Gina's fondness strengthened.

Harry said, 'I'm going backstage to turn on the lights and put a record on the deck for Mickey to dance to.'

Gina said, 'Thanks, Harry. Go ahead. Mickey, the stage is all yours. Filipo, will you sit by me?' She walked to a table as Filipo and Mickey strolled toward the wing steps exchanging camaraderie and good humour. He patted her on the back, sent her on her way. This old buddy stuff, thought Gina, between youngsters these days. Whatever happened to romance? No wonder the marriage rate is decreasing. As her brother pulled up a chair beside her, stretched out his legs, ankles crossed, clasped his hands behind his head, she said, 'Mickey seems a very pleasant person. I like her.'

He, without looking around, replied casually: 'So do I.'

'Don't faint with enthusiasm.'

He turned, grinned, winked.

Exasperating. Gina considered frying him with A Look, decided it would be futile, retracted her gaze to the side of the stage where Harry and Mickey were parting, he to disappear beyond the tabs, she to walk to the centre of the polished oak expanse.

The overhead lights faded. Soft pink illumination bathed Mickey. She stood, hands clasped down before her, and glanced toward Filipo. Gina from the corner of her eye, saw him give a thumbs-up. A scratchy gramophone rustle started from hidden speakers. Mickey tensed. Then an abrupt percussion introduction led to a jazzy instrumental *Music, Music, Music*. Mickey waited through the first few bars, snapping her fingers, picking up the tempo before jumping into her routine.

Gina watched.

To be honest, she was no expert on choreography or dance technique, but over the years she'd learned enough to know that this girl was way above average. Michelle Rooney had an exciting mixture of style and skill; above all she sparkled with that vital essence which could transmit itself to an audience, and from which stars are made.

Once more Gina thought of the girl's relationship with Filipo, and wondered if she was a practising Catholic and what her views were on combining her career with family life. Gina glanced at the strong profile of her brother, felt both loving and proud, and tried to imagine this man – not so long ago a small boy clutching her hand as she told him of their father's death – with a son of his own, a Rossi to continue the family line.

'Terrific!' Filipo was on his feet applauding. So was Suzy and the drummer, everyone in the room.

Gina pulled her attention back to the stage, realizing the music had stopped and Mickey was standing, panting, smiling expectantly in her direction. Gina arose, clapped enthusiastically, declaring, 'It made me exhausted just watching. Did you invent the entire routine? I'm sure it will be a great success.'

Mickey, wiping her forearm across her sweaty brow, asked with eagerness and surprise, 'Does that mean I might get a spot here at The First Floor?'

Gina replied, 'That'll be up to Harry.' As he appeared from the wings she called, 'Mister Dix, Miss Rooney would be grateful to receive her audition result without delay.'

Harry paused on the stage steps, cupped his long jaw in a pensive palm and in his best Jimmy Stewart drawled, 'Waaal nooow, young lady, reckon as how I'm gonna have to study on that awhile.'

'Hey,' beamed Mickey, 'what a terrific impersonation.'

'Crawler,' said Filipo.

Mickey gave him an elbow in the ribs and a peek at the tip of her tongue. He encircled her waist, pulling her to his side; and they laughed together.

Gina watched the exchange of affection with mixed emotions. Turning to Harry she asked, 'Well, sir, have you done your studying on Miss Rooney's talent?'

He nodded, slowly. 'Seems like,' he replied in his normal voice, 'The First Floor has a welcome addition to its line-up.'

'Wow!' cried Mickey, dashing to seize him and plant a loud, pink kiss on his cheek.

Then there was pleasure and congratulations all round. Within a couple of minutes champagne glasses were being clinked by everyone – including Suzy and her drummer, the two cleaners and Clara the housekeeper who burped on the bubbles exclaiming, 'Really, at this time in the morning,' adding there was no telling what state her laundry was going to get into.

The little party lasted for fifteen minutes. As it ended, Harry arranged for Mickey to discuss a contract with him at his Rossi Entertainment Management office next week. After Mickey again had thanked everyone for her chance to audition, she and Filipo went out enmeshed in their continuing celebration.

Gina said, 'Harry, you made a young lady very happy.'

'She deserves to be,' he replied. 'She has a lot of talent; a few rough edges, but they'll soon get smoothed out. I guarantee, inside six months the other clubs in town will be standing on line to sign her. No question, we'll have a new star in the family.'

'In the family?' exclaimed Gina.

'Just a figure of speech,' Harry returned nonchalantly. 'Well, must be moving along. See you later.' And with a grin that said it all he strolled away.

Gina might have said, Harumph, but at that moment a messenger arrived with a sealed grey folder. All other considerations were set aside as she opened the delivery to find a brief note from Irving Prentiss explaining that the accompanying half-dozen pages contained merely background information, and asking whether Gina wished any further investigation. On the top page was typed, MONUMENT PICTURES.

Gina hastened out, along the corridor to her office.

The door was slightly ajar and as Gina was about to push it a movement caught her eye. Someone was leaning over her desk. For an instant she imagined it was her secretary Mabel but almost at once realized it was a grey-suited man. More in puzzlement than alarm she thrust open the door to challenge, 'Who ...'

The man jerked around.

Gina exclaimed, 'Howard!' surprise pinning her on the

threshold to enquire reflexively, 'What are you doing?'

'Nothing,' he rejoined; the quick denial of a boy caught in his parent's bedroom, hands jumping into his pockets as if to hide from further inquisition, promoting truth with repetition: 'Nothing.'

Level-headedness still tilting, Gina glanced past her husband to scan the desktop.

'I wasn't pilfering paperclips,' Howard said.

'It wouldn't matter if you were,' returned Gina, offering a smile to calm the troubled moment as well as to smooth her own composure. 'You do have the right.' She read his face, observing his maturity sharpen into focus. Yet there remained a shadow of guilt behind his eyes. What had he been doing? Setting aside the question, Gina remarked brightly, 'I wasn't expecting you. Did you win the Chesapeake yacht race? How are you?' She thought he looked fit and handsome.

Howard answered, 'Yes, I won, and I'm fine, thanks. You look good too, Gina. Business putting a sparkle in your cheeks. But, then, you never need any other tonic, do you?'

The comment wasn't delivered sarcastically, rather as a simple statement of fact. Gina replied, 'You know the company has to be kept steaming ahead, Howard.'

'I've said before, it could be sold.'

'And I've explained …' Gina cut off the response. She inwardly sighed, feeling all at once weary, back once more to the familiar cause for disagreement. Yet she held back from an argument, for she understood the reasons for Howard's attitude.

Howard's mother, Alicia Cornell, widowed when he was a baby, had been single-mindedly dedicated to the running of the West Corporation, the hotel chain founded by her father; and while she had provided her son with everything money could buy, she never had given him the one thing he wanted most – her attention. Howard had grown up, increasingly seeking fulfilment from leisure pursuits, building his resentment against commerce until he would have nothing to do with it.

When Gina had married Howard she'd been aware of his lack of interest in the West Corporation, but had not realized how profoundly he'd been marked by his childhood. On his part, Howard had understood Gina's attachment to the Rossi Corporation, but had not known she could no more release her hold on the family business than could his mother.

Nowadays, they were still in love, Gina was sure, but their paths crossed only at the boundaries of their separate lives. Gina frequently told herself she was the one who must change course, yet always there was a new West-Rossi horizon to reach.

Setting the Monument Pictures report on her desk she headed off the present contention by saying, 'Are you in town for long? Will you be staying the night?'

Howard said, 'Just passing through. Meeting some friends up at the hunting lodge tonight.'

Gina was genuinely disappointed, and, briefly lost for words, simply shrugged and responded. 'Oh, well.'

Howard hesitated a moment, then he stepped toward her. He stood looking at her for several seconds before his hand moved out to grip her waist. He said, 'You're still very beautiful, Gina,' and the deep resonance of his voice, the dark fire in his eyes that had unseated her senses the first time she'd met him, caused her pulse to accelerate.

As Gina's gaze held his, her emotions convulsed. There was nothing juvenile about the fullness of his lips, the hard line of his jaw, the latent strength of his chest and arms. His hands circled her waist. It flashed across her mind to push them away as she thought of the Monument report and the business chores she had to clear before lunch; but the sudden flood of heat through her stomach caused her to sway, to reach out and hold on to Howard's upper arm for support.

His hand rose to her breast.

Gina gasped and managed to whisper hoarsely, 'Mabel might be back at any minute.'

Howard instantly released her, strode to close the door and lock it. He returned to Gina, gathered her into his arms and kissed her. A kiss that seared her lips, burned through her veins. It's been so long, she thought as she prolonged the raking kiss, experiencing the fierce movement of Howard's lips, the touch of his teeth, the hardness of his jaw.

And now the fire came. The self-control that had fettered

Gina these long months was consumed in the flames of her carnal heat. Her blood pounded in her temples as her head bent back under the pressure of Howard's desire. She melded herself to him, feeling her nipples erupt almost to the point of pain as she kneaded her breasts against his chest.

'Yes, Howard,' she rasped when he tugged at the buttons of her dress, carrying her down to the carpet.

That their subsequent lovemaking was brief was of no account. Gina was caught in a timeless delirium. Her senses were simultaneously numbed and heightened. She was in a dream while experiencing the utmost reality. She wanted to weep silently, needed to scream with pleasure as she soared toward fulfilment, her desperation mounting in ragged rhythm with Howard's urgency so that when he finally groaned, 'Gina, Gina,' it was only moments before she too cried aloud, flinging her arms outward, banging her fists on the floor in a blinding convulsive release.

They lay, recapturing their breath, for several minutes, until Howard finally propped himself on his elbow at Gina's side, surveyed her figure with appreciation and said, 'I hope that was better than studying contracts.'

Some of Gina's contentment faded. She wished he hadn't said that. Resisting the impulse to reply in kind, she sat up and answered, 'It was good, Howard. Very good.'

He said, 'I could cancel going up to the lodge tonight, and stay in town. Maybe even for a week or two. We could ...' He stopped when he saw the change in Gina's expression. 'You have things to do,' he said flatly.

Gina inwardly flinched. Next Wednesday she was scheduled to fly to Las Vegas to discuss the land purchase. She tried hurriedly to think. Could she cancel the trip? Could Irving go in her stead?

'Not to worry,' Howard said abruptly, standing and pulling on his pants. 'I remember, there's a horse show I promised to attend.' He cinched his belt with a sharp tug.

Gina arose slowly, gathering her dress and wrapping it about her. She thought she might have saved the moment, but she didn't know how; with the best will in the world she couldn't just dismiss all her forthcoming business commitments. She stood there in silence until Howard had stuffed his tie in his jacket pocket and, shirt still open at his throat, had started for the door.

Gina said quietly, 'Enjoy your stay at the lodge.'

Halting, Howard looked toward her. He responded, 'Thanks. Take care of yourself.'

For a few moments they stood facing each other across their unbridgeable gulf. Then Howard turned, unlocked the door, and was gone.

Gina dressed and went up to her apartment.

When she came down an hour later, she'd showered, donned fresh make-up, and brushed her hair into a blonde tumult about her face. She lunched at The Lady, brightly chatting to all who stopped by her table. By early afternoon she had left behind the shadow of her meeting with Howard. Nevertheless, it wasn't until the following morning she returned to her office.

Monument Pictures Corporation was founded in 1920 when a quartet of the silent screen's most-worshipped idols plus a pair of its adored goddesses, decided to pool their cash and box-office magnetism to produce and star in movies of their own choice, and, incidentally, reap one hundred per cent of the rewards hitherto gathered by their employers.

Each of the six was highly talented. Each was also wholly self-centred. Not one of them, therefore, was ever prepared to take a lesser role than any of the other five. Inside two years Monument had released only two movies. A year more and, along with its founders, the studio was sunk. Everybody in the industry said it wasn't worth salvaging.

Henry J. Jessel disagreed.

Henry J. Jessel loved motion pictures. In his mansion on his turkey ranch near Anaheim, California, the septuagenarian batchelor spent every day of his millionaire life privately viewing the flickering antics of strangers who were his only friends in the world. What was, to anyone connected with showbusiness, a disaster called Monument Pictures, was, to Henry J. Jessel, an island of fantastical escapism beckoning from beyond a monotonous turkey sea. He bought the studio.

He also bought Victor Scheer, the legendary producer

who had helped carve the fortunes of half-a-dozen major film companies. Inside twelve months new offices, production departments and four giant sound stages had been built on a wilderness tract of the Anaheim ranch. Scheer had completed eight pictures. Every one had shown a profit.

Gina turned the page inside the grey folder.

The ninety-three-year-old movie fanatic had died in 1943. In the last years of his life a group of eight producers, directors, actors and actresses had become the closest thing to a family he'd ever had. He willed them, in equal shares, the entire stock of Monument Pictures. Those heirs, however, were not commercial animals, and following Scheer's death only two years after Jessel's, the studio sailed swiftly back toward the financial rocks.

Gina read the report's concluding page.

Of the eight original shareholders, six were still living, all retired; and, according to a stipulation of Henry Jessel's will, the studio could be sold only with their unanimous consent. Monument was valued – after all tax and loan liabilities had been taken into account – at eighteen million dollars.

Gina slowly wrote the figure on her notepad – $18m – and sat regarding it as she telephoned Irving.

She thanked the accountant for preparing the report and asked if he'd heard whether Oliver Randolph had progressed in his bid to buy Monument. Irving said there was no further news. After pondering for a moment, Gina asked him to ascertain, personally and confidentially, the attitude of Monument's shareholding sextet to the sale of the studio.

When she'd replaced the receiver she stared again at the figure she'd written, and wondered what you got for that sort of money. It was some time before she returned her attention to more definite matters at hand.

Maybe it had something to do with having lived her first year in New York close to the breadline. Maybe it was an evocation of her girlhood when many of her happiest afternoons had been shared with her mother poring through French, British and American fashion magazines whose styles were, in a country where only Fascist-inspired design was encouraged, like champagne and caviar amid an enforced diet of beer and burgers. Or maybe it was simply an escape from her spotlighted role as Mrs Gina Rossi Cornell, a desire to become just another extra in the crowd.

Whatever her reasons, Gina had a weakness. She loved to clothes shop.

While the self-appointed female elite of Manhattan's *bon ton* would rather have opened their thin blue veins than be seen dead in any item of apparel which had not been stitched by the exclusive needles of one of half-a-dozen current modistes, Gina bought what she fancied, no matter where she saw it, and regardless of whose label was in it.

On this final day before she was due to fly to Las Vegas, there were a couple of last-minute chores, a few messages to deliver, and the car to collect from the repair shop. As a rule an office assistant would have handled these minor tasks, but Gina, noting that the legwork would necessitate traversing most of the shopping district, readily volunteered.

She set out at eight-thirty, toured every glittering display down Fifth Avenue, the vast department store floors around Herald Square, the small speciality shops along Thirty-fourth Street, plus everything in between. Feeling neither fatigue nor hunger, she paused only once for a lunch-counter hotdog with sauerkraut and mug of coffee when a noon clock advised she ought to stoke up a little energy.

Her expedition lasted nine hours, and it wasn't until the streets filled suddenly with hearthside-headed workers that Gina reluctantly turned for home. Still, it had been a brimful trip; and not without something to show: a bright red turban with a flamboyant bow at the back, plus a pair of silk stockings hand-painted with gardenias. Gina had no idea when she'd wear either. But she loved them. She'd loved every moment of her happy day.

She remembered to collect the car, drove homeward singing *She'll Be Coming Round The Mountains When She Comes*.

Painted on the asphalt at the entrance to the side alley of The Lady was a huge PRIVATE: NO ENTRY: NO PARKING. The same message, white-on-red on a three-foot square board, was screwed to the adjacent wall. Needless to say, the admonitions were universally ignored.

Gina negotiated her average-size blue Oldsmobile past nose-to-tail cars and vans, reflecting (as she did every time she drove down here) that it was a good thing she didn't favour a leviathan limousine and that she must, she really must, get lockable gates installed across the alley mouth.

The foot of the cul-de-sac was a T, with just enough space for Gina to turn and park. She climbed out with her packages, shut and locked the car door, walked to the private entrance and the staircase leading to the rear corridor of The First Floor, thence up a further flight to her apartment.

As a rule she rarely used this entrance, preferring to come and go via the restaurant. Apart from everything else it was a chore locking and unlocking the four doors along this rear route. 'Crime prevention is preferable to the need for crime detection,' a police security expert had averred soon after Gina had moved into the building. 'And locked doors, the more of 'em the better, are one of the finest preventers of all.'

Gina had accepted the theory that a burglar liked to be on and off the premises as swiftly as possible and if faced with too many time-consuming barriers would abandon his risky efforts. Thus all the doors here had their keys turned last thing at night. Gina took particular care with every room of her apartment whenever she went out, aware of their vulnerability amid the hundreds of strangers who thronged the restaurant and club day and night.

When she now reached her sitting room, unlocked it and entered, she immediately took her purchases through to the bedroom and tried them on. Yes, she loved them. Happy, she commenced her packing for Vegas.

It took half an hour. An early dinner tonight, she decided, then bed so as to be fresh for tomorrow's wearying cross-country flight. One final chore; check she'd left no personal items in the car. She went down to the alley – still jammed with vehicles – and walked the thirty yards to the Oldsmobile. She stepped around to the driver's door.

It was hanging half open.

Nitwit, didn't close it properly, was her first thought.

Then she saw the mangled lock. 'Damn!' she swore aloud, glaring at the crow-barred metal beside the handle, the torn bolts of the fastening mechanism. Her breath escaped in a ragged exhalation, and, slowly, her initial reaction abated to resignation. Ah well, this was the first time it had happened in all the years she'd lived here; and at least there'd been nothing of value for the villian to steal. Did he bother to take the bits and pieces from the glove-compartment? Gina opened the ruined door, bent down.

And saw the garbage on the floor.

She recoiled, hand jumping to her mouth. For the sight was loathsome. In the footwell, in front of the pedals lay a dishevelled mess of decaying vegetable matter and liquid filth. So shocked was Gina she just stood and stared for several moments until she could make out individual shreds of putrefaction, seeing that the slimy wetness was oozing across the carpet. She swung away, slamming shut the door, only to have it rebound from its buckled jamb.

Someone stepped back behind one of the parked cars.

Gina caught the movement from the corner of her eye.

A driver returned for his vehicle? But he, or she, was merely standing, unmoving. Gina could see only a dark-clad shoulder and a sliver of face between a windshield and the rear of a van. Was she being watched? She was at once both angered, on the verge of flinging invective, yet uneasy at the thought of being observed by the perpetrator of the dirty act against her car. In a way she herself felt defiled, and a shiver of distaste ran through her.

To hell with that! Gina banged her fist on the car's roof. 'Hey, you,' she yelled. 'Think this is funny? It's pathetic. Garbage? Garbage is what you've got for brains?'

She strode across the alley, obliterating her apprehension with a slash of pugnacity. 'Come round here again and you'll get what's for.' Damn these parked cars! Gina was obliged to slow her advance and edge sideways between bumpers. Here it occurred to her that confrontation was neither an adult nor a very sensible course; she might end up getting thumped, or worse. Too late – she was in the narrow space between the lined vehicles and a four-storey brick wall.

But she was alone. She flung a look right and left. The T end of the alley was deserted. At the other, Forty-seventh street bustled toward evening. Gina wasn't sure whether she was relieved or disappointed. Perhaps there hadn't been anyone here in the first place, and the lurking figure had been only a manifestation of her own anger. As for the real foulers of her car? 'Probably just kids,' she told herself. 'Twelve blocks away by now.'

She walked back to the Oldsmobile. It was a moment before she was able to peer in again at the noisesome mess. Looks a lot worse than it is, she rationalized and went into the rear of The Lady to fetch brush and dustpan and a bucket of disinfected hot water.

By the time the car was driven away by a man from the repair shop to have its smashed lock fixed, it looked and smelled as clean and fresh as new.

Nevertheless, Gina was glad she wouldn't be using it during the coming weeks.

Chapter Four

Seven years ago, this was just a blazing desert cut by a scantily used highway, with sagebrush, cactus and creosote bushes the only vegetation clinging to the sun-scorched shale and sandstone stretching to the ragged crags of the Spring Mountains. Coyotes, lizards and snakes were the only creatures to venture amidst this desolation four miles from a small town called Las Vegas.

Today, across the burned landscape, spread dozens of part-built casinos, motels and diners swarming with construction crews; and along the ribbon of cracked concrete stood a string of newly-completed palaces, their massive roadside signs sprouting outlandishly to proclaim entertainment giants starring twice nightly at the Flamingo, Desert Inn, Sands, Sahara, Thunderbird.

In the rear of the limousine carrying her from the airport Gina felt a tremor of excitement. Even in daylight, before night and neon transformed Las Vegas Boulevard into a gash of rainbow lightning crackling against black sky, there was a dynamism about this oasis, an air of recklessness, which, thought Gina with a smile of self-admission, was contagious.

Her exhilaration swelled as the limousine approached the structure now filling her vision.

The pyramid was twelve stories high, taller than any of its rivals. The sides were clad in polished steel and mirrored glass. Travellers on the highway could see it from the horizon, a dazzling jewel on the endless panorama of sand and rock. From the sidewalk, where Gina's Cadillac now turned, a white-paved driveway flanked by palms led to a forecourt lake at the centre of which six fountains spouted forty feet into the air, their fine mist drifting and settling like diamond dust on emerald turf and vistas of scarlet blooms. Beyond, above the parade of a dozen double glass doors, set across the fascia in letters twelve feet high was:

THE SILVER LADY.

Gina went in beneath the name sign to a vast blue and silver lobby. Though it was eleven o'clock in the morning, richly tuxedoed men and sveltely gowned women moved to and fro beneath the galaxy of chandeliers. Gina exchanged greetings and enthusiasm with the staff at the reception desk before crossing the lobby to take a look into the most luxurious casino in Vegas.

People thronged the room, laughing, talking, shouting as their numbers came up. The cacophony of voices competed with the rattle of roulette balls in their wheels, the patter of craps dice on their beds, the whir of slots mechanisms, and the boogie-woogie rhythm of a Steinway grand in the bustling lounge area off to the left.

Happy, Gina went down a short hallway to an elevator lettered, PRIVATE. With a key from her purse she opened the door, stepped into the car to be carried leisurely upward: past the three restaurants and bars where twenty-four hours a day guests could order anything from a cowboy breakfast to a gourmet dinner; the showroom where tonight Nat King Cole would bewitch his audience; the floors of bedrooms and suites; finally the summit of the crystal mountain, Gina's apartment and office.

She entered her sitting room.

The walls were covered with washed Chinese silk in shades of fuschia and magnolia. Swagged velvet curtains hung at the floor-to-ceiling windows. Birds-eye maple cabinets and bureaux matched the block floor and panelled ceiling. The upholstery was grey kid. On a raised dining area overlooking Las Vegas Boulevard, the black glass-topped table could easily accommodate twenty guests.

Gina smiled wryly at the decor. It wasn't exactly her idea of simplistic elegance, but, fashioned for this city, it met her visitors' expectations of unbridled opulence; and whereas she wouldn't want to live with it for too long at a stretch, she couldn't deny she thoroughly enjoyed the interludes she spent here.

After she'd showered and changed into a cream wool suit, she was returning toward the private elevator when its door slid aside and the figure which towered from the car boomed, 'Principessa. *Come sta*? Welcome. You're a sight for these old gambler's eyes.' And the giant strode forward, lifted Gina clear of the floor, and heartily kissed her on both cheeks.

Thirty-seven years ago Max Barzini had hoisted Alfredo Rossi's first-born with the same enthusiastic affection. His massive hands had enveloped the infant as his gaze examined her with wonder, delight and, above all, love. 'A princess,' he had whispered. To which Alfredo had responded, 'Your princess, old friend. Your godchild.'

From that day forth Max would have moved mountains with his bare fists to aid his principessa. He had instigated her escape from exile, accompanied her to America, watched over her, done all he could to ease her burden during their first long, hard year in their new homeland. Gina, in turn, had vowed to herself she one day would repay him.

When she opened The Lady, Max was made vice-president. 'Principessa,' he had protested, 'what do I know about running a restaurant? All I ever did for your Poppa was occasionally operate the cash register.' Gina had replied, 'And you did it brilliantly. You can check a bill in the blink of an eye. It's what comes from having been figuring the odds on the turn of a card since you were old enough to hold a deck.' Ten years later the argument had held doubly valid when it came to the choice of President in Charge of Operations at The Silver Lady.

Her feet back on the floor, Gina smiled affectionately at her godfather. Sixty-six years old now, but, seemingly, bigger, healthier than ever, his silver hair sweeping back from a wide mahogany-coloured brow, his teeth large, straight and white gleaming beneath magnificently curling moustachios.

Gina said, 'It's lovely to be back, Max. I've missed this wonderful, crazy place. And I've especially missed you.' She gave him another hug.

After several minutes of happy reunion they went down in

the elevator for an early lunch, Gina declaring the desert air always made her so ravenous.

She consumed a huge filet mignon, plus a baked potato overflowing with sour cream, chives and bacon bits, washed down with a bottle of spring water, at a corner table of one of the hotel's restaurants. As they ate, Max reported full rooms and record takings. He said that the sooner West-Rossi finalized the purchase of the extra acreage in Vegas the better. Gina confirmed she'd be seeing the landowner the day after tomorrow.

When they'd finished the meal, Gina accompanied Max to his office to discuss various business matters. The afternoon soon passed, and later, after Gina had changed into a simple but elegant white evening gown, Max into his tuxedo, they toured the casino, had dinner and ended the night in the showroom appreciating Mister Nat Cole.

The following day Gina had a full diary of meetings with suppliers, local Rossi Taverns franchisees and a party of officials from the State Gaming Commission. By the end of this busy round, however, she was far from tired, her batteries charged with the vitality of the city. 'How about a look at what the competition's up to?' she suggested to Max and he readily agreed.

They visited all the major casino-hotels on the dazzling two mile stretch of Las Vegas Boulevard which was fast becoming known by the nickname of The Strip. Wherever they called, Gina and Max were met with conviviality by managers or owners who were only two happy to show off their latest gambling and entertainment facilities.

Gina hadn't spent such a hectic evening in quite a while, and she loved every moment. But, by midnight, she had to concede that while her spirit was more than willing to continue the expedition, her feet were definitely ready to call it a day. Also she remembered she was apt to overlook her godfather's age, and perhaps ought not to keep him trailing around much longer. In the piano lounge of the Alcazar she said, 'If you don't mind, Max, I think I'll make this my last port of call.'

They stayed to hear the pianist to the end of his set and then Gina gathered up her purse. She was turning in her chair as Max began to rise when she was halted by the sight of a noisy group who had entered on the opposite side of the room. Tony Nevada was at the hub.

Max caught the direction of Gina's stare. 'Principessa,' he said with concern, 'I forget to tell you. He's opening this weekend at the Blue Moon.'

Gina remained seated, watching the ten-strong party of showy males and females take up two tables. She asked quietly, 'Do you know if Cassie's with him?'

Max lowered himself back into his chair. 'I made enquiries when I learned he was in town. I'm afraid he only has that gang of hangers-on. Cassie must have stayed behind in Beverly Hills.' Recognizing Gina's disappointment, he added, 'I'm sorry too, Principessa. I would have liked to see Cassie again. It was a sad day when she left our lives.'

Gina nodded, bit her lip as she saw in her mind's eye the woman who had been her dearest friend.

Without Cassie O'Brien's good-humoured comradeship Gina knew she might never have survived her earliest months in America toiling as a hotel chambermaid. For years they had shared their joys and sorrows, hopes and dreams; and, Gina was sure, today Cassie would still be at her side if it hadn't been for Tony Nevada.

Three years ago Cassie had become infatuated with the handsome young crooner who had made a string of hit records. No amount of advice or cautioning could make her see what a self-centred womanizer he really was; and after the subject had caused the only row she and Gina had ever had, Cassie, declaring she'd commit suicide rather than give up her lover, had gone to live with him at his Beverly Hills mansion. Gina hadn't heard from her since.

Max said gently, 'Shall we go now, Principessa?'

'Yes, please, let's,' answered Gina, and she joined him and together they started across the room. To reach the exit, however, they were obliged to pass Tony Nevada and his entourage. As Gina approached his table she was in two minds whether to ignore him.

But he gave her no choice. Standing, he said, 'Hello, Gina. Long time no see,' in the provocative drawl which had made him the heart-throb of millions. He added, 'Hi, Max,' but his gaze never left Gina.

She halted, and was unable to suppress an inner tremor; for no matter how much she disliked the narcissistic singer, she had never been able to deny his disturbing sexuality. Beneath his intensely blue eyes his high cheekbones gave him a faintly Oriental appearance, though this was contested by corn-blonde hair falling casually across his brow.

Gina said cordially, 'Good evening.'

'You're looking as ... lovely as ever,' Tony Nevada said, with just enough of a pause in mid-sentence to emphasize the suggestive tone of his words. 'Won't you join us?'

'No, thank you,' Gina answered, thinking her voice sounded too hasty. 'We're on our way home.'

'So early? But the night's young. Can't I persuade you to change your mind? We could show Vegas how to have a good time.' His lips curved, and for the barest instant his eyes flicked across Gina's figure.

Gina's scalp prickled. She said, 'We really must be going. Goodnight.' And she quickly took Max's arm, turned and went with him toward the exit. Behind her she heard Tony Nevada laugh and say, 'I'll see you again,' and she could almost feel his gaze follow her every step across the room.

When they reached the outside forecourt, Gina stood, her hot face raised to the night air as the doorman hailed one of the waiting taxis.

Max asked, 'Are you all right, Principessa?'

Gina answered, 'Yes, thanks, Max. I'm sorry I rather rushed out of there, but ... I felt ...' Actually, she wasn't sure what she'd felt; annoyance with herself mostly, she supposed, for her reflexive sexual response to Tony Nevada in spite of him being the man who had obsessed and taken away her friend. Guilt pricked her as she again thought of Cassie, and she was grateful that the taxi drew up to break this awkward moment.

Once they were heading homeward Gina avoided returning to the subject of the brief encounter with Tony Nevada, and turned the conversation to comment on all the places they'd visited tonight. Fortunately, Max, too, seemed keen to leave the episode behind and readily followed Gina's lead.

Back at The Silver Lady they said goodnight and Gina went up to her apartment where she immediately took a long, cool shower. She emerged, towelled herself vigorously, donned a white terry robe and removed from her briefcase the file on the piece of land whose owner she was scheduled to see in ten hours' time.

She read the file twice.

When she set it aside, her mind was back on an even keel. And with her clearer thinking it occurred to her that while Tony Nevada was here in Las Vegas she might take the opportunity to try to get in touch with Cassie. The day Cassie had left, she'd been in such a state over her young lover she'd told Gina never to interfere in her life again. But that had been three years ago. Surely, Gina rationalized, provided she steered clear of mentioning Tony Nevada's amorality, she'd stand a chance of making up with her old friend.

It was a tentative but an encouraging thought. Gina decided to sleep on it a while.

In the meantime, there was a piece of land to buy.

Bridging her eyes against the afternoon glare, Gina surveyed the tract, half a mile down the highway from The Silver Lady. It was a prime spot, and, Gina thought, increasing in value even as she stood here. For Max was right, Vegas was expanding faster than any city in the country: when Gina had first inspected this acreage a few months ago it had been flanked only by desert; now there were bustling construction sites with NEW CASINO OPENING SOON signs on both sides.

Of course, Mister Ortez who owned the land Gina was now looking at was fully aware of its mounting worth, and this had been reflected in his negotiations with her this morning. Still, a little haggling was the name of the game; in fact, Gina rather enjoyed it, and had not been unduly concerned when the man had said he'd take a couple more days to mull over West-Rossi's proposition.

After she'd strolled back up the boulevard, she phoned Irving in New York and told him everything was under control.

Irving brought her up to date on various items, finally

adding that the report on the Monument Pictures shareholders' attitude toward a sale would be complete by the weekend.

Gina's interest perked at the mention of the movie company. 'What about Oliver Randolph?' she enquired. 'Has he been in touch with the shareholders?'

'Yes,' Irving confirmed. 'But, from what I gather, he can't obtain their unanimous agreement.'

Gina felt a surge of satisfaction. Although she wasn't given to holding grudges, she still burned whenever she recalled Randolph's arrogant smirk. She briefly considered pursuing the subject with Irving but decided against it. So far he hadn't questioned her motives for investigating the movie studio – compiling reports on all manner of business activities was common practice for major companies like West-Rossi – and, Gina thought, it would be better for now to leave it that way; for, to be honest, she wasn't really quite sure what she intended to do about Monument.

After she'd concluded her conversation with Irving, the uncertainty still shadowed her. Could she actually buy the studio? Outdo Oliver Randolph? Originally the notion had been impulsive. But that had been back in New York. It had not faded over distance or time. Was it becoming an obsession? Of course not, Gina assured herself. It's a perfectly legitimate commercial proposition.

A few minutes later she was again on the telephone. The switchboard operator at Monument Pictures put her through to Felix Gilbert's office. Gina said with genuine pleasure, 'Felix, how are you? Yes, it's lovely to hear you too.'

When she set down the receiver she had made a date to visit the studio tomorrow morning.

Sentinel iron railings, sun-reflecting gold, marched from east and west to meet at the twenty-foot wide, thirty-foot high stone archway carved with the legend MONUMENT PICTURES. The massive bronze gates stood open, but beyond them a horizontal red and white pole bearing a circular HALT sign deterred the gaggle of twenty-odd girls, gossiping, peering into the studio grounds, glancing with constant hope at the infrequent approaching traffic, ever-ready with eager smiles, autograph books and cameras.

Gina braked her small hire car at the sign beside a neat Spanish-style lodge. An elderly man in a maroon and gold uniform and peaked cap exited from the building, saluted and enquired, 'Name, please, ma'am?'

'Cornell,' answered Gina. 'To see Mister Gilbert.'

The guard, his finger arriving at confirmation on his clipboard list, acknowledged, 'Fine. They're shooting this morning, Mrs Cornell. Go directly down past the offices.' He pointed. 'Out across the backlot, about a mile. You'll see them. Making plenty of din and smoke.' He stepped to where the red and white pole sat in a post, hooked his hand under it and pivoted it into the air.

Gina said, 'Thanks,' and drove forward.

On both sides were white stuccoed, red tiled buildings fronted by slim gold and emerald fir trees, manicured lawns and flower beds. Directional arrows indicated OFFICES, MUSIC LIBRARY, DRESSING ROOMS, PROJECTION THEATRE, COMMISSARY, POST OFFICE. Beyond these came clusters of low concrete workshops signed, CARPENTERS, ELECTRICIANS, PAINTERS, BLACKSMITH; and towering behind them Gina could see a double row of vast arching roofs, like a parade of aircraft hangars.

I never really appreciated the scale of it, she thought; for, despite her showbusiness connections, she had never before visited a movie studio. As she drove, she recalled statistics from Irving's report on Monument; 450 acres of land, 120 buildings, two man-made lakes, two miles of river, three miles of railroad track, half-a-million props, three million musical and sound effect recordings, plus more than 2000 employees. Quite an inventory.

But, thought Gina, all written in red ink.

The concrete roadway ended, became a dusty dirt track winding into scrubby, low hills.

All at once a US Army Jeep careered around the bend.

It rattled past in a cloud of grit, at the wheel a uniformed private, in the passenger seat a four-star general. Before Gina had time to decide whether it had been Eisenhower or Henry Fonda she was beyond the curve, driving between smoke-blackened, ruined houses, into a town square. An ochre stone church stood at the far side. Around the perimeter, old buildings, a trattoria with outdoor tables, a store with a hanging Tabacchini board, posters of Il Duce plastered on walls.

As Gina halted, six American soldiers bolted from a distant doorway, across the square, firing rifles at the church's bell tower. The returning machine gun clatter spat up a racing trail of bullet impacts in the men's wake. One of them cried out, pitched sprawling, his helmet bouncing across the cobbles as his companions threw themselves down amid the trattoria's tables and a voice yelled, 'Cut.'

Gina almost burst into delighted applause. She climbed from her car and headed over to a group of men and women who were now checking cameras, scribbling on scripts, talking animatedly while the shot soldier stood, dusted himself off, retrieved his helmet and strolled to rejoin his buddies.

Gina asked a youth adjusting a huge sun reflector, 'Mister Gilbert?' and was pointed toward a door beneath a Polizia sign as someone shouted, 'One more. Re-set.' She walked to the door and stepped through – onto a sun-blistered patch of barren land where two vast steel and chrome trailers, an open-countered catering truck and a trio of mobile toilets semi-circled three long trestle tables lined with foldable wooden chairs.

At one of the tables a ruddy-faced man in his late fifties, panama hat shoved to the back of his head, khaki shirt sleeves untidily rolled, was confabbing heatedly with two younger men while frequently banging his fist on a large blueprint laid out between them. None of the group registered Gina's arrival, but continued for several stormy minutes about escalating timber costs, recyclable backdrops and the impracticalities of building Rome's Trevi Fountain. At last the man in the panama slumped back, said, 'Okay, fellers. See what you can do. But please, please don't blow any bigger hole in the budget.' The others gathered up the blueprints, and left.

The khaki-shirted man stood, removed his hat to reveal a halo of grey hair. Stepping forward he gripped Gina's shoulders and said with exaggerated weariness, 'Do you mind if I just lean on you for ten minutes?'

Gina smiled fondly. 'Hello, Felix.'

He replaced his hat. 'Come inside, it's cooler.' At the nearest trailer's steps he ushered Gina over the threshold. The interior was furnished as an office with a deep pile blue carpet, mahogany desk and filing cabinets, four hide armchairs and a corner bar where an electric fan soughed from side to side.

Felix strode there, poured two tall glasses of orange juice over ice, brought them to the armchairs and handed one to Gina as he sat opposite her. He swallowed half the drink in a single gulp, breathed appreciatively and observed, 'Washes down the taste of haggling.'

Gina rejoined, 'I thought you thrived on it.'

Felix smiled, but there was more tiredness than humour in the years around his eyes. 'Sure I did, once upon a time,' he said. 'But these days it's all I can do to keep from throwing in the towel.'

Gina realized her old friend wasn't kidding. She said, 'So Monument's financial problems are as bad as they've been painted?'

'Worse,' replied Felix. 'The studio's in a swamp, sinking fast. If someone doesn't throw us a line soon we'll have had it.'

Gina ventured, 'I understand Oliver Randolph's proposed himself as saviour.'

Felix grimaced. 'He came strutting around, telling everybody how much they'd love working for him. Frankly, I'd rather drown than have to sail under that pirate. Still,' he said with a sparkle returning to his eyes, 'maybe I won't have to, if West-Rossi bails us out.'

'West-Rossi?' exclaimed Gina. 'I never said anything ...'

Felix smiled knowingly. 'When you called yesterday to say you were out west on business and thought it would be pleasant if we could get together for lunch here at the studio, I figured there had to be more to it than just a masochistic desire to eat our commissary food.'

Gina maintained her innocent facade a moment longer, then she laughed. She said, 'I wasn't trying to pull the wool over your eyes, Felix, but, you know, walls have ears, and I don't want the press picking up the story yet awhile.'

'But you're actually considering putting in a bid for this place?' Felix shook his head. 'And I always thought you were one of the few sane people I knew.'

'Would it be such a bad move?'

Felix looked thoughtful. 'I guess,' he said after a moment, 'Monument could be put into profit. But it needs a lot of investment in new facilities and equipment. Plus a lot of patience. Making movies is a slow business, and any capital injected here is going to take a long time to show a return.'

'Nevertheless,' suggested Gina, 'you think the industry's got a future? You aren't one of the doom and gloom merchants who reckons it will be wiped out by television?'

'Certainly audiences are going to shrink,' conceded Felix. 'Folks will stay home watching television because it's free. But if the studios accept that the days of the B-movie are over, look to their laurels and produce the sort of top-quality entertainment which is beyond television's capabilities, then picture-making isn't finished. I genuinely believe that.' He downed the remainder of his orange juice.

Gina remained quiet for a minute, sipping her own drink, reading the conviction in Felix's expression. I'm actually here, contemplating buying a movie studio, she thought. And a thrill of anticipation ran through her.

'Well,' said Felix, standing, 'how's about taking a look at what you might get for your money?'

Gina returned, 'I hoped you'd say that.'

Five minutes later, with Gina at the wheel of her hire car, they were heading back across the scrubby landscape toward the distant complex of buildings.

'Turn there,' directed Felix, and, skirting the cluster of workshops, they approached the double row of huge hangarlike structures. Each weather-bleached fascia was stencilled SOUND STAGE. Gina drove slowly along the wide street; slowly, in order to avoid as well as to observe the fantastic activity:

A miniature truck towing half-a-dozen palm trees on castors; a canvas backdrop of the Egyptian pyramids, big as a movie theatre screen, being trundled by two men in overalls; a gang hauling cables and a massive camera on a trolley; a score of girls running past, swishing in Hawaiian garlands and grass skirts; an elderly woman in bank teller neatness toting an alligator over her shoulder; a gang of laughing cavaliers playing handball down a side alley; a pair of Mexicans, back-to-back squatting on a parked spaceship eating hotdogs; people hurrying, calling greetings, carrying musical instruments, wheeling rails loaded with costumes, oblivious to Gina's wide-eyed peregrination.

Her excitement was fizzing.

Felix said, 'Pull in here. I'll show you where all these characters get their props.' After they'd parked in front of what looked like the biggest barn in the world, he led the way to its door and ushered Gina inside.

A cathedral, was her immediate thought. The lofty interior stretched away to indistinct shadowy distance. On each side of the central aisle marched towers of racking, and, outwards, more of the same, columned to the high roof. From up there, through hazed skylights, fell dust-moted shafts of sun to pool the floor. Footsteps rang from no distinguishable direction; voices echoed. The air was cool, unmoving on the congregation of many years.

'To see every item would take six months,' advised Felix. 'We'll just take a look down one of the aisles.' As he walked he explained, 'In here, the least-used articles. Specials. The everyday stuff – crockery, firearms, furniture, books and so on – are stored in a separate building.'

Looking to her side Gina faced a massive four-poster bed gilded and carved in lions heads and vines, burgundy canopied with velvet swags and drapes; an opulent catafalque for dead flies shrouded in dust. She asked, 'What movie did this appear in?'

'I've no idea,' admitted Felix. 'I don't even remember when I was last in here. You see, there's rarely any reason for producers, designers, directors, anybody else for that matter, to visit. Once a movie's scenes have been decided, a requisition list is issued, and it becomes the props department's responsibility. To give you an idea of what a list might read like, think about the furnishings of your own sitting room, everything in it, right down to the stack of old magazines and half-empty box of candy.'

Felix paused as Gina gave a slow, thoughtful nod. 'Right,' he said, 'now imagine the number of scenes there are in a movie – hotel lobbies, restaurants, factory floors, hospitals, bars – and how many more items they're going to contain than your sitting room.' He added, 'And, remember, wardrobe has its own additional storage facilities.'

Gina continued amid the bizarre hoard; saw Roman chariots, a stuffed elephant, suits of armour, a six-foot-high wedding cake, the prow of a pirate galleon, a severed head on a silver tray, a skeleton in a rocking chair, a papier-mâché statue of Sherlock Holmes, chess pieces as big as people, a penny-farthing, several igloos, a French guillotine, Frankenstein's monster …

These were a few of the pieces she later would recall. She was a child in Toyland, too wide-eyed to see all she passed.

When they left the vast store Felix led Gina into the production complex. She'd never realized there was so much to film-making. She looked and listened, fascinated as Felix unfolded how an initial script conception progressed through set construction, wardrobe and casting to the actual shooting which required a small army of experts in sound, lighting and special effects.

They interrupted their tour with lunch in the commissary, where the food wasn't half as bad as Felix made out; and although Gina was quite used to the backstage scene at The Silver Lady showroom, she nevertheless was thrilled dining here amid all the colourful characters she'd seen on her drive past the sound stages.

After the meal, they stepped again into the labyrinth of offices and workshops to observe and talk with the scores of post-production technicians who added mood, music and timing to a movie's completed print. 'Eventually,' explained Felix, 'As much as two hundred thousand feet of film will have been edited to end up with about ten thousand – the length of an average picture.'

It was almost four in the afternoon by the time Gina was sitting with Felix in his office. She'd have loved to go and watch some of the indoor filming which was taking place, but felt she ought not to impose on Felix any longer. She'd taken in as much as possible and, for the first time, could understand Filipo's fascination with movie-making. The thought of owning the studio was gripping her imagination.

She said, 'Thanks for a marvellous tour, Felix. I can see now why pictures cost so much money.'

'And,' said Felix, 'why Monument is valued at eighteen million dollars. Still contemplating a bid?'

Gina set aside some of her exhilaration. 'I'd have to talk with Harry and Max and the others of course, but, I admit, I am tempted. In the meantime, though I'd be grateful if you kept my intentions under your hat.'

Felix agreed to that and for several minutes went on to chat about the industry and mutual showbusiness acquaintances in general. As Gina was deciding it was time she was on her way, Felix said, 'Did you hear if Cassie O'Brien was okay?'

Gina blinked in puzzled surprise. 'Cassie?'

'Wasn't she a friend of yours, some years back?'

Gina said, 'Yes, we were close, once. But I haven't seen Cass since she came to live out here with Tony Nevada.'

'Oh, then you wouldn't know what happened?'

'Happened?' responded Gina, concern edging her voice.

Felix hesitated at the change in Gina's tone. 'Maybe nothing did,' he said, retreating. 'Sorry, I was repeating gossip. I shouldn't, of course, but, you know how it is in Hollywood, gets to be a bad habit.'

'What gossip?' Gina prompted.

'Really, it was probably nothing.'

'Felix, please.'

He paused, then sighed, 'Me and my big mouth.' He said, 'It was a couple of weeks back. There was a rumour – just a rumour – that a doc had been called in the night to Tony Nevada's place, to treat a woman.' Felix shrugged, 'Cassie O'Brien and the housekeeper were the only women there at the time, and the housekeeper was perfectly okay chatting with the mailman the following morning. Look,' he stressed, 'like I said, chances are it was simply village tittle-tattle, invented by folk with nothing better …'

Gina didn't hear any more; she was caught in a confusion of uncertainty and alarm as she recalled the final time she'd tried to persuade her friend out of her infatuation with Tony Nevada, Cassie's declaration, 'I'd rather die than live without him.' So what would she do if he left her? Why had a doctor been called? Gina thought of her encounter with the singer back in Vegas. Cassie hadn't been with him.

She asked suddenly, 'Has Cassie been seen since?'

'So I heard,' Felix replied.

'Looking all right?'

'Well, I wouldn't know about that.'

Gina bit her lip, trying to think logically. At last she questioned, 'Do you have Tony Nevada's address?'

Felix answered, 'Of course.'

Chapter Five

High firs and May blossoms cast late afternoon shadows across the quiet streets of Beverly Hills. Beyond stately gate pillars could be glimpsed English villas, French farmhouses, Spanish ranches, Colonial mansions. The Tony Nevada house was a Bavarian castle, turreted and gabled at the head of a long bricked drive.

Gina halted her car on the street, trying to steady her thoughts. Back at Monument she'd been hard put to keep her dismay under control and avoid worrying Felix. She'd left him a short time after his revelation and driven directly here. All the way she'd told herself that to imagine Cassie would attempt suicide was preposterous, nevertheless she'd felt compelled to make sure her friend was safe and well.

Leaving the car, Gina walked up the drive to stand before the iron-studded front door. After a moment's hesitation she tugged the hanging bell pull. It made no detectable sound amid the secluded acres. Gina waited.

The sunshine was warm, the birdsong clear, the scent of balsam from the pines sharply aromatic. All this was normal, and the normality gradually penetrated Gina's senses. Her resolve began to slip. Should she have rushed here so precipitiously. For what had she expected to do when she arrived? To be frank, she admitted, she hadn't really thought it through to a sensible conclusion. Not until this moment had she given any consideration to how to handle whatever emotion – distress, anger, indifference – she was met with by Cassie.

The door opened.

The dark-complexioned, middle-aged woman queried, '*Si? Senora? Que quiere Usted*? Senor Nevada he is not here. No one is here. You leave a message? I pass on to Senor Nevada's personal manager. *Me comprende?*'

Gina's mouth was temporarily stuck. The sudden appearance of the woman had taken her by surprise. For some irrational reason she'd expected Cassie to open the door. Gathering her wits she began, 'No, I'm not looking for Mister Nevada. I don't wish to leave a message. Will you please tell ...' She stopped there, seeing the woman's face struggling for understanding. '*Lo siento,*' Gina said. '*Perdone me.*' Went on more slowly, 'Senorina Cassie O'Brien? May I see her, please? Will you tell her Gina Cornell ... No. Just tell her there is someone to see her. *Entiende*?'

The woman stared, frowning. Then, slowly, her features opened with comprehension. 'Ah, *si*. Senorina O'Brien. Yes.' She nodded and her eyes became sad.

The look was unmistakable, and cold fingers of anxiety touched Gina's neck. '*Por favor,*' she requested, 'tell her I am here.'

Biting her lower lip the woman shook her head. 'No. Not possible. Not here. Senorina O'Brien not here.'

'She's out?'

'*Si*. Out. She goes out. Many weeks ago.'

Many weeks! Gina tumbled from concern toward consternation. She asked urgently, 'Did she say where she was going? Was she upset? Did she ...' Damn it, her Spanish was abysmal. She searched desperately for the words.

'Upset? Ah, *si*, Yes, very upset.' The woman's face clouded. '*Tiene usted ...*' She paused, shrugged apologetically.

The hopeless exchange was mauling Gina's nerves. She mentally railed against her inability to communicate, while her fears darkened. How upset had Cassie been? 'Where ...' she began anxiously; but the woman was turning away, saying over her shoulder, '*Un momento, por favor.*'

Gina fretted there until the woman re-appeared with a small piece of paper in her hand, presenting it, nodding, saying, 'Senorina O'Brien.' Taking the offering Gina stared at the ink-written address. She shook her mind, trying to remember the street geography of Los Angeles. The piece of paper, she thought, indicated a location along the coast. 'May I keep this?' she asked and mimed putting the slip in her purse.

'*De Nada,*' responded the woman.

'Thank you,' said Gina. '*Gracias.*' For a second she wanted to say more, to offer some nicety, but the concern on the other's face cancelled the consideration and Gina only reached out, touched the woman's hand, repeated, '*Gracias*,' then turned and ran back along the drive. She shut herself into the car, the thump of her heart intensifying her sense of urgency as she thrust the key into the ignition, revved the engine and accelerated down the hill.

Gina turned right along Santa Monica Boulevard and sped westward toward the goldening sky.

Ten minutes later the ocean was at her left side. Sunlight flashed on the blue waves, exploded like diamonds as the surf broke on the white shore. Where am I going? Gina thought suddenly. She skidded in at the side of the road, delved the glove compartment, pulled out a fistful of maps, praying that Los Angeles was here.

Thank goodness. She struggled to unfold the unwieldy sheet, cursing her own thick fingeredness as she opened it flat on the steering wheel. Rummaging amid the clutter in her purse she extricated the piece of paper, checked the address, traced her finger along the map's coastal highway. There – Las Tunas Beach, and a slip road a mile ahead. Gina dropped the map on the passenger seat, shot away from the verge in a spume of grit and dust.

Too much was in her head now; too many questions, too many rebuttals of her self assurances. The wind blasted in through the open window, tearing at her hair as confusion shredded her thoughts.

The car bounced and veered in a pothole. Gina's response was automatic, but she was negligent of the danger. She was in a havoc of distraction, oblivious to the palm trees, gas stations, bungalows flashing by. She no longer was aware of anything except her all-pervading apprehension as she peered ahead for the turn-off sign.

It came into view, pointing a parallel course to the highway, a dirt road between the beach and a string of timber houses. Gina turned down there, slowing to read the numbers on the mailboxes. As the wind on her face lessened, so some semblance of lucidity returned. She surveyed the dwellings: most two-storey, some fresh white-painted or varnished, a few the colour of old bones with a crustation of salt. In some driveways stood cars, or sailboats with folded masts. But no sign of people.

So lonely, thought Gina. Why would Cassie come to this lonely spot by the ocean? Close to the fierce surf.

Now she heard the sound of it, and she swung around to see where it crashed in a boiling line of foam. She never had liked the sea. In her darkest nightmares, visions of destruction always were born on pounding waves, death always lay in whirlpool depths. She looked back to the houses. Three more and that surely must be the one.

She pulled the car to a halt on the strip of raggedy grass separating the sand from the road, glanced at the street numbers on the piece of paper, climbed out and hurried to where a blue plastic 2400 was screwed to a weather-scarred post. Small relief loosened the chords of her nerves.

Beside a ground level garage, wooden steps climbed to the railed balcony of the house. Without hesitation Gina swiftly went up to the deck where a couple of faded canvas chairs sat with a half-barrel of geraniums. There was a wide window and a door. Gina stepped forward, all considerations of how she might greet Cassie abandoned. Finding no bellpush, she rapped with her knuckles. She scarcely heard the sound above the din of the surf. Waiting but a moment she banged again, harder. Still no response. About to strike the timber a third time she heard cries from behind. She glanced around, and realized there were distant people on the beach.

An elderly man in navy shorts and khaki shirt, strolling; ahead of him a black labrador, coat shiningly wet, bounding toward then retreating from the shattering combers; further off, two youths in swimshorts, racing, yelling, toward the deluge; in the opposite direction, a woman in a pale green dress walking along the purling water's edge; a girl in a floral sunsuit, ponytail bobbing as she did running-and-jumping-on-the-spot exercises.

Gina hit the door once more. She shivered, feeling suddenly cold. Please, answer. Please, be here. The tenebrous misgivings came sidling back, crowded her shoulders; and, despite the chill, she felt sweat bead her forehead.

She moved to the window and peered in: sofa, pine dining

table and chairs; television console; scatter rugs; on a low table a wine bottle and empty glass. Total silence locked in there. Gina hastened along the deck to where it angled around the side of the house, to the window of a bedroom: dresser, wardrobe, dishevelled sheets. She stared, besieged by a mounting disquiet. There had been life here. But now a miasma of desolation seemed to seep from the walls.

Overdramatization, an inner voice countered. Collect your thoughts. Gina slapped her hand hard against the wall in an effort to drive clarity to her brain. Still there were alarm bells; a mental discord through which she heard the ocean boom and Cassie's declaration of long ago: 'I wouldn't want to live without him.'

Gina whirled; dashed back around the front of the building; halted high up there; swung this way and that with no direction; helplessly scanned the panorama. The man and dog were further away. The youths were cavorting in the fuming breakers. The girl with the ponytail was trotting toward the road. The woman in the pale green dress was walking into the sea.

Into the sea!

Gina was frozen. Her gaze was riveted on the remote figure. The short waved hair, burnished as spun copper in the sunlight. The straight back and slim waist. The strong legs. The brisk and determined swing of the arms and hips. Cassie.

'Cassie,' Gina shouted, and the name banged across the face of the building, ricocheted from the adjacent houses, sent a gull batting, screaming from the roof. But neither Gina's nor the bird's voice survived; both were drowned in the Pacific's roar.

'Cassie!' Gina cried again. 'Cassie!'

And then she ran.

She dashed along the balcony, the gunfire of her footfalls clamouring in pursuit. All reason thrown to the wind, she raced to the staircase, too fast to grasp the handrail, hands clutching the air for support as she clattered down the wooden flight, abandoning all caution on her skidding high heels. Hitting the ground at a run she chased across the road and the strip of raggedy grass, onto the sand. Her leading foot plunged into the deep, dry drift and she lurched forward, arms out-thrown, bounced down on one knee, floundered, wrenching the foot free, staggering, willing her body to remain upright, to keep moving.

She was pumping her fists now in a vehement effort to drive onward while the hampering sand dragged at her ankles, wrenched her hamstrings with pincers of pain. Damn, damn, her mind inveighed against the crippling slow motion, the nightmare of running and getting nowhere. 'Come on!' she urged herself aloud and tripped and fell full length.

The wind banged out of her. She remained momentarily sprawled, chin buried in the gritty dust. As she sucked in breath, the muck filled her mouth and nostrils. She choked, retched, spat. Spluttering, swearing, she staggered to her feet, rubbed her knuckles across her eyes. Sharp particles scoured the lids, sent red darts to her brain. But as she blinked against the friction, some shreds of commonsense returned.

She kicked off her shoes.

When she ran again her stockinged feet thumped the yielding sand but didn't sink. Gina ran with every ounce of her strength, fixed on the far-off figure in the green dress which was now knee-deep in the frothing surf. Her breath was ragged blades in her chest. A stitch was a knife between her ribs. She was sure her heart was at bursting point. Still she ran.

Cass. Stop. Cass. Gina's lips moved but she didn't know whether her words came out, or, if they did, whether they were torn away on the surf's hurricane boom. It was beside her now, a continual explosion of liquid silver, smashing upon itself, pounding, seething up the beach. Gina could feel its spray like glass beads detonating on her face. It stung her cheeks, plastered her hair to her skull, invaded her mouth as she gulped at the salt-saturated air.

She shrank from it, ran through it. The hissing flow rushed beneath her heels. Cold, splashing up her calves, to her thighs, in seconds drenching her skirt. Don't let me fall. Struggling, wading now, feeling the ebbflow suck at her flesh. Cassie, please turn around.

The water was surrounding her. Swirling. Threatening. Gina barely could push her feet forward. The din was awesome. She knew her strength was all but gone. If she fell now she'd be snatched away. A wave crashed in. Spray filled the air. The headlong wash surged to Gina's waist, lifted her clear of the sliding sand, dropped her back onto her stumbling legs.

The green dress was twelve feet ahead.

Gina threw herself forward. God help us both, she pleaded and yelled a final time, 'Cassie!'

Her equilibrium reeled as rainbows erupted across the sky. She plunged, splashing, wallowing, spluttering, coming up in a cascade, water fuming from her in all directions, spouting from her mouth and ears, pouring across her vision. With frantic hands she swabbed her features, fought to maintain her balance, peered through shock and ocean to see …

… Cassie, standing, holding the hem of her dress above her knees, staring for an age before probing, 'Gina? Is it you? Gina. Is it you. Holy Moses, you nearly frightened the life out of me. What on earth are you doing? Trying to drown yourself?'

Thirty minutes later, 'You know what I feel like, don't you,' said Gina. 'Apart from a waterlogged skunk. The biggest dumb-bell in all the world.' She sneezed, sipped her hot toddy.

'Well,' rejoined Cassie, 'if you insist on diving head first into eighteen inches of briny, you're liable to set folks reckoning you don't exactly have a full box of marbles. Really, Hon, what a thing to think – that I was about to do myself in. Now wouldn't that have been a mite difficult with two lifeguards a stone's throw away?'

From where they were sitting in the canvas chairs on the balcony of the beach-house, Gina looked sheepishly toward the high timber lookout tower, a hundred yards distant, where the two youths in swimshorts now were perched. When Gina had been led from the sea by Cassie, they'd come running to enquire concernedly, 'You okay, Ma'am? You oughta be a bit more careful. Paddling in a wool suit isn't such a good idea. Heavy when it's wet, you know. All right? There you go. Play safe.' And off they'd gone, leaving her, a bedraggled wreck, soaked to the skin – probably the bone – feeling like the biggest dumb-bell in all the world.

Worse to come, of course. Inevitably, Cassie had persisted, 'So, what, for goodness sake, are you doing here?'

Just like that. After three years. And she'd looked so cheerful and relaxed; not at all the distraught jilted female of Gina's imaginings. Gina thought to say, Do you realize, Cassie O'Brien, I've rushed here to save you from a watery fate. You ought to be a bit grateful when I tell you. Though I don't suppose you will be. I suppose you'll laugh, or do your best not to. I suppose you'll say, Jeepers, Gina, just like a Joan Crawford movie.

And she did. Something like that.

When that was all done with, they'd walked up toward the house, Gina casting a bemused glance back at the gentle, creamy surf, the languid flux and reflux of the tide's edge as Cassie said casually, 'I've always taken a barefoot stroll in the water like that, whenever I've been down here. Now I'll be able to do it every day, now I'm shot of Mister Tony I Am God's Gift To Women Nevada.'

Gina had been too nonplussed (and sodden) to pursue the matter at that moment. The priorities were clean shower, dry robe, and stiff drink. By the time she'd taken the first, was wrapped in the blue terry towelling second, and had been handed the third (rum and hot blackcurrant juice with a spoonful of honey, which, Cassie insisted, was the world's finest chill preventative) the sun was settling toward the west, gently warming the balcony where Gina and Cassie sat in the canvas chairs.

Now they looked at each other. And Gina wasn't sure whether she would laugh or cry.

So much for anticipation, she reflected, harking back to all the times she'd rehearsed her reunion with the woman who once had been her closest friend, all the variations she'd visualized. None of them, however, remotely had approached this afternoon's turn of events.

She studied Cassie. Her short, wavy, vibrantly red, freshly-combed hair framed an emerald-eyed, dimple-chinned face which was at once elfin innocent while seeming to contain the wisdom of the world. She's a year older than me, thought Gina, but looks scarcely changed from the day I last saw her.

'You're looking good, Hon,' Cassie said, tentatively, her brisk candour of the last thirty hectic minutes faltering at last in this ensuing lull.

'Thanks,' returned Gina. 'You too.'

'A little dusty round the edges, maybe.'

Gina shrugged. 'Aren't we all.'

Cassie nodded. 'I guess.'

They traded uncertain smiles. Silence leaked across the balcony. Gina searched for something more to say, some spark that would relight their old camaraderie. She retraced her mental steps to all those rehearsals of this scene, rummaging for the pre-written lines. They were gone. Scratchy fingers of discomfiture crept under her robe. She recrossed her legs, thinking perhaps this had been a mistake after all. She stared out to the ocean, feigning nonchalance; sneaked a sideways peek at Cassie, similarly engrossed in a survey of the seascape.

Another uneasy minute dragged by.

Then Gina said, 'Cass, I think I'd better be ...'

'Please, don't,' interrupted Cassie. 'Don't say you're leaving.' She moved quickly to the edge of her seat, halting herself and Gina with the abruptness of her voice. 'Look, Hon,' she said, fresh no-nonsense in her tone. 'You said you felt like a dumb-bell out on the beach. Well, I wasn't so very confident either. Maybe it didn't seem that way, but I sort of had the advantage, you wallowing around in the water and all. Truth to tell, for the past week, since I got shot of The Great Crooner, I've been dreading you finding out, tracking me down and hanging a giant I Told You So banner on my door.'

'Cass, I wouldn't.'

'I would, in your shoes. Anyhow, look, there's no point in sitting here like daisies, pretending the last three years didn't happen, beating around the bush, making believe we one time didn't have an almighty bust-up. We did. There it is. Not a mistake on a blackboard we can just rub out. But I reckon we're both too long in the tooth not to say what's on our minds and get it over with.' She took a breath, then went on:

'You know me, never a genius with words, so ... well ... I said some pretty rotten things three years ago. Yes, I did. And they all were on account of you warning me about Tony Nevada. Because did I want to hear what you were saying? Of course not. You were right, I was infatuated. Gina, I was so far gone, I look at it now, I can't believe, even though it happened to me, that anybody could be so zonked out of their brain over a pair of pants. But ...'

Cassie shrugged, smiled philosophically. 'Anyhow, here I am. Older, though ...' she hesitated, as if considering something before adding, 'not a whole lot wiser. The thing is, I just want you to know I'm sorry, is all. Hon, I truly am. We were the best pals, ever. I can't put the clock back, undo what's been done, but ... you ...' She looked at Gina, smiled hesitantly.

Gina regarded her friend. She read Cassie's expression, and knew, as she had known when they first met toiling as hotel chambermaids, that there was no hidden side to the character in her face. A face that was free of all pretence. The face of the one person who had held out the hand of friendship when it was needed most.

Now she reached out and took that hand and held it, tight. Her throat was constricting and when her voice came it was ragged: 'Oh, Cass, what a day this has been.' She was on her feet, and Cassie followed, and they swept into each other's arms, clung together, Gina overwhelmed by her feelings as her eyes stung with uncontrollable tears.

It was Cassie who at last broke the moment when she said hoarsely, forcing a laugh, 'Hey, I think we'd better sit down before we shatter the illusions of the lifeguards.' She stepped back, delved in the pocket of her dress, produced a hanky and blew vigorously, while Gina wiped her own cheeks with the back of her hand.

Gina drew a deep, steadying breath and, realizing she still was clutching the rum toddy, took a long swig of it. She sat, feeling so much relieved; and as she exchanged a smile with her friend, the years rolled back. This was how it used to be.

This was the comradeship Gina had been missing for so very long.

Then they talked.

They talked about everything. Everything except their love lives. Cassie confessed merely that she long since had seen the light as far as Tony Nevada was concerned, had bought this beach house with her own money a couple of months ago, and come to live here permanently when she'd split up with the singer. Gina, for her part, revealed little of her relationship with Howard, said simply it was not an unhappy marriage. Neither woman pressed the other for further details.

When the sun set they moved indoors to continue their confab over bread and cheese and pickles and toasted their reunion with a bottle of Muscadet.

It was nine o'clock before Gina reluctantly said she had to be getting back to Vegas to be up early tomorrow to continue her business schedule. 'But,' she said, 'I won't be half so busy by the end of the week. When are you going to visit? You haven't seen The Silver Lady. You must come over, Cass. Please say you will.'

All at once her friend looked hesitant. 'Let me think about it a while,' she answered. 'There are one or two things I have to get sorted in my mind. I'd love to see the old gang, of course. But, perhaps not yet. Anyhow, I'm getting used to sitting watching the world go by. Maybe it'll become a habit. I wouldn't mind, until ... Well, just give me some time, Hon.'

Gina wondered at Cassie's indecision, but then put it down to the events of the afternoon. After all, it most likely wasn't every day she had a deranged old pal come rushing down the beach and back into her life. Gina guessed they both were dislocated by the reunion and needed to settle their emotions. 'I understand,' she said. 'But, please, don't let it be too long.'

They finally said goodbye.

Gina flew home on delighted wings.

Chapter Six

Bright and early the following morning, over breakfast Gina regaled Max with her tale of Cassie. Max was as pleased as Gina that the two women were again friends. He said, 'So there was nothing in Felix's story about the doctor?'

Gina said, 'I didn't mention that to Cass, but I'm sure it was just gossip. She looked as right as rain, and as happy as I've ever seen her.'

They chatted a while longer and then both had business to attend to. As they were parting, Max commented, 'By the way, Mister Ortez called to say he's decided to accept our offer for his land along The Strip. I told him you'd be in touch.'

Gina agreed she'd phone the man and went up to her office. A small sheaf of messages had been left on her desk. So had a bottle of champagne. Puzzled, Gina approached the bottle. It was vintage, very expensive. A hand-written card was tied to its neck. Gina read: You and I could share more of the best things in life. The signature was: Tony Nevada.

Gina dropped the card as if it was hot.

For several seconds her emotions were awry. She was angered by the singer's advances, yet for an instant she'd recalled their recent encounter and her inability to deny his sexuality. With a gesture of retaliation she swept the card off her desk and into the waste basket. She took the champagne bottle to a table far away across the room, then returned to sit behind her desk and slowly regain composure.

Turning to the messages she eliminated the incident.

It was a couple of hours later when a secretary brought in a special delivery packet from New York. Gina's equilibrium had returned, and recognizing the large envelope was from Irving Prentiss opened it eagerly.

Irving's report on the shareholders of Monument Pictures was succinct but thorough. The six individuals who owned equal parts of the movie company were listed with their ages, addresses, brief biographies and estimated financial worth, plus the conclusion on their preparedness to sell the studio.

Gina read the first name: an old Hollywood producer, well-known in the thirties, sixty-eight years old now, retired and living in La Jolla, California; approximate net assets in cash, property, stocks (not including his share of Monument), four million dollars.

The next four names on the list were equally familiar to Gina: a director, two actors and an actress, famous and respected for their work during the studio's heyday, today ranging in age from fifty-four to seventy, the three men in retirement in America, none less wealthy than the producer, the actress married to one of the leading vineyard owners in France, independently rich also.

After each summary Irving Prentiss had written, 'Agrees Monument valuation. No objection to sale.'

Gina reached the final name and résumé:

'Barbara Graham. Actress. 48. Only daughter of founder of Graham Quarries. Married nineteen years of age, divorced twelve months later, no offspring. New York stage 1924-28. Warner Bros. contract 1929-1934. Twice suspended by studio for 'moral conduct likely to bring the motion picture industry into disrepute.' Monument contract 1936-1946. Three Oscar nominations. Retired 1947 to Villa Arancia, Calle dei Fabbri, Venice. Approximate net assets (including holdings in family business), 15 million dollars. Agrees Monument valuation. Opposed to sale.'

Gina put down the report and lifted the telephone. A couple of minutes later she was through to Felix Gilbert. After a few pleasantries, Gina told the producer about Irving's report on the movie company's shareholders. 'Felix,' she asked, 'do you know why Barbara Graham might be opposed to the sale?'

Felix answered, 'It's years since I last saw Barbara, but

from what I remember of her, I'd guess her attitude has to do with her belief in the paternal responsibilities of employers. Her background, you know, is an old family quarrying business, the sort of company where the boss knows everyone by their christian name. Monument used to be like that in Henry Jessel's day. I'd say Barbara isn't opposed to a sale as such, only to the studio falling into the hands of some soulless conglomerate.'

Gina murmured, 'I see.'

'I'd suggest,' said Felix, 'if you're going to make a bid, rather than go through all the usual attorneys' communications, you handle it yourself.'

'You mean, visit Barbara Graham, personally?'

'Yes. Let her see West-Rossi is run by a human being. I'm sure you and she would get along fine.'

Gina mused on that a moment before she said, 'Thanks, Felix. I'll bear it in mind.' She added more chattily, 'How's *The Last Summer* coming along?'

'About the same as when you were here yesterday. We're still scratching to build sets as we go. Frankly, the budgeting's getting so's it's effecting the quality of the picture. Which is a shame, because it could've been good, maybe even great. And everybody's put so much into it, especially Fallon, done a terrific job of turning his novel into a script.'

Gina hesitated at the mention of the Englishman. She'd expected his name to crop up during her tour of the studio; when it hadn't, she'd told herself that was perhaps just as well. Now, however, she asked, 'Is he still in Hollywood?'

'I think movieland was beginning to get his goat. He's moved out to the Oasis Hotel near Palm Springs to make a start on his new novel. It's peaceful there but near enough if he's needed for any last minute rewrites on the movie.'

Gina remained silent as she dwelt on this revelation of Fallon's being only a couple of hours' drive away.

Felix went on to make a few more comments about the script. He said he hoped she'd decide definitely to bid for Monument, and then they said goodbye.

Gina, self-reproachfully, had to admit she hadn't concentrated on the latter part of the conversation; she'd been unable to keep her mind off Robert Fallon. Then, 'Pull yourself together,' she said aloud and quickly reopened the Monument report to check the Venice address of Barbara Graham.

For the following thirty minutes she concentrated on composing an introductory letter to the retired actress. Eventually, reasonably satisfied with her effort, she neatly copied it out, deciding, in view of Felix's advice, not to have it typed.

The task revitalized her optimism toward buying the studio. But, she thought, it was about time she told her fellow directors her intentions. She hoped they'd approve. She hoped Fallon wouldn't mind.

Now what on earth had it got to do with Fallon?

Gina wasn't able to come up with an answer to that until she'd addressed her envelope to Barbara Graham, then it simply occurred to her that it would be only common courtesy to let the Englishman know what was happening. After all, *The Last Summer* was currently Monument's most important production. Yes, Gina told herself, it would be wrong for him to find out from some newspaper report that his work was liable to become the property of West-Rossi. He ought to be informed personally.

She carried this notion into the afternoon. By three o'clock she'd established it as her responsibility. By three-fifteen she was driving toward Palm Springs.

The receptionist at the Oasis said Mister Fallon was working in the arbour. Gina went through to the rear of the hotel and out to several acres of Italian-style gardens. During her drive from Vegas she hadn't once let her thoughts wander back to the romance she'd had with Robert Fallon years ago. Their forthcoming meeting was a straightforward business matter, she assured herself, and she could handle it with equanimity.

Gina followed the receptionist's instructions, amid trees and statuary, until she reached a vine-canopied terrace looking toward the gold and blue horizon. Beneath a floral sun umbrella, four wicker armchairs circled a table close by the terrace's balustrade.

Robert Fallon was hacking steadily at a typewriter.

Time and weather had sculpted his features since last Gina saw him. More grey too in his hair which tumbled in all directions around a squarish face with a solid jaw. A look of strength emanated from his broad cheekbones and grey eyes. He never had been classically handsome; maybe his ears were too big, his nose too often broken, but as Gina watched him her heart began to rattle as noisily as his typewriter. In baggy green cord pants, navy open-necked shirt with notepads and pens sprouting from its chest pockets, he was all he ever had been, and more. He was all Gina had wanted when she was seventeen years old.

Quelling that thought very quickly, she walked forward to halt within a yard of where he clack-clacked unfalteringly, his gaze fixed on his unfolding words. Gina said to the man she hadn't seen in five years, 'Hi.'

Fallon leaned back, ran a sun-burned hand through stubborn hair. 'Hello. Have a seat.'

'Thank you.' Gina sat opposite him.

'How's business?' he asked.

'Can't complain. How's the novel coming?'

'As usual. Wish to God I'd been a bricklayer, ditch-digger, blacksmith, deep-sea-diver, anything but a damn writer.' He looked at Gina with a familiar sardonic smile. 'You know how it is.'

She did. She knew Fallon was a caring author. Even after all he'd seen in twenty years as a war correspondent he had not become inured to the world's pain; his written words remained deeply evocative and sensitive. Fallon was as dedicated to journalistic truth as Gina was to the well-being of her family and business.

She suddenly thought, He didn't bat an eye when I walked up on him. Now here we are discussing our work as normally as ever. She regarded him, realized she had him to thank for accepting her uninvited re-entry into his life with ease and understanding. She asked, 'What's the new novel about?'

He answered, 'Fear. The fear that's stalking America.'

Gina knew immediately what he meant. For the past three years she'd listened to the scare-mongering of the UnAmerican Activities Committee. In her darker moments she'd harked back to the Fascist terrors of her youth; but then she'd reminded herself she was now a citizen of the country which had given her sanctuary, and such persecution couldn't possibly run wild here. Gina had to believe that. She had to believe the innocent had nothing to fear.

She searched for a response to Fallon. She wanted to tell him, yes, she understood. At the same time she didn't want to plunge into a political discussion, not when she'd only just arrived.

Fallon said, 'But I'm sure you didn't come over to hear about my opus. What's up, Doc?'

Gina's senses cannoned like a pinball as Fallon's question sent her spinning back to wartime London. They'd first heard Bugs Bunny's catchphrase together at the Soho news and cartoon cinema, and thereafter Fallon had used it most evenings they met at his apartment.

All at once Gina's face felt very hot. Attempting a bright smile, which she was sure came out as a goofy grin, she declared abruptly, 'I'm thinking of buying Monument Pictures.'

Fallon responded casually. 'Uh huh.'

Damn it. He did this sort of thing on purpose, sent her objectivity reeling. Gina got a firm grip on her chair's arms and said, 'I must admit I'm no expert on showbusiness – I've yet to ask Harry's advice – but I feel sure Monument could be a good investment.' She went on with how she'd first become interested in the movie company and her subsequent investigations; all she omitted was her antipathy toward Oliver Randolph. At last she said, 'Well, there you have it.'

Fallon nodded and replied, 'Sounds interesting. But rather daunting, buying an entire film studio.'

Gina studied his craggy features. He was sincere, no longer ribbing her. Relaxing, she said, 'It's not so difficult,' adding with a smile, 'so long as you can borrow the money.'

Fallon laughed, and for the next twenty minutes they continued about business in general. Then, however, it occurred to Gina to change the subject lest Fallon think she sounded too much like a tycoon. She said, 'Here I am, prattling on, haven't even asked how you are.'

'Pretty good, thanks,' he returned. 'You're looking fine, Gina. How're Max and Harry, the family?'

'Thriving.' It took her a further quarter hour to tell him how everyone was getting along before she said, 'You ought to come around sometime. They'd love to see you.'

'And I them,' he answered, but then paused. And Gina knew they'd talked themselves into an uncertain corner. She was rather relieved when Fallon broke the moment with: 'I did see Filipo recently. Grown into quite a feller. Has he taken his law exams?'

'Another two years. He didn't mention you'd run into each other. Where'd you see him?'

'Not personally,' said Fallon. 'On television.'

'Television?'

'A news report of the AFF demonstration in Boston. American Friends of Freedom supporting those radio technicians who'd been sacked after appearing before the UnAmerican Activities Committee. Filipo was there handing out leaflets. At least, I'm fairly sure it was him.' Fallon paused, a frown coming to his brow as he searched Gina's expression. 'Is anything wrong?'

Gina remained silent only a moment. 'No, not at all,' she returned. She'd been jolted by Fallon's revelation about her brother but didn't want him to know it and feel personally concerned. She said, 'Yes, he has grown, hasn't he. And become quite as handsome as Poppa.'

'Is he still mad about movies?'

'I think it's pretty well out of his system,' answered Gina, glad she'd apparently concealed her diquiet.

'Well, it's every man to his own, I guess,' said Fallon. 'But, frankly, I've had enough of movie-making to last me a lifetime. Eternal script conferences, production conferences, press conferences. You won't see me for dust when they finally wrap up shooting next month.'

'You're leaving?'

'Going down to the Keys to get some real peace and quite to finish this.' He indicated his typescript. 'But, please,' he raised a warning finger, 'not a word to anyone. Nobody knows about my bolthole on the Gulf. Have you ever been down there? You should. If only for the sunset.' Fallon nodded toward the huge orange orb sinking in the west. 'I've seen that old girl go down in a few places, but her most spectacular performance she saves for the Keys.'

Gina said quietly, 'I'd like to see it sometime.'

Fallon looked at her.

And Gina's emotions lurched. She broke quickly from his gaze, scanning the gardens in an attempt to find something to remark upon. She felt a disconcerting fluttering of butterflies in her stomach, a sensation she hadn't experienced since she was seventeen. The tempo of her heart had increased, and she was sure her cheeks had turned bright pink.

Fallon asked, 'Would you like a drink?'

Gina stood hastily. 'No, thanks. I really must be going.' As Fallon stood also, she said, 'I won't interrupt you any longer. I only came to let you know about Monument.'

'I'm grateful,' he said.

'No problem. I just happened to be over in Vegas.'

'Yes, Felix told me.'

Gina's eyes widened as she looked into Fallon's innocence. 'You knew,' she shot. 'All that rugged nonchalance when I arrived wasn't so difficult. You were expecting me.'

'Not expecting, exactly,' returned Fallon. 'Just sort of playing a hunch.' He smiled. 'I'm glad it paid out.'

Gina almost asked, Really? but checked herself and turned to walk across the terrace. With Fallon beside her she said, 'Sorry I have to run, but, you know, work'll be piling, as usual. I hope *The Last Summer* wraps up on time so you can get away to the Keys. I'll think about you in your palmy haven when the road gangs are jackhammering outside my window in Manhattan.'

Fallon said, 'I'll think about you too.'

Gina kept her gaze dead ahead, not daring to look at Fallon's expression until they reached the path leading to the hotel; by then his features were craggily neutral. They paused, standing together in the late afternoon glow. Gina was very aware of Fallon's closeness. She said, 'No need to walk me all the way.'

He nodded. 'I'll say goodbye then. Thanks again for coming over. Take care of yourself, Gina.'

'You too,' she said, smiling a little self-consciously.

'I'll do my best.'

'Yes, well,' Gina said quietly, 'goodbye.' She hesitated, uncertain, a moment more; then she walked swiftly away. She didn't look back.

But she drove home to Vegas in a dream; and for the remainder of the evening could think only of Robert Fallon.

Her first thought the next morning, however, was her brother. As she showered and dressed she pondered what Fallon had said about Filipo and the AFF demonstration. Still, she rationalized, if all Filipo had been doing was handing out leaflets, that wasn't so serious, was it? She reminded herself he was a responsible adult, not a delinquent adolescent.

By the time Gina was at her desk she'd decided against contacting her brother in Boston. She wasn't entirely easy in her mind, but felt it would be better to let the matter rest until she could talk with him in person. That settled, she turned to yesterday's messages.

Mister Ortez had phoned twice.

Gina experienced more than a twinge of guilt, remembering she'd promised to return the local landowner's call. She quickly dialled his number, a sincere apology on her lips, only to be told he'd be away until mid-evening. Gina left a message to say she'd ring back at nine o'clock. Feeling somewhat chastened, she set about her other outstanding tasks.

She stuck at it all day, taking a lunchtime sandwich at her desk, and when the encroaching dusk necessitated switching on her office light, she'd accomplished a good deal.

Stretching, massaging her neck after the long toil, Gina stood and enjoyed the pumping of blood through her cramped muscles. For a moment she recalled that this time yesterday she'd been standing very close to Robert Fallon. She imagined his hideaway on the Florida Keys; wondered who shared his bed there.

The unbidden thought startled her and she went quickly out to the balcony, subjugating any further impulses. At the parapet she took several deep breaths. The air blew cool from the desert, chasing away the flush of her cheeks.

Obliquely across the highway, a quarter mile distant, the airport bus was discharging passengers at the Flamingo. The familiar reality of the incoming tourists decisively levelled Gina's thoughts.

As the bus started up and rolled toward The Silver Lady, Gina suddenly realized she was rather hungry after her scant lunch. Returning to her desk she buzzed Max's office intending to ask if he was free to join her for dinner. Receiving no reply on the intercom, she went down in the elevator to find her godfather.

Gina arrived at the lobby and paused, surveying the activity. She threw a smile and a small wave to the squad at the reception desk where several guests off the airport bus were checking in. Happy, she began to move away, but faltered, and looked again toward the back of one of the female arrivals.

There was something very familiar …

The woman glanced around.

Gina exclaimed, 'Cass!'

The redhead was wearing emerald, a beautifully cut, waistless dress which flared to end at mid-shin above tan slim-heeled pumps; in her hand a purse shaped like a small hatbox; on her head a neat toque with a flurry of feathers at the front. Very different from the casual figure Gina had met at the beach house.

After a pregnant pause Cassie stuck a fist on an exaggerated hip, and in her best Brooklynese said, 'So, what's it cost to get a drink around this joint?'

Gina jumped out of her trance. 'Cass, I'm sorry. You took me by surprise. I didn't recognize you. From behind, I mean. You looked so … elegant.'

Discarding her raucous accent, touching gloved fingers to her curls, Cassie rejoined, 'I figured, visiting the swankiest watering hole in Nevada, I'd better make the effort. Didn't want to get turned away at the door.'

Gina, smiling, said, 'It's marvellous to see you.' She walked swiftly forward and hugged her friend. 'But you should've let me know you were coming. I'd have collected you at the airport.'

'Well,' Cassie hesitated for an instant before saying, 'it was rather a spur-of-the-moment decision.' She seemed about to add something, but changed her mind and said brightly, surveying the reception area, 'Looks like everything I heard was true. Some heck of a place you've got here, Hon.'

Gina shrugged self-depreciatingly. 'Thanks.' Then glancing to the suitcase on the floor, enquired, 'Is this all your luggage? I'll take it,' and before Cassie could protest, had hefted the bag and was saying, 'This way please, madame.'

Gina led the way to the private elevator and unlocked the door. She ushered her friend into the car, and they rode silently upward, looking at each other like Crosby and Hope, off on the road again but temporarily out of script.

Though not for long. As they entered the sitting room, Cassie hurried to the window exclaiming, 'Oh, Gina, what a view.' And from there on they never stopped talking.

It was an hour later, after they'd both changed – Cassie into a jade evening gown with sequinned shoulder cape, Gina into a black floor-length skirt with matador jacket and white lace blouse – that they returned to the crowded foyer and were about to enter the casino when Max stepped out of his office.

The big Tuscan halted, motionless before them, his eyes widening. And as Gina recognized the reflexive look of much-more-than-fatherly appreciation flush his face as he stared at Cassie, she joshed, 'Really, Max, you could be arrested for what you're thinking.'

Cassie said, 'Don't stop, Max. I love it.'

Confusion and recognition simultaneously blew away Max's composure. He stood, swaying in a gust of embarrassment, failing to regain his balance before being catapulted into further disarray as Cassie marched up to him, hugged him, pulled his head down and kissed him, very loudly, on the lips, then leaned back to declare with huge affection, 'It's marvellous to see you again, you sexy old gambler.'

Max exclaimed, 'Cassie! *Non ho capito* ... Where ...? No matter. What a splendid surprise.' Regaining his self-command, he held her at arms' length. '*Come sta*? You look ... so ...'

Cassie grinned. 'Elegant?'

Gina interposed, 'That isn't what he was thinking.'

'Principessa ...' reproved Max. He said to Cassie, 'Certainly, elegant. And beautiful.' With an appreciative glance at Gina: 'You are both beautiful. The most beautiful women in all the world. And I am the luckiest man. To have such companions for dinner. You will join me? *Per favore*?' He beamed widely. '*Va bene*. That's settled.'

He turned to Cassie. 'Signorina, welcome to The Silver Lady. Permit me to escort you around the finest casino in America.' He offered his arm, and as Cassie responded, 'My pleasure, sir,' he crooked his other elbow for Gina. She accepted with a small, gracious bow. And Max, between them, silver hair gleaming, moustachios veritably twirling with pleasure, strode forth, the Grand Sultan escorting two exotic empresses into his domain.

They spent five hours in happy reunion. Cassie was awed by the citadel. Max was exultant at her enthusiasm. Gina was delighted to see them side-by-side once more.

It was almost one in the morning when Gina and Cassie eventually returned to the penthouse apartment. Entering the sitting room, Gina suggested, 'How about a hot chocolate before bed?' and on Cassie's acceptance said, 'Kick your shoes off. I'll be but a minute,' and went into the kitchen.

When she returned with two steaming mugs, Cassie was sitting on the chair at the head of the dining table staring down at the neon brilliance of The Strip. Gina set the drinks on coasters and took the chair alongside her friend. She said, 'I guess I've mentioned it a dozen times tonight, Cass, but, just once more, it's terrific to have you here. I hope you'll stay a long time.'

Her friend replied quietly, 'I'd like to. Very much.' She paused. 'If you won't mind.'

'Mind?' rejoined Gina. 'Don't you realize ...' She halted in mid-sentence as she saw an unfamiliar light in Cassie's eyes. A thin thread of concern tightened about her, and, frowning, she ventured, 'Is something wrong?'

The carefree expression Cassie had worn all evening had faded. In it's place was a look of uncertainty. She said slowly, 'I'd intended telling you this sooner, when I arrived. But,' she offered a faint smile, 'you gave me such a welcome, I just couldn't.' She'd taken a handkerchief from her purse and was twisting it nervously.

Gina, at once anxious, prompted, 'Cass, whatever is it?'

Her friend said, 'I'm going to have a baby.'

Gina could only stare.

In the opaque silence Cassie drew a shuddering breath, then exhaled with a gust of relief. 'There,' she said, 'the truth's out.' Some of the tension left her features, though she continued to tug at the handkerchief.

Gina found her own voice. 'Are you sure?' she asked, thinking it rather a foolish question, but in too much of a mental turmoil to produce anything better.

'It's confirmed. I'm pregnant, no mistake.'

A tremor ran through Gina as an image from the past flashed through her mind. She forcefully subjugated the memory and automatically began to ask, 'Is it ...' but abruptly cut off the question, 'No, Cass, I didn't mean to pry. I'm sorry.'

'Please, don't be. You have a right to know, and I want you to.' Cassie glanced down at her fingers twisting the handkerchief; then she raised her face to look at Gina and said, 'It was Tony. Yes, Mister Wonderful Nevada. A couple of months ago, after I'd told him I was moving out. That was what did it, I guess. Fractured his ego. Made him lose his temper. Made him ...' Cassie hesitated.

Gina said gently, 'You don't have to tell me.'

'I'd rather,' her friend returned. 'Anyhow, it's not so special. He was just trying to prove I couldn't resist him. When it was over, he knew I could. He just called me some names then and left. I went the next morning. A few weeks later, when I knew Tony Nevada was away, I went back to visit Maria, the housekeeper. While I was there I had a dizzy spell. Maria took one look at me and called the doc. It wasn't till then I realized I was pregnant.' Cassie shrugged. 'There it is. If you'd rather I took the flight back tomorrow I'll understand.'

Gina remained silent only as long as it took to fight down her emotions. She rejoined with exaggerated exclamation, 'Flight back? What on earth for? We've a perfectly good antenatal clinic here in Vegas.' She added, 'Incidentally, you're ruining that handkerchief.'

Cassie looked down at the crumpled lace. Her eyes moistened as she managed a small laugh.

Gina reached out and gripped her friend's hands. 'Cass, I'm so happy for you. I truly am. It's the most wonderful thing I've ever heard. But, are you sure you're okay?'

'The doc says I'm a hundred per cent fit.'

'Still, you shouldn't stay at the beach alone.'

'Gina, really,' the confidence returned to Cassie's cheeks, 'I'm quite capable of looking after myself. Besides, I won't be alone during the day. I'll be out, working.'

'Working?'

'To pay the bills. I've a small nestegg, but that will be for when I have to stay home with the baby.'

'But what about Tony Nevada? He ought to be providing for you. Does he know you're pregnant?'

'Oh, yes, he knows,' replied Cassie. 'At first, of course, he said it had nothing to do with him. But then he ran to his agent and attorneys in panic. I assume he told them the truth and they came to the conclusion it wouldn't do his public image a lot of good if I made a case of it – though I never intended to. They offered me a lump sum. At first I refused, but after a few days' thinking, I changed my mind. I've accepted the money and invested it. I won't touch a penny, but if anything should happen to me it'll be there for the baby.'

Gina nodded, absorbing Cassie's disclosures. At length, she said, 'Yes, I can see you'd prefer to be independent. But if you're going to work, I hope it will be at West-Rossi.'

Cassie's eyes widened.

'It's up to you, of course,' said Gina. 'But it would be so good to have you back. And there's heaps you can do. After all, you know the ropes so well.'

For a moment Cassie sat in dazed silence; then she responded quietly, 'Gina, what can I say?'

Gina smiled. 'Just say, yes.'

It was over an hour later when they finally went to their beds. Amid the scores of things they'd discussed, Cassie had agreed to spend several days here with Gina at The Silver Lady, partly as a vacation, partly re-acquainting herself with

West-Rossi to see where she might best fit into the organization.

Gina lay in the shadows, reliving the entire evening. Such an evening. Cassie was coming back. It would be so like old times. Not entirely, of course. There'd be the baby. Imagine, Cassie with a baby. Gina began to drift. The shadows shifted beyond her closed eyelids. Minutes ticked by. Gina stared through the shadows. Through the window. On the street a red London bus went slowly by in the morning fog. On the opposite sidewalk the placard before the newsboy's stand declared, ALLIES TAKE EL ALAMEIN.

Gina turned from the window to the middle-aged man facing her across the desk. 'Am I?' she asked. 'Please, Doctor, am I pregnant?'

The doctor replied, 'No, Miss Rossi. You are not.'

Gina didn't know whether she was relieved or disappointed. Since being re-united with Robert Fallon in the wartime city she'd kept thoughts of pregnancy as far from her consciousness as possible. Now she just wanted to be out of the consulting room and in some quiet place to settle her emotions.

The doctor was saying '... an accident several years ago. The damage you suffered was considerable. The results compounded by what I surmise was unchecked haemorrhaging. There is scarring to suggest ...'

Gina didn't understand. An accident? She'd had an accident. When she was an infant perhaps. Something she couldn't remember. Something her parents had never mentioned. 'Accident?' she queried. 'I didn't have any accidents as a child.'

'Not when you were a child,' frowned the doctor. 'Much later. After you had reached maturity. Surely you recall, Miss Rossi. Such massive internal rupturing could not have occurred without your knowledge.'

Internal? For an instant Gina's mind was blank. Then she was hurled back into the past; to the decrepit hut she'd shared with her father in exile; the night their Blackshirt captor had crashed drunkenly into the room, wrenching at his belt, lunging toward Gina, forcing her to the floor ...

The doctor was continuing '... you came here seeking confirmation of pregnancy. Forgive me, there is no easy way to say this.' He paused, before going on, enunciating each word, 'Such a likelihood is so remote as to be virtually impossible. Do you understand, Miss Rossi? After examining you, I believe the extent of your internal injuries preclude you from conceiving a child.'

Gina remained motionless. Her muscles were cords, tightening, clamping her hands to the chair arms, suspending her above a black pit. The doctor was speaking again but his voice was unintelligible. The only clear words in Gina's head were those he had already uttered; the words which would remain with her for as long as she lived.

Gina awoke in the daylight in her apartment above The Silver Lady. She did not remember the dream. But her face and her pillow were damp with tears.

Chapter Seven

Max said, 'I did all I could, Principessa, but it was no good. Mister Ortez says he has half-a-dozen companies, who can't wait to buy his land. I told him you'd been so busy, just hadn't had time to return his calls. I assured him of course we were ready to sign the contract. I offered to go over right away, personally. But ...' The big man spread disappointed hands.

It was the evening following Cassie's arrival in Las Vegas. Gina was sitting before her godfather's desk. Cassie was upstairs taking a shower. The two had just returned to The Silver Lady, having spent the entire day happily playing tourists. When Gina had left first thing this morning, she'd known she had no scheduled appointments. But she'd completely overlooked her list of outstanding telephone calls.

Now she felt ashamed and dejected. Mister Ortez had left town on business so she couldn't contact him, and, in any case, he'd apparently made up his mind he no longer wished to sell to West-Rossi.

Gina said, 'Max, I'm so sorry.'

'It isn't the end of the world, Principessa. We all make a mistake now and then. And with everything that's happened recently, I understand why you forgot to return Mister Ortez's calls.'

'But I shouldn't have. I shouldn't have let personal considerations take over and damage the business.'

'We haven't actually lost anything.'

'We've lost the opportunity for expansion. I know how much that meant to you. And to the company. All the other casinos are buying extra acreage, and every hotel corporation in the country is looking to get a foothold here. We can't afford to be left behind.'

The big man said, 'Don't worry. There's plenty of land along The Strip. I'll start putting out feelers tomorrow, to see which of the owners might sell.'

Gina returned quietly, 'Thanks, Max.' With a long intake of breath, recovering some spirit, she said, 'And I'll have a word with all our real estate contacts. I'm sure Cassie won't mind me getting down to work. In fact, she might like to join me on one or two personal calls. It'll help to get her back into the swing of things.'

Max looked blank.

'Oh,' said Gina, 'I haven't seen you since last night. You don't know about Cass. She ...' Gina caught herself, thinking it wasn't for her to mention the baby.

'*Si*?' queried Max.

Gina hastily gathered her thoughts. 'She's coming back to West-Rossi. We haven't decided where she'll fit in yet, but there's heaps she can do. Isn't it great news?'

Max's face lit with pleasure. '*Meraviglioso*,' he declared. 'Principessa, I'm so pleased. For both of you. For all of us. Tonight we must celebrate. To heck with Signor Ortez. I think he was looking for an excuse to accept a better offer anyway.'

Gina raised a smile.

By midnight she was sharing her godfather's fresh hopes. Yet, somehow, her vitality had been dampened. She felt vaguely uneasy; as if the small setback she'd caused was an omen. Foolishness, she reproved herself; you'll be believing in the evil eye next.

She explained the business situation to Cassie who said she'd be glad to help in whatever way she could. They agreed Cassie would remain in Las Vegas for a week then would return to Los Angeles to put her affairs in order before re-joining Gina in Manhattan to decided what permanent position she could fill at West-Rossi.

The seven days passed busily and agreeably, although little progress was made toward acquiring any additional land. Max said not to worry on that score, he'd carry on with the search after Gina and Cassie had left.

They parted at the airport. Cassie's flight left first, and Gina remained alone for an hour in the departure lounge. As she watched the incoming and outgoing planes, she pondered the fortnight she'd spent here. So much had happened. She thought of her reunion with Cassie, the tour of Monument, her meeting with Robert Fallon. All such happy experiences. Yet, recalling them, Gina again was troubled by a sense of having cracked a mirror.

The announcer called boarding for the New York flight. Gina went with the other passengers out into the hot sunshine. That was it, she decided, that was what was unsettling her; all the sunshine; too much of a good thing was likely to addle anybody's brain.

With a smile, she went up the aircraft steps, looking forward to being home in her favourite city.

She loved New York. Even when it was raining Gina loved New York. Of course, she loved Las Vegas. But that was a different kind of love. Vegas was bandbox neat, bright-eyed and bushy-tailed, a young swain with whom to spend a sparkling, sexy vacation. New York, on the other hand, was elegantly rumpled, time-etched and worldly-wise, an old lover and a dear friend to whom Gina always would return.

It was three days since Gina's return. And it was raining; a cool, late-May rain, a last reminder of the freshness of spring before the heat of summer.

The rain quickened the pulse of the streets; people clipped smartly along the sidewalks, traffic ran hissing tracks on wet asphalt as Gina hurried back to The Lady from a late financial meeting with Irving Prentiss at the West-Rossi Building. The receptionist told her Filipo was upstairs at The First Floor. He'd arrived this morning from Boston on a twenty-four hour visit, but Gina had not yet seen him. She went quickly up to her apartment to shower and change.

Pulling off her raincoat and sou'wester, Gina crossed the bedroom to draw the curtains. As she reached for the pull cord she looked down into the bustling night. The figure standing in the doorway across the street was staring up at her window. Gina had the curtains half closed before she noticed the watcher. She peered, thinking perhaps she recognized ...

The figure moved back into shadow.

Gina squinted through the rain-streaked glass, across the dazzle of traffic. A truck went slowly past. When it was gone, the doorway was empty; people hurrying by, but no one standing.

Gina shrugged to herself, unsure why the figure had looked familiar. Anyway, she reasoned, it could have been anyone, acquaintance or stranger, briefly sheltering; and it would be quite natural to be looking up at these windows. She closed the curtains on the weather and the incident.

Fifteen minutes later, in a simple amethyst cocktail dress, she went down to The First Floor.

The club was packed. Velvet darkness hung above tables whose pink Tiffany lamps flattered the expensive complexions and flawless couture of the audience semi-circling the raised dance floor where a small, curvy blonde in shiny blue flared dress was being whirled by six white-tuxedoed males to the band's bouncy, brassy rendition of *Diamonds Are A Girl's Best Friend*.

'May I find you a seat, Mrs Cornell?'

Gina whispered, 'Hi, Sam,' to the waiter who had happened by as she came in at a side door to stand in the shadows. 'No, thanks. My brother's here somewhere. I'll join him when this number's finished.' As the waiter moved silently away to deliver his tray of cocktails, Gina surveyed the crowd of faces. Even in the smoky twilight the raptness of their expressions was clearly distinguishable as they watched the dancers.

The onstage girl bounded in a final high-kicking circle as her six male partners rushed back and forth before seizing her, flinging her this way and that, climaxing on the trumpets' blare by lofting her above their heads where she balanced on their upstretched arms, her hands reaching for the ceiling, smile dazzling in the spotlight's glare.

The audience burst into appreciative applause.

Gina clapped enthusiastically too, nodded with satisfaction as the overhead lights came up, the dancers ran for the wings, and the band slid into its easy interval medley. After scanning the club, spotting Filipo alone at a side table, she swiftly negotiated the route with the minimum of stops for regulars' greetings and gossip.

Filipo rose. 'Hi, Sis. You're looking chick.'

You don't look so bad yourself, she thought fondly, taking in his pale grey suit, navy shirt and white tie. More like Tony Curtis than Clarence Darrow, but a whole lot better than his usual sloppy joe and jeans. She smiled, 'Thanks,' kissed him and sat as he drew out a chair.

'So, how was gambling-land?' asked Filipo.

For the next several minutes Gina answered all her brother's questions about her trip. She then recounted her reunion with Cassie; but didn't mention her meeting with Robert Fallon. She considered telling him about Monument, but decided she'd wait until she'd had chance to discuss the purchase of the studio with Harry who was away on business until tomorrow. Also, Gina was concerned to get around to asking Filipo about his involvement at the AFF demonstration Fallon had seen on television. They had just reached an opportune moment in their conversation for her to broach this subject when Filipo suddenly declared:

'Mickey, you were great,' pulling up another chair as the small, curvy dancer in the shiny blue dress hurried to their table, dabbing her glowing brow.

'Thanks,' Mickey replied cheerily. 'Hello, Mrs Cornell – I mean, Gina. How was your time in Las Vegas? Did you just catch my act? Was it okay? Harry says I'm improving.'

'My trip was fine,' replied Gina, smiling. 'So was your routine. I enjoyed it a great deal. Along with the rest of the audience. And a compliment from Harry – who's incurably in love with Ginger Rogers – is an item to write in your diary in gold ink. Please, sit down.'

'No, thank you. I have to change, repair my make-up for my next number. I only came over to say hello in case you didn't stay.' She turned to Filipo: 'If you don't mind missing the top spot, we can leave as soon as I'm through, get to the party a whole lot sooner. Okay?' She gave him a coaxing lift of her eyebrows.

She really is very attractive, thought Gina. And even her glossy stage hairstyle and cosmetics can't hide her youthful wholesomeness. What a word. But that's what she has. Plus an innocent sexiness. She certainly is rather special. Harry was right, Miss Michelle Rooney is going places. And if my brother intends being married to her by the time she's a star, he'd better get his skates on.

Mickey said, 'It was terrific seeing you again Gina. Must dash,' and with a small wave she skipped away through a confetti of compliments from adjacent tables.

There were only fifteen minutes of the interval remaining. If Filipo was going to a party tonight and then returning to Boston first thing in the morning, this might be Gina's last chance to talk personally with him until he was again in New York.

Turning to her brother, keeping her voice and her gaze candidly level, not wishing to seem either overly concerned or too casual, she said, 'I understand you were at an AFF demonstration a few weeks ago.'

Filipo returned a look of surprise, then with a shrug said, 'I guess you had to find out.'

'It was on television.'

Filipo nodded.

'I'd rather have heard it from you,' said Gina.

'I didn't want to worry you.'

'You agree I'd have worried?'

'You'd have had visions of a gang of radicals demonstrating against authority. You'd have imagined we'd end up the way people used to in Mussolini's Italy. Yes, you'd have worried.'

Gina had to admit to herself that this was true. She said, equably, 'Aren't the AFF members radicals?'

'No,' answered Filipo. 'They're just ordinary people, young mostly, from all walks of life, whose concern is for the rights of individuals who don't have an organization to stand up for them. You know, Sis, not everyone belongs, or wants to belong, to a union or a Church or a political party. But there are times – say, when they're sacked or evicted without just cause – when they need support. That's what the AFF is all about.'

'It demonstrates on other people's behalf?'

'Yes, and helps with claims for compensation, gives legal advice and so on. It's a worthwhile organization, Sis. The only pity is that it's necessary.'

Gina regarded her brother. A while ago she'd envisaged

this conversation as an encounter between her resolve and his nonchalance. Now, however, she could see the mature light in Filipo's eyes. Also, she realized he wasn't on the defensive, he was sincerely positive in his support of the AFF. She asked, 'Are you one of its organizers?'

'No,' replied Filipo, 'though I have been asked to join the committee. My legal training might be useful.'

'Does the college know about your involvement?'

'Several students are members.'

'And it's all right?'

'So long as we don't bring the university into disrepute, and don't neglect our studies, yes, it's all right.' Filipo smiled, reached out and squeezed his sister's hand. 'Honest.'

Gina returned his grip. 'Please don't think I was prying. But I was concerned. You understand?'

'Of course I do,' said Filipo.

'And you will be careful? I mean, you won't get mixed up in anything where you might get hurt?'

Filipo gave a good-natured laugh. 'What, and risk putting my body out of action? Sis, that would be a crime which certain ladies of my acquaintance would never forgive.'

Gina hoped she didn't blush. There were still times, no matter how adult their conversation, when she could be unseated by a sudden reminder of Filipo's manhood. She said blandly, 'I suppose there's no accounting for taste.'

Filipo grinned.

Gina said more seriously, 'I'm pleased you and Mickey are friends. I hope ...'

The lights dimmed.

Filipo said, 'She'll be on in a minute doing her stuff.' He arose swiftly, forestalling anything further Gina might say. 'I'll go and watch from the wings so's we can make a fast getaway to the party when her dance spot's over.' He bent and kissed the top of Gina's head as the band commenced its intro. 'Here they come,' said Filipo. 'See you, Sis,' and he was striding away.

Gina watched him with a co-mingling of affection and exasperation. When he'd gone, she leaned back, watched Mickey and the dancers. But her mind drifted from thoughts of Filipo's relationship with the girl back to his membership of the AFF. She understood and admired his motives; on the other hand she could never shake off her deep-seated misgivings about involvement in anything even slightly political. Not for the first time recently, she was obliged to remind herself of her brother's common sense and her fellow citizens' freedom of speech.

Sam the waiter appeared at her side to ask if she'd like a drink. Gina declined. She remained at the table until the end of Mickey's spot but then returned upstairs to her office and the familiar reassurance of a stack of paperwork.

Rossi Entertainment Management resided in ten offices in the West-Rossi Building. An air of busy, modern efficiency hummed around the agency; the rattle of typewriters and ringing of telephones infecting clients with the self-confidence of success.

As Gina passed through the glass and chrome and foliage of the reception lounge, she smiled a bright hello to the half-dozen showbusiness people waiting there. A few minutes later she was seated before Harry's desk.

She'd already talked to Harry at length on the phone when he returned from his business trip this morning, omitting only to mention Monument Pictures. Now, placing the report on the film company in front of him, she came directly to the point:

'Harry, how would you feel about buying a movie studio?'

Harry stared at her for quite some time, then down at the report to silently, slowly turn the pages, his long features growing thoughtful. At last he said, 'I think you'd better tell me about it.'

Gina did so, for over a quarter of an hour.

Then Harry said, 'I'm not sure.'

Gina couldn't conceal her disappointment.

'I'm sorry,' said Harry, 'but frankly, the state the movie industry's in, I think we'd be taking a big risk.'

'We've taken risks before.'

'Yes, and I know we came out on top. But would this one be worth it?' Harry looked doubtful.

'Monument would tie in well with West-Rossi's existing interests,' pressed Gina.

'So long as it didn't bankrupt them.'

'You're being negative,' returned Gina, a little too sharply. She was instantly sorry for her tone and quickly added, 'I mean, we ought to consider the positive side.' She offered a smile of conciliation. But there remained a corner of her patience which was restless. She thought of Oliver Randolph's beating her out of North State Roadhouses; and she wanted very much to be able to imagine his face when he learned she'd captured Monument Pictures when he could not.

Harry said, 'Word around the industry is, Monument doesn't have a lot positive going for it. About it's only prospect at the moment is the movie it's making of Robert Fallon's book.'

'Felix is very confident about it.'

'Yes. Everyone who's seen the rushes says it has Oscar potential. That could mean a box-office guarantee. Just a nomination would most likely put the film in profit. Not sufficient to get the studio permanently back on its feet, but enough of a shot in the arm to keep it breathing while major surgery is performed.' Harry stressed, 'Major surgery. You appreciate that's what the studio needs?'

Gina nodded. 'From what I hear, so do all the other studios. Seems they grew too fat too fast and are now blaming their ailments on everyone but themselves. We've kept West-Rossi fit by staying lean. I'm sure we can do the same with Monument once we've got it on its feet.'

Harry said, 'Sounds like your mind's set on this.'

'I'd like to know you support me.'

'And if I advised against?'

Gina wished he hadn't said that. 'I'm not sure what I'd do, Harry. To be honest, I've already written to Barbara Graham. Not with an offer. Just to let her know we might be interested, so she won't agree to sell to someone else before we've made up our minds.'

'Has she replied?'

'No.'

'But when she does you'll need to let her know where we stand.' Harry rubbed his jaw as he again glanced through the report. 'It says Monument is valued at eighteen million. Can we afford so much?'

Gina answered, 'Irving will have to work out the financing,' and strengthening her voice with as much conviction and enthusiasm as she could muster, added, 'but I'm sure we'll be able to raise the money.'

For a while Harry sat in sober silence. Finally he closed the report and pushed it back across his desk to Gina. With a slow shake of his head he said, 'Never figured I'd end up as a movie mogul.'

Gina's elation jumped. 'You mean ...'

He smiled. 'If Irving says we can produce the wherewithal, I'll give it my vote.'

'Oh, Harry, thanks. I promise you won't regret it.'

'I won't if I get to meet Barbara Graham.'

Slightly surprised by this remark, Gina said, 'Felix suggested I visit her personally to handle any negotiations. I think he sees her as rather special.'

'She certainly is,' returned Harry without hesitation. 'You only have to watch her on screen to know that. I admit, I was always a fan. Filipo is too.'

'But I thought she hadn't made a movie in years.'

'That's right. But I've got several in my collection. Filipo's seen most of them twice.'

Gina thought, so many men smitten by this woman.

Harry said, 'How'd you like to make her acquaintance tonight? My place, say around eight?'

Gina didn't need to consider. 'I'd love to,' she replied.

When Gina left her apartment it was raining again. Nevertheless she decided to walk to her date at Harry's. The fresh air would be welcome, would do her good after being cooped up indoors almost every minute since she returned from Las Vegas. Plus, she could take the opportunity to indulge herself, window gazing.

Wearing her fawn mackintosh and sou'wester, collar up, hands deep in her pockets, she happily strolled up Fifth Avenue, pausing frequently to study the swimwear and sunsuits posing behind the rain-dappled windows. It seemed an age since she'd mounted a real shopping expedition. She so looked forward to Cassie's arrival in Manhattan.

Together they'd raid the city.

By the time she'd covered the few blocks to the south-east corner of Central Park, Gina realized she'd dawdled rather longer than she'd intended and now quickened her pace to short cut across the park to Harry's apartment on the western avenue.

Lamps glittered in the watery air, turning benches, statues and monuments into reflecting glass. Gina hummed lightly, smiled at passers-by. Though she rarely found time to visit here these days, it was her favourite place in the city; maybe because she and Cassie, long ago during their lunchtime escapes from chambermaid toil, had spent so many happy moments here.

A poster attached to a lamppost advertised a band concert in the park next week. Gina paused to read. It was years since she'd sat here in the afternoon sun listening to a recital. Perhaps she'd find time to come. Perhaps ... Her mind cut off the musing and backtracked several seconds. Someone had been walking a distance behind her; she'd heard hard wet footsteps on the path. Now they weren't there. She glanced around.

No one. Rain misted across the pools of yellow light, dripped from trees. Traffic noise hummed beyond the far perimeter of the oasis. Gina was alone.

Imagination, she admonished herself. Nevertheless, she remained a moment with her head cocked. Then, with a shrug, she continued on her way, the heels of her own boots snap-splashing reassuringly. A first sign of old age, she thought wryly, hearing sounds that don't exist. You'll be seeing things next.

The footfalls recommenced.

Gina's mouth ran suddenly dry. Though her first impulse was to halt and swing around, she kept walking. There is someone, isn't there? Yes. The tread was wider spaced than her own. A man? And cautious; the steps were being placed with definite care. But of course they are, Gina's rationality objected, he's avoiding puddles. Still, she mentally argued, he stopped when I stopped. Are you sure? She slowed her pace, concentrating to distinguish the pursuing steps. Now she was convinced they existed, and after several moments she knew they too had decelerated.

I'm being followed.

The realization came to her as an icy gust. Simultaneously, awful statistics leapt through her head: almost three hundred murders in Manhattan last year, over six hundred felonious assaults, more than a hundred cases of rape.

She at once was afraid. Those figures from the newspaper crime reports were as familiar to her as sports scores. But these days she read them with merely detached interest, it being years since they'd been the basis of dinning into a young Paola and Filipo never to enter parks after dark, only to be on the streets in the safety-in-numbers company of friends.

Such excellent advice. Yet Gina herself had never heeded it. She was vital, strong, confident, had nothing to fear. Besides, she just didn't feel like a potential victim. This armour of nonsensical belief now fractured, fell away leaving Gina naked. She didn't know what to do. The watery landscape was deserted. Where had everybody gone? She felt suddenly, desperately alone.

Up ahead, voices, male and female, laughing.

Gina almost gasped aloud with relief as she rounded a bend and at the intersection of paths fifty yards distant saw a man and woman hurrying, clutching each other beneath an umbrella. But they were already at the intersection, joyfully intent in their companionship of haste and shelter from the increasing downpour.

Gina raised a hand, thought to shout, yet even in that moment some iota of reticence kept her from what a corner of her mind saw as an absurd act. And then the couple were briskly on their way, in the opposite direction to which Gina would turn. As they and her opportunity were lost Gina swiftly switched her attention to the tracking at her back.

It had stopped.

Gina's pace automatically slowed, and she strained to capture individual sounds amid the splash and plop of rain, rustle of leaves and creak of boughs. She halted, eliminating her own footfalls, listened intently. The surrounding rhythms of air, water and vegetation were unbroken. Gina looked around. The path was deserted. Rippled lamplight shimmered on trickling gutters, glistened on wet grass. Darkly shining trunks and their canopies cast shifting shadows on the liquid ground. Did they conceal a watcher?

Peering, Gina attempted to find the form of a person amid the lurking shapes. There was no one. So why on earth are you standing here? Heed your own best counsel and get away to the security of the crowd.

She swung around and hurried on, lengthening, quickening her stride. Throwing a glance over her shoulder she saw a piece of darkness detach itself from a patch of deeper black. Her heart lurched. And she fled. Her ears now were attacked by the rattle of hard heels as well as by the triphammer of her own pulse. Visions of assault flashed in her imagination. She snatched frantically for thoughts of self-defence. Scream, her logic ordered. Scream as loud as you're able.

Gina sucked at the air as her arms pumped and her chest heaved. With all her will she tried to force out a cry but it was choked in her gasping, jolting, racing flight. Her feet hit a deep puddle and she stumbled, skidded in a soaking explosion. For a panic-stricken instant she believed she was down, but her legs were carrying her on, pitching and tottering, remaining upright, dashing forward ...

... toward the approaching man.

He'd circled around! A tall man in a long coat, hat declined over his eyes, Gina wrenched to a halt, glanced, terrified, right and left then back whence she'd come. Another figure there, scarcely sixty feet off, a hunched, tenebrous shape. Gina flung a look ahead. The tall man was striding, advancing rapidly. Again she sought behind, saw only rain and shadows.

Confusion swirled through her senses as moisture gusted across her vision. She was caught in a cataract of alarm and uncertainty. Her powers of reasoning were drowning. She pulled back a fist, willing strength into her impotent muscles. Strike him hard, in the face, once, then run, run for your life. Gina's arm shook with tension as she squinted through the glassy, lancing atmosphere. The man was closing on her. A slap of wind smacked the soaked hem of her mac against her knees. The shock snapped her concentration.

The man raised a shoulder to the squall, his face turning toward Gina. His eyes flicked across her hesitancy and he offered a fleeting smile and a nod and without slackening pace hastened by.

Gina remained there, arms dropping limply to her sides as she watched the dark spectre of her fears become a camel-overcoated businessman departing into the wet evening. Her qualms leaked with the water dripping from the brim of her sou'wester.

A couple of teenage girls, chattering, hustled into view, followed by an elderly, dapper gent with a gambolling dalmation. Good Lord, the park's full of people. Of course you saw somebody on the path behind you: a perfectly innocent pedestrian who disappeared because he took a short cut across the grass to get out of this weather as quickly as possible. Which is what you should be doing, instead of standing here like a soggy daisy.

Gina gave a small laugh, feeling both sheepish and relieved. She pulled up her collar, walked on.

By the time she reached the park exit she'd convinced herself the episode had been conjured up by her imagination. Skipping across the gurgling gutter, she audaciously dodged traffic to gain the opposite sidewalk and hurry into Harry's apartment block.

Chapter Eight

Harry's sitting room was large with tall windows overlooking the park. It was a welcoming room with a comfortable batchelor clutter. A wide fireplace was semi-circled by sofas and armchairs, its long wooden mantle laden with letters, postcards, invitations and showbusiness magazines. Similar collections covered the sideboards and tables.

Gina had always been very fond of the room. Yet whenever she visited it wasn't the furnishings which claimed her attention. It was the walls.

Every square inch was covered with photographs. A cavalcade of world-famous faces – musicians, singers, movie stars – all autographed with love, good wishes and personal messages. All, Gina knew, pre-dated 1945, the friends and colleagues from that slice of Harry's life when, as he had said in one of his rarer maudlin moments, 'The world still put a value on excellence, before mediocrity got fancy-wrapped and folks accepted it as a gift.'

This evening, in his more characteristic cheerful mood, he'd chatted with Gina some more about the prospects of the movie industry while he hung her mac to dry and mixed a shaker of martinis. Now, with their drinks in their hands, they stood at the wall and Harry, indicating a photograph flanked by Zachary Scott and Hoagy Carmichael, said:

'Barbara Graham.'

Gina saw a woman in three-quarter profile. Black hair bobbed at the slim but strong neck; eyes part closed, looking downward above hollowed cheeks; a wide mouth with a full lower lip in a small but squarish jaw. It was a relaxed face while containing a latent vitality. Yet it was also disquieting. Gina could think of no other word as she felt an inexplicable sense of unease.

Harry remarked, 'A face that makes the camera hold its breath. William Dieterle said so after directing her first starring role. *Night Rain*. Nineteen-thirty-three.' He lingered, contemplating the photograph before turning, inviting, 'Take a seat. I'll show you what he meant.'

Gina's gaze was held by the portrait for several moments until she pulled away to sit in an armchair as Harry went to a tall cupboard and took out a large film reel can from amid dozens stacked vertically on the shelves. He carried it to a door which he opened to reveal an eight-by-six annexe wherein waited a massive movie projector on a stand.

Within minutes Harry had deftly threaded his film reel, returned to erect a canvas screen facing Gina across the sitting room. 'All set,' he declared, pulling the curtains and turning out the lights. 'Hope you've brought a bunch of handkerchiefs.'

Gina heard him cross the carpet as she stared ahead at the blackness. She couldn't remember when she last had visited a movie house, but the sense of anticipation, the tingle of her blood was as fresh as it had been over twenty-five years ago in Rome prior to the curtain-up on the silent, flickering thrill of her first *cinematografo*. It was a reflexive sensation. There was something special about motion pictures, a magic which never could be equalled by television. But could they still be profitable?

Before the question had time to set her mental wheels in motion, the sudden whir of the projector reclaimed Gina's attention as the screen flared white.

Scratches and streaks leapt about the oblong of light. Geometric shapes and a series of numerals. A hissing sound spurted from the projection room followed abruptly by an orchestral fanfare to herald the image of a sky-reaching tower against a radiating sunburst – the trademark, as renowned as Warner Brothers' shield, Paramount's alp, MGM's lion, RKO's radio mast. Next, across the base of the tower, carved into the stone, appeared:

MONUMENT PICTURES PRESENTS.

The announcement remained on view for several moments accompanied by the strident clarion call, until both ended simultaneously. An instant's silent blackness, then dramatic music and ragged capital letters being slashed across the screen to paint: DESPERATE HIGHWAY. The title held: was turned over like the page of a book to reveal:

STARRING – JOHN GARFIELD AND BARBARA GRAHAM.

Gina stared at the names until they in turn were folded back from the list of supporting players. Never before had she watched credits so carefully. She read every name, all those assistants and technicians who, under normal circumstances, she would have let roll by. There was an excitement rising in her, not only for what she was about to see, but also at the idea of being on the brink of a new horizon.

The final credit faded, to:

Night. The starkly lit exterior of a shabby roadside diner. A parked truck, its door opening, a man in crumpled pants and battered leather jacket climbing down. The camera closed in on the man's back, followed him to the sign-plastered diner and into the long, narrow interior. A counter; behind it a fat man in stained apron, leaning on his forearms reading a magazine. He looked up at the man from the truck. This man said, 'Coffee,' and turned to look down the room. John Garfield. The camera panned to trace his gaze, across the deserted tables, to the lone figure in the corner by the window. A woman wearing a dark coat, face in the shadow of her hat as she stared down at the cup before her. Garfield walked forward, the camera at his shoulder, until he halted at the woman's table. For a long moment she ignored him; at last, slowly, looked up ...

... into Gina's eyes.

The face from the photograph on Harry's wall, in animation was somehow different. The strange combination of repose and strength was there, but Gina, looking into the dark irises, was sure there was more, a secret emotion at once fascinating and disturbing.

The counterman in the diner called, 'Coffee black?'

The moment was broken. The woman returned to staring at her cup. Garfield walked back across the room. Gina felt the tension go out of her.

She watched the remainder of the movie, her emotions no

longer trapped by the real Barbara Graham but caught up in her fictional character's tale of love and murder. No question, the woman was a compelling actress, as raw and pugnacious as Garfield, able to educe the gamut of sentiments without histrionics, so that when the final condemned cell scene closed, Gina was swiftly dabbing her eyes, swallowing the lump in her throat before Harry came out of his annexe.

'Something, huh?' he said, switching on the lights then returning to unload the projector.

Gina replied quietly, 'Yes.' Behind her Harry continued to recount Barbara Graham's heyday. But Gina grew pensive. The film moved to the back of her mind and her thoughts shifted to Irving's report on the Monument shareholders; the paragraph about the ex-actress; the single phrase concerning her time at Warner Brothers:

'Twice suspended for moral conduct likely to bring the motion picture industry into disrepute.'

Gina was well aware of Hollywood's past scandals, and the stars' sexual escapades. She thought of the effect Barbara Graham's personality had on Felix and Harry and Filipo; she especially was thinking of Filipo.

When Harry re-appeared to replace the movie in the cupboard, Gina was on the edge of questioning him about the ex-actress's suspension, but at the last instant changed her mind. She told herself it was no business of hers if the woman had been promiscuous, and, besides, these days she was retired and living in Venice, thousands of miles away from Gina's family.

Harry made fresh martinis. Gina made lox and cream cheese sandwiches. They settled down to spend the remainder of the evening in easy conversation.

Gina left by taxi. As the cab pulled away she couldn't help but glance across toward the entrance to the park. Not a soul in sight. 'Of course there isn't,' she said aloud, and the driver gave her a look in his rearview mirror, and she returned him a smile and a wink and rode happily homeward.

Over the following week, Gina talked with each of her directors about the purchase of Monument, and, as she had hoped, while they were somewhat surprised by the proposition, they all eventually agreed to support a bid. Irving proved the least enthusiastic, repeating Harry's misgivings about the current state of the movie industry, and, privately to Gina, warning that the expenditure would commit every last dollar of West-Rossi's collateral.

They discussed it for an entire day, surrounded by reams of financial calculations, and only after Irving had satisfied himself that, if the worst came to the worst, the studio's land could be sold for real estate development to offset some of the eighteen million purchase price, did he finally come around to Gina's side.

Once he had given his support, however, he would, Gina knew, use all his expertise to make the venture a success. At the end of their rather exhausting conference they shared a bottle of wine and Irving toasted their plan with good luck. 'Of course,' he added, 'you haven't had a reply from Barbara Graham yet.'

Gina took that reminder to bed, wondering whether to send a second letter to the ex-actress. But the next morning as she breakfasted, she concluded it would do no good to seem too pushy, and decided to postpone pursuing the matter for another week or so.

The cable arrived that afternoon.

Gina smiled as she read:
NO BANDS STOP SMALL FANFARE WILL SUFFICE STOP ARRIVING LA GUARDIA TOMORROW FLIGHT LAX1047 STOP
It was signed: MOMMA C OBRIEN

Cassie's arrival had been worth waiting for; for not only was there everyone at The Lady and The First Floor to tickertape her with welcome, but also, it seemed, there was someone on every street corner to recognize her and say hello as she accompanied Gina on a tour of West-Rossi customers and suppliers, getting acquainted with the people and routines introduced to the company during her four-year absence.

Cassie had insisted she wanted to get back into harness as soon as possible once it was decided where she might best fit in. The latter question, however, wasn't so easily answered.

The enthusiasm Gina had felt back in Las Vegas when she'd asked her friend to return to West-Rossi, now had to be tempered with practicality.

As she'd mentioned to Harry, the company had kept fit by staying lean. No one on the payroll was run off their feet; on the other hand, nobody had time to stand around discussing the weather. And nowhere was this more so than the management offices.

As this week had worn on, Gina had become increasingly unsure about the situation. There were several positions where Cassie's experience would be valuable, but none that warranted the sort of salary Gina had hoped to pay her friend. And while she dearly would have liked simply to create an executive post, that would, she knew, be neither fair nor satisfactory for anyone.

The fact was, Cassie could easily find a genuine and challenging, well-salaried job elsewhere.

On this seventh morning since Cassie's return, on their way back from a visit to the company's bakery, they took a coffee break on a bench in Bryant Park. The June sun was warm and the small oasis pleasantly peaceful. Gina was wondering if this wouldn't be a good opportunity to broach the subject of Cassie's employment.

Cassie said, 'Gina, I've been thinking.'

'Oh?'

'About this job situation.'

'Yes?'

'Hon, I know you meant well when you invited me to join the company, but,' she looked apologetically at Gina, 'I'm beginning to think it wasn't such a good idea after all.'

'Oh, Cass ...'

'No, please,' said Cassie with concern. 'I'm not for a minute blaming you. I think we were both just carried away in the heat of the moment. I admit, I thought it would be marvellous to be back with the old gang. And I still do. Only I don't think it's going to work out.'

Gina felt smitten by disappointment. Lost for words she bit the inside of her lip as Cassie continued:

'I know this sounds terribly ungrateful, but it's simply I've realized that whatever I do it has to be for keeps. When the baby's here I can't be flitting from job to job.'

Gina ventured, 'It would be for keeps at West-Rossi.'

'Yes. But would I enjoy it? I mean, for the next twenty-odd years. That's how long I'm going to have to provide for both of us.' She glanced down at her stomach, then added, 'I've got to make the right decision now, Gina, and find a spot I'll want to stick at. And, frankly, I just don't see anything at West-Rossi that would fit the bill.' She gave a pale smile. 'I feel such a heel, after everyone's been so welcoming and all, but ...'

'There's no need,' Gina said gently. 'I understand. To be honest, I'd come to more or less the same conclusion.'

'You had?'

'I'd realized that while there was plenty you could do, none of it would exactly tax your talents. I was sure you'd want much more of a challenge.'

'That's it,' agreed Cassie. 'Like the old days, when we were just getting started with Rossi Taverns. We ran our feet off sixteen hours a day, but loved every minute. Of course, the condition I'm in, I've got to take it a bit easier than that, but if I have to work then I'd rather it was at something I can put my back into and see worthwhile results.' She paused, slightly self-conscious. 'Beginning to sound like an empire builder. More'n likely I'll finish up slinging hash at Coney Island.'

'You'll do no such thing,' countered Gina. 'In two years time you'll be on the cover of **Business Week** – with the baby on your knee, of course.' Cassie laughed and Gina asked, 'Seriously, have you considered what you'll do?'

Cassie replied, 'I've been thinking I'd like to get back into the hotel trade.' To Gina's look of surprise, she said, 'All those years I spent skivvying, in a way I enjoyed it. I mean, I enjoyed the workings of a big hotel. It always interested me. And, you know, these days there's a lot of potential in the business.'

Gina agreed, 'Certainly a growing tourist trade.'

'I think,' said Cassie, 'the future is going to be franchise hotels. Remember, we talked about it once? Years ago, when Rossi Taverns had started making money and you were wondering where to invest it.'

Yes, Gina did remember. But that had been before Cassie went off with Tony Nevada and Gina married Howard and West-Rossi shelved the idea of franchise hotels in favour of other ventures. She'd seen the concept mentioned recently in a trade magazine, but, busy with other matters, had not pursued it. Now she asked, 'No one has started up yet, have they?'

'Not that I know of,' answered Cassie. 'But I'm going to start making some enquiries. After all, I was in at the start of Rossi Taverns, so I reckon I know more about the mechanics and economics of franchising than most.'

Gina murmured, 'I'm sure you do.'

'I could help set up an operation,' continued Cassie, her enthusiasm blossoming, 'and then manage its day-to-day running – training courses for the franchisees, special promotions and so on – just like we did for the Taverns. And, best of all, I could do it from one place, wouldn't have to be running around the country, which would be perfect once I had the baby.'

Gina nodded, caught in a web of thought. She said, 'I'll be sorry to lose you, Cassie.'

'Well, we'll still see each other won't we? I mean, even though I'm working for a competitor we'll stay friends?'

Gina returned quietly, 'Of course.'

Cassie, seeing the small frown between Gina's brows, ventured, 'You don't mind, me doing this?'

'Not at all,' answered Gina. 'It's just that ...' Her head was full of questions, suppositions, notions, put in train by her friend's discourse. She needed time to think. She stared across the sunlit park, and was looking directly at the tall, narrow rear windows of the Public Library. All at once she said, 'Cass, I just thought of something. Can I see you later at The Lady?'

Cassie, only slightly surprised by the sudden cut in the conversation, replied, 'That's okay. You go ahead. It'll give me chance to catch up on some family calls.'

Fifteen minutes later Gina was at a table in the magazine and newspaper room of the library, commencing a sortie into a stack of hotel trade journals. It took her over an hour to find half-a-dozen brief items on hotel franchising, but these were sufficient to convince her that Cassie's faith in the new concept was not misplaced. She made some notes and wrote down a few speculative figures. When she left the library she was on the horns of a dilemma.

Wrapped in thought Gina returned to the park bench.

She had, she believed, found the solution to what Cassie could do if she joined West-Rossi. And franchise hotels would be a logical step for the company. But, the cost of launching such a venture on a national scale would be substantial. Two or three million maybe.

A couple of months ago that wouldn't have presented much of a problem. Today, however, Gina was all but committed to the expenditure of eighteen million for Monument, and she recalled Irving's warnings about the strain that purchase would put on their resources.

But she wanted so much for Cassie to have a place at West-Rossi. Gina felt she owed it to her friend after barging into her life and encouraging her to come all this way.

She bunched her fists with frustration. 'There has to be something we can do,' she said fervently.

Irving shook his head. 'The bank would never agree.'

Gina sagged. She'd come directly to the accountant's office from the park, had spent an hour explaining about Cassie and franchise hotels. Irving had listened sympathetically, but, he'd said finally, they couldn't possibly fund both the purchase of Monument and the launch of a franchise hotel company.

He said, 'I can see the potential, but I'm afraid it will be a couple of years before we can afford to get involved.'

Gina said unhappily, 'But Cass will be working for someone else by then. Isn't there anything we can do.'

'We could forget about the movie company.'

Gina remained silent. She thought of her tour of the studio with Felix; her meeting with Robert Fallon. For several moments she dwelt on Fallon; the film of his book *The Last Summer*; the fact that it would be scrapped if Monument closed. Then she thought of Cassie, and her shoulders dropped in defeat.

Rising, she said hoarsely, 'Thanks, Irving. I appreciate

your help,' and before he could respond hurried out.

Gina returned to The Lady and lunched with Cassie and did her best to maintain a cheery facade as Cassie chatted about her plans. After lunch Gina had a number of business appointments and she was grateful to be able to leave her friend to her own devices, at the same time, she was hard pressed to give the meetings her fullest attention.

There was a further respite for the remainder of the afternoon and evening as Cassie had gone to visit relatives. When Gina went up to her apartment, she switched off her phone, having left a message downstairs that she'd prefer not to be disturbed. From seven o'clock to nine she sat on her sofa doing nothing, feeling alternately miserable and angry.

Eventually she stirred, thinking a shower and change of clothes would at least freshen her up for when Cassie returned. Under the hot, lancing water some of the tension went out of her; and by the time she'd donned a simple blue cotton dress, she'd accepted that the corner she was in was of her own building, and the surest fact of life was that nobody could have everything.

There was a knock at the door.

Thinking Cassie must have forgotten the key she'd been given, Gina crossed the room and opened the door.

Irving said, 'Have you got half an hour?'

It took him less than that to explain what he'd been doing all afternoon; working out the economics of franchise hotels; the fees and royalties payable by franchisees; the cost of launching such an operation throughout the country. 'At least two million,' he said. 'And, I have to confirm, we just can't afford it.' He handed over a set of figures.

Gina, glancing resignedly at the calculations, said, 'Thanks, Irving. You shouldn't have gone to so much trouble.'

He said, 'But we can afford half a million.'

Gina stared as he produced more typewritten sheets. Taking them, she read the sums that could be gleaned from the barest corners of West-Rossi's operations. She acknowledged, 'Yes, half a million. But you agreed we'd need two.'

'Certainly, for a nationwide launch,' he returned. 'But do we have to begin on such a scale?' He handed over further statistics. 'These are only rough estimates,' he stressed, 'but with half a million we can afford to set up a hotel franchise operation in a single region of the country, with perhaps a dozen franchisees. I know that's very modest, but at least it would be a start, a foot in the door.' He added encouragingly, 'Better than nothing.'

Gina slowly read the statistics. When she reached their end, she read them again. At last she looked up. She wasn't sure whether she would cheer or cry. Holding on to her conflicting emotions she asked, 'Have you any idea when we might get it under way?'

Irving answered, 'Say, for the opening of the first franchise, early next year.'

'So soon?'

'We have the advantage of having the operational machinery of franchising already running. The only major aspect we're going to have to plan from scratch is the style of the hotels, once we've decided which market sector to aim for.'

'And then publish a prospectus.'

'Interview franchisees.'

'Hold a press conference.'

Irving said, 'Of course.'

Gina caught the humour in his voice. She smiled. 'Getting a bit ahead of myself,' she admitted. 'But, really, this is such good news. And I'm so grateful, Irving, for your making it possible. Thank you.'

He gave a small shrug. 'It would have been a shame if Cassie had had to leave,' and for the briefest instant he broke from Gina's gaze. Before she had time to even think about his fleeting hesitancy, however, he reasserted his businesslike stance, saying, 'I must emphasize, the half million is absolutely all we can commit to the scheme. There can be no question of starting with more than a dozen or so franchiseships. We cannot possibly go nationwide.'

Gina said, 'I understand.'

'Fine,' said Irving. 'I'll leave these figures with you so you can discuss the situation with Cassie.'

Gina glanced at her watch. 'She'll be back shortly. Won't you stay and talk to her yourself?'

'Well ...'

'And you can make arrangements to get together with her to prepare some outline proposals. After all, the sooner we start moving on this the better.'

Irving asked, 'Are you free to meet with us tomorrow?'

'I don't see that I need. Besides, I don't want Cass to feel I'm looking over her shoulder. If she's a bit rusty on office procedures, I know you'll help her out.'

They debated where Cassie would be accommodated in the West-Rossi Building, and then went on to discuss the venture in general. As they talked, Gina thought of how despondent she'd been only an hour ago, and now here she was, her spirits brimming. But, watching the accountant as he underlined some of his figures, she was reminded of the serious financial implications of the commitment they were about to make, and she wondered if Irving had come here tonight against his better judgment.

A key rattled in the lock.

Gina swiftly shelved her thoughts.

Cassie entered and said, 'Hi. Oh, hello, Irving.'

Irving, standing, returned, 'Hello.'

Gina said, 'Cass, there's something we have to tell you.'

Chapter Nine

The letter from Barbara Graham arrived a few days after Cassie and Irving got down to the nitty-gritty of the franchise hotel scheme. Cassie had been over the moon with the turn of events. And Gina had been delighted to see her so; nevertheless she couldn't help feeling a little left out even though it had been her own decision to take a back seat in the new venture. The letter with the Venice postmark was therefore doubly welcome.

Its contents were brief. Barbara Graham apologized for the delay in replying, thanked Gina for her interest in Monument, and invited her to Italy to discuss the matter.

Although there was nothing to indicate the ex-actress's attitude toward the sale of the studio, at least she hadn't dismissed the possibility out of hand, and Gina thought she had every reason to feel optimistic.

She cabled a reply just as soon as she'd booked a flight and hotel accommodation. She then made telephone calls to the West-Rossi directors, appraising them of the situation and stressing the need for secrecy. The last thing Gina wanted was to antagonize Barbara Graham by having their meeting splashed across the newspapers before it had even taken place; her visit to Venice was to be passed off as a holiday.

She now felt far more content about her self-exclusion from Cassie and Irving's hotel discussions. All Gina's thoughts now revolved around her forthcoming meeting with Barbara Graham. And as the time for her departure fast approached, her optimism grew. The more she thought about Monument, the surer she became that the studio could be turned into a success.

The day before she was due to leave, she spent the

morning on routine office chores, had a snack lunch then walked to her hairdressing appointment in the Rockefeller Centre.

When she emerged from the salon into the shopping arcade, Gina was feeling especially chipper. She strolled in front of the exclusive stores, pausing at each tempting display of silks and cosmetics and perfumes, thinking to treat herself to some small extravagance, a good luck token for her assignment in Venice.

She'd been thus engaged for about ten minutes when she all at once had the unsettling sense of being watched. She glanced left and right, but saw only the busy crowd. And then, as her eyes focused on the reflecting window before her, she realized there was a man standing in a doorway on the opposite side of the arcade.

She swung around.

The man started toward her.

Surprise rooted Gina to the spot as she recognized Tony Nevada, and it took her mind a few moments to adjust to the situation. Her first consideration then was to walk away; but she decided that would be both a childish and a futile gesture. She stood her ground as the singer approached.

In his usual provocative drawl he said, 'Hi.'

Gina had an unreasonable feeling of being trapped. She said as levelly as possible, 'Good afternoon.'

'It is now that we've met. You've made a boring business trip worthwhile.' He was wearing a blue sports coat and an open-necked cream silk shirt which accentuated the deep gold of his tan. His smile held all its customary bravado.

Gina was lost for a response.

He said, 'But we really must stop meeting in such public places,' and he took a further step toward Gina so that she was obliged to retreat into the recess of a shop doorway. Tony Nevada moved in with her, his back to the passers-by. 'Much cosier,' he said.

Gina clenched her teeth in self-annoyance at being manoeuvred into this position. She said, 'I really don't have time ... If you'll excuse me ...'

'Do you have an appointment?'

'Not exactly ...'

'Nor do I. Such an opportunity for an intimate chat.'

'I don't think you and I have anything to chat about.'

Tony Nevada grinned. 'I'm sure you're kidding. Come on, across to Pierre's. We can take a rear booth. Very private.'

'No, thank you. I have to go.'

'You said that in Vegas.'

'And it was equally true.'

'You never thanked me for the gift.'

Gina stared. 'Gift?'

'Small token. The bottle with the gold top.'

Gina remembered the champagne.

Tony Nevada said, 'But it wasn't thanks I wanted. Only to share it with you. That, and ... who knows?' His high-cheekboned face glowed with self-confidence as his gaze moved downward over Gina's throat to touch her breasts before returning upward to lock on her eyes.

Gina stared into the intensely blue irises, into the black pupils. And, despite all she knew about the man, she experienced a sexual tremor. She couldn't help it; and anger, at her own reflexes, sharpened her voice as she clipped, 'I have a great deal to do. Goodbye.'

'Running away again?'

'Don't be absurd.' Gina sought a way past him.

'Then why the rush?' The singer's smile was half mocking, half challenging as he barred her path.

Gina said, 'Please, let me by.'

His hand moved out and gripped her arm.

Startled, Gina tried to pull away; but he held her fast. She looked over his shoulder to the bustling arcade and for a panicky instant almost cried out, but rationality straightened her shoulders and she said coldly, 'Do you intend to keep me here all day?'

'Only long enough to arrange our date.'

'There isn't going to be any date.'

'I'm not used to being turned down.'

'Then it will be a novel experience.'

Tony Nevada shifted his hold on Gina's arm, drawing her toward him. His other hand rested on her ribs and he said, 'I know the sort of experience you really want.'

Gina flamed. Yet she remained pinioned, not so much by

the singer's grip as by his penetrating gaze. She imagined she could feel the heat of his body, while knowing it was her own sweat which had broken out beneath her blouse. She said hoarsely, 'Take your hand off my arm.'

He laughed.

Gina tugged sideways, trying to break free, but realizing she couldn't do so without causing a commotion. Desperation mounted within her as Tony Nevada leaned forward, his lips curving and parting. Gina felt frozen.

His hand cupped her breast.

Gina's paralysis was instantly shattered. She wrenched from his grip, at the same moment rammed her free arm forward, slamming her palm into his chest, sending him staggering backward from the doorway. Her eyes blazed, searing him with all her contempt.

Tony Nevada regained his balance, and he stood, arrogance destroyed, the blood draining from his cheeks.

Gina held her gaze on him only a moment longer, then she stepped past him and began to walk away.

He rasped, 'Bitch. Frigid bitch.'

Gina halted. She was aware of passers-by slowing to glimpse the confrontation; one or two people had stopped. An inner voice exhorted her to leave immediately. But she remained, to say icily, 'Go home, Tony, before you make a bigger fool of yourself.'

'Afraid of it,' he retaliated. 'You're afraid of it.'

Gina clenched her teeth, turned to leave.

'That's right, run away,' the singer threw, his voice rising. 'Go on. Run away. Run back to your loving buddy. Cassie sexless O'Brien. Another one who's afraid of men.'

Gina swung toward him. Warning bells were loud in her head, urging her to end the scene. But there was too much anger in her as she faced the singer's spite.

He took a step toward her, his mouth venomous. 'Yes, I know she's here,' he hissed. 'I know all about you. You and her. Two of a kind. Bloody lesbians.'

Gina recoiled. The entire arcade seemed to have been struck silent and motionless, as if everyone had been tranfixed by the singer's words. Gina imagined hundreds of eyes scouring her, boring into her. Then her control snapped and her arm arced around, driven by fury. Her open palm slashed across Tony Nevada's cheek, snapping his head sideways, causing him to stumble against the store window.

Pain and surprise contorted his features and he reflexively threw up his arm against further blows. When none came he stood, stunned, the air sucking into his nostrils as his name was whispered among the gaping onlookers.

Gina bunched her fists at her sides, fought down her boiling emotions. She looked into Tony Nevada's eyes a moment more, watched his hate bloom, then she quickly turned and strode away.

The radio reporter was saying '... food poisoning at Smith's Restaurant in Wilmington was the cause of several diners being hospitalized. A Department of Health spokesman said the restaurant kitchen was below hygiene standards in a number of areas, and salmonella or similar contamination could not yet be ruled out. Investigations are continuing. Meanwhile, in the Little Town Baseball League, front hitter Jim Hansen ...'

Gina switched off the set on the bedside table and returned to packing her suitcase. She shook her head at the food poisoning report. That was the sort of occurrence the catering trade could well do without. But she held scant sympathy for the restaurateur; there was no excuse for a dirty kitchen. She recalled, not for the first time, her father's strictures on the subject.

Gina paused in her packing, fondly remembering Alfredo Rossi. She thought he'd be satisfied today if he visited The Lady's kitchen. She hoped he'd be proud if he saw their family name on over fifteen hundred Taverns across the country. She was sure he'd be more than somewhat surprised if he knew his eldest daughter was off to buy a movie studio.

Smiling, Gina completed her task, shut the case, took it through to the sitting room. She checked her purse: passport, ticket, traveller's cheques. She was ready. And she was feeling good, had buried yesterday's incident with Tony Nevada, telling herself she had far better things to think about.

The telephone started to ring.

Gina thought to ignore it, but occupational habit got the better of her and she lifted the receiver, said, 'Hello.'

The man's voice said, 'Hello, Gina.'

She exclaimed, 'Oh, Howard!' She was so surprised she hardly caught his next couple of sentences. It was so long since she'd heard from her husband. Not that that was anything new, but over the past few weeks Gina had been so involved with business and personal affairs she'd scarcely given Howard a second thought. Now, pricked by guilt, she listened to him recount his hunting and fishing trip.

He said, 'I'll be back in town tomorrow.'

Gina said, 'Fine. I'll see you when …' She cut off the sentence as her mind returned to the moment and the suitcase at her feet. She searched for words.

'Yes?' said Howard.

Gina kept her tone as light as possible. 'I'll be away tomorrow, Howard. I'm just leaving for Venice.'

There was a pause. Then: 'Business, I suppose.'

'Yes. Someone I have to see. It's important. Very important. Can you keep a secret? Of course you can. We're going to buy a movie studio.'

There was silence on the line.

Gina said, 'Howard? Are you still there?'

At last, 'Yes,' he answered.

'Well, please don't sound so glum,' Gina pressed brightly. 'It's a chance we can't miss. But, don't worry, I promise it won't take any more of my time. Someone else, of course, will be running the studio.' She paused. 'I'm sorry I won't be here tomorrow. But, are you staying in town? Will you be here the day after?'

Howard said, rather quietly, 'I don't know.'

'Oh, please say you will be. I'll fly straight back from Venice. We haven't seen each other for so long. And we should. We really should, Howard. Will you stay?'

After several moments he said, 'I'll see.'

'Thank you,' returned Gina, pretending she didn't hear the complaint in his voice. 'We can go somewhere special. Or have a quiet dinner, just the two of us. Whatever you like. Now, I must go. Take care of yourself. See you in a couple of days. Goodbye, Howard.' She waited until he answered:

'Goodbye, Gina.'

Some places, thought Gina, are like certain people. Whatever circumstances, good or bad, befalls them, they never intrinsically change; and no matter what assembly they join, or are obliged to join, they remain wholly individualistic. She always had felt that way about Venice. Venice always had been, and still was, a citadel, a place of retreat.

Was that why it attracted people like Barbara Graham?

Gina had arrived yesterday, spent a happy evening at a table in the square outside her hotel where the folk of the quarter gathered to chat, play cards, maybe sing, share a corner of their day. The same sociality had been a part of Gina's youth in Rome. In New York too, before the war, after dinner families would stroll, pause in cheerful groups to put the world to rights. Nowadays, those people sat all night in front of a stream of gasoline and soap commercials. Gina wondered how long it would be before the neighbourly squares of Europe were emptied by television.

This morning, that grey prospect was reflected in the weather. 'Glorious June,' Gina muttered to herself, knotting a navy silk scarf in the throat of her salmon jersey suit, peering out at a sky as dull as slate. She gathered her purse, went down to the narrow street beside a lugubriously slopping canal.

The gondolier ferryman at the foot of Calle Gritti was hunched on a bollard smoking a cigarette. As Gina approached, she said, '*Buon giorno*,' the man nodded, scrutinizing her from beneath the brim of his straw hat. He pinched out his smoke, dropped the remnant in the pouch of his white smock.

They poled out into the Grand Canal.

To their left, the waterway's wide mouth to the leaden bay; to the right, the Byzantine, Lombard, Gothic and Baroque palaces, curving around and beyond the Porte dell'Accademia. Despite the dreary light, even though many of the facades were sadly crumbling, this was still the most majestic sweep of buildings in the world.

A rusting green water-bus chuntered along the opposite bank; another distant gondola of gesticulating tourists; several barges. A burbling roar and a motorboat, brass and bright varnish, raced by ploughing a bow wave which slapped and sloshed across the prow of the ferry so that Gina was obliged to cling to the bench as the gondolier swayed precariously and bawled loud and lewd abuse after the fleeing culprit.

Gina, in Italian, said, 'I entirely agree.'

This spurred the man to further vituperation on the subject of the proliferating power boats. When they reached the quay he secured his craft, sat on a bollard, relighted his cigarette, concluded acrimoniously, 'Progress,' and spat into the canal.

Gina walked along a narrow side canal, between high, old buildings. This area of the city was normally far quieter than the right bank, the commercial and tourist centre of the city. On a morning such as this the alleys were deserted. Gina hadn't visited here before and it was only after several wrong turnings that she came upon Villa Arancia.

There was a stone wall, six feet high, draped with lichen and moss; a timber gate, bleached as old bone. Gina went through into a courtyard where glaucous plants sprouted between damp slabs, and a pale-limbed tree reached upward, its foliage filtering the light to a faint green hue.

Gina involuntarily shivered.

The villa, with narrow, arched windows, wooden shuttered, was four storeys of ochre stucco, the lower eight feet patchy and stained by centuries of flood tides. A dark door was similarly scarred. As Gina approached, the door opened.

Barbara Graham said, 'I saw you coming.'

The actress was not as tall as Gina had expected, was perhaps five-feet four. She was wearing loose black trousers and a white blouse, sleeves rolled on thin, sinewy arms each with a wide, plain gold bangle. Her straight, black hair, fringed, bobbed at her neck, was held behind her ears with mother-of-pearl clips. Gina's first impression was that she had a rather Oriental appearance.

The actress invited, 'Please, come in,' and led the way up

a stone staircase. At the top of the flight she opened another door. Gina followed, into a long and wide, light and airy hall. The ceramic chequer tile floor ran between a wall of tapestries and a parade of leaded windows beyond which flowed the Grand Canal.

Barbara Graham turned as Gina paused to watch a gondola emerge from a tunnel beneath the facing villa. The ex-actress remarked, 'Three hundred years ago that was the route used by Pietro Dini, the young actor, to visit his lover here, Villa Arancia's owner, Cardinal Corno. When their affair was finally discovered, Dini was publicly executed, by strangulation, the cardinal was allowed to poison himself.' She looked out of the window. 'Such a beautiful city. Created by such cruel people.'

Gina regarded the woman's three-quarter profile; the dark eyes above hollowed cheeks, wide mouth with full lower lip in a small but squarish jaw; a face at once beautiful but disquieting. Gina experienced the same sense of unease she'd felt on seeing Barbara Graham's portrait in Harry's office.

Barbara Graham went ahead. 'This way.'

The large room was elegantly furnished: pale Chinese rugs on the cobalt tile floor; gilt-framed mirrors and pastoral scenes; a vase of creamy roses filling the fireplace. No signs of eccentricity or egocentricity. The only photographs were half-a-dozen, black-and-white in silver frames on a table between the windows. Gina saw all were children, with perhaps a family resemblance to Barbara Graham.

The actress led the way to two beige satined chairs. She asked, 'Coffee or tea? A glass of wine?'

'No thank you,' Gina replied, sitting, removing her gloves, laying them on her purse.

'Did you have a bearable flight?' asked the ex-actress.

'Not too bad,' smiled Gina.

'Long-distance travel is so hectic these days, so crowded. I avoid it if at all possible.'

'You haven't visited the United States in quite a while,' Gina commented conversationally.

'As you well know from your investigations.'

Gina's smile dropped.

'Please,' said Barbara Graham, 'don't be offended. I didn't intend to be provocative, or critical. I appreciate it was necessary. Sensible too. It's only when companies start spying on their employees that the practice becomes diseased.'

This last word startled Gina, its virulence seeming alien to its deliverer as well as disproportionate to the statement. Then she remembered Barbara Graham's being suspended by the studio for 'moral conduct likely to bring the motion picture industry into disrepute'. Maybe she had cause to feel bitter about company investigations. But with justification? Gina said calmly, 'I understand you've spent the past five years in Venice. Are you ever homesick?'

Barbara Graham answered unhesitatingly, 'Only for jelly doughnuts.' She smiled. 'Venetian pastry chefs are superb, but none of them can make sinkers like Harry's Broadway Bakery.'

'The truth,' agreed Gina, warming. 'I used to eat at his storefront counter, just after we'd emigrated, when I was tramping Manhattan looking for work. Miss Graham, one thing we have in common is great taste in doughnuts.'

'Please, it's Barbara.' Again the smile, richer. And, thought Gina, beautiful. When the woman's face lit that way it became deeply alluring. Barbara Graham asked, 'Do you miss living in Italy?'

'I love the country,' answered Gina. 'I always will. But my roots are in America now. My sister's two boys were born there. My brother Filipo was only ten when he arrived. Now he's twenty-five and doesn't have a trace of Italian accent. He'd enjoy being here today. He's been a movie fanatic since he was a mere infant.'

'Does he work for West-Rossi?'

'He's at law school in Boston. When he's qualified I'm not sure what he'll do. Of course, he'd love to work for Monument.'

'Perhaps he will. If I vote my shares.'

Gina winced. Mentioning the movie company had been a slip of the tongue. Still, there wasn't any point in beating about the bush. She said, 'I hope you will.'

'Why?'

'Pardon?'

'Forgive me, that was rather brusque,' Barbara Graham apologized. 'Old habits, you know. Once upon a time it seemed not a single conversation went by without me having to fence for every word.' She looked away, through the window, the slate grey of the afternoon reflecting nail points of light in her eyes. She turned back to Gina and her lips curved back into a smile. 'Still, my question stands. Why do you want to buy Monument?'

Gina replied, 'I believe we can make it profitable.'

'To what end?'

'The benefit of the West-Rossi Corporation.'

Barbara Graham acknowledged, 'At least you're candid. Thank you for that, for not offering a string of platitudes about saving a fine old studio, protecting jobs, preserving creative merit. They're the lines I've been thrown by all the other would-be buyers.'

Gina asked, 'Are you considering any of their offers?'

'No.'

'Might you consider West-Rossi's?'

'Now that we've met, yes. Forgive me if that sounds rather patronizing. I don't intend it to be. I didn't invite you here to assess your character. More, I suppose, because I was inquisitive. You see, I think I already knew you quite well.' To Gina's questioning look, Barbara Graham said, 'I must confess, I too have been making enquiries?'

'About me?'

'And your company. That's why I took so long to reply to your letter. I liked your letter. Of course, apart from anything else, it was the first business approach I'd ever had from a woman. That in itself was enough to arouse my curiosity.'

Gina said, 'Did you find out all you wanted to know?'

Barbara Graham nodded. 'West-Rossi is a family company. That's the important point I learned. And you, personally, care about what happens to it. That's how it used to be at Monument in the old days. And, I think, how it would be again if West-Rossi took over.'

Gina did her utmost to contain her turbulence. 'Is there anything I can tell you to help your decision? Would you like to discuss any finer contractual points? If it's a question of the price ...'

'Not at all,' cut in Barbara Graham. She remained silent for several moments looking directly into Gina's face, frowning slightly, until she said suddenly, 'It would be unfair to have brought you all this way and not give you a decision.' She took a breath. 'I'll be happy to approve the sale to West-Rossi.'

Gina almost jumped out of her chair, but, with a supreme effort of will, she kept still to respond, 'That's marvellous. Thank you. I assure you you won't regret it. If ...' She hesitated as the ex-actress raised a palm and said:

'On one condition.'

'Yes?'

'I'd like Monument to re-release my old movies.'

Gina was somewhat nonplussed.

'Just seven movies, actually,' said the ex-actress. 'Not for myself, but for the writers and directors who were involved. Four men. Very talented men, who haven't worked – haven't been permitted to work – for several years.'

For a moment Gina remained puzzled. Then she thought: She means they're on the blacklist. She mentally frowned.

Officially the blacklist didn't exist. If certain showbusiness people couldn't get a job, that wasn't so unusual; at any one time half the industry was out of work. No one was unemployed because of their political beliefs. And a handful of West-Rossi Management clients who had recently moved to Europe, had done so, said Harry, because that's where they preferred to be. Gina had left it at that.

Barbara Graham said, 'I want you to understand, I'm not making a political gesture. Rather, a financial one. Those four men had a stake in the seven movies. They're entitled to a share of the box-office receipts.'

Gina said quietly, 'I see.' She pondered for several moments before adding, 'But even if the pictures are re-released the income wouldn't be a fortune.'

'Nor would it be a drop in a bucket. Not if Monument promoted a special Barbara Graham season around the country.' The ex-actress smiled wryly. 'After five years of silent retirement – you know, there've even been rumours I'm dead – I do have a certain curiosity value.'

Gina nodded, thoughtful. She accepted, there wouldn't be anything political about a Barbara Graham season. In fact, come to think of it, it might prove rather a good publicity stroke to follow the announcement of West-Rossi's takeover of the studio. She looked at the ex-actress, who was watching her, awaiting an answer. Gina knew she had to make a decision here and now.

She said, 'I'll have it written into our contract.'

'Your word is good enough,' said Barbara Graham.

'You have it,' returned Gina.

'In which case,' smiled the ex-actress, 'you just bought yourself a movie studio.' She extended her arm and firmly gripped Gina's hand for several moments before standing, saying, 'And now, how about that glass of wine?'

'I'd love one,' answered Gina.

Chapter Ten

She was, to say the least, cock-a-hoop.

When Gina got back to Manhattan she could scarcely contain herself. Yet, she decided, she must. So must everyone else. 'We can't just let the news leak out,' she said to Harry and Irving when she met them at West-Rossi headquarters immediately following her return from Venice. 'We don't want it going off like a damp squib. We want to startle folk with a big bang.'

'We'll keep the lid on,' said Harry, 'till we can arrange a full-blown media conference.'

Irving agreed the importance of making publicity capital out of the studio takeover. Then he went on to say he'd get the contracts under way and would hustle the attorneys to complete matters within a fortnight.

Gina said that would be perfect to give the public relations department time to prepare press releases and information kits and set up the conference. 'It'll be terrific,' she enthused. 'A great boost for West-Rossi. Maybe we could arrange some sort of tie-in with all the Rossi Taverns. Or,' she mused, 'perhaps we should leave that till we do the Barbara Graham season, then, say, offer free movie house tickets to selected diners.'

Harry stopped her there to enquire about the Barbara Graham season. Gina explained. Harry pondered it, but eventually said he couldn't see where anyone might think there was a political motive in screening the seven movies.

That out of the way they spent a further hour discussing various aspects of the Monument deal. Gina then thought to ask how Irving and Cassie were getting along with the franchise hotels concept.

Irving said their proposals would be ready shortly. He and Cassie were happy with the scheme. The only bugbear was the finance; the half million budget would mean a more modest start than originally anticipated, but, the accountant repeated his previous warning, the company's finances could be strained no further.

Gina again agreed, the hotels would not play a major role in West-Rossi's expansion. Besides, she said, Monument would be a big enough firework to explode for the time being.

They continued to chat for a while longer, but Gina began gradually to wind down. Having caught the plane late last night, she'd managed a little sleep during the flight, but, really, since leaving Villa Arancia she'd been running more on nervous energy than anything else. Now, with her news delivered, her adrenalin stopped pumping and she was obliged to stifle a yawn as Harry and Irving sidetracked into discussing Barbara Graham and her movies.

Gina listened for a while, but eventually, gathering her purse, said, 'If you don't mind, I'm for an early night.'

The two men arose. A few more enthusiastic comments were exchanged, arrangements made to get together again tomorrow, then Gina went down, out through the lobby, and walked up the street to The Lady. She stood for a moment or two talking with Joe, the doorman, before going in to tell the receptionist she was back and preferred not to be disturbed.

After the receptionist had passed a pleasantry or two she said, 'Cassie – Miss O'Brien – said to tell you she'd be staying at the Carlton tonight. Mister Cornell's upstairs in the apartment.'

Gina drew a sharp breath. Then, slowly, she released it as she remembered the brief telephone conversation she'd had with Howard before leaving for Venice.

The receptionist asked, 'Is anything wrong?'

Gina raised a smile. 'Not at all,' she replied. 'Have a pleasant evening,' and she went along to the private staircase and up to the apartment.

Howard was in the sitting room listening to the radio – a boxing match. As Gina entered and said pleasantly, 'Hello,' he glanced up and rejoined, 'I expected you earlier.'

Gina held on to her brightness. 'I had to pop into the office, let them know how I got on in Venice.'

He watched her a moment. Then he returned his attention to the radio as the commentary rose urgently.

Gina inwardly sighed. She blamed herself for not coming here directly from the airport. On the other hand, Howard ought to appreciate the importance of the long and tiring round-trip she'd just made; he could at least ask about Monument. Gina thought to prompt him, but decided perhaps he was genuinely engrossed in the radio fight and interrupting him would only make matters worse. She asked quietly, 'When will that be over?'

'When one of them wins.'

Gina murmured, 'Yes.' Then, briskly, 'I'll just go and shower and change,' and she smiled as genuinely as she was able and went through to the bedroom. She stripped and stepped beneath the cascade of steaming water. And, slowly, the tension flowed out of her. She remained there several minutes, luxuriating in the hot massage of the lancing jets. When she emerged, she vigorously towelled herself to a rosy glow, brushed her hair and felt a whole lot better.

Wrapped in her white robe she peeped in at Howard, saw him still involved with the noisy fight, so returned to her bedside table and the small stack of personal mail which her secretary was accustomed to leaving there.

Gina read the couple of invitations, a postcard from her sister holidaying in Canada, a letter from a friend in England. The final envelope was rather grubby, addressed in a blunt hand Gina didn't recognize. It was postmarked Manhattan. Gina slit it with her opener, extracted and unfolded the single sheet of paper.

Scrawled in green crayon:

YOUR GOING TO BE SICKER THAN A PIG LADY HIGH AND MITY

Gina flinched, dropped the letter on the table. She stared down at it as she reflexively wiped her hands on the sides of her robe. She'd experienced a sudden sense of defilement. It wasn't so much the message that had caused this reaction, as the dirty stains all over the paper.

With a shudder Gina strove to suppress her repugnance. They always made her feel this way, these poisonous communications which were the price of being in the public eye. Over the years she'd received half-a-dozen or so. All had been handed to the police, though none of the threats had come to pass and none of the writers had been heard from again. A detective at the local precinct house had told Gina that was usually the case. Such reassurances, however, did little to lessen the impact of the vile notes.

Howard asked, 'What's the matter?'

Gina jolted, catching her breath as she glanced around to see her husband in the doorway. Swiftly recapturing her composure, she answered lightly, 'Nothing.'

'You looked as if you'd had bad news.'

'No, nothing like that,' returned Gina, putting on a good face. She abandoned the idea of telling him the truth in favour of keeping their reunion as normal as possible. She quickly gathered all the personal mail, including the green crayon note, and slipped it into the table's drawer. Turning, she asked brightly, 'Is the fight over?'

'In the tenth.'

'Oh.' Gina would have liked to show more interest but, knowing next to nothing about boxing, decided it would be best not to pursue the subject. 'Well, then,' she said, 'are you ready for my news?'

Howard walked into the room, swivelled the dressing table chair and sat facing Gina. 'Your business news?'

'Yes.'

His face remained impassive but he said, 'Go ahead.'

With as much enthusiasm as she could muster, Gina declared, 'We got it. The studio. Monument Pictures. Barbara Graham has agreed to sell. Isn't that terrific?'

Her husband said, 'Is it?'

Gina thought, Please, Howard, don't let's start a fight over this. Not tonight. I'm too weary. She'd thought that even Howard would be interested in the purchase of an entire movie studio, but, she realized, this just wasn't the time for bridging the gulf which separated their lives. She shrugged, 'Well, fairly terrific. I mean, for someone like Harry, or Filipo, movie nuts.'

'And for you?'

'You know I was never what you'd call a fan.'

'Will it be good for West-Rossi?'

'I hope so.'

'So the company's in good shape?'

A little surprised by the question, Gina said, 'Yes.' There was no point in telling Howard about financial problems. She saw him nod, as if to himself, and his expression grow thoughtful. She walked over to him, stood before him as he looked up at her. The strong lines of his features were deeply mature. And in his dark blue suit he appeared serious and capable; not at all the sort of man whose childhood had caused him to resent all aspects of business.

Gina reached out and stroked his black hair. She wanted very much not to widen the rift between their lives. And yet she felt a pang of bitterness that her husband would not share her enthusiasm. She wished she had a partner she could talk to.

Howard placed his hands on her hips. He stared silently up at her for several moments before moving his hands to the loosely tied belt of her robe.

Gina looked into the dark fire of his eyes, at the set of his jaw and the fullness of his lips. But tonight her pulse did not accelerate. A wave of melancholy suddenly washed through her and she felt unbearably lonely. She sensed Howard's fingers working at her belt. It entered her mind to step away. But then her robe fell open and Howard's hands were on her naked waist.

She closed her eyes as his hands slid around and down to her buttocks. And her body began to respond. Gina willed herself to respond. With a backward movement of her arms she shrugged the robe from her shoulders, let it drop to the floor. Reaching out, she circled her hands around Howard's neck and slowly drew his face forward.

His breath touched her flesh. His lips touched her flesh, travelling across her ribs; upward, under the curve of her breast; around her nipple; over her nipple.

Gina gave a small cry as her reflexes answered to the heat of Howard's tongue. She dug her nails into his hair, kneading his scalp in rhythm with the increasing urgency of his mouth. Then she was on her knees, between his knees, pulling off his jacket, his tie and shirt, grasping the taut muscled ridges of his chest. Their mingled odours swirled around her as she rapidly uncinched his belt.

Gina heard Howard's voice but she didn't distinguish the words. Her head was full of drums. She wanted this, wanted it desperately, yet wished it wasn't so.

A delirium of confusion was in her. Howard was with her on the floor. She felt the hard familiar lines of his body. But images of other bodies flashed across her mind. She knew the strong sure touch of his hands. But memories of other hands burned on her flesh. This was wrong, she knew. This wasn't how it should be. She gasped, 'Howard,' and opened her eyes wide to stare up into his face and for an instant she saw another face.

Gina saw Robert Fallon.

No! her inner voice cried and she locked herself to her husband, thrusting him sideways, rolling onto him, bearing down on him. Now there was a fierceness in her. A desperation. An urge to subjugate all feelings except her feral need.

Gina drove herself. She devoured her husband. She was drowning in a booming surf. Squeezing shut her eyes she plunged and surged on the titanic breakers. The whirlpool roar filled her head, pounded in her veins.

Gina was hurled forward, liquid streaming down her arms and sides and back, blinding her eyes, plastering her hair to her brow and neck. She flew on the racing tide.

And then the wave she was riding crashed upon the beach. The explosion consumed Gina. It was all around her. It was within her, blasting her emotions to smithereens, detonating her senses into momentary oblivion.

She slumped, gasping.

The savagery of her instincts was gone.

At last she opened her eyes. She was kneeling astride Howard. Her body was drenched in sweat, and her breath was sawing in long, harsh strokes. With an effort, she controlled her lungs and pushed her wet hair from her forehead. She looked down at her husband's face. And saw shock written there.

'Howard,' Gina said hoarsely, 'I'm sorry.'

He gave a short, sharp laugh, raising himself awkwardly on one elbow. The uncertainty in his eyes retreated. 'No need to be,' he said, but his voice was toneless.

Gina didn't know what to say; for despite what had just happened, and although she still wanted to believe in her marriage, the feeling of discontent at Howard's attitude toward the business hadn't left her. Tonight she was unable to suppress the wish for someone with whom to share her enthusiasms.

Howard said, 'I'd like to take a shower.'

'Yes, of course,' returned Gina, moving from him to gather and pull on her robe. As she watched him go into the bathroom she considered joining him. She wanted to comfort him and be comforted by him. But, she thought dully, what good would it do?

She went through to the sitting room, sat on the edge of the sofa and flipped slowly, distractedly through the pages of a magazine. After several minutes she set the magazine aside. She had seen none of it. Howard was back in the bedroom. Gina listened to doors and drawers and the sound of him dressing. When he came into the room he was immaculate in a grey suit. He was, thought Gina, very handsome.

He said, 'I think I'll spend tonight at the club.'

Gina, with genuine disappointment, said, 'Must you?'

'I'm sure you'll want to be up early in the morning. To get on with business. Your movie studio deal.'

'Will I see you tomorrow night?'

'I think I'll have left town.'

'You've only been here a couple of days.'

'I don't have anything to stay for.'

Gina wanted to counter that, but felt she hadn't the strength for either argument or persuasion. She arose and stepped to him and asked gently, 'Are you all right?'

'Yes,' Howard answered. 'I'm fine.' As he stood staring at Gina, she thought the very air ached between them. Howard seemed about to say something, but he turned and walked from the room. Gina remained standing, alone.

It was some minutes before she returned to the bedroom.

She moved around a little aimlessly, shifting things on the dressing table, turning down the bed covers, winding the alarm clock. As she replaced the clock on the bedside table she noticed the drawer slightly open. And she remembered the threatening letter.

Gina opened the drawer, looked down at the grude green crayon scrawl. A shudder ran through her. In a harsh sort of way the dirty piece of paper resettled her equilibrium.

The detective at the precinct house asked, 'Have you any idea who might have sent it, Mrs Cornell?'

Gina shook her head. 'Maybe someone who didn't like The Lady's fettucini,' she said jokily.

The man smiled. 'I'm sure there aren't many of those.'

'You can't please everybody,' said Gina, 'no matter how hard you try.' She thought, Nor can you run a business the size of West-Rossi without making enemies, but I don't think they're the sort who go in for sending grubby notes.

'Well, hopefully,' said the detective, 'it's just another harmless crank. Although ...' he paused, rubbing his chin thoughtfully as he stared at the piece of paper.

'Is there something?' asked Gina.

'Not much. But, the stains. Looks like whoever sent the thing spat on it.' Seeing the reaction to that on Gina's face, he added, 'I'm sorry. But that's what it looks like. And, I have to say, it's usually the characters who defile their messages in some way who are the ones with a screw loose.'

'You mean, they're the dangerous ones?'

'Not so much dangerous as unpredictable. Look, Mrs Cornell, I don't want to alarm you. You know, the Manhattan police force gets thousands of these things handed in every year. Not one per cent of them comes to anything. What I'm saying is, maybe, just maybe, this one is from somebody who imagines they've got a genuine grudge against you. So, be a bit careful that's all. Make sure you lock up at night. Don't open the door to strangers.' He smiled. 'Though I'm sure I don't really need to tell you any of that.'

'It never does any harm to have a reminder,' said Gina.

'Though I guess you don't need one for birthday cake.'

Gina frowned, utterly uncomprehending.

'I was thinking of Wilmington,' said the detective.

'Wilmington?'

'They thought it was food poisoning at first.'

Gina suddenly remembered the radio report she'd heard shortly before leaving for Venice. 'Of course. Smith's Restaurant. But, wasn't it food poisoning?'

'Didn't you know? It was in the papers.'

'I've been away.'

'So you didn't read the story. About the laxative.' The detective explained, 'That's what it was gave those folks the runs – excuse me, diarrhoea. They were having a small birthday party at the restaurant. A couple of weeks previous to that the girl whose birthday it was had walked out on her boyfriend. He figured on getting his own back. To cut a long story short, he managed to get at the birthday cake, and laced it with laxative. Unfortunately, it wasn't only his girlfriend who ate the stuff.' He suppressed a grin, and added, 'The guy just couldn't stand being jilted I guess.'

Gina stared. A picture of Tony Nevada had flashed across her mind; the livid weal of her fingermarks on his cheek; the venomous look of revenge in his eyes. But, she quickly told herself, it couldn't possibly have been the singer who'd sent the threatening letter.

Reading her troubled expression, the detective asked, 'Did something occur to you, Mrs Cornell?'

Gina thrust aside the memory of Tony Nevada. 'No,' she answered. 'So, are the people who ate the cake okay?'

'They're all right. No real harm done, I suppose. Except to the restaurant. I mean, the business. After the story of the sick diners hit the papers, the place couldn't give meals away. Everybody was scared, thought it was food poisoning, you see.'

Gina nodded. She did see, knew only too well what bad publicity like that could do to a restaurant's trade.

'Anyhow,' the detective concluded, 'that's all by the by as far as this,' indicating the green crayon note, 'is concerned. I'm glad you brought it in, Mrs Cornell. I'll do what I can.'

Gina thanked him. There wasn't a lot more to say, and ten minutes later she was walking back up Fifth Avenue. She repeated to herself, the note had been harmless, from some sad soul who was more to be pitied than blamed. By the time she reached The Lady, she was almost convinced this was true.

She loved it. Gina loved the rush toward a new frontier. Right now her horizon was filled with Monument Pictures. The media extravaganza which would announce the studio's takeover by West-Rossi consumed her every waking moment. And the fact that it had to be kept more hush-hush than a Pentagon secret weapon only served to exhilarate her the more.

During this headlong fortnight the sun climbed from June into July growing brighter every day. It was surely an omen of good fortune. Gina told herself all her clouds had been left behind. She'd heard nothing more from the green crayon letter writer; Tony Nevada had returned to the west coast; the bank had given its blessing to the franchise hotel scheme.

The only spot of rain to fall from Gina's otherwise clear sky, was Cassie's move to an apartment of her own.

Gina protested that Cassie was more than welcome to stay. She'd already told her friend there'd been no need for her to camp out at the Carlton the evening Howard had turned up. 'After all, Cass, your bedroom is the other end of the hall to mine, so it isn't as if we'd've kept you awake all night.'

She'd flinched slightly at this effort to hide the crack in her marriage but the moment had quickly passed as Cassie had been prompted to rejoin, 'Not like Big Bess and her howling dry goods salesman.' And they'd gone on to spend a somewhat raucous few minutes recalling this ribald tale of their chambermaid days.

Finally Cassie had concluded that it simply would be more practical all round if she had a place of her own. Gina had, with regret, concurred. Soon, however, the continuing rush toward the Monument media conference blew away the shreds of her melancholy.

The days counted down.

With twenty-four hours to go they were all set.

Filipo and Mickey had arrived for the event; Felix Gilbert had flown in from Hollywood; Max had arrived from Las Vegas. Along with Cassie, Harry and Irving, they gathered in Gina's apartment the evening before the conference.

Everyone was talking nineteen to the dozen. Celebration was fizzing in the air. Gina reflected that they hadn't had such a convivial get-together since Christmas.

Harry rapped on a table, brought quiet to the assembly, and, raising his glass, said, 'Here's to being in the headlines.'

With much good cheer they all joined the toast.

There was a knocking at the door.

Gina went to open it.

David McKay, West-Rossi's head of publicity, stood on the threshold. 'Mrs Cornell,' he said, 'I'm sorry to interrupt, but ...' he glanced around the small crowd and his expression clouded. 'I didn't realize you had guests.'

'That's all right,' said Gina. 'Come in,' issuing him forward and closing the door. 'We were just drinking to tomorrow afternoon. Would you like a martini, something else?'

'No ...' the fair-haired man hesitated, 'thank you.'

'Please,' encouraged Gina. 'You're not intruding. You know everyone here. Besides, I'm sure you could do with a drink after all the running about you've done to get tomorrow's show together in such a short time. Won't you ...'

'No, really,' David McKay interrupted, glancing urgently at his watch. 'I came to tell you ...' Again he surveyed the smiling faces, and his own expression grew taut. Then he said, 'Oliver Randolph is holding a press conference. Tonight.'

Silence fell like a bomb.

For several moments no one spoke. And then everybody was firing questions at once. Gina broke in with, 'Just a second. Give David a chance.' Though her nerves were rioting, she said levelly, 'Please, David, go ahead. What's it about?'

He shook his head. 'I've no idea. I only know that late this afternoon Randolph's aides contacted all the media – press, radio and television – to say he had a major announcement to make. Apparently, he apologized for the short notice, made some excuse about finalizing last minute contracts.'

Harry said harshly, 'He's going to steal our thunder.'

'I'm afraid so,' agreed David, a bitter edge in his voice. 'Randolph will be front page news tomorrow. The media coverage we get for Monument will be the day after.'

Gina, still holding on to her anger, said, 'But at least that's better than nothing. It's still something worth shouting about. Something to give Mister Oliver damn Randolph a surprise.'

Irving asked, 'David, when might Randolph be broadcast?'

'Any minute now. That's why I ran over here.' He checked his watch. 'I'm sure it will be on the seven o'clock news.'

Gina was already hastening across the room to switch on the television. As the screen flickered into life all heads turned toward it. Gina stood back, fists tight at her sides.

A report on the Presidential campaign was finishing. Another item came up, speculation on a rise in oil prices. No one in the apartment spoke; but anxiety crackled like static electricity. The oil news ended. The announcer's face reappeared and he said:

'And now, following our earlier report, we're going live to Randolph Corporation headquarters to talk with Oliver Randolph, who, just ten minutes ago, announced his company's intention to build the largest, most luxurious casino in Las Vegas.'

A stunned silence held Gina and her guests.

The television picture showed a room of several hundred people, talking excitedly, gathered around a vast table. On the table, a model – trees, roads, buildings.

Max exclaimed, '*La Striscia*! The Strip.'

Gina stared. Yes, she could see the familiar facades of the Flamingo, the Thunderbird, the Desert Inn, and, there, The Silver Lady. Her heart was thumping. The buildings were growing larger as the camera closed in on the model. The scene looked very real. As the camera moved lower it seemed to be travelling along Las Vegas Boulevard. Cars and people appeared lifesize. The camera stopped, panned around, to a building. An immense building.

Gina caught her breath.

The building was drum-shaped, at least fourteen stories

high. It appeared to be built entirely of glass. Surrounding it were lush palm trees amid gleaming white sand dunes. At the roadside in front of the building, a sign board towered thirty feet above the ground; in shimmering letters: BIKINI BEACH.

Filipo, puzzling, asked, 'Max, where's that location?'

Max peered at the scene, studying the landmarks around the proposed casino. 'I'm not sure. I think ...' He squinted, frowning; then he breathed, '*Ah, questo e tragico.*'

Gina said anxiously, 'Max, what?'

The big man spread disconsolate hands. 'Principessa, that place, it's on the Ortez land. The land we were going to buy.'

Gina's blood drained. She was caught in a blizzard of anger, grief, guilt as she recalled her failure to return Signor Ortez's calls. She could scarcely meet Max's eyes.

Irving said, 'You've heard nothing about this, Max?'

'Not a word. It has been kept most secret.' The big man stared at the screen, his face crumpled with disappointment.

David McKay said grimly, 'Certainly Randolph has had the whole thing under tight wraps. Nobody in the media had an inkling what this conference was to be about.'

The television camera had moved back and a reporter holding a microphone had appeared. Turning, he asked, 'Mister Randolph, when do you expect completion of the Bikini Beach?'

Oliver Randolph's face came into close-up.

Gina almost recoiled from the gross features.

Smiling confidently, Randolph said, 'Within five months. When construction begins it will continue twenty-four hours a day. We will open the doors of Las Vegas's newest, finest casino-hotel the first week in December. And, I can assure you, we will have the most spectacular opening show ever seen.'

'With an all-star line-up,' prompted the interviewer.

'The Randolph Corporation wouldn't settle for less. In fact it gives me great pleasure, and pride, to announce right now that our first headline celebrity for the Bikini Beach's inaugural season will be America's number one recording star, Mister Tony Nevada.'

Cassie released an oath.

Harry said, 'You might've known – birds of a feather.'

Gina felt stricken. She could only stare as Randolph went on to extol the forthcoming magnificence of his casino-hotel, its restaurants, its facilities, its superiority.

After a few more obviously pre-arranged questions allowing for glib answers, the interviewer commented, 'The Randolph Corporation certainly is making dynamic strides. Could you tell our viewers, are you still considering expanding into the movie industry with a bid for Monument Pictures?'

'No, we are not,' returned Randolph without hesitation. 'We abandoned that line weeks ago. After an exploratory tour of the studio, we found that Monument was far below the standard we were seeking. Also, I have to say, its current productions were not of the type commensurate with the image of the Randolph Corporation.'

'In what way would that be?'

'Shall we say, they didn't reflect certain ideals, American ideals, which I personally believe in.'

Felix rasped, 'The mealy-mouthed hypocrite.'

'Of course,' Randolph continued, 'I'm sure such movies might well appeal to certain people. And, after all, this is a free country, where our citizens have freedom of choice.'

'Absolutely,' the interviewer agreed self-righteously.

'And I'm sure,' said Randolph, 'that sort of choice will continue to be offered by the Monument studio once it is under the direction of the West-Rossi Corporation.'

The interviewer's mock surprise was reflected a hundredfold in the genuine shock of everybody in Gina's apartment.

'West-Rossi?' queried the interviewer. 'Have they taken over Monument? I didn't know.'

'Did you not?' said Randolph blandly. 'Well, I only heard it myself a few days ago. Perhaps they'll be informing the media in due course.' He turned, smiling fatly to the camera. And Gina was sure he knew she was watching. There was no mistaking the mockery and the triumph in his eyes as he said. 'They must have decided there's no point in holding a press conference.'

Chapter Eleven

'Cancel it,' rapped Gina. 'Cancel it.'

For the past fifteen minutes consternation had reigned in the apartment after Gina had stabbed the gloating television face of Oliver Randolph into oblivion. To add to the racket the phone had kept ringing repeatedly with clamorous calls from reporters until David McKay had been obliged to tell The Lady's receptionist to stonewall all further enquiries.

Everyone had been talking at once; opinions and counter-opinions of what to do, flying about like distraught bees.

'Shouldn't we go ahead with the conference?' Harry had argued. 'Show Randolph we aren't on the run.'

Filipo had declared, 'We can't let him get away with that mud-slinging against Monument's productions.'

Felix had suggested, 'Somehow we just have to make our media campaign even bigger and better.'

As the unhappy debate had continued, Gina sat saying nothing. Her throat had been too tight to utter a sound. The feeling of having been defeated was almost too much for her to bear. But, she knew, she had to think rationally; a decision had to be made. She strove to make her brain function.

At last, as the commotion in the room had subsided, all eyes had turned upon Gina. Then, her fists tight on her chair's arms, she had rapped, 'Cancel it.'

Controversy erupted anew. But it lasted only until Gina said sharply, 'If the conference goes ahead tomorrow, all any of the interviewers will hammer on about is the sort of movies Monument is currently making. We'll be hauled into a public inquest on what that loathsome creature called

American ideals. Well, we've got better things to do than give the media a field day.' Gina knew her rancour was showing but was unable to mask it. She fervently hoped she wouldn't have to argue her case.

The room remained on a brittle edge for several moments. It was Irving who broke the strained silence:

'I believe Gina's right,' he stated firmly. 'We've lost the element of surprise. No useful purpose will be served by continuing with the conference.'

Felix glanced sideways to Harry and Filipo, and they traded looks of quiet frustration. Looking back to Gina, Felix gave a ragged sigh and said resignedly, 'I guess our guns are spiked.'

Before any further dialogue could break out, Gina turned to the publicity man. 'David, I appreciate this will cause you a terrible headache, but will you please take care of all the necessary steps for the cancellation.'

'I'll start on it right away,' he responded. 'If you'll excuse me, I'll get over to the West-Rossi Building, call up some assistance and begin contacting the media.'

Cassie asked, 'What will you tell them?'

'More or less the truth. That we can't see the point in wasting everybody's time tomorrow.' He said to Gina, 'But we'll still have to issue a statement about buying the studio or all manner of rumours will start flying.'

'Yes,' agreed Gina. 'Can you come back later this evening and we'll draft something. We'll use the basic press release you've already prepared but will change a paragraph or two to emphasize the high standards achieved by Monument in the past, as well as the quality and integrity of its current productions. A strong refutation of Randolph's remarks. But,' she stressed, 'from a positive standpoint. We are not on the defensive.'

'I understand,' said the publicity man.

Within a few minutes Gina had seen him on his way and returned to the others. The practical requirements of what to do next were helping to rein her emotions. Nevertheless, she kept seeing Oliver Randolph's mocking features, and her anger was dangerously close to the surface. She was very grateful when Cassie said:

'I reckon we ought to call it a night, Hon. No point in sitting here grieving over spilt milk.' She arose, and after some hesitation the rest followed.

There was a muted exchange of farewells at the door. Felix said he'd go back to his hotel and start contacting the movie people who'd been invited to the conference. Irving said he'd call Wheldon Hoyt, the banker, at home to put his mind at rest. Gina apologized to Mickey for such an abrupt end to the evening before they'd scarcely had a chance to talk.

But as each one went out, it was Max for whom Gina felt most heartache. While everyone's concern had been toward the debacle of the Monument conference, Randolph's announcement of the Bikini Beach in Las Vegas had retreated into the background. Gina knew, however, the new casino would remain the major blow to Max; and she once more reminded herself that she was wholly to blame.

At the door she faltered, 'Max ... I ...' but had to swallow hard as her larynx constricted.

'Principessa,' her godfather responded, 'please, don't look this sad. There is no need. So, we got a little hurt. We've been hurt before. But we didn't spend too long licking our wounds. That isn't what your poppa would want us to do.' He put a big, gentle knuckle under her chin, raised her face. 'So, come on. *Sorridi*. Smile. *Per favore*.'

With an effort, Gina did.

Cassie was the last to leave. Gina thanked her for prompting the exodus. Cassie asked if she should stay awhile, but Gina said she preferred to be alone to make some notes on what she personally would say when she was inevitably cornered by the press. The two women said goodbye.

Gina was alone.

She walked back into the room, stood motionless.

And now the leashed demon of her anger reared. Gina let it tear free, gave herself to its ferocity. She felt its fangs at her throat, its claws on her heart. As she remained there in its grip, Gina focused her thoughts. She understood that Oliver Randolph's victory had to be countermined. West-Rossi's reputation must be reasserted. And it was her responsibility. To Gina this was unattestable. But how to do it?

For two days this question dominated her thoughts.

She said to Irving, 'I intend to do it, come what may.'

From behind his desk the accountant responded, 'Gina, I'm sorry, but we can't possibly raise the money.'

'I intend to do it,' Gina repeated without emotion. 'I intend to launch a nationwide chain of franchise hotels, at a stroke. One in every major city in the United States. At least two hundred. You and Cassie are already all geared for ten. The increase in number is only a question of logistics.'

'And cash.'

'But you do agree it would boost West-Rossi's reputation, put us squarely back in the forefront of the hotel trade?'

'Certainly, it would be an exceptional move.'

'Would it fail?'

'No, I'm sure it wouldn't. The research we've done has proved there are scores of independent hotel owners who'd be more than willing to become members of a new West-Rossi franchise operation. But, Gina, you've known all along the company simply doesn't have the resources to launch on anything but a modest scale.' Irving leaned forward, his face very serious. 'And even if we had the money, I would not recommend the investment.'

Gina, for the first time since arriving here, felt a chill of caution. Irving, she was aware, did not make statements lightly. Nevertheless, she held on to her determination. She was resolved to wipe the sneer off Oliver Randolph's face; and when an inner voice warned, Revenge is the most dangerous of all motives, she rejoined, I am not seeking revenge, only reaffirming the integrity of my company.

She asked, 'Why wouldn't you recommend the investment?'

Irving replied, 'Because we're already in the most precarious financial situation. The Monument purchase has left us virtually nothing for emergencies.'

Gina said, 'Irving, I appreciate your concern, but what possible emergency could arise? We aren't destined for another Wall Street crash, are we?'

'On the contrary,' he conceded. 'The national economy has never looked healthier. We're heading into a boom.'

'So now's the time to expand?'

'Unquestionably.'

'And franchise hotels would be an exceptional move?'

'Ten would be a step in the right direction.'

'A small step.'

Irving didn't respond to that, and Gina was at once sorry for her sharp retaliation. She was deeply appreciative of Irving's expertise; he had never advised her wrongly in all their years together. She valued his quiet friendship too, and would be very hurt to lose it. Still she said:

'A small step won't put us ahead of the opposition. And we have to get ahead. Because any day now someone else is going to launch franchise hotels – Hilton, Hughes, worst of all Randolph – and we'll be left looking like also-rans. We can't let that happen. I won't let it happen.'

In the oak-panelled and leather-upholstered seclusion of Eastern Bank & Trust's topmost sanctum, Wheldon Hoyt, grey-haired and placid-faced, removed his gold-rimmed spectacles and looked up from the pages of figures. 'Gina,' he said, 'you know we were already stretching a point when we agreed to back the scheme at half a million. To quadruple that amount is absolutely out of the question.'

Gina suppressed her impatience.

She had nothing against Wheldon personally; it was just that all those years ago when she'd been seeking financial backing to open The Lady, she'd been turned away from every door on Wall Street where several of the bankers had made no bones about the fact that they simply had no intention of entrusting their money to a woman. This had rankled with Gina ever since; and even nowadays, when she was received into the bank president's office with courtesy and welcome, she still felt on the defensive.

For the past half hour she'd been pleading her case for franchise hotels. The royalty figures, she was sure, spoke for themselves: an income from two hundred franchisees of at least a million dollars by the end of the first twelve months. 'That,' she'd pointed out to Wheldon, 'will cover half the launch cost.'

Still he'd shaken his head.

Now, he said, 'Gina, it's simply a question of collateral. West-Rossi has nothing more to offer as security for a loan.' He gave a small, apologetic quirk of his lips.

On her lap, out of Wheldon's sight, Gina was scraping frustrated nails on her purse. To be honest, she'd expected this would happen. And, beneath her old scars of resentment, she respected the banker's professionalism as much as she did Irving's. But there was in Gina a new kernel of determination, and she now gripped this like a talisman, placing in it all her faith as she said:

'I can personally provide the collateral.'

Two hours later she was once more before Irving's desk, watching as he read the list of all she'd pledged as guarantee against the bank's one and a half million dollars. It was with grim humour she recalled how difficult it had been to persuade Wheldon to take her stocks and bonds, shares in various properties, the deeds of her Park Avenue apartment.

'Everything,' said Irving, stunned. 'Everything you own.'

'Except The Lady,' said Gina. As the accountant stared at her she thought she had never seen such concern in a person's eyes. Before he could voice the anxiety, however, she said, 'I know it's contrary to all your advice, and I'm truly sorry for that. But, it's done. I believe it's for the best. And I won't undo it.'

In the silence that followed, for the first time since she'd made her monumental decision, Gina wondered what she would do if Irving said he would have no part in her precipitate venture. And for a split second her resolve faltered. But only for a second; for then the accountant said:

'One and a half million dollars. And you intend to invest the entire sum in the franchise scheme?'

'Plus the half million you've already funded.'

'For a national launch of two hundred hotels?'

'So long as two million dollars is enough.'

Irving said, 'It will be enough.'

Gina said, 'Then, please, will you help me?'

At the boardroom table Cassie addressed the West-Rossi directors. 'Throughout the country,' she said, 'there are plenty of luxury hotels, and ample cheap ones. But, what do we have in between? Who's providing first-class, family lodging facilities, with standardized top quality and service, at a price that isn't out of this world?

'And why,' she asked, 'should reasonably-priced accommodation only be available in faceless, usually tacky motels or rooming houses. Why should comfort and elegance be offered only to guests who can afford to arrive by chauffeured limousine?

'A feller who works the line is entitled to be treated to a touch of class too – and not just on his honeymoon or when his horse comes in at a hundred to one. The same, of course, goes for single women or widows, with or without children.'

As her friend continued, Gina gave her a smile, and permitted herself a silent sigh of satisfaction. She took a glimpse around the table of rapt faces; and at Irving, his presence beside Cassie a tangible validation of the franchise scheme she was presenting.

It was a fortnight since Gina's visit to the bank and her subsequent meeting with Irving. When the accountant had agreed to back her, it was as if great chains had been struck from her limbs. The oppression she had felt since Oliver Randolph's television appearance was gone.

She knew Irving remained very troubled about her huge personal financial commitment, but, she was relieved to say, he accepted her fixity of purpose without further argument. Having thanked him profoundly for his support, Gina had said, 'There's one more favour I have to ask.' And then:

'Please, don't tell anyone where the money's coming from. If they know the truth they'll all want to help. But this has been my decision. It's my responsibility. And,' she'd added, 'I especially don't want Cassie to know. She'd worry, and that's the last thing she must do right now, in her condition.'

The following morning Gina had gone to Cassie's office.

'What! Holy smoke! Moses! You're kidding!' Gina was pretty sure her friend made all these exclamations, and probably a few more, when she heard the news.

After her initial euphoria had subsided, however, Cassie had said, 'But, Hon, this means the whole operation is going to be so much bigger. I mean, enormous, I hadn't envisaged being involved ...' She lapsed into a wondering silence.

'Well,' Gina had prompted, 'I hope you will envisage. I'd be grateful if you could outline your plans to the directors within a couple of weeks so that we can hold a press conference by, say, the end of next month.'

Cassie breathed, 'Whew ... I don't know.'

Gina, suddenly recalling her own remark to Irving about Cassie's condition, said, 'Of course, all this is only if you feel up to it. We don't have to rush ahead quite so fast.'

'Certainly we do,' Cassie asserted, throwing off her hesitancy with a positive set of her chin. 'If the company has got enough faith to invest two million dollars in the scheme, I sure as heck have got the energy to get it rolling as soon as possible.'

'You're sure now?'

'I'm as fit as a flea?'

'Fine,' Gina had smiled. 'But, in any case, you don't want to be running all over the place. Irving has rustled you up three more assistants, he'll be putting one of his deputy accountants on to it full time, and David McKay's department will be taking care of all the publicity.'

'Sounds terrific,' said Cassie. 'But how about you? Will you come and share this office?'

'Not unless you want me to,' replied Gina. 'This was all your idea in the first place, Cass. All I did was pay a visit to the library. I was hoping you'd stay in charge. That is, until you want to call it a day, I mean because of the baby.'

Cassie rejoined, 'Call it a day? What on earth for? I'll get a bed fixed up here in the corner, then I'll only have to knock off for five minutes while Junior makes his debut.' Straightfaced, she queried, 'Will that be okay?'

Gina regarded her friend, and, equally deadpan, replied, 'I'll check with the Fire Department.'

Now, at the boardroom table, Cassie detailed the concept of the hotel scheme. 'West-Rossi won't own the properties,' she pointed out. 'Existing establishments will be franchised to trade under a corporate identity. Cornells,' she said, 'I'd like to call them Cornells.'

She went on to explain. 'Each hotel will retain its existing name, coupled to that of the new franchise corporation. So, for example, a hotel called the Mayfair would become the Mayfair Cornell.' She looked around, 'See?'

Yes, they all saw. And they declared it a fine idea.

Gina had known about it for several days. At first she'd baulked at Cassie's suggestion, feeling it smacked too much of self-glorification, but, on second thoughts, she'd had to acknowledge the repute and tradition in the Cornell family name. Also, it had occurred to her, it might please Howard.

Max said, '*Si*, I understand. All the hotels will have the same name. But, Cassie, will they all look alike?'

'Not on the outside,' she replied, 'except for the name sign. But on the inside, yes, the idea is to make them instantly recognizable as Cornells, so folks, as soon as they arrive, will feel at home, secure in a familiar, hospitable place.'

Harry asked, 'And what will they look like?'

All eyes turned to Cassie with wide expectation.

She gave a shrug and a small, apologetic smile. 'I don't know,' she confessed. 'It's the one point I'm stuck at. The stipulation is there must be lots of lobby space, where guests will want to linger, where they can buy a drink, a snack, their souvenirs, instead of taking their custom around the corner to some place else. It's all a question of economics.' She looked at Irving.

He explained, 'We, and the franchisee, will need all the income we can generate from such incidentals to offset the extra overhead of the large lobbies plus the initial refurbishment costs. The latter could be substantial. Few existing hotels have so much open ground floor space, so conversion to the Cornell standard could entail considerable demolition and reconstruction.' Irving opened a manilla folder. 'I've prepared some figures.'

Gina watched as he distributed sheets of typed estimates. She leaned back, happy and excited. And confident. While the enormity of her personal financial commitment continued to occasionally prick her with concern, it no longer was a cause of dire worry. Gina was convinced the franchise scheme would be a success. Listening now to her directors' enthusiasm, she felt doubly reassured.

For four hours they avidly discussed Cornell Hotels.

And they were still talking exuberantly when they eventually quit the table, leaving dunes of scratchpad sheets amid the debris of their lunchtime sandwiches and coffee.

As they began to leave for their own offices, Cassie turned to Gina and queried, 'Hon, can you spare a minute?'

Gina replied, 'Of course.'

'It's about the hotel lobbies,' Cassie said, her brow slightly puckered. 'It was true what I said, I'm really stuck on what they should look like. They have to be different, memorable, something nobody's ever seen before. But not like a set from Flash Gordon.' She paused, then asked, 'Could you spare time to help? Come up with an idea? It'd be a problem off my plate.'

Gina said calmly, 'I'd love to, Cass.'

What she thought was, Hurray!

They were off and running. The drifts of bumf, miles of red tape necessary to the formation of a new company had been shovelled and sheared in double quick time by Irving and the attorneys, and the documentation for Cornell Hotels Incorporated was signed, sealed, notarized, its registration set on Gina's desk three weeks after Cassie's boardroom presentation.

Gina had spent all the intervening time sailing her ship of exhilaration across the oceans of interior design, architectural detail and building regulations which would lead to the specification for every Cornell hotel lobby in the country. Of all the tasks which Cassie might have asked her to do, this was the one which Gina would have chosen herself.

She loved every moment of these busy days. They more than made up for the cancellation of the Monument press conference. Gina had firmly put that behind her; the ability to do so helped by the fact that no one else wanted to rake over the miserable ashes of the affair.

In private Gina had asked David McKay if he had any idea how Randolph might have found out about Monument, but the publicity man could only admit there had been so many people in the know about the takeover he supposed it really had been asking a lot to expect it to stay under wraps.

He and Gina had then agreed that the Cornell hotel proposals, while being subject to the usual company security, would not be treated as top secret. Gina rationalized that the concept was so revolutionary, even if word did leak out it would only serve to sharpen the media's appetite. And, she added, franchising was not currently within Oliver Randolph's province, so there was no way he could put together a scheme and again beat West-Rossi to the punch.

This latter thought alone, the outpacing of the malicious wheeler-dealer, was sufficient to boost Gina's spirits into realms of fresh optimism.

Even when she phoned Howard, over in Saratoga Springs for the beginning of the racing season, to tell him about the use of the Cornell name, and he responded with only an indifferent, 'Good luck,' she refused to be dejected. Admittedly, she felt enough of a twinge of disappointment to make her think fleetingly of Robert Fallon, but, as there was no way she knew of contacting the Englishman at his incommunicado hideaway on Key West, she soon put him from her mind.

Gina forged ahead on her lone but sunny path.

She faltered for only one moment, three days before the franchise hotels press conference, when Filipo said:

'We're going on vacation, to Europe, tomorrow.'

Gina looked from her brother to Mickey. 'Oh, must you? I was hoping we'd be together for the Cornell announcement.'

Mickey said, 'We may not get another chance for a while.'

Filipo declared, smiling, 'Mickey's landed the second lead in the new production of *High As The Sky*. She has to start rehearsals in a fortnight, and after that there's no telling when she'll be able to take a break.'

Gina's brief disappointment of a moment ago quickly evaporated. 'Mickey, what wonderful news. Congratulations.'

'Thanks,' replied Mickey. 'I only found out yesterday,

which is why the last-minute decision to go away.' Her freckled face was dimpled with a happy smile, but all at once this faded slightly and she ventured, 'It is all right, isn't it? I mean, you don't mind, us taking a vacation, together?'

Gina rejoined, 'Good heavens, why ever should I mind? You're both adults.' She glanced at Filipo, who gave her an exaggerated wink which put her instantly off her stride so that she hurried on, 'After all, this is the second half of the twentieth century. Mind you, some places in Europe are still rather conservative about ..., well, you know.' She gave what she imagined was a worldly shrug and said, 'You'll just have to be discreet about it.'

Mickey went mildly pink. 'Actually, we weren't ...'

'Heavens,' exclaimed Gina, 'the passatelli!' and ran out to the kitchen stove where several pans were simmering. She swiftly turned the heat under one pan down, hoisting the lid to check no harm had come to the cheese and egg dumplings. They were fine. She relaxed.

'It'll only be a few minutes,' she called over her shoulder, and began to move around, seeing to the meal.

This was the first get-together they'd had, just the three of them. Gina had invited Mickey, promising she'd cook her a genuine Roman dinner, and was truly glad to have the opportunity, for these days she rarely had time or occasion to indulge this personal pleasure.

As she prepared the salad, she thought of the news she'd just received. It took a bit of getting used to, imagining her brother and a girl actually spending an entire fortnight – days and nights – together. On the other hand, to be honest, she hadn't suggested this little party entirely without ulterior motive, feeling sure the warm conviviality of a family evening would foster irresistible instincts in Mickey.

Such blatant matchmaking.

No harm in giving nature a gentle shove.

She paused in the slicing of a radish; saw in her mind's eye a full-scale Italian wedding; a couple of years later, a christening. She hoped they'd choose Alfredo as one of the baby's names. Imagine, Filipo's son continuing the family tradition.

'Gina,' Mickey's voice, 'can I help?'

'What? Oh, no thanks.' Gina smiled around to the girl in the doorway. 'I'll be with you in a moment.' She swiftly returned her attention to the radish, and a few minutes later, having seen that all was safely nearing completion, went back into the sitting room to finish her martini.

Filipo and Mickey were watching the television news.

Gina stood, looking at the set, but not really paying much attention, until it occurred to her that the gang of noisy demonstrators milling about outside an office block was brandishing AFF placards. Before she could focus her attention, however, the report ended, the newscaster moved on to another item, and Filipo switched off the set.

Gina, trying not to appear unduly concerned, remarked, 'That looked to be a rather unruly demonstration. The AFF wasn't it? No one was getting hurt, were they?'

Filipo exchanged a look with Mickey. Turning to Gina, he said, 'One of our members was taken to hospital.'

'Hospital!' Gina couldn't contain her alarm. 'Why?'

'He had his arm broken.'

'There, on the street, in broad daylight? But you assured me the AFF was a non-violent organization.'

'It is.' Filipo looked slightly doubtful, but said, 'Sis, please don't start worrying. It was an unavoidable incident ...'

'Unavoidable?' Gina's voice was tightening. 'Someone's arm was broken. How could that be unavoidable?'

Filipo hesitated. 'He was ... jumped on.'

The words struck Gina in the face and a childhood memory leapt into her head: on the busy street where she lived, two Blackshirt troopers ferociously kicking the writhing body of an anti-Fascist. She obliterated the mental image, and asked as calmly as possible, 'By whom?'

Filipo replied, 'A couple of characters sent out by the company the AFF was picketing. Hired bully boys. It happens. And with the best will in the world it can't be avoided.' He considered a moment and then in a positive tone said, 'Gina, you know that whenever and wherever somebody stands up for what they believe in, there'll always be an opposition prepared to use violence to put them down. It's an inescapable fact of life.'

Gina inwardly flinched at the harsh truth, and again old

memories reared. She swiftly quashed them. Don't tumble into the past, she warned herself. The churning within her settled and she drew a breath and said, 'How is the person who was injured?'

'He's okay,' replied Filipo. 'It was a simple fracture.'

Gina said with quiet sympathy, 'That's good.' She would have liked to ask more, about the demonstration, but somehow could not. Besides, too much of a cloud had already shadowed their bright evening. Abruptly, she declared, 'The dinner, it'll be dried out. Mickey, please, take the seat by the window. Filipo, will you pour the wine?'

Mickey said, 'I'll come and help.'

'No need,' replied Gina. 'I'll be but a minute,' and she hurried out to her simmering pans.

Chapter Twelve

The past weeks had seen a busy schedule for New York. Following the Celebration of Our Lady of Mount Carmel in Italian Harlem came the Swedish Folk Festival in Van Cortlandt Park. The Empire City Race Meet opened, and the World Labor Athletics Championship was held. There were record throngs at the Coney Island Mardi Gras, an unprecedented number of participants at the Women's Exposition of Industry. Also jammed into the calendar were the Rose Show, the Model Yacht Regatta, the Beaux Arts Ball, the National Shotgun Tournament, The Miss Physical Culture Contest, and the Summer Ice Carnival at Madison Square Garden.

But none of these raised the same rumpus of publicity as West-Rossi's new franchise venture.

On the twenty-seventh day of August at the company's headquarters, at a table bristling with microphones, before five hundred media sharp shooters and a battery of television and newsreel cameras, flanked by Cassie and Irving Prentiss, Gina, in a deep mauve suit and pearl-pinned lace jabot, announced, 'Ladies and gentlemen, America's Favourite Home From Home.'

She then pressed a button beneath the table, and the curtains at her back covering the entire hundred-foot-long wall slid aside to reveal in huge three-dimensional bronze letters, CORNELL HOTELS, and a series of vast colour illustrations of a hotel lobby which was a paved Italian piazza around a wide central pool and fountain, surrounded by curving arcades of small stores, bars, a beauty salon, barber shop, restaurants and cafés with umbrellaed tables 'outside' amid trees and statuary.

Gina crossed her fingers behind her back.

Since the architects and designers had translated her mental vision into pictorial reality, she'd been on a bed of nettles awaiting this moment of truth. The five hundred people before her now were judge and jury. By this time tomorrow they would have presented their verdict to virtually every human being in the United States. On their approbation Cornell Hotels would tower to success; on their derision the venture would crumble before it even got off the ground.

The awestruck silence seemed to last for minutes. Then:

'Book me a double room for tonight,' a reporter shouted.

'I'll take mine right now,' called another.

And then they all were yelling at once, jokey comments, compliments, congratulations, encouragement. Applause clattered. Camera flashes burst one upon the other to become a continual glare. Thank goodness, thought Gina with huge relief. It's a winner. We're on our way. Smiling, she raised a delighted hand, waited for the hubbub to quieten.

'Thank you,' she acknowledged sincerely, 'you make an old Manhattan saloon keeper very happy.'

They liked that.

Gina added, 'I hope you'll appreciate the real thing even more. Ten of the first two hundred Cornell Hotels will be the venues for a special inaugural weekend. You're all invited, early next year.'

They liked that too.

After the fresh applause had subsided Gina continued, 'Question time in thirty minutes. First, Mister Prentiss, whom many of you know, will outline the financial details of our scheme. Then, Miss Cassie O'Brien, who, I'm sure, won't be long in making your acquaintance ...' she paused for a ripple of appreciative laughter as Cassie patted her curls and winked at the front row, 'will present the philosophy behind what we hope you will agree is the most exciting and innovative step in the hotel world since Mister D'Oyly Carte installed hydraulic elevators in his London Savoy seventy-five years ago.'

Gina again said, 'Thank you,' gave a smile they'd feel at the rear of the room, and sat as Irving arose.

Two hours later she was hoarse from answering questions. More precisely, the same question asked a thousand times. The question Cassie had asked when Gina had unveiled the illustrations last week to the West-Rossi directors:

'But, Hon, where did you get the idea?'

To which Max had said, 'You remembered your homeland, of course, didn't you, Principessa.'

And Gina had smiled, but said nothing, not wishing to dent her godfather's chauvinistic faith with the admission that the entire notion had sprung from her memory of the Monument studio backlot where she'd visited Felix during the shooting of *The Last Summer*.

Now, as she watched the last of the journalists departing, she knew the concept was a success. This evening and tomorrow, Cornell Hotels would be headline news; ironically, today's event would be far more fruitful than the cancelled Monument conference could ever have been. Gina experienced a pang of bitter pleasure remembering how she'd felt seeing Oliver Randolph's mocking face on television, imagining now the sneer erased, the face stricken by the blow of West-Rossi's triumph.

She took out a handkerchief and wiped her palms, quenched the invidious emotion. Looking around she realized she was alone with Cassie. Smiling, she said, 'Remember, Cass, you said you wanted it to feel like the old days. Well, what do you think after today's little exercise?'

Cassie sank onto a chair beside the table littered with press releases and empty wine glasses and replied, 'What I think is, I need a new pair of feet.' She eased off her shoes and, massaging her insteps, observed, 'Time was I could run around from dawn to dusk, no problem. Right now I feel like I've hiked the Sahara.'

Gina said with sudden concern, 'Oh, Cass, I'm sorry. I haven't been thinking. This past couple of weeks I've been so involved with the hotels I'd completely overlooked your condition. I shouldn't have expected you to spend so long standing today.' She peered worriedly down at her friend's lower legs.

Cassie grinned. 'Really, Hon, they're not so bad. Well, to be honest, I was thinking of spending the next hour with them in a steaming mustard bath, but that doesn't have anything to do with Junior.' She patted her stomach. 'Moms-to-be don't get swollen ankles till the rest of their bodies are inflated. So it says in *Pregnancy, The Ultimate Joy*. No kidding, that's the title. By a feller, wouldn't you know – most of them are.'

Gina gave a small smile, but didn't respond, only pulled up a chair to sit opposite Cassie, who continued:

'Still, I confess I've got them all. Maybe every book ever written on the subject. Reckoned I'd better be prepared. Never knew there was so much to it. All your life you see females waddling around like over-stuffed sofas, and unless you've actually talked to them – and I avoided discussing it as resolutely as I did getting it – you figure growing fat is more or less all there is to it. But, I tell you, when the doc explains all that's happening inside you ...'

She leaned forward, lowering her tone:

'I mean real strange stuff. Some of the technical talk I didn't really understand. The doc – obstetrician – fed me this jaw-breaking medical jargon, must've figured me for a Bryn Mawr biology graduate. Which, by the time I've read all the books, I'll be as good as. Not that I'd recommend such literature, Hon, especially the illustrated volumes.' She shuddered. 'Too gruesome.'

Again Gina smiled, but still remained silent.

Since the night in Vegas when Cassie had divulged her condition, Gina had kept all specifics of the subject in the shadows. Naturally, she'd asked frequently if her friend was feeling okay, but had delved no further into the visits she knew the mother-to-be was making to the obstetrician, nor had enquired about the contents of the stacks of tomes she'd seen toted from the library and bookstore. Fear, she accepted, was the reason. Gina was undeniably afraid all her long-buried instincts would come surging to the surface to rekindle the pain of her own inability to conceive. Darker still: might she be jealous of her friend's pregnancy?

'... morning sickness has finished, thank goodness,' Cassie was saying, 'but I still have to keep running to the john umpteen times a day. That's apparently normal though – something to do with extra pressure on my bladder. Oh, sorry, Hon, I'm sure you'd rather not hear these grim details.' She shrugged apologetically.

Gina murmured, 'Just so long as you're all right.' Then, more brightly. 'Certainly you look terrific.'

'Feel it too. I admit, at the outset I was worried, frightened even, from some of the stories I heard. You know, soon as word's out you're in a delicate condition – that's how *The Wonder of Nativity* describes it – seems all of a sudden everybody you meet is an expert. And some of the old wives' tales they tell are enough to scare you hairless. But I straightened it out in my mind after the doc said I was fit as a marine and that there was no reason in the world to think me and Junior weren't going to have a completely normal pregnancy and birth.'

'That's great news,' said Gina. 'I'm truly pleased, Cass. But, you will take it easy, won't you? Less running around town, more time in your office. And the minute you start feeling tired, have some days off, finish work altogether if you want. Promise?'

Cassie grinned, 'Yes, Ma.' She stood. 'But, for the present, I'm fighting fit. No question, sufficiently fit to go dancing. And still curvy enough,' she smoothed her maternity dress over her hips, 'so's I don't look like a foxtrotting avocado. In fact, the weight I have put on around my middle is almost balanced by the extra inches on my bust.' Inhaling: 'Impressive, don't you think? Something for Irving to keep his eyes on while he's steering me round the floor.' She made a cheeky face.

Gina queried, 'Irving?'

'Yes. This last couple of weeks when we've had our heads together over Cornell Hotels he's mentioned a few times some of his favourite bands. Tommy Dorsey, who's way up there on his list, is at the Biltmore's Roof Garden this month. Irving asked if I'd like to go tonight. I tell you, I can't remember when I last went out with a feller, so I figured why not. Irving's rather good company. We have plenty to talk about with the business, and also movies, he's really quite a fan.'

Gina managed, 'Really?'

'Mind you,' Cassie went on, 'it's just an evening out.

Nothing more. You know, nothing ... personal. Hey, you could join us. I'm sure Irving wouldn't mind. How long since you spent an evening on the town? Why not come along tonight? We'd have a good time.'

Gina's concentration had been so startled by Cassie's revelation it was racing as rapidly but ineffectually as a mouse on a treadmill. 'No ... I ...' She got a flimsy grip on the whirring mechanism. 'There's a stack of paperwork on my desk. Thanks all the same. Some other time, okay?' She arose, forestalling Cassie's persistence with, 'Is it all right, I mean, safe, for you to be dancing?'

'No problem,' assured Cassie. 'The doc said to ignore all the myths about having to creep around like an invalid. So long as I use my common sense, don't enter the Olympics, I can walk, dance, swim, even ride a bike, plus, if I get lucky, you know what.' She winked broadly.

The humour further helped to slow Gina's mental spin. She said, straightfaced, 'You mean, play the saxophone?'

Cassie laughed aloud.

They went out of the room, stood in the hallway for several minutes, discussing the press conference, until Cassie declared she must hurry to shower and change.

Gina said, 'Take care. And have a lovely time.' She watched her friend leave, feeling vaguely like a child who hasn't been invited to the party. Nonsense, she reproved herself. It's a very good thing Cass and Irving should be friends ... as Cass said, there's nothing more to it than that – and, as you were told, you'd have been most welcome to join them.

She went into her office and quietly closed the door.

Gina remained there working until past ten pm. She then left the building with an armload of files and walked up the street to The Lady. To avoid the evening crowd in the restaurant lobby, she went down the side alley to enter by the private door and climb the stairs to her office off the rear corridor of The First Floor.

She set the files and her purse on her desk, sat and glanced through the messages left by her secretary. Nothing too important. She thought to go up to her apartment, now, but remained at the desk feeling restless. Gina told herself that in fact she felt fine. Happy. Of course she must be happy after this afternoon's success. Somehow, though, she couldn't quite convince herself. Overtired, she reasoned, recalling the headlong rush of the past month, I'll go up and get an early night.

Three hours later, however, she was still at the desk, reading a financial report on Monument sent by Felix from the studio. By the time she set this aside it was almost two in the morning.

The club and the restaurant had closed. The building seemed very still. Gina was wide awake. She thought of Filipo and Mickey in Europe; Cassie and Irving dancing closely at the Roof Garden. A memory of her last meeting with Howard sidled into her head. She saw herself and her husband upstairs in the bedroom. A co-mingling of sexual need and melancholy began to pervade her senses.

Gina stood abruptly.

'Enough of this,' she declared aloud. 'What you need is a very cold shower and a very large sherry to put you to sleep.' She gathered up her purse, strode purposefully out of the office, along the corridor and up the stairs. She started along the hallway of her apartment.

The lights went out.

'Oh!' exclaimed Gina, halting. A fuse? Of all the times to choose. No, not a fuse – all the lights had gone, as well as the air conditioning. Gina could hear no electrical murmur whatsoever. Local power failure? She peered back along the pitch black landing toward her bedroom. Under the thin gap at the bottom of the door she could distinguish an amber glow spilling into the room from the neon sign across the street. There hadn't been a power failure.

Gina remained still, puzzled, unsure of what to do, half expecting the lights to come on again. They didn't.

With a small, 'Huh,' of vexation she decided the sensible course would be to call the company's emergency maintenance contractors, have them send somebody right away to check the system, make sure nothing had shorted out and was likely to set the building afire. She cautiously made her way forward, running her hand along the landing wall, toward the sitting room.

Something creaked downstairs.

Gina froze.

She strained to catch a further sound. All she could hear was the thud of her own heartbeat, interrupted by the rising-falling drone of a passing car. Imagination, she reproved herself. The building settling. It settles, expands, contracts all the time. You hear its life movements every night when you're in bed and never question them. What is the matter with you? Get on and phone the maintenance company.

The bump came from the lower corridor, close to the foot of the stairs, striking Gina like a physical blow.

Fear seized her. Burglars, was her first thought, but that was gone as quickly as it had come and her mind jumped back to the evening in Central Park when she'd supposed someone might be following her. The brief panic she'd felt then, now clawed at her chest like a frantic animal. She automatically, uselessly, looked this way and that as if seeking an escape route. But all was blackness. She couldn't remember ever before confronting such blackness. It hung all around, an almost tangible inky fog, so dense Gina couldn't see her hand in front of her face.

Her flesh began to crawl, her scalp to tingle, and she knew unequivocally someone was climbing the stairs. Whether or not she could hear the whisper of feet on the carpet, or the low breathing of a person moving very slowly she wasn't sure. Yet in her own utter stillness she was positive the air was being shifted by an advancing presence. Her heartbeat became thunderous, nightmare waves booming on an unseen shore.

For God's sake think, her inner voice exhorted. Get out of here. Run. You must run.

There was nowhere Gina could run. The fire escape was in the lumber room, back the way she'd come, beyond the top of the flight from the lower floor. If she fled in that direction she might dash directly into the arms of the unseen intruder. Hurl herself past him? But it was pitch black; she didn't know whether he was approaching on the left or right. Desperation sobbed in her throat and she almost choked aloud.

Her chest, she realized, was so tense she could hardly breathe. Gripping her ribcage she forced herself to drag air into her lungs; exhaled, inhaled. The oxygen cleared her senses, and in her mind's eye she saw the telephone in the sitting room. Hope charged her veins. Logic returned.

Contain your panic. Think rationally. You can't see him; equally, he can't see you, perhaps doesn't even know you're here. With infinite care Gina unclasped her purse so as not to make a sound. Delving silently, her fingers edged between comb, compact, handkerchief, lipstick. There were six keys on the ring. Slowly, so slowly, she gathered them, explored their shapes. In the light they were as familiar as her own fingers. In the dark all the incised pieces of metal felt the same.

Remember, the sitting room key has an oval head. In a moment it was between her thumb and forefinger, its fellows tucked securely into her palm.

Bending, finding she was disconcertingly unsteady in the blackout, Gina removed her shoes, set her purse beside them on the floor, arose and moved as silently as possible, as rapidly as she dare along the hallway.

Her stockinged feet seemed to roar and thud on the carpet. Her hand ran across the storeroom door; the alcove with the flower urn; the mirror. In the nick of time she remembered the chair, stepped around where she guessed it would be. She reached the sitting room, panting, couldn't help but pause and listen.

For several moments Gina could hear nothing.

Self-doubt crept in.

What have I been thinking of, she began to ask, prepared to believe she was a victim of her own overwrought imagination. Then she caught the faint rasp of something – a fingernail? – on the distant wall. It came again. The stealthy intruder had reached the head of the stairs and was prowling along the landing. Now Gina could distinguish the furtive rustle of approaching footfalls. But he still doesn't know I'm here, does he? And who is he? Even in these menacing seconds Gina couldn't help posing the question.

The door! Unlock it, before it's too late.

With an arm so desperately rigid it ached, Gina extended her empty hand, slid it down the wooden panel until it located the keyhole. With her other fist she cautiously guided the key to the spot. It was all she could do to stop her muscles from spasming with tension as she eased the metal shaft, millimetre by millimetre, into the opening. Sweat slicked her fingers. Time stretched interminably.

The key reached its limit. Wincing with concentration Gina tentatively twisted her wrist the fraction of a degree necessary to bring the teeth into contact with the tumblers.

That was as far as she could go without noise. When she fully turned the mechanism and the locks shot back her position would be revealed. She'd have but the fleetingest instant to plunge into the room, slam and relock the door. The moves flashed through her mind; a simple sequence, plus, the element of surprise on her side.

Do it, she commanded herself, and jerked the key.

The bang leapt like a gunshot.

Gina yanked the key. Metal shrieked against metal. It was jammed. God help me, Gina's mind screamed with dread as, struggling, she heard the gutteral exclamation along the corridor. In awful lucidity she understood it was a man's voice. The key jumped free. She wrenched open the door. Street light flooded through the window, betrayed her in drenching amber. Sudden footfalls rushed toward her and she knew she was destroyed.

'No!' she yelled.

A tumbling thump and a furious curse.

He fell over my shoes! Gina threw herself across the threshold, crashing shut the door with terror-driven strength. It bounced open, cracked against her wrist sending the bunch of keys flying, skittering along the top of the sideboard, pitching into a cavern of shadow. Gina spun, in a full circle, made mad by fear. Her hands involuntarily clawed the air. Her body was flayed by a blizzard of despair. No rational thought was visible in the maelstrom of her shattered senses. She was stricken mute, inert, impotent.

A growl from the hall broke the moment.

Gina swung around, raced across the room, toward the table by the window with the telephone. She seized the receiver, ripping her nail as she slashed at the dial, knowing there was no hope. He was running toward her open door. She heard him collide with the chair, swear, lunge onward.

A weapon? There must be something. Gina flung frantic eyes around the room. Nothing. Nothing to stop a man.

He was suddenly silhouetted against the corridor wall, hunched, faceless, formless, a black grotesque.

'Stay away,' screamed Gina and snatched up the big brass, parchment-shaded tablelamp. Tearing the flex from the wall socket, she swung the lamp upward, above her shoulder, willed every ounce of strength into her muscles as the creature started over the threshold. She whirled, arm straightening, powering forward, the brute force of her fear hurling the heavy object into space, toward the window.

It exploded through the glass, blasted outward amid flying shards. Gina threw up a hand against the detonation and the din. For suspended seconds she watched the projectile spinning in the air, the shade rent and twisted, the flex lashing in pursuit of the globular brass body flashing orange and yellow like a burning cannonball. Then it plummeted from sight.

A moment's silence, followed by the crash on the sidewalk. Gina dashed to the gaping hole in the window, prepared to screech her lungs raw, thinking all at once to break off a jagged tooth of splintered glass, use it in desperate defence. It would lacerate her own hand. Imagination lanced pain up her arm. She flung a look over her shoulder, stumbled against the table, grabbing it to prevent herself pitching backwards through the jagged opening.

She was alone.

Was she?

Her battered senses sought shadows, whispers, smells. Menace crouched all around. The surface of the table beneath her hand was hard reality. A breeze touched the back of her neck. There was no one else in the room. From down the street, running footsteps, coming in this direction. Others approaching from the intersection. A voice calling:

'Joe, what in heck was that? Up there. Look.'

Gina realized she was shaking violently. But in the realization was a sort of relief, like waking from a nightmare, still afraid yet knowing the threat is past. Wrapping her arms about herself, she peered down to the street and the two policemen beside the ruined tablelamp. One of the men shouted, 'Mrs Cornell? Is that you? Are you all right?'

It was several seconds before Gina was able to reply.

Chapter Thirteen

'Feeling better now?' Detective Sergeant Shaughnessy peered into Gina's eyes with the professionalism of a man who'd seen shock in all its forms. He was sitting opposite Gina across her desk, downstairs from the room where the glaziers were replacing the shattered window.

It was eleven am. The sun was shining into the office. Gina had spent the night in her bedroom with a patrolman at the door. She'd refused to let the police call any of her friends, insisting she felt all right and that there was no point in hauling people from their sleep at that time of night.

Surprisingly, she herself had slept like a log. (Sergeant Shaughnessy had told her this was not an unusual reaction.) When Gina had awoken at nine o'clock, it had been to find that word had spread from the early-morning cleaners, and Cassie, Harry, Irving and at least a dozen others were camped anxiously in her sitting room.

The task of assuring them all that she was uninjured and none the worse for her experience had gone some way toward restoring her own fractured confidence.

At last Irving had left for the West-Rossi Building to quell any exaggerated rumours, Harry had gone downstairs to make as little of the incident as possible to the several reporters who'd picked up the news at the local precinct house, and Cassie had remained in the apartment to tend the incessant phone.

The detective sergeant had arrived thirty minutes ago.

Gina had recounted her brief story. This had been her third or fourth telling of it, and each time the reality retreated to become more like the memory of a grim dream.

She'd watched the detective as he wrote in his notebook.

He was a stocky man with sandy hair and a pugilistic but not unpleasant face. Gina was genuinely grateful for the calm consideration he'd shown during his inquiry.

Now she said, 'Thank you, yes, I'm feeling much better.'

He said, 'Well, then, if there's nothing you have to add ...' His eyes asked the unspoken question, Do you?

Gina bit the inside of her lip. Should she mention the incident – imagined incident? – in Central Park? She didn't want him to think she was an hysterical female who saw lurking figures around every corner, or he might begin to wonder if last night's episode had been largely a fantasy of her overtired brain – he'd already shown some surprise at the fact that she'd been working until two o'clock in the morning.

She said, 'No, there's nothing else I can tell you.'

He nodded. 'Finally then, Mrs Cornell, you still can't recall any detail of what the intruder looked like?'

'No, I'm sorry. All I can remember is an awful black shape in the doorway. I wish I could be more helpful.'

'That's okay. I understand,' said the sergeant with a kind smile. 'But, if anything should come back to you, please get in touch right away and I'll arrange for you to come over to the office to take a look through our photo files.'

'You think he might be there, a professional burglar?'

'We always hope. Certainly I think he must be a professional, the way he turned the power off at the fuse box. And if, as you say, the door to the alley was definitely locked, then he picked it very cleanly, didn't leave a scratch. Same with all the inner doors – though you do admit you might've overlooked those.'

Gina gave a guilty nod. While she was sure she'd secured the door from the alley, she couldn't for the life of her remember locking the others. Again she felt this tolerant but hard-worked man might think her an utter scatterbrain. She was beginning to think it herself.

She ventured, 'So you don't believe there's any connection with this and the person who sent the note?'

The detective had already mentioned he'd seen the green crayon threat in the precinct files. He pursed his lips and replied, 'It's a possibility we can't overlook. But,' he added, leaning forward to emphasize his words, 'remember what my colleague told you when you brought the note in. The characters who send threatening letters very rarely follow them up. It's only the real psychopaths, who imagine they've got a genuine grudge, who resort to violence. So, please, don't get to thinking there's a madman out there stalking you. Be extra careful, by all means, but don't let it prey on your mind. Sounds sort of contrary advice, I know, but I hope you'll see what I mean.'

Gina said positively, 'Yes, I do, thank you, Sergeant. Don't worry, I have far too much to do to sit around fretting about burglars or note-scribblers.' She hoped that didn't sound dismissive, she was genuinely trying to reassure the man she wasn't hyperimaginative. She gave an inward sigh, experiencing a wave of aftershock, an enervating sensation which left her feeling drained and shaky.

As if reading this in her face, the detective put away his notebook and arose, saying, 'I won't trouble you any longer, Mrs Cornell. Thank you for your co-operation.' He took a card from his pocket, wrote upon it. 'That's my number at the precinct house. If you think of anything else, please don't hesitate to call.'

Gina stood, took the card, glancing at it and acknowledging, 'Thank you, Sergeant Shaughnessy.' She walked with him across the office and opened the door.

'By the way,' he said, 'good luck with the hotels.'

'Hotels?' frowned Gina.

'In the papers. This morning.'

Gina responded vaguely, 'I haven't read the papers.'

'Oh, of course, I can see you might not have. Well, you should,' said the detective encouragingly. 'I'm sure it'll help throw a blanket over last night.' He smiled. 'If I may say so, the *Post*'s is a very attractive photograph.'

It was certainly a large one: Gina in front of the huge bronze letters CORNELL. Beside it, one of the illustrations of the Italian piazza hotel lobby. The accompanying report covered almost half the page beneath the headline, WEST-ROSSI CHECKS IN FOR FRANCHISE SUCCESS.

The other seven major dailies published in New York were equally generous. Gina had them all spread out on her desk. Until the detective had mentioned the hotels, she'd completely forgotten yesterday's press conference. Now, nothing could have restored her morale quicker than the tonic she'd just consumed.

'It's been on all the radio stations, too,' said Cassie. 'And the TV. And, apparently, in just about every other newspaper from here to the west coast.'

Irving said, 'Our switchboard down the street has been jammed with calls all morning. It seems half the independent hoteliers in America want to become Cornell franchisees. At least fifty have turned up in person, and there are more arriving all the time.' He smiled. 'Congratulations.'

Gina took a long breath. 'It's marvellous,' she said, the enervation she'd suffered earlier, replaced by a light-headedness of elation. 'But it isn't me you should congratulate. It was Cass who started this ball rolling.'

Cassie swung her shoulders with exaggerated mock modesty and responded, 'Aw shucks, twarn't nuthin.'

Gina smiled at her friend, but from the corner of her eye saw that Irving was also looking at Cassie and there was more than a colleague's admiration in his expression. Gina glanced toward him and his features instantly re-assumed their characteristic professionalism. Gina now wasn't sure what sort of a look had been on his face. Her senses, she was aware, were still far from stable.

For the remainder of the day, however, she put on a good face, realizing that everyone was doing their best to keep her from dwelling on last night. When late afternoon arrived it was obvious there was a well-intentioned conspiracy not to leave Gina alone. She silently accepted this along with Cassie's invitation to dinner downstairs at The Lady.

That, however, proved not to be the world's greatest decision: they were constantly interrupted by good wishes from all who'd learned about the hotels, and sympathy from those who'd heard about the intruder.

At their corner table, at nine-thirty Gina said, 'Much as I appreciate all their considerations, Cass, I must admit it's wearing me down a mite. Please don't think I'm being ungrateful, but I'd rather like to be alone now.'

Cassie's face grew at once uncertain. 'Wouldn't you prefer to come over to my place for the night?'

'Thanks all the same,' returned Gina. 'But I think it would be better if I stayed here. There's no point in avoiding it. You know, like falling off a horse; the thing to do is get right on again, or you might be afraid of it for the rest of your life.'

Cassie nodded, but didn't look too convinced.

Gina insisted, 'Honestly, Cass, I'm not worried.' She added emphatically, 'Nor do I intend to be. I'm not going to let some creepy burglar frighten me out of my own home.' She gave her friend the most reassuring look she could manufacture.

At last Cassie sighed in acquiescence.

As Gina watched her friend leave she felt an uncomfortable mixture of relief and trepidation. She also felt suddenly weary; worn out by the day's traumatic extremes.

Upstairs, after a swift wash, she went directly to bed. She closed her eyes. But she remained awake.

In spite of knowing there was an extra police patrol on the street and one of the security guards from the West-Rossi Building to make regular checks outside, still Gina could find no substance for herself in the empty assurances she'd given Cassie. Where last night she'd slept as if in a coma, tonight she lay helplessly conscious for several hours, her nerves mauled by indistinguishable phantoms, until, around dawn, she at last fell into a fitful slumber.

It took Gina's senses almost a week to return to anything like normal; and even then, when alone on the street, she still couldn't entirely rid herself of the need to throw a watchful look over her shoulder. More than once she was prompted to sympathy for similar victims who had little to keep their minds off their experience; at least her own days were filled with absorbing activity.

Even before the Cornell Hotels' prospectuses had been issued, West-Rossi had received more than ten thousand enquiries. And as David McKay's publicity department made sure the burgeoning success continued to fill newspaper columns almost every morning, Gina was able to further boost her spirits with the grimly humorous thought that Mister Oliver Randolph's breakfast eggs would be daily turning an increasingly unpalatable shade of green.

Gradually, the memory of the night intruder, while remaining harshly clear in Gina's mind, faded in potency. Ten days after the incident she was able to believe it was just one of thousands which happened throughout the city every year.

The telephone call she received that afternoon blew away the final wraiths of her misgivings.

Through the crackles and bleeps of intercontinental static she heard Filipo say yes they'd had a fabulous time. They'd seen so many places and so many relations. He said stop asking all these questions Sis this call is costing a fortune and it isn't my phone. We'll be home the day after tomorrow he shouted above the oscillating row. Can you hear me? Arriving late-morning. Leaving Venice tonight. Venice he repeated. Yes that's where he was calling from. Villa Arancia. Yes Barbara Graham's home. She'd be going with them.

'Barbara Graham? Going?' called Gina. 'Going where?'

Filipo called back, 'To New York, where else.'

Barbara Graham's return to her homeland caused almost as much of a media furore as Cornell Hotels. The celebrity spotters had recognized her at Venice airport and the news was all over the European papers before she and Filipo and Mickey landed in New York. There the army of reporters was out in force. Gina had known what to expect, however, as Filipo had phoned during the plane's stopover in Paris. The long-distance interference hadn't been so noisy this time and he'd told Gina he'd remain with the ex-actress at La Guardia's VIP arrivals lounge for the inevitable media barrage before bringing her to the West-Rossi Building for lunch (they'd decided it would be impossible to cope with the midday throngs around The Lady; at least the security men would be able to keep the crowds out of the company headquarters.

'They're overdue,' said Harry for the umpteenth time, restlessly pacing the office lobby in an immaculate blue check suit (which Gina had seen only once before at a very ritzy showbusiness wedding), while Irving, equally splendid in oyster grey, stood to one side imperceptibly tapping an eager foot.

The two men had agreed (with the ill-concealed excitement, Gina had thought, of small boys invited for a trip to the moon) to make up the informal reception committee. Gina wished Cassie hadn't been obliged to attend the antenatal clinic and was here to give her moral support. Since when, Gina's inner voice demanded, did you need any such thing?

'They're here,' declared Harry, and he and Irving were hastening toward the entrance doors as if the *Dawn Of The New Age* had just occurred on Forty-seventh Street.

Gina remained a model of composure. As Filipo and Mickey came through the doors, she walked to meet them. 'Mickey, welcome back,' she smiled. 'How was Italy? Heavens, what a tan. Did you have a good time?' She kissed Mickey's cheek as the girl replied happily that they'd had a great vacation.

Gina stepped back, glimpsed Harry and Irving hefting luggage from the limousine while Barbara Graham waited looking up at the fascia of the West-Rossi Building. The ex-actress was wearing a beige linen skirt with matching cotton shirt, sleeves rolled to her elbows, holding a wide-brimmed straw hat, purse and two large paper carriers. With little make-up, her hair caught by the breeze, she looked, thought Gina, a decade younger than her forty-eight years.

Filipo was saying, 'Well, Sis, seems you managed to keep the old company tub afloat in our absence.'

Pulling her attention around to him, Gina responded, 'I struggled through.' She surveyed his handsome features, then hugged him and said, 'It's good to have you home.'

The door was swinging open, Barbara Graham was entering, followed by luggage-laden Harry and Irving. Gina walked forward and greeted warmly, 'Barbara. Welcome. It's lovely to see you again.' She briefly touched cheeks with the actress. 'Let me help you with those,' taking one of the carriers and leading the way toward the elevators.

'Thanks,' Barbara Graham responded. 'Just a few presents I brought for family and old friends.'

'It was such a surprise when Filipo phoned. I do hope you didn't mind him turning up on your doorstep.'

'Not at all.' Barbara Graham glanced toward a smiling Filipo. 'His visit was just what I needed. We – I mean Mickey too, of course – had a marvellous couple of days together. And they finally persuaded me to return to the land of the living – at least for a vacation.'

They reached the elevator, waited for Harry and Irving to stow the luggage behind the reception desk, then everyone squeezed into the car and rode up for lunch at the boardroom table where, for the ensuing two hours, the conversation revolved entirely around the current state of the movie industry.

'What it boils down to,' observed Harry, 'is that the golden age of Hollywood is over. The era we're into now is mid-life crisis. What Monument, and all the other studios, have to ensure is that it doesn't result in premature death.'

'But,' asked Barbara Graham, 'what's their answer?'

Harry said, 'Several see the future in 3-D. At Fox, Zanuck is putting his money on a wide screen image he's registered as Cinemascope. A couple are experimenting with stereophonic sound. And there's even a rumour somebody's working on an idea called – no kidding – Aromavision.'

'So which one will save the day?'

Harry raised a thoughtful eyebrow but before he could produce his reply, Filipo said:

'In the long term I don't believe any of them will prove to be the answer. They're just gimmicks. Like when automobile manufacturers stick on extra fins or flashy dashboards. They catch a few customers for a while but once the fad has passed they've got to start over, dream up yet another novelty. What none of them ever seems to think of is simply building a better product. It's going to be the same with the movies. When all's said and done, I'm sure the industry will stand or fall on the quality of its product. The bottom line is, pictures people want to watch.'

As Harry agreed with this and the subject moved along, Gina listened to her brother with growing admiration. She hadn't before realized he'd kept such a close and expert eye on the development of the motion picture industry.

But also, after the discussion had reached fresh technical

levels, it occurred to her that she herself was injecting precious little. Gina had to admit even Mickey was better informed. Here she was, the person who'd committed eighteen million dollars to the purchase of Monument and she didn't understand half of what the others were talking about. She decided she'd better do something about it.

At last Harry was rising, saying he had an appointment with one of the TV companies. Irving also had a meeting, at the bank. Filipo declared he was going to take an incredibly long, very hot bath – why did European hoteliers insist on producing only lukewarm water? Mickey stated she was going to get three days sleep, ready for rehearsals of *High As The Sky* next week; she said they'd all be welcome at the show's try-out in Buffalo in December.

Gina observed the men's reluctance to tear themselves away from Barbara Graham, but eventually they were gone and Gina was alone with the ex-actress.

Barbara Graham was delving into one of her paper carriers. 'I'll be on my way too in a moment,' she said. 'Up to Vermont to see the family. I just wanted to give you this.' She handed over a small blue paper package.

'You shouldn't have,' said Gina, mildly embarrassed. Within the blue paper was a carton. She lifted the lid to reveal a green figurine, a slim, nude female, tiptoeing on a plinth, arms outstretched. 'It's exquisite,' Gina exclaimed.

'Just a token,' said Barbara Graham. 'A keepsake of our first meeting. I'm glad you like it. Filipo said you would. He was with me when I bought it.'

Gina said, 'Oh?'

'He's quite a fellow, your brother.'

'Yes,' said Gina, 'he is.'

'We had some fascinating conversations while he was in Venice. He's very knowledgeable, for his age, about so many things. Astute too. It was his idea I come back to the States, so that I could give some extra publicity to the Barbara Graham season.'

Gina frowned, puzzled. Then, 'Of course,' she recalled, 'the seven movies you'd like Monument to re-release.'

'You haven't changed your mind?'

'Not at all. It had slipped from my thoughts for a while. But it's been put in hand. I'll ask Felix Gilbert to give you a call, let you know what's been arranged.'

'No need,' returned the ex-actress. 'Filipo said he'd do just that. I gave him my number in Vermont.'

Gina almost said, Oh, again, but managed to keep it in. She felt somewhat unsettled by the relationship which seemed to have developed between her brother and this woman. Don't be absurd, she reproved herself; the situation is perfectly normal.

'I said he'd be welcome to visit in person,' remarked Barbara Graham, lifting her carriers and starting toward the door, 'when he's up in Montpelier next month.'

'Montpelier?'

'My parent's home is quite near.'

'I didn't know Filipo was going there.'

'To attend an AFF meeting.'

'He told you that?'

'And all about the AFF's aims. It seems your brother is helping a very worthwhile organization.'

They'd reached the door and Gina opened it. 'Yes ...' she said tentatively. 'But I wouldn't want him to become too politically involved. His law studies must come first.'

'I don't think it's so much a question of politics,' said Barbara Graham. 'Rather a matter of standing up for what one believes is right. And it's good to know there are people like Filipo who are prepared to do just that. I told him he has my wholehearted support.' She looked directly at Gina, her dark eyes intense.

Gina experienced once more the tremor of unease she'd felt on first seeing this woman on Harry's movie screen; and she imagined what effect the ex-actress's dramatic personality, and thus her acclamation, might have on Filipo. She couldn't deny she was angered by Barbara Graham's encouragement of his involvement with the AFF. She said, 'I'll walk up to the lobby.'

Ten minutes later she was back in her office. If the ex-actress had noticed Gina's slight brusqueness, she hadn't betrayed it and had left with warm promises to keep in touch. Gina spent the remainder of the afternoon persuading herself she had no logical basis for her fitful emotions.

Chapter Fourteen

She had every reason to be happy.

These last weeks of summer were golden. The stream of franchise applications to Cornell Hotels had swelled to a flood. Barbara Graham's return had generated even more publicity for West-Rossi. Wheldon Hoyt, the banker, had phoned Gina several times to compliment her on the burgeoning success and assure her of the security of her personal investment. The memory of the intruder in Gina's apartment had retreated, and she rarely gave a thought to the green crayon letter sender.

The traumas of the past months, Gina told herself, had been a passing phase, a trough into which all businesses as well as individuals must periodically fall in order to rise again, and there was absolutely no reason for imagining they presaged disaster.

She re-applied herself to the future. And that meant Monument.

Since the lunchtime confab the day of Barbara Graham's arrival, when Gina's ignorance of the film industry had become more than somewhat apparent, she'd determined to rectify her failing. Thus, almost every morning, she buried herself in technical manuals, fan magazines and history books. She learned everything she could about movie making, from the earliest flickering efforts in Paris before the turn of the century to the foundations of Hollywood two decades later, from the spectacular rise of the American moguls to the plateau of uncertainty whereon they fretted today.

During the afternoons she studied the product.

This was the year when Crosby, Hope and Lamour

trekked the *Road to Bali*; Martin and Lewis parachuted as *Jumping Jacks*; Abbott and Costello were *Lost in Alaska*; Ray Milland was *The Thief*, and Charlton Heston was *The Savage*; Judy Holliday was *The Marrying Kind*, and Lana Turner was *The Merry Widow*; Rita Hayworth had *An Affair in Trinidad* while Gene Kelly was *Singing In The Rain*; and as James Stewart clowned, Betty Hutton trapezed to create *The Greatest Show On Earth*.

And Gina was right there with them all.

By the beginning of October, while she still couldn't call herself an expert, she at least felt a growing competence during the frequent phone calls she made to Felix at the studio to discuss progress of their current productions.

It was during one of these calls that Felix said, 'When are you coming out to your eighteen million property?'

Gina hadn't committed herself to a definite answer. She wanted very much to visit Monument as well as West-Rossi's other interests on the west coast; and, even more importantly, it seemed far too long since she'd seen Max. But, here in New York, there was Howard.

Howard had returned to the city a week before Felix asked his question. The only way Gina could describe his mood was peculiar. He'd decided to stay at his club, but he did turn up at The Lady or the West-Rossi Building almost every day briefly to see Gina. Ostensibly this was to make some effort at their marriage, but Gina couldn't help feeling he was checking on her whereabouts.

She told herself not to be foolish. Why should Howard do such a thing? Then it occurred to her he might be concerned for her welfare following the incident of the intruder. But she abandoned this theory, recalling he'd scarcely wanted to discuss the matter when she'd first mentioned it.

Still, perplexed as she was, Gina felt she must play her part in preventing the rift between them growing any wider. She cut down on her movie-house visits, even delegated some of her office chores in order not to have to rush off when Howard was around.

He'd been back over a week, however, before they made love, one lunchtime in the apartment when Gina, deciding to take the initiative, led the way to the bedroom, quietly undressed Howard and herself, then drew him down onto the bed. But she couldn't lose the inhibiting memory of their last encounter, and this ragged fifteen minutes left her feeling neither satisfied nor satisfactory.

She didn't see Howard again for three days.

When he did turn up, around noon, Gina put on her brightest face, suggested they lunch together, and kept their conversation light and general while she signed a few letters. Then, as she gathered up her purse, Howard said:

'Have you thought any more about leaving the company?'

All Gina's good humour drained. But she said equably, 'No, Howard, I haven't. I couldn't possibly at the moment. Nor do I see why I should. We've had plenty of time together this past fortnight, and could have had more if you'd wanted. I wish you weren't staying at the club. Why don't you move into the apartment, or ...'

'So you aren't even considering it?'

Gina drew a breath, told herself to count to ten. 'No, but ...'

'I see.' Howard stood and started for the door.

'I thought we were having lunch,' called Gina.

In the doorway he said, 'I wouldn't want to keep you from more important matters, or people.'

'Howard, don't be ...' Gina bit back a harsh retaliation. Keeping her voice as calm as possible, she said, 'If you won't stay for lunch, please let's have dinner together this evening.'

'I have things to do.'

'Tomorrow then? Will you meet me here?'

'I may be leaving town.'

Gina inwardly sighed, at once wearied by the exchange. With an effort, she asked, 'Will you be away for long?'

He shrugged. 'A month, or more. Does it matter?'

'Must you go?'

'Why shouldn't I?'

Gina remained at her desk. No more words were said.

The franchise applications had been winnowed: the genuine but unsuitable hopefuls courteously rejected; a thousand possibles held on file; two hundred hoteliers' petitions stamped APPROVED. It had been a hugely consuming round of interviews and visits to premises to ascertain the suitability of each individual as a franchisee and the potential of his or her hotel for conversion to the Cornell standard.

Cassie, Irving and their growing squad had taken care of all this while Gina was occupied with her usual tasks as well as her self-education in movie-making and her involvement with Monument. This afternoon, however, they'd all been together making the final choice of the hotels where the grand openings would be held, those ten to which the press would be invited for the inaugural weekend.

At the board meeting back in August when this idea had been originally mooted, Max had frowned, 'But, I don't think I understand. Ten grand openings? *Per che?*'

'Because,' Gina had explained, 'these States of ours may be called United, but when you come down to it America consists of a collection of regions which are as fiercely independent as the counties of England or the provinces of France. And with better reason. Distance. You can't really blame a citizen of Los Angeles for feeling somewhat remote from New York three thousand miles east; or a resident of Bangor, Maine thinking Tucson, Arizona, almost seventy driving hours south-west, is a world away.

'So, if we were to hold a grand opening at just one Cornell hotel, no matter where it was, more than half the population of the country would be, at best, indifferent, at worst, resentful. To avoid that, to keep everybody happy, we'll have simultaneous openings, in ten strategic cities throughout the country.

Thus, following nationwide counsel with Chambers of Commerce, trade allies, media contacts, friends and relations, a map had been blue-lined into ten sections in each of which an appointed franchisee would be the pennant-bearer for all the Cornell Hotels in that region.

Now, those ten had been chosen. The only decision not yet made was which of the grand openings the directors would attend. Gina, Cassie and Irving discussed it without conclusion before calling it a day at five-thirty.

When Gina and Cassie started up the street from the

West-Rossi Building to The Lady the late October evening was dark, and a cold, blustering wind carried a threat of winter.

Passing a poster for Walt Disney's *Dumbo*, Cassie remarked, 'Beginning to look like that feller. Feel it too.' She swayed, halted, hands in the small of her back, wincing.

Concerned, Gina asked, 'Are you all right? Shall we step into this store so's you can sit down a minute?'

'No, thanks,' declined Cassie. 'I think it's the sitting all afternoon got to me. Not that standing's much better. Or lying down. Hon, it tells you plenty in all those books I read, but it never mentions how it actually feels to be in this so-called delicate condition.' She glanced down at the voluminous flare of her maternity coat. 'Delicate? Hah!'

Gina smiled, but took Cassie's arm to stand away from the hurrying pedestrians in the lee of a news-stand. She'd similarly caught her friend's elbow a few days ago when Cassie had tottered as they were crossing the street. Cassie had laughed aside the incident:

'Don't worry. The doc says if pregnant ladies fall over, there's little chance of their babies being bruised. Anyhow, Junior is a tough little guy. I know. Days I feel him sparring away like Rocky Marciano in there.'

Gina had kept her response in a similar lighthearted vein, reminding herself that of course millions of women carried their babies through nine months of hectic urban life. Nevertheless, she couldn't help worrying about her friend.

'Right,' said Cassie, moving away from the news-stand, 'let's stagger on, get in out of this wind.' She pulled up the collar of her coat, tugged down the brim of her hat.

Reaching The Lady they went into the bar where Cassie said she preferred to stand. In an out-of-the-way corner they sipped tomato juices, while they warmed themselves at a radiator. They didn't speak for a while, watching the lively cocktail crowd beginning to gather. It was Cassie who broke their silence:

'Hon, I've been thinking,' she said, her expression tentative. 'These ten grand openings of the Cornell Hotels. I'd rather like to attend the one in San Francisco.'

Gina, taken unawares, only stared.

'I shouldn't have wasted Irving's time this afternoon,' said Cassie, 'hedging around it. But I really hadn't made up my mind. And now I guess I better had. I hope you'll understand.'

Gina found her voice. 'If you prefer San Francisco, that's fine. Is there something special about the hotel there?'

'Not really, although I think the reconstruction is going to make it one of the best of all, but the reason for choosing it …' Cassie gave a small shrug, 'is simply the weather.'

Gina's eyes echoed, The weather?

'Frankly,' said Cassie, 'I'd forgotten just how cold New York winters can be. This past week has been a sharp reminder, and – I know this sounds sort of faint-hearted – I'd prefer Junior to make his debut in the sunshine rather than a howling blizzard.'

Gina smiled. 'I can't say I blame you.'

'Also,' Cassie went on, 'I reckon I've only got a few more weeks before I have to sit back awhile. I'd like to spend them close to one of the flagship Cornells, maybe help the franchisee if I can, then I'll be able to pick up the reins early next year in time for the grand opening.'

'Seems like a good idea,' agreed Gina.

'So it'll be okay?'

'I don't see why not.'

'Then I'll tell Irving,' said Cassie. 'We've already made arrangements for my workload to be taken over.'

Gina asked, 'Will you have the baby in San Francisco?'

'I haven't really decided. Maybe I'll go to LA, though I'm not too keen – too many memories there, I think.'

Gina pondered. 'What's wrong with Vegas?' she asked.

Cassie looked thoughtful.

'The new hospital is excellent,' said Gina. 'And as soon as you decide you've had enough in San Francisco you could go down and stay at The Silver Lady before, and after, you have the baby. Vegas is perfect at that time of year, not too hot but sunny almost every day. Plus, you can walk the streets without being bowled over by either swarming pedestrians or runaway trucks.' She looked enquiringly at her friend. 'How about it?'

Cassie slowly nodded. 'Sounds fine. I'd like it. So long as

Max doesn't mind a fat lady waddling around the place.'

Gina laughed. 'He'll love having you. I was only thinking a while ago that it was too long since any of us had been out to visit. I'd have liked to go myself then, but ...' She hesitated, caught by her sudden thought of Howard. In the four days since he'd walked out of her office, Gina hadn't heard a word from him, wasn't even sure whether he was still in town.

Cassie probed, 'Yes?'

Gina pulled away from the image of her husband. 'Oh, nothing,' she said. 'Cass, when were you thinking of leaving?'

'Maybe the beginning of next week,' her friend replied.

Gina hesitated only another moment. 'Would you mind a travelling companion?' she asked.

To be honest, she'd be glad to get away. The day before she and Cassie were due to leave, Gina looked out of her office window at a thin, sleeting rain and shivered at the very sight of it. Must be my bones getting old, she joshed herself. At her desk she checked the list of all the friends and business contacts who'd been informed of her move to The Silver Lady. She nodded, satisfied. The only person she hadn't told was Filipo; whenever she'd called his Boston number he'd been out.

She lifted the phone now and dialled.

A male voice answered, 'Hello.'

Gina recognized her brother's room-mate. 'It's me again, Jake,' she said. 'Is Filipo there?'

'No. Sorry Gina. Haven't you seen him?'

'Seen him?'

'He was talking with some other guys in the cafeteria last night. I thought I heard him mention New York.'

'That he was coming here, you mean?'

'Can't be sure, really. You know, I was only half listening. I'm not involved in any of the AFF business.'

'They were discussing the AFF?' queried Gina.

'Something about a demonstration, I think.'

'Here in Manhattan?'

'Yes. That's why I figured you'd have seen him. It's today.

The demonstration. This afternoon. Let me think. Some of it's coming back. Yes, they said this afternoon, two-thirty.'

Gina glanced at her watch. Two-fifteen. 'Where was it going to take place?' she asked as evenly as possible.

'I couldn't tell you,' began Jake, then, 'no, wait a second,' he added. 'I remember, it's one of the chain snack bars. A branch that had fired a waitress for no good reason, something like that.' He paused. 'I can't recall the details.'

'But can you recall which snack bar chain?'

'Oh, sure. I wouldn't forget that. They were bought out last year. It was in the papers. The one with the catchy name – if you like that sort of thing. The Kwik Koffee Kup.'

Gina caught her breath as the name pierced her memory. 'Which branch?' she asked urgently. 'The address?'

'Heck,' muttered Jake. 'I really don't remember.'

'Please try,' pressed Gina. 'There are eight branches around Manhattan. I have to know which one.'

'Well ... I ...' Jake seemed to remain silent for an age as Gina scraped her anxious fingernails on the desktop. Then at last he blurted, 'I got it. I remember. Herald Square.'

'Thank you,' gasped Gina and in a moment was hurrying across her office to snatch her mac and rainhat, pull them on as she ran downstairs and out to hail a taxi. Icy rain blew into the cab with her. But Gina's blood was already chilled; had been from the instant Jake had mentioned the Kwik Koffee Kup. Yes, Gina knew the chain of garish snack bars had been bought out last year – by the Randolph Corporation.

Consternation beat around her. Of all the foolhardy acts Filipo could have committed! Wouldn't the media just love to find out a West-Rossi director had been demonstrating outside Randolph Corporation premises. Worse: what might Oliver Randolph do with such knowledge? Gina daren't even begin to consider the consequences.

She checked her watch; coming up to two-thirty. She was too apprehensive to think of what she was going to say to her brother out on the street in front of his fellow demonstrators; she only knew that one way or another she had to get him away from that snack bar before the press arrived on the scene.

The taxi came to a halt in bumper-to-bumper traffic. Gina

peered fretfully ahead. 'What's the hold-up?'

'Who knows in this city,' grumbled the cabbie.

The taxi crawled forward; in five minutes it moved only a hundred yards. Again it halted. Gina said exasperatedly, 'I'll walk,' and thrusting the fare into the cabbie's fist clambered out and hurried to the kerb.

Her heels rattled her anxiety amid the impeding sidewalk crowd as the sleet cut across her vision, stung her cheeks. Half running, half striding she dodged umbrellas, bumped shoulders, hastened across two busy streets, until, at last, up ahead she could see the wide intersection which was Herald Square. She ran the final yards to the corner.

Halting, catching her breath, Gina tiptoed to scan beyond the frenzied traffic.

Over there, among the mosaic of store and restaurant signs, The Kwik Koffee Kup. So bustling was the far sidewalk, however, Gina couldn't make out anybody gathered in front of the snackbar. For a moment she dared to hope the demonstration had been cancelled, but then she realized that the twenty or so pedestrians approaching from the subway were all moving at the same pace. She watched as they came to a ragged standstill and with some fumbling inside coats and macs raised a rash of multi-coloured placards.

Gina hardly bothered to read the angry messages, she was too intent upon trying to distinguish Filipo.

But it was impossible with so many passers-by. Hanging on to her hat, she ran for the other side of the street, vehicles bleating as she skated their frenetic lanes. She arrived at her goal, rapidly surveying the demonstrators' faces. Hurrying along their line she could not find her brother. 'Filipo Rossi?' she enquired of the placard-carrying young man, and when he negatively shook his wet head she pressed, 'Are others coming?'

'Other what?' parried the youth.

He's being purposely obtuse, Gina fretted, grasping the wind-blown edges of her collar and patience. She offered a friendly smile, but the youth's suspicion only deepened and he turned away. 'Please,' she appealed, 'I must ...' She jolted as a passing pedestrian clipped her with a shopping bag. Nerves rattling, she re-approached the youth, catching at his sleeve. 'I only want to …'

A yell came from behind.

Gina swung around to see, twenty yards along the block, half-a-dozen people scuffling. Perplexity was her first reaction. What had happened? Who was causing the trouble? Suddenly, it was very noisy. Voices were raised up and down the line of demonstrators. Several people began to shout. Automobile horns blared.

Still Gina couldn't find Filipo.

Beside her a man rasped, 'Quit shoving.' She returned, 'Sorry,' beginning to turn. Hands pushed into her back causing her to stumble forward. A shoe trod hard on her instep. She cried out loud and her own sound frightened her. There seemed to be many more people than there had been moments ago, jostling, exchanging threats, starting to shove each other. Aggression charged the air.

A placard flew overhead, clanged against the snackbar window. Another arced around and struck a woman full in the face. The woman screamed and blood gushed from her mouth.

Gina saw this as if in a nightmare. The violence had erupted so unexpectedly, her mind seemed to have been pitched into a different dimension. She felt suddenly trapped. I have to get out of here, she thought with rising alarm.

Then someone cannoned into her, sent her tumbling, snatching hopelessly at the air for support. Her knees hit the ground and pain flamed up her spine. Before her she could see only a battling mass of legs. God, let me get up, she pleaded, grabbing a coat hem, only to have it ripped from her grasp as something caught her a glancing blow across the ear. 'Help!' she yelled and a fist seized the scruff of her raincoat, jerked her bodily upright. Gina gasped, 'Thanks,' but her saviour was lost in the tumult while she tottered there gulping for air.

As her lungs filled and her vision cleared she reached up to straighten her hat, and the absurdity of the automatic reaction pierced some clarity through her mental commotion. She understood she was against a store front. To her right was a gap between the buildings and the havoc of bodies, a twenty yard run to safety. Throwing up an arm to protect her face she dashed forward.

A whistle shrieked.

So loudly startling was the blast, Gina halted.

Another whistle. And sirens. The crowd abruptly retreated backward over the sidewalk, cutting off Gina's escape route. She cast this way and that, scalded by the feverish contagion of alarm, pressed back against the wall as men and women dashed in all directions. Momentarily she was paralysed by the chaos, then she knew she too must run. She turned swiftly, only to find her path barred by a policeman. Before she could begin to form a rational thought, the man had seized her and was hauling her along the sidewalk. 'No, you don't understand,' Gina protested, defensively raising her hand.

'Don't!' warned the policeman, pointing his baton at the tip of Gina's chin while simultaneously yanking up on the shoulder of her mac so that she was obliged to rise on tiptoe with her head bent sideways at an acute angle.

'Please,' she rasped through her trapped jaw, 'let me explain. I wasn't in the demonstration. I ...'

'Over there.' The officer propelled her sideways and she bumped into someone. A hand steadied her and a male voice snapped at the policeman, 'Take it easy. We don't want any trouble.' Gina turned to see the young placard carrier.

'Just stand still,' he advised. 'Do what you're told.'

Gina nodded, grateful, but too dismayed to speak. She saw she was one of a group of perhaps ten, corralled against a wall by four policemen. Several other officers were up and down the rainy street, deterring onlookers. The traffic was passing slowly. Drivers and passengers stared out at the bedraggled detainees. A voice yelled, 'Lousy communists.'

'In the truck,' ordered a policeman.

Gina and her companions were hustled up the rear steps of a patrol wagon. The vehicle interior, including the benches down each side, was scabrous black metal. The reek of disinfectant was so strong it caused Gina's eyes to water. She wiped them with the back of her hand as she sat between the young man and a girl who was perhaps eighteen.

The truck's rear door was slammed and an officer sat beside it, baton across his knees. The motor rumbled and with a jerk the truck started forward.

Gina looked at the people facing her. Everyone was wet and dishevelled. No one spoke or smiled. Gina glanced down at her own condition: raincoat dirty, shoes scarred, knees bloody through torn stockings. All at once she felt unutterably afraid. She tightened her grip on her purse. Her purse! The surprise of discovering she still had the small, cream leather bag jolted her back from the brink of panic.

The ride lasted only a few minutes.

When the truck halted and its door banged open, the officer ordered, 'Out,' and the group was hustled across the sidewalk, up a flight of steps and into a stark lobby where a sergeant sat at a high desk fielding the complaints and demands of a dozen petitioners. The place smelled of carbolic. Overhead yellow bulbs were caged in wire mesh.

After a few moments the ten demonstrators were herded past the desk into a side corridor and ordered to stand still while a tired-looking patrolman walked their line taking names and addresses. Gina's disconcertion re-arose. How could she admit who she was?

When the patrolman and his notebook reached her, she mumbled under her breath, 'Gina Cornell, Ninety-seven, Broome Street.' The lie – the address of the old apartment she'd rented when she'd first arrived in America – seemed to echo in the confined space. She was sure her identity would be questioned, but the officer had already moved on, and no one was pointing an accusing finger. Gina told herself everything would be all right; she'd silently accept whatever ticking-off was given and get quickly away from this place.

After the last name had been noted, a woman officer arrived, the group was split into males and females, the latter led down a flight of stairs and through a steel door.

Gina almost cried out in alarm.

There were six cells along each side of the central aisle, bar-fronted, separated by solid walls. Two were empty. Each of the others held two or three occupants, women of various ages, some talking, some lying silently on their bunks; few took much notice of the new arrivals.

Gina's heart was racing. This was wrong. She wasn't supposed to be locked up. She'd assumed ...

'Don't take all day about it,' snapped the policewoman, and before Gina could decide on any alternative course she was stepping into the cell behind three young demonstrators. The door clanged shut. Gina looked around the bleak cubicle: double bunks at each side; a stained sink beneath a high barred window; a toilet with a wooden lid; a white globe ceiling light in the inevitable wire cage. Gina's impulse to swing around and shout for the policewoman was broken by one of her companions remarking:

'Clean,' as she examined a blanket. 'The last time, over in Allentown, the bed was crawling.'

The second girl said, 'And this is a flusher,' cranking the toilet handle. 'Some places still got buckets.'

The third remarked, 'Makes for real sociability.'

They all laughed, rather crudely. Gina managed to raise a smile. She looked around the young, brash faces. A sorority allied in youth and experience of prison conditions. Gina felt like a middle-aged innocent. She said, 'What will happen to us?'

The girl in a motorbike jacket replied offhandedly, 'Your first time, huh? They'll hold us overnight. Maybe they'll feed us, chances are they won't. If we complain, they'll go on about overwork and undermanning. We'll get the same bull for not being given the opportunity to call our lawyers till midnight. We'll go into morning court and plead guilty to causing an affray or disturbing the peace or whatever else they call whatever it was we didn't do. The judge'll hand us a twenty-dollar fine, and the gang of loonies on the courthouse steps'll spit at us when we leave.' She gave a flippant laugh.

Gina ventured, 'And if we plead innocent?'

The girl said, 'You must be joking.'

Gina sat on the edge of a bunk as her companions began to gossip among themselves. She was cold and aware of the soreness of her knees. And she was once again afraid. The unshakable fear of prison. No matter how hard she tried to reassure herself, she was beset by memories of the Fascist persecutions of her youth. She looked around the cramped cell, shivered at its harsh shabbiness, tasted its acrid atmosphere at the back of her throat.

'Play gin?'

Gina glanced up. Though she didn't really care for card games she'd welcome a means of occupying her mind. She nodded as the trio gathered on the bunk. She told them her name. They introduced themselves as Eileen, Shirley and Jo. This was apparently all the information they were interested in trading. Their banter was mainly about men and movies. After a while, however, Gina did gather they weren't AFF members, simply acquaintances of the girl fired from The Kwik Koffee Kup. She also began to realize they'd been at the demonstration more out of habitual dissidence than any real sense of justice. The three weren't exactly trouble-makers, but nor were they genuine protesters.

This knowledge only deepened Gina's concern over her brother's involvement in such activities.

She concentrated as well as she was able on the card game. It lasted for almost two hours. By then, the daylight had gone and the cell was illuminated by the harsh yellow ceiling lamp. The girls lay on the bunks and continued to gossip and joke. Gina's fractured confidence began to crumble.

The door to the stairs opened, footsteps came along the aisle, a key rattled in the cell lock.

'Mrs Cornell?'

Gina looked up. The man was stocky with sandy hair and a pugilistic but not unpleasant face. He stared, perplexed, at Gina. She exclaimed, 'Sergeant Shaughnessy,' recognizing the detective who'd visited her following the episode of the mystery intruder at her apartment.

He pulled his gaze from her dishevelled condition and said urgently, 'Please, come with me.'

Gina was too surprised to ask questions. She stepped out of the cell, stood while the sergeant relocked the door, and realized that the three girls were sitting up watching her. She sought for something to say but her own emotions were as indefinable as theirs.

'Please, Mrs Cornell.' The detective reached for her elbow. 'We don't have much time.'

Gina took a last brief look at the bleak cell and its staring occupants, then she turned and went out with the sergeant. Pausing on the bottom tread of the stairs while he secured the steel door, she asked, 'Where are you taking me?'

'Out of here.'

'Out where?'

He put the key in his pocket. 'I'm releasing you.'

Relief flooded through Gina so suddenly she swayed on the step and the sergeant reached out to steady her. She raised a small laugh and covered her perturbation by asking, 'But how did you know I was here?'

'In this afternoon's shindig,' he replied, 'an innocent pedestrian received a broken jaw. The Why-Isn't-The-Law-Protecting-Our-Safety brigade is up in arms. The mayor's office has been bombarded by phone calls. Though there's little the police can do, we have to be seen to be making an effort. So the Detective Division has been roped in.' He gave a weary shake of his head. 'My partner and I got stuck with checking the list of detainees. When I saw your name I didn't really think it could be you but figured I'd better take a look all the same.'

'I'm grateful,' said Gina. 'Honestly, I wasn't one of the demonstrators. I went there to see ...' She hesitated, reluctant to mention Filipo's involvement with the AFF.

'Please,' the sergeant interrupted her thoughts, 'frankly, the less I know, the better. The main thing is to get you away from here, keep your name out of the reports.'

'You can do that?'

'Fortunately. With everybody in the department currently up to their necks in real police work, no one's yet had time to fill in the arrest book. So far you're still only on a detainees list. I can get it scrubbed without much problem.'

'I wouldn't want you to get into any trouble.'

'I reckon I'd be in a lot more, Mrs Cornell, if the newshounds caught wind of your being here. Right now they're not showing too much interest in what looks like just another street rumpus. If we, the department, handle the situation quietly and diplomatically, the Outraged Citizens will soon forget it. Which is what my Lieutenant and his Chief and right on up to the Commissioner are all praying for. And which is why you're leaving by the rear exit, and why, afterwards, we're both going to tell ourselves we're just like everybody else in this world, trying to get by the best way we know how.'

Gina faced this man in a long silence. She wanted to offer some further mitigation for her actions, but was lost for words. She wanted to make a plea for Eileen and Shirley and Jo, but knew it would be useless. She only said, 'Thanks for your help.'

Sergeant Shaughnessy nodded.

A few minutes later Gina was hurrying home.

She picked up all the evening papers at the news-stand, and as soon as she was into her apartment, before even taking off her coat or hat, searched every page of every one. Then she searched them again.

Thank the stars. Gina had found only three brief reports of the disturbance. Each one mentioned the AFF, but none named any of the demonstrators. She sagged as if a great weight had dropped from her shoulders.

Looking back across the past four hours, they seemed wholly unreal; so much so that Gina actually glanced down at her raw knees for proof that she'd really been caught up in the nightmarish drama. How could she have behaved so recklessly? Think first, act second had always been her advice to her young sister and brother. She'd have done well to heed it herself this afternoon. As she again thought of what the consequences could have been if she'd been recognized in Herald Square, a shudder ran through her.

The phone rang. Gina lifted it and said, 'Hello.'

'Sis, hi. You've been trying to reach me?'

It took Gina several moments to gather her wits. 'Filipo,' she replied at last, 'thank goodness. Where are you?'

'The college cafeteria. Jake told me you'd called.'

The college cafeteria? Gina struggled to grasp the significance of the words, and then to try to calculate whether her brother could have travelled back to Boston from New York since the demonstration broke up.

'Sis? What's the matter? Are you okay?'

Gina realized he couldn't have made the trip in the time. He'd never been here today! Finding her voice, she said in what she hoped was a conversational tone, 'Yes, I'm fine. I was just reading about an AFF demonstration this afternoon in Herald Square.'

'Made the papers, did it?' said Filipo, a little angrily. 'Just as Oliver Randolph intended.'

Surprised, Gina could only respond, 'Randolph?'

'It was his bully boys who caused the trouble. On purpose. To get the blame laid on the demonstrators and have the AFF pilloried as a gang of trouble-makers.'

Gina queried, 'You know that for a fact?'

'We had word it was likely to happen. Which is why the committee didn't support the demonstration. It was entirely unofficial. A bit hot-headed, actually, on account of a few militant members. Now look what's happened, damn it.'

He sounded hurt as well as annoyed. Gina's sympathy went to him, while she was also greatly relieved he hadn't been involved. She wanted to ask him more but was chary of inadvertently letting slip anything which might reveal her own headstrong actions. A flashback of the brawl and her imprisonment crossed her brain. She instantly blotted it out; determined to forget the entire dangerous incident.

She said lightly, 'Well, so long as you're all right,' and added. 'What I was calling you about, earlier, was to let you know I'm flying to Vegas to spend some time with Cass before she has the baby. So I shan't see you till Christmas.' She hoped she didn't sound too dismissive of his concern for the AFF and was relieved to hear his old self respond:

'You will, Sis. In Buffalo. Had you forgotten? The try-out of *High As The Sky*. Mickey's expecting you.'

'Of course,' Gina returned, remembering. 'Yes, I'll be there. I'm looking forward to it. How is Mickey?'

She listened as Filipo told her about Mickey's busy rehearsal schedule, and everyone's hopes for the musical. He said what would really be terrific would be if *High As The Sky* was a big enough Broadway hit to set the Hollywood studios bidding for the movie rights because he was sure Mickey could make the successful transition from stage to screen. As Gina listened to his enthusiasm, her own thoughts turned from the AFF to indulge in pleasanter speculation of her brother's future.

When they eventually said goodbye, Gina leaned back on the sofa and released a grateful sigh. Though her afternoon's ordeal continued to chafe her nerves, the chat with her brother had been a welcome anodyne. Later, having bathed her physical sores, she completed her preparations for tomorrow's flight to Las Vegas. Before going to bed she took a last look out of the window. It was still sleeting.

Gina swiftly pulled the curtains on the scene.

Chapter Fifteen

Las Vegas was quite as sunny as Gina had hoped it would be. The only blot on her horizon – literally – was the huge glass tower rising from the desert, teeming with construction workers, beyond a massive roadside sign: OPENING DEC 12 * NEVADA'S MOST FABULOUS CASINO * THE RANDOLPH CORPORATION'S SENSATIONAL * BIKINI BEACH.

Gina couldn't avoid it; could see it every time she stepped out of The Silver Lady; had to pass it whenever she drove to or from the airport; almost had to shield her eyes from it at night as it blazed under hundreds of arc lamps.

She took consolation, however, from the continuing success of all West-Rossi's ventures, and, gradually, the presence of the Bikini Beach cast less of a shadow across her bright landscape until, by the time she'd been in Vegas for a couple of weeks, she was even beginning to let Oliver Randolph's dark image fade, reminding herself of the futility of vendettas and that Randolph could now do nothing to harm either her or her company.

Gina grew increasingly relaxed, as pleased as Cassie to be away from New York's worsening weather.

Before leaving the city she'd tried, twice, to contact Howard, but without success. Although, apparently, he'd still been staying at his club, he wasn't there when Gina called, nor did he respond to the messages she left. With a co-mingling of sadness and vexation Gina had decided she was quite justified in flying west.

In Las Vegas, however, her good mood rebloomed as she helped Max with his busy run-up to The Silver Lady's traditional Christmas celebrations. While Cassie was in San

Francisco, she had also taken the opportunity to visit West-Rossi's office in Los Angeles, her sister in Phoenix, and the Monument studio in Anaheim.

The latter she'd found particularly exciting. The thrill she'd felt the first day she'd visited the backlot was rekindled the moment she drove beneath the studio's grand portal. She spent two days with Felix discussing various aspects of the business, including the re-release of the Barbara Graham movies which was scheduled for next spring. Felix had been in touch with the ex-actress and she'd agreed to remain in America for a while to help generate publicity for the Barbara Graham Season.

Gina said she too would boost it to the press whenever she got the chance. She'd already been interviewed by most of the fan magazines as well as the movie trade papers and had taken all these opportunities to underline not only West-Rossi's but also her personal commitment to Monument's future.

Her interest was genuine and vigorous as, in her office at The Silver Lady, she studied film costings, production reports, distribution schedules, even movie stars' contracts, and kept in regular telephone contact with Felix.

It was during one of these calls that Felix said, 'We're doing a final reshoot on one of the outdoor scenes for *The Last Summer* tomorrow. Why don't you come over?'

Gina thought it would make an interesting day.

Warren Curtis removed his hat, held it up against the afternoon sun, surveyed the bullet-scarred Italian town square. He nodded satisfaction, returned to his canvas director's chair, replaced his hat, folded his arms and commanded, 'Right, let's get this picture finished.'

Cameramen uncapped lenses, lighting technicians adjusted reflectors, the continuity girl checked her script, a dozen other people clicked their expertise into top gear. A youth stepped forward, announced, '*The Last Summer*, scene twenty-two, take four,' and snapped his clapperboard.

The assistant director shouted, 'Action!'

Six American soldiers burst from a distant doorway and dashed across the square firing rifles at the belltower. Bullet impacts spat up a racing trail in their wake. One of them tumbled, sprawling, his helmet bouncing away across the cobbles.

Warren Curtis called, 'Cut! Perfect.'

The assistant director declared, 'That's a wrap.'

Felix Gilbert breathed, 'Thank the Lord.'

Gina enquired, 'Is it all over?'

They were standing a few yards behind Warren Curtis's chair on the Monument backlot where Gina had arrived an hour ago to watch the setting up of this scene, the re-shooting of which had taken, in actual camera-rolling time, five minutes. No wonder, she thought, movie-making is so expensive.

'Yes,' replied Felix, 'apart from the final editing and dubbing. The first rough cut should be ready for you to take a look at in about three months' time.'

'I'm looking forward to it,' said Gina. 'How were all the rushes?' she added, brandishing her technical jargon.

'Good,' answered Felix. 'Everyone's very pleased.'

'The story worked out as you'd hoped?'

'Perfectly. Just the way Fallon intended.'

Gina's pulse jumped. 'Oh, yes, Fallon,' she said, and hoped Felix didn't think her voice sounded as loud as it seemed in her own head. Affecting a nonchalant air, she remarked, 'He went away, didn't he? Is he back?'

'A few weeks ago,' said Felix.

'Wasn't he working on his novel?'

'Yes.'

'Did he get it finished?'

'Why don't you ask him.'

'What?'

'He's just coming through that doorway.'

Gina's eyes almost popped out of her head.

Fallon was wearing faded green cord pants and an open-necked denim shirt, sleeves rolled to his elbows. His hair, as usual, tumbled over his brow and ears, its streaks of grey accentuated by the deep mahogany tan of his craggy features. He strolled forward and, lips curved in a smile, said to Gina, 'Hi.'

Her face felt red hot. She said casually, 'Hello.'

Fallon turned to Felix and said something about scripts. But Gina didn't hear it. All her senses seemed to have been numbed by shock. She watched the two men exchanging words and gestures as she strove to gather the pieces of her fragmented emotions. Then Fallon was looking at her again, and she heard him say:

'By the way, congratulations on becoming a movie mogul.'

Gina managed to reply, 'Thanks.'

'Enjoying it?'

'Yes. It's interesting. Rather different from restauranting.' Gina realized she was calming down. 'But it all takes so much time,' she added, indicating the set.

Felix turned to Fallon, 'Gina's learning film-making isn't quite as straightforward as canning beans.' He gave the Englishman a wry smile. 'And that we have to make certain allowances for the artistic temperament.'

Fallon retorted, 'That'll be the day.'

'Actually,' Felix said to Gina, 'it's grizzle-headed ink-slingers like this feller the industry needs. They're tried and tested, adaptable and reliable. They'll work any time, any place, so long as you feed and water 'em regular, and give 'em an encouraging word.' He grinned. 'Just like old hounds.'

'You mean,' growled Fallon, 'just like old whores.'

Warren Curtis looked around. 'Someone mention me?'

The three men laughed and Warren joined the group. As they stood sharing movie anecdotes, Gina gradually began to feel drawn into their close circle. She ventured an opinion and the men voiced agreement and Fallon gave her an encouraging smile. A sensation of warm intimacy spread slowly through her veins.

When the general chat ended, Warren said he only had a couple more close-ups to shoot and walked away to talk to the cameraman. Felix declared he wanted a word with his secretary and went to phone from his trailer-office. Gina remained standing beside Fallon.

She was very aware of his presence.

He said, 'Have you seen the studio from the hill?'

She replied, 'No.'

'Would you like to?'

'Very much.'

Without a further word Fallon turned and led the way.

The path climbed a grassy slope, between boulders and up a gentle hillside of trees. Shafts of sunlight fell amid the branches, shimmering with winged insects. Birds sang. The sounds of the activity on the movie set gradually faded. Underfoot the earth was soft with moss, untrodden. Glancing about, finding the mock Italian piazza had been lost from sight, Gina felt they were in a wood in the middle of the countryside. But even more private, for here the land was wholly enclosed by the perimeter fencing of the studio. We're utterly alone, she silently told herself as she walked beside Fallon.

He was talking generally about movies.

Gina responded only as his pauses demanded.

As he talked on she watched him from the corner of her eyes, examining his sun-bronzed features, noting how rugged he was, yet admitting she always had thought so. She was back beside him in Ristorante Rossi, Rome, 1936, awash with his words as he shared wine and politics with her father and Max Barzini.

Total recall of those convivial evenings came surging forth from her memory. She saw every detail. Most of all she saw Fallon there – his laughter, the nuances of his voice, the eloquence of his big hands, craggy brows and wide mouth – just as she saw all this now, reacting to it exactly as she had all those years ago, with a quickening of her blood which she felt powerless to prevent.

He halted and said, 'There it is.'

Gina found they were out of the trees on a green knoll. Turning, she saw the distant piazza, from this angle the rear of the pretend buildings supported by tangled frameworks of timber and scaffolding. Over to the right were other sets – a cowboy town, a London street, a Paris square, a mediaeval castle. To the left was the river and the lake. And, far off, the studio offices and workshops and the parade of sound stages.

It was the first time Gina had seen it all spread out this way, and she stood surveying it for several minutes. When she finally turned around Fallon was sitting on the grass, leaning against a jutting rock, hands behind his head, eyes closed.

The scene at Gina's back was forgotten in the instant. She stared at Fallon. Even in repose his face had a hard vitality, suffusing her with that flush of exhilaration and unease she experienced in uncensored dreams. She stared at his mouth, stared for a long time, the impulse to kiss him consuming her like slow fire. She almost could taste his mouth on hers, his lips and teeth and tongue ...

Stop it! she commanded herself and quickly sat a few feet from Fallon, her legs tucked beneath her spread skirt.

Fallon opened his eyes, and Gina was sure he could see to the depths of her soul. After only a moment, however, he said easily, 'So, how's the dish-of-the-day trade?'

Gina's sexual urge subsided, though she didn't know whether she was relieved or disappointed. She gave what she hoped was a casual shrug and replied, 'About the same as always. You know, so long as you don't shortchange the customers and can make them smile once in a while, they'll keep coming around to see what's cooking.'

Fallon nodded. 'Much the same as novel writing.'

'Felix said you'd finished your latest.'

'Apart from the editing.'

'When will it be published?'

'Around the middle of next year in Britain; Europe and Scandinavia too. Maybe never over here.'

Surprised, Gina said, 'Doesn't the US publisher like it?'

'He doesn't like what's in it,' answered Fallon. 'Or, rather, he's afraid of what's in it.'

Gina remained puzzled only for a second before remembering that the last time she'd seen Fallon he'd said his novel was about what he'd called 'the fear that's stalking America'. She ventured, 'Surely they wouldn't stop publication because of that. You're established here. Both your last books were bestsellers.'

'If some libraries and stores can ban W.H. Auden and Sherwood Anderson, they're certainly not going to shed any tears for the loss of Robert Fallon.'

'I didn't know those authors had been banned.'

'Plus a few others. Word hasn't generally got around yet.

But it will. Then the panic to get rid of all suspect literature will start. Pretty soon they'll be burning books in public.'

Gina said unbelievingly, 'That couldn't happen here.'

Fallon returned, 'A year or two ago I'd have agreed. There was a moment back then when the UnAmerican Activities circus might've begun to run out of steam. But that was before McCarthy raised his reptilian head. He'd crucify anybody just to further his own ambitions.'

Gina inwardly flinched at the harsh words.

'And his disease is catching,' continued Fallon. 'A while ago so-called friendly witnesses were denouncing Communist sympathizers just to protect their own necks, to preserve their Beverly Hills mansions and inflated Hollywood salaries. Now they've started using the system to square off old grudges, get rid of their enemies and rivals. The whole rotten business hardly has anything to do with politics any more. It's corruption, the pursuit of personal power, plain and simple.' Fallon halted there, staring out across the studio vale.

Gina remained still, lost in his words. She hadn't heard him talk this way since wartime London. It unnerved her, but at the same time drew her to him in greater intimacy.

Fallon turned to her and said, 'Sorry. Climbing on my high horse again. I appreciate the vast majority of Americans are neither McCarthyites nor Communists. They're just ordinary people who want to believe in their Government. That's how it always is.' The hard light in his eyes softened. 'Anyhow,' he added, 'I brought you up here to show you the view, not bend your ear. Habit. You remember?'

Gina struggled to produce a casual smile. She remembered only too well her time with Fallon; it was what she had tried so hard to forget. Now she was fully aware she should not have walked up here with him this afternoon. But, perversely and undeniably, she was glad she had.

He said, 'Maybe I shouldn't have brought you at all.'

Gina heard herself ask: 'Why?'

He answered, 'Because you're very beautiful.'

Gina's mouth ran dry.

Fallon muttered, 'I'd told myself I wouldn't say that.'

Gina swallowed to bring moisture to her throat. Taking a breath, she said, 'So you'd imagined you might?'

'Of course I'd imagined I might. I've been imagining it ever since you walked into the Oasis in Palm Springs.'

'Well,' Gina tried to sound nonchalant, 'there's no harm in imagination.' Her heart was hammering in her chest.

'The hell there isn't,' returned Fallon.

'Did you know I'd be here today?'

'Felix phoned last night. But, please, don't suppose he was an accomplice. It was all my own idea.'

'I'm very flattered. But …'

'But had I forgotten you were married? Of course not. So, what was I thinking of? I wasn't thinking at all. Just responding to instinct. Maybe playing a hunch.'

'A hunch that I'd want to come up this hill?'

Fallon ran a hand through his tumbling hair, exhaled. 'Which makes it sound as if I figured you'd be easy. I'm sorry, Gina, I didn't intend …' He lapsed into silence.

Gina said quietly, 'Don't be. You know me very well. Perhaps better than I know myself.'

Fallon reached out. 'Gina …'

'No …' Gina drew her hand away, but not abruptly. Although she remained afraid of her emotions all at once she felt strangely in control of the situation. She said, 'I can't Fallon. Not at this moment. Don't ask me why, because I'm really unsure. I admit, I'm a little mixed up. But that isn't your fault. And, believe me, I'm not sorry I'm here, nor angry with you for inviting me.'

Fallon searched her face. At last he nodded. 'I guess we'd better be getting back.'

Gina let out her breath with a small smile. 'Yes.' She stood, reached around to brush stray grass from her skirt and almost automatically asked, Are my seams straight? and although she bit back the words, the rush of butterflies in her stomach caused by the simple thought of Fallon looking at her legs, underlined how dangerously close she still was to the brink.

Fallon said, 'They're packing up.'

Gina saw that he was standing surveying the distant Italian piazza where a truck was being loaded. She said, 'The final shots of *The Last Summer*. Will you be here to watch the editing?' She started slowly across the slope.

Fallon walked at her side. 'Not right away. I'm flying to England next week, to see my publisher, and complete a couple of magazine pieces I've been asked to do.'

Gina kept the disappointment out of her voice. 'When will you be back over here?'

'After Christmas. Felix has some publicity interviews lined up. But I'll want to get down to some writing too.' He looked toward Gina. 'So I'll be at the Oasis again.'

Gina glanced at him without breaking her stride. 'I'll know where to get in touch with you then.'

Fallon said, 'Whenever you want to.'

They went on down the hill.

She was hugely relieved he'd gone to England. For, despite the composure she'd demonstrated during their brief encounter, over the following days, back in Las Vegas, Gina was clawed by her emotions. She told herself she still loved Howard, but she could not get Fallon out of her head. She desperately wanted to believe in the sanctity of her marriage, yet was unable to repel the seduction of her thoughts. Whenever she imagined the Englishman she re-experienced the sense of intimacy she'd felt on the Monument backlot as they shared their mutual interests. But each time she mentally turned to her husband she could see him only at a distance, across the gulf which separated their lives.

Gina felt trapped in this tormenting web.

She had to break free. And work, she was certain, was the answer. She thrust her mind into a mill of documents, letters, reports and costings. But, ultimately, it was none of these which snapped the threads.

The sun had set by the time she returned from the downtown business meeting and drove into the car park at the rear of The Silver Lady. It was shadowy here, the exterior floodlights not yet on. As Gina carried her briefcase and a couple of box files toward the building's service entrance she caught a movement from the corner of her eye.

She quickly turned, halting, to peer into the semi-darkness amidst the ranks of silent automobiles. Nothing stirred. Gina scanned the scene. The car park was deserted. And yet ... Scratchy fingers of apprehension crept up her back and she was sure she was being watched.

'Mrs Cornell.'

Gina's heart leapt to her throat.

The floodlights flared.

'May I help you with those?' The blue-uniformed security guard stepped out of the doorway and walked toward Gina, hands extending for the box files she was clutching. 'Nights are drawing in fast now,' he remarked. 'Better set the lights to come on earlier.'

Gina found her voice. 'Yes, it was rather dark out here.' Allowing the guard to take the files, she surveyed the now brightly-lit car park: shining metal and glass; but no person. 'Did you see anybody else over there a moment ago,' she asked, trying to sound casual.

The guard shook his head. 'Can't say I did. You figure you saw something? Coyote more'n likely. In off the desert. Sniffing in the back of the kitchens. Around the swill bins.'

Gina nodded and she started with him toward the entrance doors. Something plucked at the chords of her memory. She hesitated; but the thought was gone. With one look over her shoulder she went into The Silver Lady.

Ten minutes later, at her desk, she relived the incident. Had there been someone? Could it have been a prairie dog? The more she thought about it the less sure of her senses she became. Should she phone the police? And tell them what? About the burglar in New York? Then they'd deduce she was still suffering from nerves. Perhaps she was. No denying, these past few days her brain had been far from relaxed.

The phone rang.

Gina cried out in alarm.

The bell jangled again. 'Idiot,' she reproved herself and lifted the receiver and said, 'Hello.'

'Hi, Hon,' said Cassie.

Gina let out a silent sigh. 'Cass,' she said, a smile coming into her voice, 'it's good to hear you.' She got her mind into second gear. 'How's it going there?'

'Fine. Everything's under control. The Embarcadero

Cornell sign arrived today. Looks terrific, but we've covered it up so's the press can't get any pictures till the opening. I was just ringing to say I think I'd better be getting back there now.'

'Are you all right?'

'Sure. Just a bit wobbly, that's all. But I don't want anything premature happening here. Less than a month to go. I reckon it would be best to spend the time closer to home. I mean, in Vegas.'

'I'm sure you're right,' agreed Gina. 'Can't be too careful. When will you be coming down?'

'Say the day after tomorrow. How are you fixed for some free time? I'd like to do some Christmas shopping, and maybe spend a while in the sun with my feet up before I have to start keeping an eye open for Junior's arrival.'

'That will be lovely,' returned Gina, her thoughts now firmly back on their rails. 'I have to fly over to Buffalo – you remember, for the opening of Mickey's show – but I'll be there and back inside forty-eight hours. Then we can spend as long as you like doing as little as possible. Cass, I'm already looking forward to it.'

They exchanged another five minutes gossip before cutting the connection. Gina leaned back. A simple telephone call, but it had been all she needed to set her senses to rights. The shadow in the car park was consigned to her mental OUT tray. And when, an hour later, she went down to join Max for dinner, for the first time since last week's visit to Monument, Gina was free of the images of both Robert Fallon and Howard Cornell.

The first-night try-out of *High As The Sky* at the Buffalo Little Theatre had success written all over it. Harry said so. And Harry knew more than a thing or two about audience reactions. Even before the interval he whispered in Gina's ear:

'Listen to them. Look at them. They love it. Most of all they love Miss Michelle Rooney.'

Gina reached out and squeezed his hand. She really felt quite thrilled for Mickey. Since the bubbly blonde had danced her first solo spot ten minutes into the show, an almost audible crackle of excitement had greeted her every subsequent appearance. And not only was Gina happy for the girl, but for Filipo too; she couldn't remember when she'd last seen him as ebullient as he was tonight.

He'd been backstage almost until curtain-up, and immediately the interval lights came on, with a few hurried, enthusiastic words, was on his way back there.

Gina declined Harry's suggestion of a drink in the bar, and they spent the interval discussing the show, Harry reiterating that he was sure it would be a success when it reached Broadway. Certainly his optimism seemed well-founded.

When the final curtain came down, the audience practically leapt to its feet. Gina didn't count the calls but they went on and on, and each time Mickey took her individual bow there was no mistaking the swell in the ovation.

Eventually the crowd began its jostle toward the exits.

Filipo said, 'Come on, let's go and give them our congratulations,' and led the way toward the side door.

Gina willingly followed, pleased for the opportunity as she had turned down the invitation to the later after-show party, preferring to be in time for the midnight train to New York in order to manage a little sleep before catching tomorrow's early flight back to Las Vegas.

As Filipo went on ahead, Gina and Harry were waylaid several times by show business acquaintances. At last, however, they were through the backstage door, and into a bigger racket of activity than there'd been in the auditorium.

Everybody was milling around the corridors and dressing rooms, congratulating themselves and each other, laughing, singing, swigging from all manner of pots and glasses, entertaining friends, posing for photographs, clustering at the pay phones, and jubilantly sharing the success which they all knew was coming their way.

Gina, Harry behind, struggled forward and eventually spotted Filipo and Mickey amid the throng.

'Hey, Sis, shove in here,' called Filipo above the din, hauling her forward with one hand, sticking a mug of something fizzy into her fist with the other.

Mickey, still in her bright stage make-up, beamed, 'Gina, it's super to see you. Wasn't it fantastic? I mean, the audience, the applause, everything. I can't get over it. Really, I'm just so excited I could jump up and down. Isn't it great? And isn't it going to be marvellous on Broadway. We'll have such a time. Barbara says we'll have such a time.'

Gina's own sparkle faltered. 'Barbara?'

'Yes. Where is she? Barbara, there you are.'

Barbara Graham turned from a nearby group. 'Hello, Gina,' she smiled, her voice strongly confident amid the babble. She was wearing purple silk evening pants and a paler toning shirt with half sleeves and a neck widely open to reveal the lines of her collar bones. A single large amber stone rested in the hollow of her throat. Her jet hair was swept to one side, pinned with a tortoiseshell comb.

As she came forward, the press of bodies opened before her. She halted between Mickey and Filipo, touched darkly nailed fingers to their cheeks then slipped her arms about their waists. 'Aren't they both wonderful,' she said to Gina. 'And aren't I lucky they came to bring me back to life.'

Gina managed to respond with a smile. But all at once she felt vaguely ill at ease at the ex-actress's presence here, beside Filipo. Later, it transpired that Barbara Graham was an old friend of the producer, was here at his invitation. Still Gina couldn't fully recapture her earlier cheeriness and wasn't too sorry when Harry said they'd better be on their way to catch the train.

Filipo said he'd come to see them off at the station, but Gina told him to stay and enjoy himself. She kissed him at the theatre door, told him to keep wrapped up in this cold weather and that she'd see him at The Silver Lady for the family Christmas party.

In the taxi she rubbed her gloved hand over the misted window to look out at the dark, frosty streets. She shivered. Someone walking over her grave.

'Cold?' asked Harry.

Gina shook off her premonitions, raised a smile. 'I certainly won't be sorry to be back in the sun,' she said.

Chapter Sixteen

Not a breath of breeze stirred the spiky yellow grasses sprouting amid the boulders along the deserted shore. No sound, save the quiet lap of water on shingle, and the occasional faint cry of a bird. The shelf of flat ground a hundred yards from the dirt road gave an elevated view across Lake Mead. Far to the south a tourist steamer plied its leisurely course, laying a thin wake like a trail of white paint on the perfect blue. The distant shore was a sliver of antique gold; beyond, the mountains hung like smoke against the cloudless late afternoon.

Gina sighed with warm relaxation.

She and Cassie were sitting in folding canvas chairs on the shelf of flat ground. Between them, a small table with a butterfly and several bright insects picnicking amid the remains of lunch. Gina was wearing old blue jeans and a chambray workshirt. Cassie was in a pale green smock embroidered across the bodice. Both were hatless, make-upless, heads back, arms draped beside their chairs, sheens of perspiration on their closed eyelids and upper lips.

It was three days since Gina's trip to Buffalo. She and Cassie had completed their Christmas shopping, card writing and gift wrapping and had elected to spend today doing absolutely nothing.

They'd come out to Lake Mead this morning, spent their time pottering, gossiping, lazing along this unfrequented stretch of north-west shore, seeing not another living soul apart from a similarly dawdling shaggy big-horn sheep and the half-dozen brown-and-blue ducks which were currently ahead of them down the slope paddling and bobbing in endless soporific circles.

Cassie yawned and opened her eyes. 'I think I could get used to this. Too used to it. If I don't move soon I maybe never will.' With a wheeze she hauled herself to sit upright. 'How many times did I fall asleep today?'

Gina smiled. 'Thirty three.'

'One more than you. Must be my greater age.'

'Twelve months can make all the difference.'

'So can twenty pounds.' Cassie, with a sideways-forwards-upwards lurch, rose to her feet.

Gina watched. Though she'd been witness over the past months to her friend's increasing size, she still at odd moments was hard put to reconcile the present ungainly, dumpling figure with the svelte, curvy female who'd set Max's moustachios twirling the May evening she'd arrived at The Silver Lady.

As if sharing the remembrance, Cassie planted her legs apart, set her hands on her belly. 'Pretty elegant, huh?'

'You look great ... I mean, wonderful,' responded Gina, rising to join her friend. She gazed toward the distant crags; behind them the sky was deepening from cobalt to indigo and their smoky peaks were beginning to burn orange in the setting sun. 'I guess we'd better head for home,' she said, 'before the mountain lions start looking for their supper.' She lifted the picnic hamper, began to load it with the crockery and cutlery.

Everything was soon stashed; the furniture folded. 'No, don't you start lifting anything,' Gina vetoed when Cassie bent toward a chair. 'I can manage it all in a couple of trips.'

'Perhaps you're right,' conceded Cassie, slowly, straightening. She took the remains of a loaf from beside the table. 'Not much point in carting this back. I'll give it to the ducks.'

Gina cautioned, 'Don't fall in – not without shouting a warning to Hoover Dam.' She sidestepped, grinning, as Cassie raised a mock fist, then gathering half their kit she set off toward the distant, parked car.

It took her but a few minutes. By the time she returned, Cassie had negotiated the slope to the pebble beach, was standing at the water's edge pulling the bread into pieces. Gina joined her.

'Come on, Donald,' called Cassie, tossing a rag of crust upward and outward. It plopped onto the water a few feet from the shore, yards short of the intended recipient. After a moment's deliberation, a couple of ducks paddled warily forward, but veered away before reaching the morsel.

'Hopeless,' joshed Gina good-humouredly, taking a piece of bread, winding up her arm, firing the tidbit like a baseball over the heads of the chary birds. 'Cass, you'll never make pitcher for the Yankees.'

'Well DiMaggio wouldn't have been so brilliant if he'd had a fifty-inch waist.' Cassie poised for another shot.

'Joe was a batter, not a ...'

Cassie flung wide and high, and as the bread sailed into the air, her right foot skidded on the shale, shot upward, apparently to pursue the flying dough. With a yell which sent the ducks flapping, splashing skyward she toppled back, landed with a thump on her rear.

Gina gasped, 'Ohmygoodness ...' starting forward.

Then she halted, staring at her friend: the globular figure, legs stuck out, toes pointing vertically, hands planted flat on the ground. And, try as she might, Gina was powerless to suppress the laugh which started as a deep chuckle in her belly, burgeoning as it bubbled toward her chest, into her throat, to burst so loudly from her lips that she clapped her hand to her mouth. Even then she was unable to prevent further eruption as her mind refused to obliterate the memory which Cassie's dumpling pose had bidden. 'I ... I ...' she attempted, but Cassie's wide-eyed indignation only convulsed her the more and she swung away, clutching her sides, hooting like a loon.

The attack persisted for a full minute.

At last Gina, gasping for breath, choked back the spasms of mirth and wiped the streaming tears from her eyes. She turned to her friend, stifling a final giggle. 'I'm sorry, Cass. Truly ...'

Cassie fixed her with mighty gall. 'I'm glad you find it amusing. Really ...' She struggled to roll sideways in an attempt to stand, but didn't make it. 'People who get a ...' Puffing, she tried the other direction. '... a rise out of other folk's ... misfortunes ...' Again she failed, flopped back to her sitting position with a grunt of exasperation. Glowering at Gina she declared, 'Well, they're just ... warped, that's all.'

Gina dropped her grin in exaggerated repentance. 'I know. I'm terrible. I'll never go to heaven. It's just that you reminded me of ... something.' She looked down at her friend from beneath contrite brows, slowly offered both hands, and an irrepressible smile.

Uttering something like, 'Harumph,' Cassie accepted the assistance and after much heaving and blowing eventually was on her feet facing Gina. For a long moment they traded stare for stare. Then Cassie's features wreathed into a grin and she said, 'I guess I should be thankful I wasn't alone. I could've been stranded on my duff for days. Like a beached whale.'

They both laughed at that and, arm in arm, reclimbed the slope to the desert flat. 'By the way,' said Cassie, waiting with her hands in the small of her back while Gina gathered the remaining picnic equipment. 'You said I reminded you of something. So? Confess. What?'

Gina bit her lip as they commenced the trek to the car. 'Well ... Promise you won't bop me. Okay. When I was in London, during the war, they had fearful air raids. As a precaution against enemy planes the Ministry of Defence raised, on wires, hundreds of ...' She glanced at Cassie's rapt expression. Then down to her figure. And ...

Here it came again. She couldn't prevent it. She must. How utterly foolish to be beset by such giggles. She swallowed and clenched her teeth, looked dead ahead, not daring to take so much as another glimpse of her portly pal and tramped determinedly forward, trying so fiercely to stamp out the memory of the great, wallowing, wobbling thing she'd seen tethered to the ground like a gigantic captive caterpillar in Hyde Park. How childish, she reproved herself. How childish.

'Yes?' prompted Cassie.

Gina's jaws were locked.

'Are you going to tell me?'

Gina halted, slowly swivelled her head toward Cassie. She knew she couldn't contain the laugh, but in the split second before it burst forth she blurted:

'A barrage balloon.'

Then she was stumbling the final steps to the car, banging against it, braying and wheezing in an awesome effort at self-control. She sucked in air; nailed her concentration on the dusty black gleam of the car's roof; strove for a rational thought. Cass, I couldn't help it. Bop me if you want. Gina's mind formed the words. She turned to deliver them. Saw Cassie's lips pulled back in a grin, her hands clasped to her stomach; heard her rasp:

'Oh, God. Oh, God.'

Gina's humour drained. For seconds a hail of uncertainty stormed her brain until all at once she recognized reality. In an instant she was dashing to her friend's side, reaching for her but hesitating, piniioned by fear as she stared at the ashen face, the bared teeth, the eyes that beseeched release. Gina whispered raggedly, 'Cass,' breaking her own spell to seize the redhead's shoulders, tightly grip them, willing strength through her own fingers, praying for the agony before her to pass.

Cassie gasped, 'Moses,' and the paralysis of her features abruptly dissolved as she slumped, panting, against Gina. When at last her breathing steadied, she moved back a pace and raised a feeble but stoic smile. To the question in Gina's eyes she said, 'No, it wasn't indigestion.'

'You mean ...' But Gina really needed no explanation, and in her mental tumult she scarcely heard Cassie add:

'I reckon falling on my butt must've bounced Junior awake. Didn't do his patience a lot of good either.' She winced. 'And I've got more'n a sneaky feeling he isn't about to wait another three weeks for his birthday.'

Gina hesitated only one more second before responding, 'So we'd best get all three of us out of here, and soon,' the briskness of her tone as much to bolster her own shell-shocked confidence as Cassie's. Gripping her friend's arm she started carefully toward the car. 'Feeling better now? You look fine. Here we are. Hold on to the roof a minute while I find the keys.' She bent to open the dropped picnic hamper, found her purse as Cassie leaned against the car. 'Won't be a second.' She inserted the key in the lock, turned it ...

Cassie groaned.

Gina jerked around. And realized how fast night was falling. She barely could distinguish her friend's face. But she could see lividly the wide open mouth. The silent scream pierced her eardrums, raw anguish sending knives down her spine. This shouldn't be happening; not another contraction so soon. Sweat burst across Gina's shoulders, flowed suddenly, icily beneath her blouse.

She prayed, prayed for the spasm to pass.

'Dear Jesus,' gasped Cassie, beginning to crumple.

Gina's arms went around the heavy figure, holding strongly. 'Take it easy, Let's get you inside.' Her own voice surprised her, its calm assurance belying her inner turmoil. 'Everything's all right, Cass.' She pulled open the rear door. 'Just lower down there. Mind your head. That's good. Feet up.' The struggle in the confines of the doorway was mercifully brief. As Gina looked into Cassie's face she almost recoiled from its yellowness before realizing the colour was a reflection of the car's interior lights. 'Hey,' she smiled encouragingly. 'How're you doing?'

Cassie gave a single, slow shake of her head. 'Oh, Hon, it hurt. I never knew it'd hurt so much.' Closing her eyes she fell back against the upholstery, her breath coming in short, hard gasps.

Again Gina reached for rationality. How many contractions should there be? When might the last one come? Damn it, why didn't she know these things. A co-mingling of anger and anguish welled through her, while into her head reared ominous memories: her mother in bed, face so drained it was whiter than the pillow, lips as translucent as dying leaves; in a crib, the new-born son; gathered around, the family, nurses, a doctor, the priest.

Stop wasting time, Gina's inner voice warned.

She said determinedly, 'Don't worry, Cass. It's going to be okay. I'll have us back in Vegas before you know it.' It actually would take, she guessed, over twenty minutes. Of course that was time enough. With a reassuring pat to Cassie's clasped hands she shut the rear door, opened the front, slid swiftly behind the wheel; paused to reinforce her self-control. Be calm. Drive carefully. Don't take unnecessary risks.

Gina started the motor, switched on the headlamps and rolled the car onto the desert road.

Blackness surrounded them, so impenetrable beyond the lamps' cone of light they seemed scarcely to be moving but Gina hastily lessened her pressure on the gas pedal when she saw she had the speedometer needle actually hovering on 60. Steadying the velocity along with her nerves she glanced in the rearview mirror, realized it was too dark to see Cassie. 'Is everybody back there happy?' she called, hoping such cheeriness wasn't misplaced, heartened to hear a strained but spirited:

'Just peachy.'

To underline the optimism, Las Vegas came into view.

Fourteen miles across the valley, yet the individual casinos – splashes of crimson, yellow, orange – were unmistakable, and beckoning spectacularly white and blue in their midst, The Silver Lady. Never had Gina been so pleased to see the lights of home. With an exhalation of relief she announced, 'Land ho! Cass. Not long now. Then we'll all be calling you Momma.'

What a monumental thought that was. Gina took strength from it, concentrated on it to keep her mind from retreating into fear. She told herself how wonderful it was going to be to have a baby in her life. Remember, like when Paola's children were born. There'd be so much to do for the new member of the family. I wonder where Cass will choose to live? Out here, the countryside is fine, fresh air, sunshine. But, you know, a young mind shouldn't be allowed to become too insular, it ought to know the marvels of the city – museums, galleries, libraries, movie houses, even department stores. I wouldn't trade the years I grew up in Rome, Cass. I saw so much, learned so much, even though I didn't realize it at the time. How about you? You recall your childhood in Manhattan. Don't you agree it ...

Cassie's scream tore through the car.

Gina's fists convulsed on the wheel. Her foot reflexively stamped on the brake, and she saw the hood dip but hold its course as the car skidded forward. Dust and grit splattered alongside. Abruptly they were still. Cassie's scream continued to batter within the closed space, agony-laden, pleading for release, and quivered on the air long after it had ended.

Gina was scrambling over the front seat, her hair snagging in the ceiling light, her ankle tearing on something as she tumbled into the rear compartment and struggled to her knees in an attempt to gather Cassie into her arms but recoiled as the scream came again.

It ripped around the walls like a demented bird so that Gina clamped her hands to her ears, shrank as if from a physical assault. She thought it would go on forever; but at last it began to die, trembling to a whisper, finally shuddering to a series of racking sobs.

Gina's blood was roaring. In the blackness, fear was a rake of talons on her flesh, shredding her reason. What am I doing down here? I shouldn't have stopped. I should be speeding us on to the hospital. Her impulse to return immediately to the driving seat was snapped as she felt Cassie's fingers grasp her hand. Returning the pressure she whispered, 'I'm here, Cass.'

The broken voice appealed, 'Don't ... leave ... Gina.'

'Of course I won't. Just let me turn on the light.' She reached up to the ceiling, found the switch.

Once more they were bathed in pale yellow. As Gina's gaze returned to Cassie she bit her lip to stifle a cry. The redhead seemed to have aged ten years. Dark circles shadowed her eyes; the muscles of her jaw were tensed, drawing her skin taut on the bones; and over all her face perspiration stood in glistening beads, ran in strings to her throat, plastered her hair to her brow in dark coils.

Cassie rasped, 'Not ... going ... to make it, Hon.'

Bunching her fists, Gina fought to subdue her own harsh breathing, to blot out all thoughts save the practicalities of what to do. Regaining some of her self-control she rigidly rolled the sleeves of her blouse past her elbows. This simple move strengthened her grip on rationality. She found a handkerchief in her pocket, gently wiped Cassie's face.

'Do you think ... I woke the neighbours?' Cassie managed, her lips beginning to curve but wrenching into a rictus of pain as her head snapped back on rigid shoulders.

Gina flinched, expecting the scream. But, mercifully, it

didn't come. Cassie remained braced against the seat, apparently paralysed save for the heaving of her breast. Gina could hear the creaking of it, as if the straining of it would break Cassie's ribs. She was sure she could feel a pressure around her own heart, a fist closing and closing, cutting off the blood to her brain. Her vision blurred. Panic pounced onto her shoulders.

Cassie drew a huge, jagged breath.

Her chest didn't fall.

Gina was so still, so aware of the passing moments she thought she could feel the very earth turn beneath the car. Despairingly her mind sobbed, God, don't let them die.

She would hold the following minutes in her memory for the rest of her life; and yet she'd be unable to recall the details of any of them. Whenever she brought the episode to mind she'd experience only fractured pieces of sights and sounds; Cassie's face rupturing from rigidity to shattering contortion; her voice choking and scraping in shreds of incoherence; her fists, viced bone-white into her own hair; her stomach convulsing.

Gina would remember sweat, swamping her eyes. She'd remember heat boiling within and around her as if the car were drowning in steam. She'd remember somehow lifting Cassie's legs and tearing the skirt of her dress. She'd remember her friend's sounds, all her sounds, on and on. And she'd remember the water, pink water everywhere, streaming, swimming, saturating her from waist to toes.

All this was confusion.

But then she saw the baby's head.

And clarity returned in an instant. Automatically, Gina reached out to cradle the head in her palms as it exited so slowly. Cassie had fallen suddenly silent. The entire world seemed to be silent. Gina felt and saw the tiny figure imperceptibly appearing. She could scarcely believe her eyes; was no longer certain whether any of this was reality or just a fantastic dream.

Then there was a squelching sound.

Cassie gasped.

Gina cried, 'Oh!'

The object of her amazement was suddenly in her hands.

She was holding it. All of it. It was squirming. Alive. This shiny, scarlet, slippery being was alive, legs bending, fingers clutching, tiny lips moving. What a monumental miracle; a brand new person arrived on earth, stranger in a strange land. Gina was speechless. For several heartbeats she was awestruck to the point of paralysis.

It was the cry which broke the moment.

A single yell, so loud, so unexpected, Gina almost dropped the fleshy bundle from which it had burst. Thank God, she thought as she saw the small chest rising and falling, and her own breath returned. Elation as well as a sort of exhaustion rushed upon her and she whispered, marvelling, 'It's a boy, Cass. You've got a son.'

Cassie strained to peer downward. 'Is he all right?'

'What?' Gina blinked away the tears which were blinding her sight. Dragging her senses back on a straight course, she surveyed the miniature man. 'He's perfect,' she assured. 'Look,' turning him, shuffling her knees with infinite care to display the infant. 'Isn't he incredible. He's real. What a silly thing to say. But, see, he's got hair, and eyelashes, and everything. Cass, it's just too marvellous. Here, take him, you ... Oh!'

The umbilical cord was still attached.

'There's cotton thread in my purse,' Cassie said practically. 'It'll do until we reach the hospital. Don't look so surprised. I read all the books, remember.' She took her son, held him to her side, delicately touching the back of her fingers to his cheeks. Fatigue still shadowed her face but the pain had disappeared, and in its place glowed a deep and utter joy. Looking up at Gina she said quietly, 'Thanks, Hon. From both of us.'

Gina's throat was too tight to speak.

Chapter Seventeen

'And then we simply drove back to Vegas,' Gina said nonchalantly to her sister on the telephone, telling the story for the thirtieth time some eighteen hours later.

It had been mid-morning today before Gina finally quit the hospital. Last night she'd fretted for two hours until a doctor had reported mother and child to be one hundred per cent fit. Cassie had been given a mild sedative and couldn't be visited but Gina had insisted on staying. She sat on a wooden chair by the wall amid the to-ings and fro-ings of casualty reception and fell into a well of dreamless relief. No one disturbed her and she didn't wake until six am.

Her reunion with Cassie and baby was timeless happiness, until, eventually, she'd had to be almost forcibly removed from the premises. Even then, for several more minutes she'd remained sitting in the car, oblivious to the shambles in the rear seat, reliving the night's events, repeatedly murmuring to herself, 'Amazing. Absolutely Amazing.'

It wasn't until a sudden, sirening ambulance jolted her back to reality that she realized she hadn't phoned a soul. Yesterday, before leaving on their trip, Gina had left word at The Silver Lady she and Cassie might spend the night at Lake Mead Lodge. Nobody would be questioning their whereabouts. Nobody knew what had happened.

Inside an hour about half the world knew.

Cassie and the baby were kept in hospital for the next five days until the doctors were satisfied there were no adverse effects from the premature birth. At last the all-clear was given. Gina made a final check of the bunting and WELCOME HOME banner bedecked party room, practised with everyone their 'Surprise! Surprise!' routine, listened one more time to the band's rehearsal of *Baby Face*, then took off in The Silver Lady's largest, shiniest limousine to collect mother and son in presidential style.

She got as far as the first intersection.

She'd forgotten. Gina had overlooked entirely the fact that this was the day of the parade. In her stationary vehicle she drummed her fingers on the wheel, rapped both feet on impotent pedals as another float – the eleventh, maybe even twelfth – rolled by.

She'd known about the event for weeks, but since the birth her mind had been too filled with Cass and the baby to find space for recall of the opening of the Randolph Corporation's casino. It had not jammed itself back into her consciousness until she'd been halted here by a traffic cop to discover she was in the splendid (she didn't think) pole position for the passing display.

The theme was America Through The Ages, commencing with a replica of the Mayflower (Columbus, needless to say, did not figure in the Randolph version of history), followed by a series of showy floats, bands, all manner of marching clubs, and platoons from all branches of the armed forces. There was plenty of noise, colour and movement to captivate the onlookers' attention, and, at frequent intervals, pairs of long-legged females in pink two-piece bathing suits, gold capes and stiletto heels flourishing above their heads the orange-on-turquoise proclamation:

WE'RE ALL GOING TO THE BIKINI BEACH

Gina was unable to salve the prickliness of her emotions, but she held on to her temper, strove to subjugate her darker memories of the gross man, determined not to let him spoil her day.

To be honest, if the cause of her being stuck at this intersection had been anyone other than Oliver Randolph, she would have conceded, willingly, the passing spectacle was, though somewhat jingoistic, a crowd-stopper. Witness the throng: very nearly every resident and visitor in the city seemed to be lined along both sides of the street.

'Thank goodness for that,' Gina breathed, noting the half-dozen girls on the next trundling tinselled platform were wearing short shimmery dresses, charlestoning precariously. This meant they'd reached the 'Twenties. Only a couple of decades to go. Let's hope Randolph hadn't devoted too much of the procession to the patriotic exploits of World War Two.

Four more floats and Gina craned frustratedly forward in an effort to see if the end was in sight.

A spaceship (or it might have been a giant bomb) painted with stars and stripes and the message 'Into The Future' came rolling on the rear of a silver-sprayed truck. The final pair of swimsuited girls high-stepping past with their flaring banner, the one on this side turning to wave and flash dazzling teeth in Gina's direction.

Gina growled and switched on the ignition. The policeman swung around, gave a small salute and an arm-sweeping gesture, his lips mouthing, Go ahead now. Gina drove forward, smiled tautly through her side window and mouthed back, Thank you so much, officer.

'He was only doing his job,' remarked Cassie.

'His job,' insisted Gina, 'does not include facilitating Oliver Randolph's publicity stunts.'

'Facilitating,' repeated Cassie to the infant in the carrycot. 'Big word. Educational stuff. I hope you're taking note, Junior.' She smiled at Gina, winked broadly.

They were in the hospital lobby where Gina had arrived a few moments ago – half an hour late – to collect her friend as arranged. Cassie had been waiting on a bench, suitcase at her feet, son in the cot at her side. 'Hi,' she'd greeted blithely as Gina came hurrying in. 'Did you stop to watch the parade?' Now she suggested, 'Maybe you should send a stiff postcard to the Chief of Police.'

Gina could contain her indignation only another moment. With a laugh she blew it out. Affectionately touching a hand to the baby's tan elflocks, she asked, 'May I carry him out?' and when Cassie responded, 'Since when did you have to ask?' she reached for the blue-smocked infant and lifted him, happily making boo-boo-boo noises into his cheery, chubby face.

She loved him. Gina loved the feel, the sound, the smell

of him. She'd visited Cassie each day since the birth, declaring she was positive he was growing, his grip was getting stronger, his hair longer, his eyes greener, that he for sure recognized her. At every opportunity she'd raised and snuggled him, constantly marvelled that here was the result of the traumatic events beside Lake Mead. And, thankfully, she had experienced no recurrence of grief at the reminder that she herself could never be a mother. She felt no jealousy toward her friend. Gina was content in her acceptance of her place in the baby's life.

She walked with him out to the sunny parking lot.

'There,' she said, partly turning him to face across the highway to the desert, mountains and gentian blue of December sky. 'The world.' The infant looked. A breeze touched the silken hair above his ears and he made a small sound, raising a hand, tiny fingers opening and closing as if he might catch the invisible stranger.

A few minutes later Gina was back in the driving seat, Cassie was in the rear of the limousine with the cot. Gina was about to start the motor when Cassie appealed:

'Hold on, Hon. There's something I want to tell you before we get back to The Silver Lady. Don't try kidding me there won't be a reception committee waiting. I don't mind. I'm looking forward to it, even practised a short speech, to say thanks, on behalf of Junior and me, for all the visits, cards, presents, and, most of all, the affection everyone's given.'

'Lovely,' said Gina to the rearview mirror. 'They'll be pleased. I mean, anybody who just happens to be around when we arrive. So, better be going ...'

'But that wasn't what I was getting at,' said Cassie. 'The thing of it is, they're all going to be repeating the question they've asked a thousand times already this past week. I want to announce the answer before they get the chance.'

Gina stared bemusedly at the reflection of her friend.

'Junior,' said Cassie. 'Everybody keeps calling him Junior. From the moment I woke up the morning-after-the-night-before you've been telling me I have to make up my mind on a name, a proper name. Well ... I have.'

'Wonderful,' returned Gina. 'Yes? What?'

'You know I've had hundreds of suggestions, searched through dozens of lists and books. There are a lot of new names around right now, after movie stars mostly, but I don't really care for any of them. This was the one I wanted all along. I've always liked it. It's plain, but, I think, manly. And we're both used to it now,' tickling under the baby's chin, 'aren't we? We've been kind of practising with it in this last couple of days. Plus, I wrote it in my diary.' Cassie found the small leather volume in her purse, opened it. 'See. That's when it happened. The date.' She handed the book to Gina.

Written in blue ink, beneath December 6th was: Robert's Birthday'.

'Is it okay?' Cassie ventured. 'You don't mind?'

Gina stared at the name for several moments. She hadn't seen it hand-written for a long time; six years, since she thus addressed a letter, and, when she was seventeen, on a slip of paper she carried in her purse. She turned and handed back the diary, looked at the child engrossed in examination of his mother's hand. 'Of course I don't mind,' she said, smiling. 'It's a fine choice, Cass.'

'I'm truly glad you think so,' her friend said happily. 'Does he know I had the baby?'

'I don't suppose he does.'

'Will you write and tell him about the name?'

Gina hesitated. 'I think it might be better if you did it yourself. More personal.' She gave Cassie a quick smile and before the subject could be pursued, turned back to the front, switched on the motor and said briskly, 'Now, time we got going.'

Cassie said, 'Or the party'll be over without us.'

Gina did not say, What party? merely gave her friend a very nonchalant look in the mirror.

Cassie turned to her son and said, 'Bet you five bucks the band plays *Baby Face*.'

What Gina said was, fortunately, foreign to small ears.

Word had it, the Bikini Beach was packed every night, not least of its attractions being Tony Nevada whose gigantic photographic image smiled provocatively down from the casino's roadside sign onto the horde of females who gathered daily to catch a glimpse of their sexual fantasy as he arrived in an ivory Cadillac emblazoned with the Randolph Corporation logo.

When she'd first seen the sign, Gina had been worried about the effect it might have on Cassie who was obliged to pass it every time she went to the postnatal clinic. Only once, however, did Cassie say, 'One of these days folks'll learn the truth about that snake and then he'll be smirking on the other side of his face.' She didn't mention the singer again, apparently had exiled him to the backyard of her memories; rather as Gina had decided to banish unwanted recollections of Oliver Randolph.

There were far pleasanter things to think about.

Christmas glittered in the downtown store windows while platoons of jovial Santas rang good cheer at every street corner. The lobby of The Silver Lady was festooned with holly, balloons and streamers as Gina sparkled about her daily round, happily looking forward to everyone's arrival for the traditional family celebrations.

Just four days to go.

Gina spent the first hour of this morning opening the stack of festive cards forwarded from New York and hanging them on red ribbons around her office. The usual grandiose calendar from the bank was accompanied by seasonal greetings from Wheldon Hoyt. Gina was too full of good cheer, however, to regard it with cynicism; in fact it further boosted her spirits as she recalled that after next year's launch of Cornell Hotels the personal collateral she had put up would begin to be returned.

Humming *Jingle Bells* she sat beside her desk.

The door opened and Howard entered.

'Howard!' Gina was unable to contain her surprise.

He walked forward. 'Am I interrupting?'

Gina reclaimed her composure. Was there a sarcastic edge in her husband's voice? She dismissed the suggestion and responded, smiling, 'No, of course not. You startled me, that's all. I wasn't expecting you. I mean, I was hoping you'd arrive soon but didn't know when it would be. I tried to contact you in New York at the club but you'd checked out.'

He didn't respond to that, merely stood looking around the office as if examining it for the first time.

Gina wasn't sure what to say, but at last asked, 'Have you been anywhere interesting?'

He regarded her. 'Have you?'

Gina held on to her smile although she felt disturbingly unsettled by Howard's demeanour. 'Not really,' she answered. 'I've been here and there but nowhere special.'

'I heard you were in Anaheim.' He came and sat in front of the desk, glancing over the papers there.

'Yes. At Monument.' Gina sidestepped the image of Robert Fallon. 'You ought to come over with me some time. It really is a fascinating place. Or, if you wanted, you could go on your own. If you fixed it up with Felix beforehand I know he'd be pleased to show you around. He'll be here for Christmas Eve. Why don't you ask him?'

'I wasn't thinking of staying.'

The words cut Gina to the bone. 'But ...' she managed, 'we've always spent the vacation together, every year since we were married. It's the family party.'

'Your family.'

Gina flinched. 'Our family,' she rejoined. 'They're our family. Yours and mine. And you know I don't just mean Paola and Filipo, but also Max and Harry and Cassie and Irving, everyone.' She heard her voice rising and pressed her lips together for a moment telling herself to count to ten. 'Besides,' she went on, 'you've always got along fine with them all. You've never said you didn't like them. Certainly they like you.'

Howard hesitated. 'That isn't the point.' The hard light that had been in his eyes began to soften.

Gina said gently, 'I wish you hadn't walked out of my office in New York. Up till then we'd seen each other almost every day for a fortnight. I thought we might have started to put things to rights.' She really wasn't sure whether she believed this but felt she had to push out a bridge on which they could meet. She said, 'Please don't leave, Howard. I want to spend Christmas with you.'

'Then come to Aspen with me.'

'To ski? You know I can't ski.'

'You've never tried to learn. Try now.'

'How could I possibly learn in a few days?'

'It doesn't have to be a few days. In a fortnight you could learn. In a month you could be proficient.'

'A month? Howard, you know I couldn't possibly ...' Gina bit her lip as she saw her husband's jaw clench. She felt suddenly trapped, talked into a corner and not knowing which way to turn. But warning voices were sounding. She saw determination in Howard's face and realized this wasn't merely a juvenile gesture on his part. Fleetingly, she wondered why he had chosen this particular moment to be so adamant; but she cast aside the speculation, instinctively knowing there was no more time for prevarication or argument. Without pausing to consider the practicalities, she declared:

'Very well, I'll take a month off. We'll go to Aspen.' Gina put on a lighthearted approach. 'Though, I warn you, you'll spend the entire time digging me out of snow drifts.'

Howard looked her straight in the eye. 'You mean it?'

Gina smiled. 'Girl Scouts honour.'

'When can we get started?'

'As soon as you like, immediately after Christmas.'

Howard said, 'I want to go before Christmas.'

Gina felt thin wires tighten on her nerves, but, keeping the smile in her voice, she responded equably, 'That isn't fair, Howard. The family party's all arranged. Everyone will be here in the next forty-eight hours. You can't expect me to just leave. Please, don't be unreasonable.'

'You mean don't rush you away from business.'

'No, that isn't what I mean at all.'

'Then leave with me right now, and come back for the party here on Christmas Eve.'

'That would be foolish.'

'Why? We can fly to Aspen in less than four hours.'

Gina held on to the edge of her desk as if it might prevent her from falling into the pit she saw opening before her. But was there any point in holding on? And did she truly want to? She regarded her husband; his dark eyes and firm mouth and strongly sculpted features. And in this moment she remembered the day they'd met, the first time they'd kissed, the first time they'd made love. The blood came into her face. But, she insisted, I won't capitulate under force. She said levelly:

'All right, I admit, the family isn't the sole reason I can't leave before Christmas. There are certain matters I have to take care of. Yes, business matters. Items that are important. I'm prepared to clear them up quickly, more quickly than I should, but I won't abandon them, Howard. And you shouldn't ask me to.'

Howard stood. He said flatly, 'It's always been like this. And it's never going to be any different is it?'

'It can be,' rejoined Gina. 'I'm trying ...'

'Hah!'

The cords around Gina's nerves bit deeper. 'Howard, stop it.' She rose quickly and stepped around the desk, stood a yard from him. 'We can't go on this way.'

'You're damn right,' he shot.

'I didn't mean ...'

'It's got to come to a finish.'

'You're being purposely obstructive.'

'Don't tell me what I'm being. I'm not a child. Nor am I one of your bloody employees.'

The retaliation slashed Gina and her anger reared. 'Maybe it would be better if you were. Certainly it might have made a difference if you'd ever done a stroke of work in your life.' The instant the words were out of Gina's mouth she was desperately sorry, but before she could apologize, Howard flared:

'Well if you're an example of what work does for somebody, I'd rather stay idle.'

'That's a hideous thing to say.'

'Work. It's an obsession with you. Just the way it was with my mother. You're exactly the same as her. Always pleading your need to support the family. But your real need is the parenthood of the company, your beloved business. You can't help yourself. You have to go on and on, getting bigger and bigger. And why? What are you trying to prove? That you're as good as any man? Is that it? Maybe you should have been a man, Gina. Maybe that would have made you happy. God knows you act like one. You've even begun to make love like one.'

Gina's face blazed. Out of control, she flung vehemently, 'Well, that's more than can be said for you.'

Howard's hand jumped up, his shoulder swinging back. For an instant Gina flinched against the expected blow. But it didn't come. Slowly, Howard lowered his arm. His anger, however, remained carved into a face as bloodless as scraped bone. For her part, Gina felt emotionally frozen. She was all at once possessed by an icy calm. She didn't speak, knew that her husband also would keep silent, both of them understanding that all their words had been used up.

After a moment Howard turned and walked out.

Gina followed to the door, closed it and went back to sit behind her desk. She told herself she would not think about what had happened, more especially would not recall what had been said; for, she knew, deep in the darkest corners of her mind were whispered questions and, perhaps, answers she'd prefer not to hear.

She looked about the room – bright with its profusion of cards on their red ribbons. Everything was as before. Nothing had changed. All was normal here. Gina was in control. She opened a ledger and began to trace the columns. There was no one to see the trembling of her hand on the page.

Chapter Eighteen

Christmas Eve came to The Silver Lady. Beneath the huge, tinselled tree in the lobby, Max played Santa Claus in crimson costume and foaming beard, handing out brightly wrapped gifts to every guest, before the entire congregation of the building gathered in the showroom for the midnight carol service. Gina stood here with her family and dearest friends and sang with all her heart.

While she could not entirely forgive Howard for scarring their lives at this particular time, nor could she wish him ill. She'd made no excuses for him not being here, had told everybody the truth, that he'd elected to go to Aspen. No one had pursued the subject.

For the past four days she had gone about her chores, taking strength from the familiar routine of their transaction. She'd been sustained too by the festivity of the season. Well-wishers were constantly at her door or on the telephone; and she, in return, had a thousand and one tokens and greetings to deliver.

Good cheer was in the air, and Gina couldn't help but be infected by it. Only once did she teeter toward self-pity, when, at the private party in the apartment, she saw across the happy room Cassie and Irving standing very close and exchanging a warm smile. In that moment Gina's heart ached and she might have hurried to her bedroom to give in to tears had Filipo not walked up, put his hands on her waist and said:

'Hey, Sis, how about a dance with a good-looking guy?'

Gina turned to him, quickly recapturing her brightness. 'Why?' she said, scanning the room, 'who came in?'

And so Christmas went on its way, along with most of Las Vegas's visitors. Now the hotel guests were either folk looking for some desert peace and quiet, or professional gamblers seeking some undisturbed casino action. In this start-of-the-year lull The Silver Lady took the opportunity to dust herself down, polish herself up, prepare for the spring tide of tourists.

Three weeks into January and West-Rossi was back to business. Everyone but Harry had returned to homes and routines; Harry had remained here to conduct some agency business on the west coast. Cassie, having insisted she was fit to work, was installed in a temporary office, regathering the Cornell Hotel reins. Gina too had decided to stay and operate from The Silver Lady rather than go back to New York.

She still thought about Howard, but not so frequently, and when she did it was with a growing belief that while she must share some of the blame for their situation it was Howard who had been wholly intractable.

She'd discreetly checked with the Aspen hotels and learned he was still at the resort, but she left no message for him. The fact that he might be spending his time in female company neither saddened nor angered her. For years she'd lived with the thinly veiled thought and now she accepted it in the open. Gina was not jealous. So she told herself.

And there was plenty to keep her fulfilled.

Especially there was Robbie. (Thus had Cassie's baby been dubbed by one and all.)

Despite her busy schedule Gina always made time to walk Robbie in his high white carriage four or five times a week. And she would have done so more often had it not been for the battalions of other would-be baby escorts.

The young O'Brien must have had more fresh air than any child in Las Vegas, perambulated as he was up and down the boulevard almost every daylight hour by secretaries, croupiers, cooks, movie stars, blackjack dealers, crooners, showgirls, bartenders and a man built like a granite mountain who, when carrying persistently rumbustious customers out of the casino's rear exit, issued warnings never to return in a voice guaranteed to make the grizzliest bear head for the hills, but who, when accompanying his little buddy, trilled, 'Oochy coochy coochy coo,' in tones not unlike those of a besotted dove.

'Everyone's so marvellous to him,' remarked Cassie, buttoning her blouse after the infant's afternoon feed and laying him in his wickerwork cot in the corner of her office. 'He's going to grow up terribly spoiled.'

She returned to sit opposite Gina in an armchair and they continued their discussion about the launch of Cornell Hotels, particularly the grand opening they would attend at the Embarcadero – soon-to-be Embarcadero Cornell – in San Francisco, where reconstruction was progressing apace toward completion by the beginning of March.

They finished crossing t's and dotting i's in a further half hour and were just closing their files when there was a rap at the door and Harry walked in.

'Hi,' he greeted the two women and went directly to the cot to peer down at the now slumbering infant. 'Sleepy bye, sleepy bye,' he whispered and would probably have remained there another ten minutes if Gina, after exchanging a smile with Cassie, hadn't prompted softly:

'Was there something you wanted, Harry?'

'What?' He straightened. 'Oh, yes ...' With a parting gaze into the cot he came across the room and parked on the corner of the desk. 'Just delivering a message, sort of. I was over at the Springs talking with a couple of agents this afternoon – we were at the Oasis – and who should I run into but Bob Fallon.'

Gina felt her muscles tighten.

'He'd just checked in,' continued Harry. 'Said he thought you might like to know he's there.' Just for an instant he paused before adding, 'In case you wanted to discuss Monument's publicity for *The Last Summer*, anything like that.'

Gina's entire body now seemed to be a rigid knot, but it was with the utmost nonchalance she responded, 'Well, thanks, Harry. Yes, I suppose there just could be the odd point to iron out. Maybe I'll give him a ring sometime.'

Cassie put in, 'Can't we call him now?'

Gina faltered, 'I don't see any reason ...'

'I would so like him to come over,' said Cassie, 'to see Robbie. After all, they are namesakes.'

Harry commented, 'I'd forgotten that. Hey, I'll bet old Fallon would be tickled pink to see the little feller. Gina, how about a get-together tomorrow? Max will love it too; it's ages since he and Fallon got to chew over old times.'

Gina looked from Harry to Cassie, scrabbling to gather her scattered wits. She managed to shrug while vivid images of the Englishman flashed in her head. 'I suppose there's no reason why he shouldn't visit, if he wants to.'

'Great,' said Harry, 'I'll leave you to call him,' starting for the door, 'while I go tell Max.'

'No ...' Gina rose abruptly. 'I just remembered something I have to do. Why don't you call him, Harry. I'd be grateful. Cass, sorry I have to run. I'll see you both later.' And with rapid strides she left the room, went swiftly up to her apartment to drop onto the sofa and try and regain her composure.

Running out like that, she realized, hadn't been a very sensible thing to do. But she'd had to; she'd felt she couldn't possibly talk to Fallon on the phone in front of Cassie and Harry. Since her fight with Howard she'd done everything she could to occupy her mind, to leave no room for Fallon to enter. For, she knew, with the constraints of her marriage bonds almost severed, just the thought of him would set ablaze the torch she always had carried.

Now, alone in her room, she felt that fire start. For just a moment she shied from it. But then its heat was in her veins, spreading through her breasts and into her stomach, slowly consuming the last shreds of her resistance.

Gina trembled; turned toward tomorrow.

He said, 'Pick him up? Well, now ...' glancing from Cassie to Max to Harry to Gina to the infant in its pram beneath the palms alongside The Silver Lady's swimming pool. 'I ...' Again Fallon's eyes travelled the encircling faces with the uncertainty of a small boy prompted by his confidently experienced fellow gang members toward the initiation of lifting his first live frog.

'He won't bite you,' assured Cassie.

'Just sort of gum you a little,' said Harry.

'Well ...' Fallon faltered another moment before capitulation. 'If you're sure he'll be okay.' He bent slowly, sliding his big hands under the infant's armpits, dubiously raised him forwards and upwards, held him in mid-air a few seconds until finally manoeuvering him onto a forearm. Man and child regarded each other with mutual surprise at their revolutionary position.

'Hello,' ventured the larger Robert.

Pin-drop silence. Then:

'Ppprrrpp,' replied the smaller.

And from there on they were old mates.

Max brought his camera, took several photographs of the pair, took several more at the suggestion (insistence) of Fallon who, gripping his gurgling pal with waxing confidence, stood, sat, squatted, even at one flabbergasting moment lay supine with the infant hornpiping on his chest.

Later, as they all sat chatting around the poolside table, Fallon excavated the entire treasury of his pockets, lengthily discussed each item with his small fellow archaeologist. When their inventory was complete, 'How about a bit of a stroll,' he proposed, with 'We'll see you later,' for the enlightenment of anyone misguided enough to think it had been a general invitation. He set off, pointing out features of the surrounding architecture, pausing frequently that his charge may pass the time of day with all on route.

Gina murmured, 'Who'd've thought.'

Max chuckled, '*Padre orso*. Pappa Bear.'

Upon the wanderers' return Fallon continued to dangle the infant for a further half hour, releasing him only when Cassie explained it was time for his afternoon tea. Harry and Max declared things to do and after arranging to meet Fallon tonight in the poker lounge took their leave. Cassie stood, instructing, 'Robbie, say goodbye now,' and when he'd dribbled excellently she headed for the hotel entrance.

Gina thought, Alone at last.

Fallon said, 'Cute little feller.'

Gina said, 'Only about the cutest in the world.'

'That was quite something you did out in the desert.'

'Thanks. Though, actually, Cass did all the hard work.

Still, if ever the bottom falls out of the restaurant trade I guess I might qualify as a midwife's assistant.'

Fallon smiled. 'Cassie looks well.'

'I think she's content. Doing what she enjoys.'

'There can't be anything better than that.'

Gina thought, Except doing it with someone you love. She was glad Fallon couldn't read her mind. Or was she?

He seemed about to say something, but turned and looked away across the pool.

Silence crept between them. Gina wanted to break it but for the life of her couldn't think of a word. She began to feel awkward and constrained. For the past two hours, since Fallon's arrival, she'd been quite self-confident. But that had been in the reassuring company of the others, with their non-stop gossip not permitting her a moment to dwell on what she'd say or do when left alone with the Englishman.

She took a sideways look at his strong profile, and there was no denying her desires were as acute as ever. But, she questioned, were his? For the first time since she'd given in to romantic imaginings last night, she was beset by doubts. How serious had his interest been on the hill at Monument? Had he merely been pursuing an afternoon's flirtation? Had he come here today only in response to the invitation to see Robbie? Was he staring at the swimming pool wondering how he could avoid any unwelcome intimacies?

Gina's confidence was ebbing. Perhaps the best thing to do would be to make an excuse to go inside, to save them both from further embarrassment. Yet still she felt an overwhelming need to remain close to him.

She said, 'Will you be at the Oasis for long?'

He pulled back from wherever his thoughts had been taking him and replied, 'A couple of weeks.'

'Doing publicity interviews for the movie?'

'They've got me booked solid. Typical Hollywood ballyhoo. Be glad when I'm out of it.'

'I think I know how you feel,' sympathized Gina. 'But we do need *The Last Summer* to be a success, and that means getting as much media coverage as possible.' She smiled, hoping he wouldn't think she sounded too commercial.

'I understand,' he said. 'It's just that I'd been hoping to

spend a little time in private, to do only the things I want.' He looked directly into Gina's eyes.

She willed herself not to become flustered. 'So, are you leaving once the interviews are finished?'

'The minute the last reporter packs his pencil. If I don't, your Monument PR beavers will line me up for something else. And, apart from being tired of jumping through hoops, I have to get away to put some time in on the new book.'

'Will you go back to England?'

'No. To the Gulf. Did I tell you about my hideaway?'

'On Key West.'

Fallon nodded. 'No phone. No radio. I don't even take the papers. And folk down there don't ask questions. It's like retreating up a mountain. But better.' He raised a droll eyebrow. 'You can buy liquor.'

Gina said, 'And watch the sunset.'

Fallon stared.

'You said it was one of the most spectacular sights you'd ever seen. And that Key West was the only place for it.' Gina was aware of a tremor starting in her stomach. Fallon was apparently examining every minute movement of her mouth and features. His own face was impenetrable. He looked down at his knuckles, bunching and unbunching his fists. Returning his gaze to Gina, he said:

'Everyone should see it.'

Gina was on the brink of a cliff. She said, 'I'd like to see it.' For several moments she remained with her toes at the cliff edge. There were no warning voices; no cries of encouragement. Gina was entirely alone. She took a breath and stepped into space. 'I'd like to see it with you, Fallon.'

He didn't respond.

'Of course,' Gina added hastily, 'if you'd rather not, I mean, if you'd prefer to keep your hideaway a secret, I'll understand. I wouldn't want to intrude. I ...'

'No, no,' he stopped her. 'It isn't that.' He gave a small shake of his head and pushed his hand through his hair as if just waking up in a strange place. 'It's simply, when we were up on the hill, at Monument, I thought I'd made a damned fool of myself, and insulted you into the bargain. That was why I told Harry yesterday I wanted to see you. To apologize again. To make sure you hadn't decided I was a complete hound. So what you just said, about seeing the sunset, was kind of a surprise.' He studied her. 'You did say it, didn't you? My ears aren't malfuctioning in their old age?'

Gina was grateful for this small piece of humour. 'Yes, I said it.' She smiled gently, and realized she felt quite calm. 'You told me Key West was a special place, somewhere you could leave the world behind a while. And that's what I want right now. Not to talk or even think about business or politics or ...' She hesitated on a momentary thought of her marriage, but almost at once set it aside and added, 'I'm sorry if my change of mind seems perverse. Though I'd rather you didn't ask for an explanation.'

Fallon said, 'None needed. I'm not looking for salves for my conscience. Besides, we aren't a couple of teenagers who need to know each other's motives. We want to spend some time together. Let's leave it at that.'

Gina said quietly, 'Thanks.' She had a strong desire to reach out and touch Fallon, but her present level-headedness kept her hands in her lap. She added, 'I'd like to leave it at that on Key West too. No soul-searching. No asking whys and wherefores. I know we can't ignore the future, but, just for a time, I'd like to try and put it on hold. Am I making sense? Maybe not. I suppose I'm a little mixed up, Fallon.'

He said, 'Which is why you need Key West.'

Gina remained silent, looking into Fallon's face, held in the grip of his words by the simple strength of their understanding. She glanced away and surveyed the sunny scene. People were still sitting, talking, laughing; just another day around the pool. Gina was almost surprised nothing had changed. But it would change, wouldn't it, if she spent this time with Fallon; afterwards it would never be quite the same again.

Fallon said, 'When will you come down?'

Gina turned back to him. For just a few more seconds she hesitated. Then she said, 'As soon as you want me.'

Three weeks. The time crawled.

Gina ached to tell Cassie, but knew she couldn't burden her friend with the secret. For wouldn't that be asking her to share the guilt? Was Gina guilty? She constantly asked herself the question, went through the prosecution and defence a thousand times. Yes, she understood the opposing arguments; right and wrong; mitigating circumstances; the penalty for defying the Sixth Commandment. But, still, she could not decide whether or not she was guilty. If she was guilty, surely she should feel it. And she did not. Gina felt happy. A little afraid too, but, above all happy. She searched her conscience.

Three weeks. The time had flown.

Chapter Nineteen

What to wear? For the first time in her life Gina had been unsure what to wear. Down on those Florida Keys what on earth did people wear? To be more precise, for a clandestine rendezvous with a secret lover what, for goodness sake, should a thirty-eight-year-old-prickling-with-teenage-excitement wear?

I am not at all prickling – the very idea! – with excitement, teenage or otherwise. I am sophisticatedly composed. The prospect of spending five whole days with Robert Fallon does not unnerve me in the slightest.

This Gina had told herself as she'd tried on the umpteenth outfit from her wardrobe for the nth time yesterday afternoon. She'd repeated the assertion this morning as she'd piled, and pinned her hair, pulled it down, combed it back, fluffed it up, settled, eventually, with the clock rushing toward flight time, for rapidly brushing it into a halo around her lightly mascaraed eyes and corally lipsticked lips.

As she looked out of the window of the bus chuntering along the Overseas Highway she was wearing a cream cotton safari-style suit, panama hat and navy neckerchief. She appeared unpretentious but casually adventurous.

So blue, she kept thinking.

The sea, to both sides, was the bluest she'd ever seen. Sometimes, as they crossed the bridges linking the Keys, it was an unbroken expanse, at others it was glimpsed through the mangroves, Caribbean pines and silver palmettos. The islands; shiny, rough-cut gems hanging on the string of road from the tip of Florida: sun-glaring sand, salt-scoured timber houses, palm trunks beheaded by old hurricanes, trees with clouds of white butterflies fluttering like bedsheets caught in the boughs, the remains of beached boats with gulls picking as if among the skeletons of marooned sea monsters, open-fronted shacks advertising bait and tackle and camping gear with the jaws of real ocean terrors nailed above their doors.

It was a world at once wonderful and utterly alien to Gina, like nowhere she ever before had experienced. Yet already she loved it (told herself she loved it), wanted to be loved in return by this place to which Fallon belonged.

Now the mainland was far behind, it was as if the bus were driving over the rim of the earth. Gina reached out and held for a moment to the seat in front of her. She'd been fleetingly disorientated. And a little afraid. She'd perceived that Fallon was the denizen here, at home amid the land and people. While she was the interloper. What if she didn't fit in? What if he saw her as a showy and inviolable city lady? She wished this suit didn't look so new. She wished she had a tan.

But the trepidation retreated after the bus stopped to pick up an old boy as runnelled and knotty as driftwood who sat across the aisle from Gina, gave her bare legs a good once-over and then threw her a grin and a wink which lit up the rest of the ride.

When she finally stepped down to the hot sidewalk of the Key West end-of-the-line, a brief shadow returned. For as the other passengers dispersed she thought she was alone, except for a youngish fellow in T-shirt and jeans leaning on a faded orange jeep on the opposite side of the street.

Had Fallon forgotten? Had he assumed she'd forgotten? Had he never really expected her to arrive?

Then the youngish fellow was walking toward her.

And he was Robert Fallon.

Gina thought, God he looks gorgeous.

He said, 'You look gorgeous,' and kissed her on the mouth, tilting her head back so that she had to hang on to her hat. As he released her she drew back to cast an anxious look around the street, but Fallon smiled calmly, 'Not a press photographer in a hundred miles. Welcome. I'm glad you came.'

When they'd climbed into the jeep and were on their way Gina surreptitiously studied Fallon. He really did look so much younger. Her gaze moved down his throat, lingered on his chest, traced slowly to his denim-clad thighs. She paused on his bare, sun-bronzed ankles above battered loafers before returning upward to his profile. The line of his jaw was dark with afternoon beard. His mouth was gently curved. His skin seemed to glow in the goldening light. Gina had a very powerful urge to lick his neck.

What an erotic thought! Still, she smiled to herself, it was what she wanted to do. And the admission of it didn't trouble her. No guilt. No anxieties. She felt she truly was in another world. Nothing and no one could touch her here. She was free. The sensation settled on her like thistledown, and she turned from libidinous imaginings to the surrounding reality of quaint stores, fretted fences, iron lampposts, a passing tram, scarcely any traffic, many cats sleeping on walls and window ledges, folk wandering, gossiping, lazing.

'Everybody takes it slow,' remarked Fallon. 'No more road for them to rush down.'

Dusk was following from the east. When they halted the sky ahead was brush-stroked with pink.

'A gingerbread house!' exclaimed Gina, swiftly clambering out to survey the two storeys of cream-painted, brown shutters and full-width veranda and balcony with ornamental wooden grillework of intricate vines and leaves and fruits. 'It's lovely,' she cried and hurried up the lilac-bordered path.

Fallon unlocked the door, ushered Gina inside where she was further delighted by the polished plank floors and walls. She stepped amid the simple pine furniture and colourful cushions, ceiling-high bookshelves of much-thumbed volumes, rag rugs, framed watercolours of beachscapes, a scarred twin-pedestal desk in the window bearing Fallon's battered old Remington. Though there was no fireplace, the room glowed warm and welcoming. Gina turned to Fallon. He gathered her into his arms and they kissed deeply and lingeringly.

He asked, smiling, 'Can you wait an hour so so?'

Such a question.

Fallon: 'For supper.'

'Oh ... yes ... of course.'

'So we can catch the sunset. Then we'll wander back, I'll cook – no arguments thank you – I'll fry you the best spotted sea trout you ever tasted anywhere, including that fancy whatsitsname place in Manhattan.' He said, 'Now, ten minutes for you to wash up, then we'll head for the show.'

In less than that time they were walking down the street, Gina wondered if she were dreaming; it really was hard to believe she was actually here. For it was as she had imagined it would be: all her teenage romantic fantasizing become true. She felt positively light-headed; one moment boldly seductive, the next timidly maidenish. She wanted very much to hold Fallon's hand, and dare not, because, she realized, the street was filling with people.

Close by a fat Mexican woman with flowers in her hair walked with a skinny grinning black man. Ahead, a trio of sailors. On the opposite sidewalk, two women in evening gowns; an ancient in a straw hat with a live iguana around his neck; an old biddy picking a banjo; an elegantly-suited male couple, arm-in-arm. They came out of bars, houses, and alleyways, without urgency but with lively expectation, as if they were heading for a football game.

So caught up was Gina in the spectacle, the quayside came upon her unexpectedly. Before her was sea and sky.

'A couple more minutes,' said Fallon, taking her hand. 'We'll find a spot out on the jetty.'

Gina went wordlessly. We're holding hands, she thought, yet accepted it with no drama, for it seemed the most natural thing to do. People were all around now, spreading along the quay, meeting and greeting, standing, sitting on their bicycles, perching on bollards and barrels. Some had brought paper bags of seafood, bottles of wine, clay pipes which they puffed mellowly. The banjo lady was plinketty-plinking accompanied by a boy on a concertina. A man was juggling coloured balls. A patch-eyed dog was turning back somersaults.

Fallon led Gina onto the wooden jetty, swapping pleasantries with folk along the way. Halting, he drew her to his side, arm circling her waist. 'All right?' he asked looking down at her as he might at a child brought into his strangely exotic world of grown-ups.

Marvellous, she thought. 'Fine, thanks,' she smiled.

'Watch,' he instructed.

Ahead, the sea stretched like hammered copper to an horizon so distinct Gina was sure she could distinguish the curve of the earth. The sky was palest mauve, flamingo blushed around the sun which was an orb of molten gold. As Gina watched, the sun seemed to expand while burning to a deeper amber. Conversations grew hushed. The music ceased. A murmur of voices rustled with the lap of waves. It was darker now along the waterfront, the audience in silhouette, flushed with rose.

A narrow streak of carmine had appeared across the western farness. For several seconds the heavens remained as still as a painted backdrop. Then without warning they were torched into flame. Gouts of orange and scarlet flared horizontally, outward and outward. Shreds of cloud ignited into tongues of smoky fire. The rubescence swirled and fumed, towering and spreading until the very ether seemed to be ablaze. Within moments the entire vault of the sky was a furnace. And at the heart of the conflagration the solar disc appeared to pulse with red heat, its rim a visible cauldron of seething lava.

Gina was awed. She searched for words. The crowd began to applaud. And that was comment enough. She joined them, celebrating in pleasure and wonder.

As the clapping died down, the clamour of voices broke out again and the music recommenced. Wine bottles were passed around. A peddler, head tied in a green pirate scarf, came along with a vast tray of oysters. Some people began to drift away, others remained to watch the day burn down to rufous embers.

Fallon observed, 'Though you'll see a lifetime of sunsets, this is the only spot you'll see one like that. Of course it's all to do with the reflection and refraction and atmospheric pressure over the Gulf and dust rising from Mexico, but it's good to forget all that awhile and believe, like the Calusa Indians who used to live here, that it's the gods lighting up a bonfire to frighten away the demons of the night.'

Gina chided quietly, 'Why, Robert Fallon, the crusty

novelist, hard-boiled war correspondent, you're really just an old softy, a romantic at heart.'

He reached out a slow, large hand and tweaked her ribs and when she exclaimed, 'Ow!' said, 'We'll see about who's so old, later.' Then: 'But first, this is one sunset-worshipping Indian who needs his supper.'

As promised, he cooked.

And it was excellent.

Gina had watched with initial amusement but mounting admiration as he'd butter-fried the trout with almonds, mixed a salad of palm hearts, dates, pineapple and crystallized ginger. She'd been even more impressed after consuming the meal with crusty pumpernickel and a bottle of French chablis which Fallon said was most likely 'imported' via the same West Indies route used by the bootleggers of Prohibition. Gina had sunk back on her chair, hands on a well-contented stomach and complimented, 'Delicious. Mister Fallon, if you ever decide to mothball your typewriter, there's a job waiting for you at The Lady.'

He acknowledged, 'Your appreciation is much appreciated. But you ain't seen nothin' yet. Wait until you taste my Key lime pie. You might just stay here forever so you can have it every day.' He looked at her across the candlelit table. But if there was any double meaning behind his eyes he didn't let it show.

Gina said nonchalantly, 'We'll have to see.' What a puny riposte. Where was her witty repartee? Gone, along with her self-assurance. She gave him her best alluring smile; imagined it came out like a goofy grin. 'Yes, well,' she was on her feet, 'I'll wash the pots.'

'We can leave them till morning.'

'Certainly not,' countered Gina, rapidly clearing cutlery and plates. 'You sit. Cook's privilege.' She eyebrowed him back onto his chair, and that recharged some of her confidence – though not too much.

In the kitchen she got busy with plenty of suds and steamy water, sloshed and polished vigorously. Of course she wasn't nervous. The very idea! Yes, she was about to go to bed with Robert Fallon. So what? Nothing alarming about that. After all, she'd been to bed with him hundreds of times. In

London, during the war, she used to come home to his apartment from the Red Cross Club, they'd chat, maybe listen to the wireless, have supper, and go to bed, and plenty of nights go straight to sleep.

Gina's face was very hot.

She dried the dishes, found their places in the cupboard, stacked them. She wiped the draining board; neatly folded the washcloth; hung the tea towel over a chair; inspected the kitchen; wiped the draining board; inspected the kitchen.

'Are you through yet?'

Gina almost jumped out of her shoes. 'Yes,' she replied blithely, 'all through.' She walked to where Fallon stood in the doorway. 'Time to turn in. Shall we go up?'

'I'll check the doors, follow you in a few minutes.'

'Fine. Don't be long.' And off she went.

He really is a romantic, she thought, letting me come ahead, giving me chance to get ready for bed. Or putting off the fateful moment. 'Nonsense,' she retorted entering the bathroom. She stripped, stood in the centre of the floor beneath the unsympathetic yellow light. And she felt considerably more naked than she actually was. It shouldn't be like this, she sighed, losing heart. In all the best passionate romances the lovers grapple each other to a sheepskin rug in front of a flaming log grate; their clothes come off to reveal rippling limbs, gilded by firelight.

She peered downward beyond her bust. Wrinkly knees!

The thought ran between her shoulderblades like a string of cold water. But everyone has wrinkly knees. Do they? Do eighteen-year-olds have all those lines and asterisks? Damn it, stop worrying. He isn't going to see your knees. And what he will see will knock his eyes out. It's a pretty good body. It's a pretty good body – for a woman of almost forty. Gina sagged. The reality she'd left behind in Vegas caught up with her now; common sense arriving to end her pipe dream. What possessed you to embark on this insane adventure? Why didn't you, for one minute, stop and think? Did you, in all seriousness, believe you could recapture the past? Fool. No fool like an old fool.

'Stop it!' hissed Gina and stamped her foot. I am not

trying to recapture anything. I accept that I'm not a girl any more; but it does not bother me. I admit this situation makes me nervous; but I'll bet it does Fallon too. He isn't downstairs giving me time to get to bed; he's pacing the room, plucking up courage to appear without his pants. Because, I'll warrant, his knees are a whole lot wrinklier than mine. She laughed.

Fallon's voice: 'You okay? Thought I heard a bump?'

'Fine. Thanks. Dropped the soap.'

A few minutes later Gina peeped out, carried her clothes into the bedroom. Having stowed her outfit in the wardrobe she folded back the bedcovers to reveal the nightdress she'd laid there on arrival. It took her but a minute to decide to exile the ivory lace and silk confection to a dresser drawer. She slid beneath the sheets and lay on her back.

What a disturbing sensation. Truth to tell, she had never slept naked in her life. In the Italy of her youth, even in a household as enlightened as the Rossi's, for a girl to go to bed nude was inconceivable; and to Gina, by the time she was into womanhood, the practice of night attire was as everyday as the wearing of shoes in the street. Her London months with Fallon had caused no abandonment of the habit, for she had arrived there in bitterest winter when wartime fuel rations gave barely a glow in the grate so that while sleep garments might have been shed during the heights of passion, in the sub-zero depths of before and after their renunciation was thermally unthinkable.

How shamelessly bold I've become, she thought.

Then it occurred to her she perhaps looked like a disembodied head lying on the pillow. She pushed the sheet down to her collar bones, posed one bare arm behind her head, arranged the other across her ribcage. But, she discovered, she could see the door, beyond the foot of the bed, only by peering down her nose over the escarpment of her toes. She sat up. The covers slipped to her waist. She snatched them, tucked them beneath her armpits, poised, felt like a patient awaiting visitors.

Exasperation.

Fallon entered and said, 'Hi.'

Radiantly, 'Hello.' Her entire body was aflame.

He switched off the light, crossed the amber glow of the street lamp, removing his shirt, dropping it on a chair, discarding his loafers, unbuckling his belt …

Gina's eyes leapt to his face. Beamed into his face. Locked on his face as it dipped slightly to the sound of his jeans rustling down his thighs. Oh my God, I think I'm going to faint. This actually went through her head, because she really didn't know whether she was in a scarlet lust or a blue funk and she remained paralysed as his face loomed toward her, the mattress sank, the sheets swished and his hand arrived on her naked hip.

'Well, g'night, then,' he said and pecked her cheek.

'I'll give you goodnight,' she shot and fell on him and kissed him and melded herself to him, entwined herself with him, wanted him with a desire beyond imagination.

The floodgates of Gina's pent-up longings disintegrated and she was deluged by a tide of sexual heat. She was shocked by the intensity of her need. Even in her wildest dreams her craving had never been as overwhelming as this. It was a demanding hunger, mounting and mounting, and she could feel it raging in Fallon as fiercely as it was in herself. She saw again the heavens ignite, soared upward to be engulfed in the exquisite fire.

Fallon's mouth raked her breasts, her throat, her cheeks, tasting and biting before fastening to Gina's lips and kissing her deeply and searchingly. And she returned his voracity, with her tongue and her teeth, wishing to eat him, to devour him utterly while herself being consumed.

It was as if these minutes lasted for hours. Yet at the same time they fled like seconds. Time was deranged as Gina rolled with Fallon, rode him, plunged and towered with him, was a very part of him. She sailed on a fantastic cloud of sensuality, upward and upward, hearing a high-pitched cry and vaguely recognizing it as her own. She ground her jaws, holding to the blazing moment, willing it to last forever. But then Fallon's arms were pinioning her, he was gasping, she was erupting, wanting to weep, needing to shout for joy as they both collapsed, Gina looking down into the dark mirrors of Fallon's eyes, seeing her own savage satisfaction reflected there.

She couldn't remember when it last had been this way for her. And the thought brought a wisp of sadness. She brushed it aside. No regrets, not this lilac-scented night. Tonight was for fresh hopes, and new beginnings.

Gina moved gently, lay on her side facing Fallon. She traced a finger down his chin and his throat, into the sweat-damped hair of his chest. She said softly, 'You certainly know how to make a lady feel wanted, mister.'

He smiled, 'Not so tough, when the lady's so easy to want.' He drew her into his arms.

Later, much later, they slept.

Gina awoke to sunlit birdsong. She felt marvellous, having slept like a log for – glancing to the round old alarm clock's 9.15 – seven hours. She'd never been so thoroughly out to the world in donkey's years. Must've been all that fresh air down at the jetty, and the wine, and the food, not to mention all the physical exercise. Twice in one night! (Actually, almost three times.) 'Fantastic,' Gina laughed aloud.

She threw back the sheets, lay, hands behind her head.

Her dream had come true. Through all the past months, since the day last spring when she'd met Fallon at the Oasis in Palm Springs this was the feeling – this co-mingling of relaxation, accomplishment, happiness and love – she'd longed to capture. Why did I wait so long? she asked herself. Fallon and I are right for each other. We always were. Therefore this can't be wrong. Everything's going to work out now. We aren't dizzy teenagers carried away on passion's flood. We're two responsible adults who fully understand the implications of our course and its destination.

On this assertion, Gina swung out of bed.

In a faded pink blouse and white cotton skirt, hair tied back with a ribbon, she went to discover Fallon in a cane chair on the front porch. She kissed him on the mouth – yes, in broad daylight – murmured, 'Yum. Did I ever tell you you're delicious?'

Fallon deliberated. 'I think you might have. Last night, maybe.' Puckering his brow, 'I don't remember. After we ate supper everything went blank.'

She gave him a light bop on the dome. 'How about I take you inside and refresh your memory?'

Fallon banged the heel of his hand beside his ear. 'Pardon? Didn't catch what you said. Must've gone deaf as well as amnesic.' He stood. 'Hungry again? We'll breakfast at Tante Jeanne's.' He added, 'Incidentally,' surveying her face and figure, 'you taste pretty good yourself.'

Gina became mush. Another moment of standing so close to him, with him looking at her like that, and her entire body would have melted into a romantic blob. Fortunately he turned to lead her down the path and into some semblance of solidity.

Tante Jeanne was two-hundred-and-forty pounds, polished ebony with a laugh that was more gold than teeth. Her café was done up like the Hollywood version of a smuggler's den. When Gina remarked this later, Fallon said in fact it was the real thing and the wine they'd drunk last night was the least lethal of the diverse tonics which arrived in the USA via Jeanne's back room.

After they'd eaten platefuls of grits and eggs (Gina was amazed at her own appetite), Fallon walked her around the town. Spanish, southern Colonial, Bahamian, the mishmash of architectural styles was as colourful as the population. The circus of characters Gina had seen at yesterday's sunset were all here this morning. And Fallon knew them all by name. Pausing frequently to pass the time of day, he played tour guide around the narrow old streets.

Around noon they stopped in at Sloppy Joe's, the hostelry wallpapered with newspaper clippings of the island's famous folk and several of which featured Fallon. Gina felt more proud than she'd ever been about any of her own press appearances.

In the afternoon they wandered along the beach; lay beneath placid palms; watched sea birds wheeling serenely above an ocean as tranquil as the polished sky; talked and laughed and kissed and touched.

Once, in a quiet moment, Gina was visited again by sadness as she thought of all the beaches she'd seen, alone; all the years of sunny days she'd spent, alone; all the nights she'd slept, alone. But a soft breeze came to whisper at her ear, to remind her she no longer was alone. She pressed her mouth to Fallon's then with a fullness yet a tenderness which caused him to murmur, 'Why do I deserve that?' To which she answered, 'Simply because you're here.'

When dusk came they remained on the sand and watched until the canopy of deep purple night had closed over their world, and they discovered their divining stars amid the zodiac, foretold each other's happiness for evermore.

Later, in the small café, with men and women who knew of hurricanes, pirate treasures, the hours when the best marlin would be running, and the cove where several cases of Jamaican rum soon would be washed up on shore, Gina and Fallon sang old songs and narrated old stories.

They stayed long past midnight, and when Gina walked slowly home, arm around Fallon's waist, she felt she'd lived here always. People who a few hours ago had been strangers now accepted her, if not quite as one of their own, certainly as a welcome immigrant. She was deeply content.

After they'd climbed into bed, Gina snuggled into Fallon's embrace, murmuring, 'It's been a wonderful day,' and made love with him quietly and langorously, exploring joyously the lights and shades, the hills and valleys, the hardnesses and softnesses of him. She was glad they'd drunk so much, for it tempered their desire. They moved together in a strong but easy sexual sharing, erotic but peaceful, powerful but considerate, a mutual giving and taking between two people who knew and understood each other's passions and needs.

On their second full day on the island they swam, fished, played street boules with two ex-patriot French painters and a Cockney girl (who, Gina learned, did extraordinary things twice-nightly with a very large snake at the Blue Parakeet Club), strolled, shopped and Fallon made his Key lime pie.

'No looking over my shoulder,' he ordered. 'Plus, don't you dare write down the recipe.'

So, Gina looked over his shoulder, and when he'd beaten egg yolks with a can of condensed milk, added yellow juice from the tiny Key limes they'd bought, folded in whisked egg whites, poured the mixture into a baked pie shell, topped it with a thick layer of meringue and popped it into the oven set at 350 degrees, she said innocently, 'Must run upstairs a minute,' and hurried there to scribble ingredients and quantities in her notebook.

After they'd eaten double helpings of the golden dish, Gina confessed her sinfulness but pleaded it would make such a perfect addition to The Lady's dessert list. Fallon said he was well aware all restaurateurs were inveterate recipe thieves and he therefore forgave her but said that if he wasn't accorded a full credit on the menu he'd sue for breach of copyright.

They were delighted with each other then and almost made love there on the rag rug beside the table, but what with the large amounts of pie, on top of the day's exertions, they fell asleep on the sofa and didn't wake until the moon was on the wane.

This was their time together. It was a magic time. Gina wished it might never end. Yet, knowing it would, she told herself this was not an ending, rather a beginning.

As the days wore down she felt ever more confident. Never had she been so sure of her emotions, nor of her closeness to Fallon. One of her greatest pleasures had been their conversations. They'd talked and talked; and yet, as they'd promised, they'd avoided any subject which might lead them into a discussion of their future.

On the evening before Gina was due to leave they watched the sunset again. It was as spectacular as ever, and they lingered on the quay until the final ember of the day had died. They walked home and sat in the cane chairs on the porch amid the scent of the lilacs.

Gina said softly, 'It's been lovely, this whole week.'

He remained silent in the semi-dark, until presently he asked, 'Will we do it again, sometime?'

Gina turned to him, could see the pale light on one side of his face. She said, 'I want to, very much. And I want it to be more than a vacation. You understand?'

'Yes.' He paused. 'So, what next?'

'To be honest, I'm not sure. I need some time. I imagine we both do. After all, I still have a business to run and you have a book to write. Let's keep our pact and not talk about it any more for now. Please, give me the chance to think about what will be for the best.'

Fallon answered, 'Take your time, Gina. I won't pressure you. As soon as you're ready, we'll talk.'

Reaching out, she found his hand and held it. She said quietly, 'Thanks, Fallon. Thanks for everything.'

Their day drew toward its close.

Chapter Twenty

Howard said over the phone, 'Where were you last week? I called. Nobody knew where you were.'

Gina inwardly groaned. When she'd first decided on her trip to Key West she'd told those few to whom it mattered that she was going away on a private break and preferred not to give a contact phone number or address as she wanted the opportunity to study various company files without interruption. She hadn't liked to lie – especially as both Cassie and Max had urged her to go saying it was time she took a vacation – but she'd felt she couldn't share her secret until she'd spent her days with Fallon and begun to put her thoughts in order. It simply had never occurred to her that her husband might phone.

She said, 'I was away on business, Howard.'

'Away where?'

'Does it matter?'

'I think I have a right to know what you do.'

'I could say the same. When I called Aspen a few weeks ago they said you'd checked out. I tried New York, and some of your friends, but you weren't there either.'

'Why were you trying to find me?'

Gina hesitated. After a moment she replied, 'I wanted to talk about ... the argument we had.'

'What about it?'

'We need to discuss it.'

There was silence on the line.

Gina prompted, 'Howard, did you hear me?'

'Yes. I'm listening. Go ahead.'

'What?'

'Go ahead, discuss it.'

Gina clung to the fraying edges of her composure. 'It isn't something we can talk about on the telephone, Howard. I need to see you.' Again there was no response but Gina could hear him breathing. She briefly wondered whether she should cajole him or speak sharply. The former seemed, under the circumstances, treacherous; the latter, hypocritical. Gina's overriding feeling toward her husband at this moment was sympathy. Her irresolution was broken by him saying:

'It will have to wait.'

'I don't think it should, Howard. We ought to ...'

'I have things to do.'

Gina decided not to push. 'But we will talk?'

'When I'm ready.'

'Where will you be? If I need to get in ...'

'Goodbye, Gina.' He cut the connection.

Gina sat with the receiver in her hand for several moments before she set it down with a sigh. She felt weary. And that was all she felt. The brief exchange with Howard seemed to have drained her, left her in emotional limbo. She wished Fallon had a phone down on Key West. But then she decided that even if he had she wouldn't contact him; before parting from him she'd promised not to disturb his writing for at least a couple of months, by which time, she'd assured herself, she would have spoken with Howard about the future of their marriage.

She went and stood at her office window and looked down at the neon brilliance of night on The Strip, determined, for now, to put both men from her thoughts.

Gina watched, way below, the limousines and taxis turning in to The Silver Lady's driveway. Plenty of customers. Business was good. Business in Vegas was building faster than new casinos were being constructed. Gina looked along the highway to the green-lit tower of the Bikini Beach. Plenty of business for Oliver Randolph too. Her distaste rose at the memory of the gross man. But she strove to quell it. What was the point in bearing grudges?

Also, she thought, what was the point in driving herself to compete so fiercely? All the West-Rossi ventures were running surefootedly. Cornell Hotels would be under way in a fortnight. Gina's own finances would soon be secure again. Surely she then could cease to race so fast; take time to put her personal life in order; go forward on a less headlong course.

Gina turned from the window. Yes, she could do it. She'd talk with Howard. There'd be heartache, she knew, but, in the long run, it would be for the best, for them both. She nodded decisively, feeling very much restored.

The phone rang and she went to answer it.

Filipo said, 'Hi, Sis. How are you?'

Gina experienced a further boost on hearing her brother's voice. 'Fine, thanks,' she answered. 'Are you?'

'Couldn't be better. I was just ringing about the Cornell Hotels' launch in San Francisco. I'll be there as arranged, and Mickey's managed to get a few days off before the Broadway opening so she'll be able to come too.'

'That's lovely,' said Gina.

'Have all the invitees said yes?'

'As far as I know.'

'Going to be a bit packed is it?'

'Not so's the hotel can't cope. And we've kept the numbers down so that the press and newsreel cameras can see all around the lobby – which is the whole point of the exercise.'

Filipo said, 'I understand. It was just that I was wondering if there'd be room for one more.'

'One more guest,' returned Gina. 'I don't see why not. Was there someone special you wanted to bring?'

'Yes. I was thinking of asking Barbara.'

Gina's grip tightened on the phone.

Filipo went on, 'She was coming out to the coast anyway, visiting old friends, and I thought it wouldn't be a bad thing if the media saw her at the Cornell party. She could get in a plug for the Barbara Graham Season as well as Monument. It all helps, don't you agree?'

Gina responded slowly, 'Yes, of course.'

'On the other hand, if there isn't going to be room ...'

Gina quickly got a hold of her thoughts. 'I'm sure we can use all the celebrity publicity we can get,' she said. 'By all means bring Barbara along.'

'Thanks, Sis. I know she'll be pleased.'

Gina changed the subject: 'How's it going at college?'

'Okay. Keeping busy, as usual.'

Gina really wanted to ask about the AFF which Filipo hadn't mentioned since before Christmas, but, on the brink of broaching the subject, decided to leave it alone; there'd be ample opportunity when she saw him in San Francisco. 'Well, then,' she said cheerily, 'we'll have a good long chat in a couple of weeks' time.'

They exchanged their farewells and Gina set down the phone. As always, she felt warmed after talking with her brother. And, she told herself, his reasons for bringing Barbara Graham to the Cornell party were straightforward and sensible. She remained standing still for a few seconds reclaiming the equilibrium she'd been gathering before Filipo's call. Presently, with a fresh smile, she went out to find Harry who she knew would be more than somewhat pleased to learn of the ex-actress's impending visit.

One television reporter said it looked as if the entire population of California had come to San Francisco. Certainly it seemed like the entire population of the city had gathered at this spot on the bay. Beneath a sky of purple velvet, touched by gold in the west, sprinkled with stars in the east, the crowd billowed along the sea front, while out on the water hundreds of craft of all sizes bobbed and tacked, their lights as myriad as fireflies above the darkly marbled swell.

Back and forth the throng flowed. But always it returned to its vortex, to be pulled into the swirl around the circular forecourt where gleaming limousines discharged their evening-dressed passengers, newspaper and radio legmen jostled to capture a fleeting interview, flash bulbs exploded in a constant barrage, and excitement crackled like summer lightning. The sign above the open doors glowed golden:

EMBARCADERO CORNELL

The celebrity guests entered.

Inside, a carnival of light and movement and noise. Everyone gesticulating, exclaiming, staring in surprise and wonder at the encircling parade of shops, arcades, vaulted porches, balconied windows. In one corner, the 'outdoor' tables of a trattoria. In another, wooden benches beneath a pergola of vines and roses. At the centre of the piazza, a lichened stone fountain spouting fifteen feet into the air to splash into a fish-darting pool. Trees in full leaf. Wrought iron street lamps haloed in amber. And, twelve stories overhead, the night sky, clear through the arching glass roof.

'It has to look as nearly the real thing as possible,' Gina had said when she'd first presented the concept to her directors. 'It must be bricks and mortar, not plasterboard and paint. Above all it must be in good taste. With the best will in the world we'll never please everybody. There'll be those who insist the lobby of a luxury hotel should always look like a Greek mausoleum. It's therefore imperative, whatever we do be done well; so that not even our severest critics can accuse us of shoddy workmanship or gimcrack style.'

Through all the financial and personal upheavals of the past months Gina had been pursued by her own words.

She needn't have worried.

Tonight, the awe on the faces of the milling guests was sufficient to dispel all her doubts. The shower of compliments was a bonus. They congratulated her, kissed her, pumped her arm, one loud male in a sky blue dinner jacket even clapped her on the back. And a handsome, tanned middle-aged man declared, 'Mrs Cornell, it's a marvel. Tonight you've set the hotel world on its ear.' Gina had replied, 'Thank you, Governor.'

Cassie's voice said, 'Hon, isn't it fantastic.'

Gina smiled at her friend as she stepped from the crowd. In a low-cut, lace and chiffon, tan and emerald gown, Cassie looked as royally glamorous as any of the attending movie queens. Gina said, 'All thanks to you, Cass. You've worked wonders.'

Cassie said, 'I'm just grateful to've had the chance.'

Amid the hubbub they shared a quiet moment.

Gina then said briskly, 'Well, can't stand here chin-wagging all night. Better go and do our party piece.'

They made their way through more congratulations toward a dais at the far side of the piazza where a forest of microphones and an arc of newsreel cameras was waiting. Here Gina turned and looked back across the scene, the seven hundred guests whose names read like a roll-call from the pages of *Time*, *Newsweek* and *Screenland*.

She searched the faces.

Over there stood Max, silver hair gleaming, moustachios positively twirling with pleasure as be beamed upon a diminutive but very chic lady tennis star. Nearby Felix was happily involved with the World Heavyweight Champion and his wife. Beneath the archway to the bar, Mickey, vivacious in a spangly yellow dress, was performing animatedly for a trio of Hollywood directors. Harry, no doubt was swapping reminiscences with that famous clarinet player. Paola, Gina's sister, and her husband were being entertained by those two top movie comedians. The banker Wheldon Hoyt had come here to look over the security of his loan but was presently keeping both eyes on the scarlet sheathed assets of Miss West Coast. Irving, immaculate, was engaged in relaxed conversation with the hotel's owner and the city's mayor.

Gina once more scanned the crowd, frowning.

Where was Filipo? There, with the young blonde? No. Was that him? Again, no. Gina bridged her eyes against the dazzle of the fountain. At last, yes, she saw her brother, couldn't mistake the tumbling, shiny curls, the dark laughing eyes as he traded some intimacy with Barbara Graham.

Gina's happy mood faltered. The ex-actress was leaning in close to Filipo, her vermilion nailed fingers resting on his forearm. She was looking up at him from beneath heavy lashes, the tip of her tongue travelling her darkly moist lips. Filipo said something. She replied. And they glanced around as if they might have been overheard.

Gina nibbled the inside of her mouth, scraped her fingers on her purse. She told herself there was nothing to get upset about. Her brother and the ex-actress were merely exchanging social chit-chat. Nevertheless, her eyes remained locked on Barbara Graham as she threw back her head in a theatrical laugh accentuating the strong line of her throat and the taut swell of her breasts beneath a purple silk blouse.

A man's voice called: 'We're ready, Mrs Cornell.'

Gina turned to the West-Rossi public relations organizer. 'Thank you,' she answered and she and Cassie went around to the rear of the dais where the mayor was now standing waiting to proceed with his speech of civic welcome.

Several more moments passed while sound engineers adjusted their recorders, and cameramen checked light levels. Then the celebrity master of ceremonies was stepping to the microphones, the cacophony of voices gradually died down, everyone in the huge lobby turned toward the dais.

It took thirty minutes.

The Embarcadero Cornell was officially open.

Applause battered up to the high atrium dome, and music began to issue from the surrounding hidden speakers. A further half hour was spent posing for photographers, producing quick quotes for reporters, signing autographs. Gina amiably performed her duties, and was happy to see Cassie enjoying her evening in the spotlight.

Presently there was a lull in the questions and compliments thrust at Gina and as she drew a couple of steadying breaths she was touched by a wisp of sadness, a few moments loneliness amid the close throng. She thought of Fallon, couldn't help but wish he was beside her tonight.

Harry stepped from the crush. 'Gina, it's been a sensation. Across the country. I put in calls to the other nine hotels. The openings went off without a hitch. We made just about every radio and TV station coast to coast. Cornell Hotels have arrived. In aces. And they're here to stay.'

Gina mentally shook herself. She'd almost forgotten the simultaneous opening ceremonies. Now she imagined them. Foresaw the company's name splashed on every front page tomorrow morning. Her enthusiasm rebloomed. 'That's fabulous news,' she responded, and proceeded to bombard Harry with questions about every one of the other nine venues to whom he'd spoken.

When at last Harry was drawn away by old acquaintances, Gina went on her own round of playing hostess. The evening wore on. The huge cold buffet of savouries and sweets had been consumed but the wine continued to flow, and although, eventually, the guests began gradually to leave, at ten-thirty there were still a hundred or more lingerers.

Gina had kept away from the main doors lest she had to remain there on hand-shaking duty until dawn. Now she meandered toward a rear staircase intending to slip out, prise her shoes off for a secluded fifteen minutes in the hope her absence would encourage a final exodus.

She paused as it occurred to her she hadn't seen Filipo for some time. She turned to look around.

Maybe he'd also taken the opportunity to duck out for a while. Gina was held at the foot of the stairs by a vague disquiet. She stepped onto the bottom tread to peer past the fountain, between lampposts and tree trunks to the farthest reaches of the piazza. Couples and small groups stood amid the pools of light and shade. Gina squinted to distinguish part-hidden faces.

Why are you doing this? an inner voice demanded. Your brother isn't a child to keep an eye on. Does it matter where he is? Or what he's doing?

Gina turned a deaf ear. Who was that, in the far corner, beneath the vines? She could make out the figure in the dappled amber glow. A woman in a pale clinging long skirt and dark blouse. As Gina craned, the distant face half turned, and she saw Barbara Graham, laughing, speaking to someone in deeper shadow. The ex-actress reached out to the screened figure. Her own face was lit in dramatic contours, her body a curve of sensuous lines. She again spoke, glancing around before moving in close to her companion, disappearing all but for a highlight on her jet hair and bare arm.

Gina was propelled from the stair as if by a fist in her back. Her heels cracked sharply on the paving, echoing with the louder percussion of the pulse in her temples, drowning all inner cries of caution. Her rationality had flown; she had no idea what she was about to do or say as she was spurred forward by a confusion of anger, hurt and protectiveness, pursued by a swarm of anxieties for her brother.

Oblivious to the surprised stares of several guests who stepped out of her path, with impulsive strides Gina reached the arbour. She halted, catching her breath, glanced around the shadowy place.

She was alone.

But at the rear an archway gave on to a wide corridor. Without hesitation Gina hastened down there; along silent carpet, past muted wall lamps. She rounded the far corner to a shorter hall and open double doors to the hotel's ballroom. The ballroom was in darkness.

From within came a woman's laugh.

Gina stopped several yards short of the doors. Her chest was pumping as if she'd run miles. She now knew she had no right to pursue her brother this way. But still a corner of her mind refused to retreat. She had to know whether her suspicions had any foundation. After all, Filipo and Barbara Graham might be doing nothing more than capturing a short respite from the crowd just as Gina had intended to do a few minutes ago. If it was more than that ...

Gina was unable to follow the thought, couldn't imagine how she might handle the circumstances. But, come what may, she had to know what was happening in the ballroom.

Moments later she was standing to the side of the open door. Pinpricks of sweat popped on her back and shoulders as her deepest instincts of sisterly concern warred against her self-reproach for the act she was committing. Slowly, she inched the side of her face beyond the door-jamb and peered into the vast, black void.

For seconds she could see nothing, but then, as her sight adjusted to the darkness, gradually the lofty room took on form. Chandeliers, tables and chairs, mirrored columns reflecting some light from the hall where Gina stood. No movement. No sound. Had the laugh from within been a figment of her imagination? She strained to heighten her senses, to see and hear, even to smell a hint of perfume amid the myriad fragrances on the cool air.

In the constricting stillness Gina's mind was transported back to the night in her apartment above The Lady when she'd been tracked by the unknown intruder. And the fear she'd experienced then crept up on her now. But a contrary fear; not for what was happening to her, but for what she was doing. For here she was the lurker in the dark, a stealthy peeping Tom. She flinched at the harsh truth.

Someone whispered in the secluded room.

Gina saw Barbara Graham in the pale shine of a distant mirror. The ex-actress was reaching to touch her unseen companion, her faintly luminescent arms seemingly disembodied, her hands invisible in the semidarkness. She moved forwards and all but disappeared, the line of her neck remaining as fugitive white flame. A second figure was in front of her, gathering her to form a tenebrous silhouette among the indistinct shadows.

Murmurs and soft rustling. Light on a naked shoulder; on cheekbones; on smiling teeth. The two forms were separate. Had their oneness been illusion? Gina couldn't be sure. Though she had only one eye beyond the door frame both were stinging wetly from forced staring. She squeezed shut the lids; opened them to peer through a watery veil, and see Barbara Graham standing against a patch of opalescence. The ex-actress took a step backward, raising an outstretched arm in a gesture of proposal. A silent laugh was on her mouth. Her other arm lifted to form an invitation of embrace. Filipo stepped toward her.

Gina slammed herself back into the angle of the walls, taloning her fingers so tightly around her purse her nails snapped, but feeling nothing as she froze beside the jamb. Her brain was momentarily unable to form a coherent thought as a riot of real and illusory images stormed across its inner vision.

Gina shrank from the mental rampage. Then all at once a door along the hallway opened to spill bright light, and a voice called. Gina jolted out of her trance and immediately was hastening away from the ballroom, around the corner and toward the hotel piazza. Scores of guests were still out there, chatting and drinking. A group glanced toward Gina as she almost ran from the carpeted corridor and pulled up sharply.

A few yards away Max and Cassie broke from their gossip. Max started forward. 'Principessa, *che cosa c'e?*'

For a moment the words conveyed nothing to Gina as she tried to reweave her tattered senses. Then Cassie was approaching, saying, 'Hon, is anything wrong?' and Gina managed to reply, 'No. Nothing's wrong. Won't these people ever go home?'

Cassie smiled. 'I don't see why we can't shoo them out now.' She studied Gina. 'Are you all right?'

Recovering some balance, Gina nodded. 'Just tired.'

Cassie said, 'I must admit, me too.'

Max put in, 'Which is no surprise. Both of you, you have been running around all day, saying your speeches, shaking hands a thousand times. You should finish now. Go. Upstairs. I'll make your apologies and say our farewells to these stragglers. Harry and Irving will help. Filipo too.'

Gina looked around. Her brother was standing beneath the arbour with Barbara Graham. As he caught Gina's gaze he threw back a wave. Gina returned a pale smile; but she was still harrowed by what she'd witnessed in the ballroom. Too many conflicting thoughts were now in her head. She did need to get away, especially as she was sure her face would betray her if Filipo and the ex-actress walked over here.

Turning to Max, she said in as natural a tone as she could muster, 'Well, if you're sure you don't mind …'

'Go,' he ordered with mock fierceness, 'before I scoop you up and carry you.'

Gina managed a small laugh. 'The way my feet feel I might let you.' She tiptoed and kissed his cheek. As she stepped back Cassie followed to kiss his other side.

He beamed upon them. '*Buona notte.* Sleep well.'

'Goodnight, Max,' smiled Cassie.

'And God bless,' said Gina.

They turned away.

A crash rang from the other side of the piazza.

Both women instantly swung around. Gina sought the source of the noise. Over there, she saw a woman on her knees, clutching the edge of a buffet table cloth, smashed glasses and plates on the paving beside her. It was a moment before Gina understood that the woman had collapsed, snatching at the cloth, pulling its contents to the floor.

Cassie said with a note of aggravation, 'If they're going to get that drunk, they could at least wait until they're outside to fall over.'

Gina exclaimed, 'Oh dear, and now she's going to be sick,' as the woman doubled forward and retched violently.

Several people had now gathered about the sufferer. Gina hesitated, then said, 'We'd better go over.'

Cassie sighed. 'Another minute we'd have been out of here.' She started forward with Gina. 'It's bad enough when a man gets into that state, but, I can't help it, I always think it's so much worse with a woman ...'

A cry came from a few feet away.

It halted Gina and Cassie in their tracks, pulled their heads around – to see a man gripping his stomach, sagging, his mouth open in a face contorted with pain.

Gina began, 'Not another ...' A chill of alarm froze her words. Something was wrong here. She shot a look at Cassie and saw dismay dawning in her eyes. Turning back to the stricken man Gina hurried toward him as two others eased him down onto a chair. Reaching them she asked anxiously, 'What's wrong?'

The man in the chair groaned. One of his helpers said, 'We've no idea. It just hit him.'

Apprehension plucked at Gina with cold hands. She peered into the victim's anguished features before straightening, getting a hold on practicality and saying, 'Cass, is that woman over there the same? Please, can you go and see. I'll stay and ...' Her attention was snatched by a commotion on the far side of the piazza – people hurrying toward a man who was writhing on the floor.

Gina swung this way and that, caught in a net of consternation, literally not knowing which way to turn.

The man in the chair lurched to the side and vomited.

One of the others recoiled with a shocked oath.

Cassie gasped, 'Hon, what on earth's happening?'

A blue uniformed bellboy ran from a nearby doorway, halted, surveying the piazza, then, seeing Gina, hurried toward her. 'Mrs Cornell, I'm sorry to trouble you at ...' He saw the man on the chair. 'Bloody hell,' he exclaimed. 'Oh, I'm sorry,' he apologized to Gina. 'I ...'

'That's all right,' clipped Gina. 'What did you want?'

'Pardon?' He was staring past her to the activity around the two other nausea victims, his eyes wide. Pulling his attention back to Gina, he said dazedly, 'In the toilet ... there were two men ... sick to their stomachs for the past quarter hour. We called the doctor. Thought you ought to know.'

Before Gina could respond a wailing siren cut across her already lacerated thoughts. People all around were beginning to talk loudly and anxiously. The siren howled nearer. A woman gave an agonized cry and as she fell with a smash against a trolley of wine bottles another screamed. Panic sped in all directions like burning gasoline. The lurid emergency lights of an ambulance flashed past the hotel entrance, the vehicle's siren blaring around the side of the building.

Gina knew it had halted in the car park, and as the siren died the frightened babble of surrounding voices again filled her ears. But her brain recommenced to function; with terrible clarity she suddenly understood what was happening.

As if the realization was universal, there was a second's lull. People exchanged shocked stares. And then a woman close to Gina breathed, 'Oh, God, we've been poisoned.'

The racket burst forth anew. People started yelling for help even though they hadn't been stricken. A man blurted, 'I've got to get out of here,' and charged toward the exit as if he could escape the threat. Someone started to shriek hysterically. Pandemonium was on the loose.

Cassie, ashen-faced, said, 'Hon, what can we do?'

Gina groped for an answer, but could find none as she looked helplessly around the confused scene.

Harry hurried up to them. 'Are you both okay?'

Gina replied numbly, 'So far.'

'I just spoke with the hotel manager,' said Harry. 'They've been getting reports for the past half hour from doctors all over the city who've been called to folks who left here earlier. Dozens of guests have been hit. Vomiting. Diarrhoea. Stomach cramps.'

Gina nodded, said desolately, 'Food poisoning.'

'Looks like,' said Harry. 'And pretty bad. Is there anything we ...' He bit off the words.

Gina saw his teeth clench and his eyes squeeze shut. Paralysed, as another siren came yowling out of the night, she watched Harry slowly begin to buckle.

Chapter Twenty One

Of the 734 people who attended the launch party at the Embarcadero Cornell, by eight o'clock the following morning 522 had been felled by salmonella poisoning. 121 had been sticken badly enough to require hospitalization. Four were in a critical condition. The victims included seventeen West-Rossi personnel and three of the company's directors: Harry Dix, Max Barzini and Filipo Rossi. These three men's photographs appeared in all the morning papers along with those of numerous celebrity guests who had been afflicted; among the latter were Michelle Rooney and Barbara Graham. Every paper also carried a picture of Gina Cornell, accompanied by the only statement she'd made throughout the unfolding of the disaster: 'I have no idea how it could have happened.'

In a spare office of the hotel, bare save for a grey metal desk and two wooden stacking chairs, Gina said hoarsely into the telephone, 'Thank you,' and set down the receiver.

The door opened and Irving entered. He was without a jacket, his shirtsleeves were untidily rolled, his tie loose. He hadn't shaved. As he slumped onto a chair, Gina said:

'I just spoke to the hospital again. Most of the victims have now pulled around. The four critical ones are no better, no worse.' She pushed her tangled hair from her brow, and made some effort to wipe her grubby hands on her handkerchief. She hadn't washed for hours. She couldn't clearly remember what she had done.

The past night had been a havoc of doctors and ambulance crews and people being laid on emergency beds set up amid the trees and statuary of the hotel piazza. Gina and Cassie and Irving had helped where they could: trying to hold receptacles for guests in the throes of sickness, comforting those who were in pain; later, toward dawn, assisting with the cleaning of some of the mess; and, all the while, dreading the moment when they themselves would be struck down.

Mercifully, they'd been spared.

In the bare office, Gina now asked Irving, 'Have any more cases been reported?'

He said, 'Thankfully, not for the past hour.'

'Have all the guests been contacted?'

'Every one. And all those who didn't eat the potted shrimp are still okay. Looks like the other buffet food was clean; though the lab is checking it out just to be on the safe side. I guess we can be grateful we don't care for shrimp.'

Gina nodded wearily. Last night, such had been the scale of the poisoning, City Health Department officials and technicians had been roused from their beds, and after a swift round of interviews of the sufferers, the probable cause of the epidemic had been pinpointed. Immediate laboratory examination of the remains of the buffet's potted shrimp had revealed massive salmonella contamination. The press army, camped on the laboratory doorstep, had had the results in time for their early editions; and Gina had been obliged to provide her feeble statement: 'I have no idea how it could have happened.'

Gina asked Irving, 'Is Cassie still all right?'

'Yes. I called in her room. She's playing with Robbie. But she looks all in. I told her she should get to bed.' He looked at Gina. 'So should you. You've done all you can down here.'

Gina returned, 'I'd never sleep, not as long as those four people are on the critical list.'

'Then at least go and lie down for a while. You must get some rest, Gina. Dozens of reporters are still besieging the building, and it's you they want to see. You need to at least have your wits together when you eventually face them.'

Gina exhaled raggedly as a wave of depression swept over her. She said, 'This terrible affair is going to hit West-Rossi very badly, isn't it?

The accountant, with strained casualness, replied, 'All businesses have to cope with a downturn occasionally.'

'Thanks, Irving,' said Gina tiredly, 'I appreciate your trying to minimize the situation. But I'd prefer to accept and face the worst. We both know what just a small salmonella scare can do to the trade of a single restaurant. We've just poisoned over five hundred people. Four of whom might yet die. And by this time tomorrow there'll be scarcely a human being in America who doesn't know it.' Her shoulders sagged. 'Oh, God, of all the times for this to happen ...'

Irving reached quickly across the desk and gripped her hand. 'Take it easy,' he said.

Gina held his hand, tightly, as she fought to regain her self-control, willing the tears not to spring to her eyes. After several seconds, with a shudder she pulled herself upright. 'Sorry,' she said, offering a pale smile. 'You're right, I'm overtired.' She realized she was still holding his hand, and, briefly, she didn't want to release it, needed to hold onto the strength of it, needed someone to cling to ...

Abruptly she broke her grip and stood, then stepped out from behind the desk. In as level a voice as she could manage she said, 'I'll go upstairs, get a little rest.' Irving had also risen, and Gina, looking at him, dishevelled and bleary-eyed, added, 'But only if you promise you will too.'

He rubbed his palm around his densely bristled jaw, and presently smiled. 'That's not such a difficult pledge to give. Although, believe me, I'll feel at least fifty per cent better simply for a shave.'

Gina drew a steadying breath, and, returning Irving's effort to raise a little good humour, said spiritedly, 'For me it will be washing my hair.'

Twenty minutes later, she'd proved her point.

In the bathroom of her suite she stepped from the shower and vigorously towelled her head. The simple act of shampooing and hot rinsing really had made her feel a good deal better. She was still tired, but now it was a calming, acceptable tiredness, rather than the grim fatigue of a short while ago.

Wrapped in her white terry robe, still rubbing her hair, Gina went through to the bedroom, sat on the chair by the telephone table. When she eventually set aside the towel she considered phoning Cassie but decided against it lest her friend had gone to bed. She did, however, call the temporary medical office which had been set up downstairs, and asked the duty nurse for the latest reports on Filipo, Max and Harry who were here in their hotel rooms. The nurse said all three had been checked an hour ago, were considerably improved and now sleeping.

Thank goodness. Setting down the phone, Gina breathed a further sigh of relief. She decided to just give her hair a quick blow with the drier then she too would get between the sheets. She had started across the room to where the drier lay on the dressing table when a knocking came at the sitting room door.

Gina turned and went to answer it.

The hotel's assistant manager stood in the hallway; a slim, fair-haired man in his late twenties. Gina had met him earlier when he'd arrived on duty at seven am to discover all his superiors stricken by the contamination. He'd coped well, however, remaining relatively cool in the crisis. It was with some surprise, therefore, that Gina now clearly saw considerable anxiety in his face.

'I'm sorry to disturb you, Mrs Cornell,' the man said, 'but ...' he glanced at her damp hair and then up and down the hallway, 'please, may I come in?'

'Of course.' As she led him into the room, Gina asked worriedly, 'There aren't any more victims, are there?'

'No, its nothing like that, I'm relieved to say. Although ... well ...' He reached inside his jacket.

Gina watched him take out a manilla envelope.

He said, 'It was amongst this morning's mail. No one's name on it, just the hotel and address. I opened it.' Hesitation troubled his features. 'I don't know what to think ... Forgive me, but under the circumstances, I thought you ought to see this ...' he slid a sheet of paper from the envelope, passed it to Gina, 'before I show it to the police.'

Gina stared at the green crayon scrawl:
YOUR GOING TO BE SICKER THAN A PIG LADY HIGH AND MITY

She almost dropped the malignant page as her mind catapulted back to the day last year when she'd received an identical message. Her hands felt suddenly soiled by the dirty splatters covering the paper, and she involuntarily shuddered.

'I'm sorry,' said the assistant manager with concern. 'I didn't mean to shock you.'

'That's all right,' said Gina, regaining some composure. 'It's just so ... nasty.' She stared at the stains. The first note had been similarly defiled, where the sender had spat on it, according to the New York Police Department.

'Looks like garbage stains,' said the assistant manager.

'No,' returned Gina, 'it's ...' She faltered. She held onto the note but didn't see it. Confused images were flashing across her mind's eye. Something was plucking insistently at the chords of her memory. As it had done once before. When? Gina strove to concentrate, and recalled the car park at The Silver Lady; the evening she'd thought she was being watched but the security guard had said it was most likely coyotes, in off the desert, sniffing around the swill bins.

Swill bins. The words thumped in her head. She continued to stare unseeing at the note. She saw a scene, far off, through a mist. The mist shifted and coiled, across a walled yard, around two tall metal bins. A man came toward her out of the mist.

Gina remembered.

'He was short. Squat. Rather sullen-looking.' Gina stared into the past as the detective lieutenant wrote the details in his notebook. She remembered vividly the cropped-haired man in overalls, slouching across the kitchen yard of The Lady after he'd urinated against the wall beyond the swill bins. Her own words rang sharply from her memory: 'Collect your belongings. Get off these premises. And don't come anywhere near here, ever again.'

That was already in the detective's notebook. He was sitting with Gina in the privacy of her hotel room. She was now wearing a plain grey suit, having dressed and finished drying her hair during the hour that her call to the Police Department had been relayed to ever higher authority in the light of the seriousness of the events of last night. The lieutenant was a big man with a florid but friendly face and crinkly grey hair.

He said, 'Is that all, Mrs Cornell?'

'I'm afraid so. I only saw him twice.' Gina found a business card in her purse and handed it to the detective, explaining,. 'Our restaurant in Manhattan. The maître chef, Mister Chang Leung, will be able to give you a much more detailed description of the man, plus, of course, his name and the address he was using at the time.'

The lieutenant slipped the card into his pocket. 'When you ordered the man to leave, did he retaliate? Did he threaten you verbally or, in any way, physically?'

'He didn't do or say anything. At least, not that I recall. It was all rather abrupt, you understand. I simply turned around and walked away, left him standing there.'

'And you haven't seen or heard from him since?'

Gina hesitated, unsure whether to mention the thoughts she'd had during the hours before the detective arrived. Remembrance of the incident in the swill bin yard had dropped several more of the jig-saw pieces into the puzzle. That is, perhaps it had; it might only be her imagination which was making them fit.

She ventured, 'Not unless he was the one who chased me in my apartment above The Lady one night. And who dumped wet garbage in my car. And who – though I can't be certain this actually happened – followed me in the rain in Central Park.'

The lieutenant stared. Eventually, he said, 'I think you'd better begin at the beginning, Mrs Cornell.'

It took Gina over a quarter of an hour.

After she'd told it all, the lieutenant said, 'Thank you. It looks as if your whole run of mysteries is solved. I'll talk to Detective Sergeant Shaughnessy in New York and, with luck, we'll soon nail this lunatic, get him behind bars where he belongs.' He offered a smile. 'I'm sorry it couldn't have been sooner.'

Gina nodded, was burned by guilt as she thought of all the times she'd been too busy to sit down and think through the situation as she had this morning. If only she'd made the effort, five hundred people wouldn't have been struck down. If only ...

'Incidentally,' said the lieutenant, 'have you told anybody

else yet about this morning's note?'

'No,' replied Gina. 'All my colleagues are resting. As far as I'm aware, Mister Collins, the hotel's assistant manager, who you've already seen, is the only other person who knows.'

'Good. If you don't mind, I'd like to keep it that way.'

Gina frowned, puzzled. 'I have to give a statement to the press later. Shall I not mention the note?'

'Better you don't. Mad-Poisoner-At-Large headlines would have folk panicking all over the place. You know how these scares get out of hand. Restaurants – not just West-Rossi's – all over the country would be hit. If you don't mind, I'd prefer to keep this under wraps until your green crayon scrawler is under lock and key.'

'Very well,' Gina responded vaguely. Tiredness was upon her again; a darkening cloud in her head. She really was getting past the ability to think straight. She listened to the lieutenant offering a few pleasantries and repeating his sympathies over last night, and she managed a smile with the occasional nod, but was very relieved when he arose, saying he'd keep her informed of progress, and at last left.

Gina hauled herself to the bedroom. As she passed the window she glanced out. So vast was the crowd on the sidewalk, the police had erected barriers to prevent it spilling onto the street. Newsvendors were selling special editions as fast as they could hand them out. Scarlet headlines screamed from the placards: EPIDEMIC SAVAGES HOTEL PARTY; SICKNESS RUNS RIOT; POLLUTED FOOD FELLS HUNDREDS.

Gina turned away, and exhaustion claimed her. She collapsed onto the bed into a black and tortured sleep.

Irving said, 'I see the lieutenant's point about preventing a panic, on the other hand it would have been some help to West-Rossi if the public could have been made aware of how the shrimp had been contaminated.'

Gina sighed. 'Yes, I see that now. I just wasn't thinking clearly when he talked to me. Still, I've given my word. We'll just have to hope the police can catch Gant.'

Twenty-four hours ago, shortly after the lieutenant had

left Gina, Alfred Gant had been identified by Chang at The Lady as the man who had been dismissed last year. Since then Gina had slept, fitfully, twice. Now, though she still mentally ached, her brain was functioning logically.

This morning she'd learned with huge relief that all the victims of the poisoning were on their way to recovery, even the four guests who'd been most severely stricken were off the danger list. On the reverse side of the coin, however, was the devastating whirlwind of media coverage whipped up by the disaster and now storming the country.

Newspapers, radio and television stations had rushed out special features on food contamination and the need for stricter Government control of the catering industry. Every report contained as many emotive and frightening words as the writers and broadcasters could muster. And always at the centre of the verbal hurricane was the name of West-Rossi. That the San Francisco Department of Health, immediately following the cataclysm, had conducted a thorough inspection of the Embarcadero Cornell kitchens and found them to be 'of the highest possible standard' was of scant account. The core fact was that the potted shrimp, prepared by the hotel's own chefs, had been massively tainted. No one could deny it.

Nor could they explain it. Except by proving that someone had intentionally introduced contaminated shrimps into the Embarcadero Cornell's food store.

The best hope, as Gina could now see, was to catch Alfred Gant. 'But,' she said mutedly to Irving, 'I suppose there isn't much chance. We have to be realistic. Gant is hardly likely to be still around here. He could be anywhere in the country by now.'

'Yes,' agreed Irving, 'but the lieutenant has issued a national APB. And I'm sure every police force will give it priority.' He gave Gina an encouraging smile.

Although Gina couldn't really raise much optimism, she was grateful for Irving's consideration. He looked his usual self today: shaved, hair combed, re-assuringly businesslike in dark suit and blue-patterned tie. Gina genuinely wondered if she could have made it through the past day and a half without his supportive presence.

He said, 'I think I'd better be getting back to New York tomorrow. Everyone over there's coping but I'd like to keep a personal eye on our financial situation.'

Gina nodded, disappointed but understanding. The banker, Wheldon Hoyt, had been among those who hadn't eaten the shrimp. Gina had seen him this morning before he returned to his Manhattan office. He'd said little, but the gravity of his expression had been more than enough to warn Gina she was on a knife edge.

She asked Irving, 'How big an income drop can we stand?'

He responded, 'There's no need to worry right now.'

'Please,' urged Gina, 'tell me.'

The accountant pursed his lips. 'Very well,' he said at length. 'There are a couple of plus factors to take into consideration – outstanding franchise fees and tax liabilities we can get postponed – which is why I want to get back to my office to see the exact figures, but, on the broad calculations I've already made, I estimate we can survive a fifty per cent drop in revenues for a period of two months.'

Gina registered this silently. Taking a breath, she asked, 'And after that?'

'Put simply, we'd be beyond the point of bankruptcy. The bank would have little option but to foreclose on all the collateral it's holding.'

Irving delivered these words with deliberate evenness, but to Gina they were as jagged as broken glass, for she knew he was including her personal commitment – virtually everything she owned. Self-controlled, she enquired, 'When you phoned West-Rossi headquarters this morning, did they have any idea yet of the immediate effect of the poisoning on business?'

Irving answered, 'From reports received so far, the drop in trade appears to be around eighty per cent.'

Gina couldn't contain a gasp.

'But,' said Irving positively, 'that's attributable to sudden panic – people shunning our restaurants, cancelling reservations. Once the initial shock waves have passed, trade will begin to pick up. A confident publicity campaign for Rossi Taverns will help. Please, Gina, try not to worry. We'll see this through.'

Gina realized her hands were opening and closing spasmodically. She clasped them together, tightly.

Irving enquired, concerned, 'Are you all right?'

'Yes,' Gina returned briskly, 'I'm all right?'

He looked into her eyes.

'I am,' she said. 'Truly.'

But her nerves were raw. When Filipo came in thirty minutes after Irving had left, Gina was studying the estimated profit and loss figures the accountant had given her. 'Just a minute,' she said edgily, tracing the columns with her pen as her brother came and stood close by. She'd been over and over the figures but no matter how she tried to juggle them she couldn't escape Irving's predictions. And no matter how hard she strove to turn a deaf ear, still she heard the grimly persistent question: What if business does not improve within two months?

'Sis, I just wanted …'

'Please, Filipo, can't you see I'm …' Gina bit back the reproof, struggled to steady her uncertain temper. Looking up at him, she observed, 'You seem much better.'

'I feel fine. Are you all right?'

Gina wished people wouldn't keep asking her that. Again she had to curb her tetchiness. 'Yes, thank you.' She took a couple of deep breaths. Really she was very glad to see her brother. The sole patch of brightness under her leaden sky was the early recovery of all her family.

He said, 'I just came to ask if you've time to spare to see Barbara. She's flying to Los Angeles this evening and would like a word with you before she leaves.'

Gina's grip had spasmed on her pen the instant Filipo had mentioned the ex-actress. She vividly saw the scene in the hotel ballroom, and her nerves re-tightened. 'I can't see her,' she said. 'I'm far too busy at the moment.'

Disappointment clouded Filipo's eyes. 'It wouldn't take too long,' he pressed. 'How about later?'

'I'm sorry. It will have to wait.' Actually, she didn't wish to meet Barbara Graham ever again. As for her brother, Gina knew she must talk with him about the older woman. There was so much to say to him. But now was not the time;

Gina couldn't trust her overwrought emotions. She asked, 'Are you well enough to travel back to Boston?'

Filipo frowned at the abrupt change of subject, but responded, 'Don't you need me here?'

'There isn't really anything you can do.' Gina was genuinely grateful for his concern. She smiled. 'Thanks, but I'd rather you returned to college. I'll be leaving myself in a couple of days, for Las Vegas. Once I'm behind my own desk I'll feel more able to get a grip on the situation.'

'How is it, the situation?'

'Under control.'

'Sis, you wouldn't keep the truth from me?'

'Filipo, I promise you, Irving has evaluated the state of business. He says there's no cause for immediate concern. I was going over his figures when you came in.' She indicated her notes. 'Do I look worried?'

'You look tired.'

'Thanks for the compliment.'

He reached out and put his hand on her shoulder and squeezed gently. 'Just take it easy. Okay?'

Gina returned a nod. She didn't grip his hand, was too afraid her self-control would fail. 'Of course I will,' she said briskly. 'Now, when will you leave for Boston?'

Chapter Twenty Two

Gina felt as if she was slowly dying. Despite the warmth of the Las Vegas spring, she was permanently cold. Three weeks after her return to The Silver Lady she sat hunched at her desk, shivering as a chill ran through her. Someone walking over her grave. She recalled thinking that once before and dismissing it as foolish fancy. Now she couldn't rid herself of images of death.

She scanned the columns of figures in a leather-bound ledger, as she had scanned them that day in San Francisco, and every day since. They always told the same story; but each time the grim ending occurred sooner.

Gina banged shut the ledger. 'Hold on,' she said raggedly and bunched her fists.

The door opened and her secretary brought in a sheaf of letters. Gina saw that the top sheet was a covering memo from Irving in New York. She said, 'More cancellations?' Her secretary replied quietly, 'Only three.'

Gina murmured, 'Thanks,' and the secretary left. Setting aside Irving's note she glanced at the letter beneath, recognized the name of the man who'd signed it. Samuel Marks had been one of Rossi Taverns' first franchisees. Now, following over a hundred others who'd already written or phoned, he was asking to be released from his franchise contract. He explained that his reasons were wholly financial, not personal; he just couldn't afford to be associated with the name of West-Rossi any longer.

Samuel Marks's Tavern was in one of those small parochial towns where the storm raised by the poisoning had raged strongest – thanks to his competitors.

This had happened in numerous places where there were

few restaurants; West-Rossi's rivals had seized the chance to sing the praises of their own premises' cleanliness while, by implication, denigrating the local Tavern. In several instances this had even included not-so-veiled references to the foreignness of the Taverns' menu. The town media, knowing a good, contentious, circulation-boosting story when they saw it (and with a keen eye on the advertising revenue received from the anti-Rossi eateries), played it for all it was worth. Political opportunists and religious fanatics also grabbed their moment to jump on the clamorous bandwagon, calling for everything from a Presidential committee of enquiry, to divine vengeance, demanding the gamut of castigation, from a boycott of individual West-Rossi restaurants, to the outlawing of all 'non-American' catering companies.

The bigotry underlying these attacks hurt Gina more than the resulting financial losses.

'It'll pass, Hon,' Cassie had insisted. 'They can only get so much mileage out of us. Soon as their mud-slinging stops being profitable they'll pick on some other poor devil.'

Cassie and Robbie had returned with Gina to The Silver Lady. Gina was hugely thankful for that; yet at the same time, her friend's presence constantly refuelled her sense of guilt. She believed she was somehow personally responsible for the ordeal visited on West-Rossi, all her family and friends. Her conscience was especially stricken by what had happened to Cassie.

For while the dismayed chorus from the Rossi Tavern keepers had been loud enough, the outcry from Cornell franchisees had been deafening. Of the original two hundred hoteliers who'd jubilated at being chosen to have their names married to Cornell, during the past three weeks over half, with varying degrees of vehemence, had petitioned for divorce. More than fifty were suing for damages.

Gina was devastated that all Cassie's hard work and enthusiasm should have come to this. And she assumed the blame. For she was the one who'd persuaded her friend to stay with West-Rossi to develop the franchise hotel scheme. If only I'd let Cass go to another company, she reproached herself time and again. If only I hadn't been so selfish. If only ...

At her desk she thrust aside the letters from New York. Her intercom buzzed and her secretary's voice said, 'Miss Barbara Graham is on the telephone.'

Gina was too surprised to answer.

Her secretary enquired, 'Shall I put her through?'

'Pardon?' Gina got a grip on her senses. 'I mean, no. Don't put her through. Tell her I'm unavailable.'

'What should I say if she asks when she can call back?'

Gina's nerves rattled. 'Just tell her you don't know.' When the intercom clicked off she sat scraping her nails on the desktop. Since Filipo had mentioned the ex-actress in San Francisco Gina hadn't given her a thought. Certainly she had no wish to do so now. Even less did she want to speak to her. The dark scene in the Embarcadero Cornell ballroom reared in her head: her brother and Barbara Graham. Gina's anger flamed.

The intercom buzzed again.

'Very well,' Gina rapped before her secretary could speak. 'If she won't take no for an answer, put her through. I'll give her something to think about.'

'It's Mister Hoyt,' her secretary said defensively.

Gina was left floundering.

The secretary asked, 'Are you unavailable to him too?'

Regaining some equilibrium Gina would have liked to say yes. She didn't relish a conversation with the banker. But, 'I'll speak with Mister Hoyt,' she said and lifted her telephone and greeted firmly, 'Hello, Wheldon.'

'Gina, how are you?'

A formal nicety, Gina knew, at once aware from the tone of his voice that his prime concern was not her health. She replied, 'I'm very well, thanks,' deciding not to spend any time on further socializing. The banker obviously was of the same mind for he went directly on to say:

'I've just been talking with my directors, Gina, and we're extremely concerned about the situation. As far as we can see it's showing no improvement.'

'It's only been three weeks,' said Gina.

'Twenty-four days,' corrected the banker.

Gina held her breath, restraining herself from any snappish rejoinder. Presently she said, 'But I thought we'd agreed – based on Irving's calculations – we had two months in which to see an upturn in business.'

'What we agreed,' said Wheldon, 'was that West-Rossi must achieve a certain level of cash flow within that period. That didn't mean the company could reach that point on the sixtieth day. It meant showing a degree of stability had been established.'

'Yes,' agreed Gina without inflection.

'Frankly,' Wheldon went on, 'there is no sign of a move in the right direction. In fact, taking into account the future losses which will accrue with the cancellation of franchise contracts, by the end of this year the company could well be in a worse financial state than it is at present.'

Gina was only too aware of this. But she said determinedly, 'Still, you agreed we had two months.'

Wheldon sighed. 'Yes,' he accepted. 'However, my directors felt I should let you know they have already decided that if your cash flow target is not achieved within the period, the bank will offer no further leeway. We will foreclose on all your loans.' He paused. 'Do you understand, Gina?'

'You'll put West-Rossi into bankruptcy.'

'I'm sorry, we'd have no choice.'

And, Gina thought, there was genuine sympathy behind his tone. 'But,' she enquired, 'you're not, at this moment, reneging on our two months' grace?'

'You have just over five weeks left.'

'I know.'

'So long as nothing further happens.'

'You mean another food poisoning? I assure you it would be impossible. The security at all West-Rossi premises and franchiseships is now tighter than at Fort Knox. And every item of food is checked and double-checked, Gant doesn't stand a chance of getting to us again.'

'Are the police any nearer to tracing him?'

'I haven't heard from them.'

'Well, the sooner he's caught the better. Gina, I must stress, absolutely nothing must occur which would further damage West-Rossi's reputation. Absolutely nothing. Otherwise the bank would have no alternative …' He faltered, obviously reluctant to complete the warning.

'I appreciate you'd have to foreclose immediately,' said Gina. 'However, I'm perfectly confident.' Her voice wore an optimism which wasn't on her face.

Wheldon had little more to add then, and after a few strained pleasantries he said goodbye.

Gina set down the phone, saw it was wet with the imprint of her sweating palm. She waited a few steadying moments before pressing her intercom button and saying to her secretary, 'Mabel, sorry I was a bit snappy earlier. But, please, for the rest of the day, no more calls.' She slumped back, holding onto the arms of her chair. Ranged before her on the desktop were the ledgers, letters of cancellation, adding machine, financial files. Yet what Gina saw most clearly amid all this, staring at her, hard black numerals on white, was the calendar. Five more weeks. So little time. But all the time she had left in the world.

Gina willed herself to endure.

She didn't know whether the days or the nights were worse. During the day she could at least keep busy, though these were the hours when she most dreaded the ring of the telephone in case it was a prelude to more bad news. Each night she lay, cold, staring into the darkness, trying to see some hope for the future, until, toward dawn, she fell into semi-consciousness and the recurring nightmare of the black void from which a taunting voice echoed, What future?

'I'd like to discuss the future, Mrs Cornell.'

The man was tall and angularly thin, but immaculate in a grey mohair suit. He was bald with hollowed eyes and sharp cheekbones which gave his head a sallow skull-like appearance. His bony hand held a black alligator document case under his arm. He had walked across the quiet lounge of The Silver Lady to where Gina was sitting behind a low table with her mid-morning coffee and the mail from New York.

She'd been about to read Irving's latest financial projections when the man had approached her and made his declaration. A salesman who'd tricked his way past the reception desk, was Gina's immediate thought, and she looked toward the distant archway to the lobby, seeking one of the casino's plain-clothes security guards.

'Please, Mrs Cornell,' the man read Gina's expression, 'I assure you I'm not here to sell you anything. On the contrary.' He deftly produced and presented an embossed ivory business card: Charles Scheer – Attorney at Law.

Still Gina felt uneasy; a sense of being trapped here in this corner. Standing suddenly and stepping out into the open, she said, 'What can I do for you, Mister Scheer?'

'More to the point, it's what I can do for you, Mrs Cornell. I represent the Randolph Corporation.'

Gina snatched her breath.

'Yes,' the man smiled thinly, 'I thought that might be your reaction. Which is why I had to arrive unannounced. However, I'm sure when you've heard …'

'I have nothing whatsoever to discuss with the Randolph Corporation,' Gina declared icily.

'Not the sale of West-Rossi?'

Gina was speechless.

Scheer said, 'We're prepared to make a generous offer.'

Anger spurred Gina to recover her wits. 'I've had an offer from your company before,' she rejoined. 'A year ago. From Oliver Randolph in person. And he received my answer.'

'Ah, but,' Scheer's tone was coldly confident, 'circumstances are more than somewhat changed, are they not?'

'If you're referring to West-Rossi's present temporary setback,' Gina raised her chin with a determined tilt, 'let me assure you, Mister Scheer, you and Oliver Randolph, that's all it is – temporary. The idea that we might have to sell our company, to you or anybody else, is quite absurd – and therefore out of the question.'

'Really,' said the attorney. 'That isn't how I understand it.' To the flash of denial in Gina's face, he went on, 'Come now, Mrs Cornell, you surely don't imagine West-Rossi's current financial state is a secret? You employ someone to keep track of all your competitors' circumstances, do you not? Every major company does. The Randolph Corporation simply happens to be more thorough in its investigations than most.' Scheer gave his thin, knowing smile again before continuing, 'And those investigations tell us, irrefutably, that within three weeks, the entire West-Rossi group of companies will have been taken into the hands of your bankers.'

Gina felt cornered, as if by a snake. The attorney's sharply gaunt face was deadly self-assured. She searched vainly for some retaliation, but Scheer went on:

'When that happens, Mrs Cornell, you know as well as I, the bank will sell West-Rossi, either as a single corporation, or, more likely, piecemeal. And, in the latter event, it is doubtful whether even the company name will survive.' He raised a matter-of-fact eyebrow. 'I would have thought you'd be only too willing to see your company taken into the fold of a dynamic and expanding corporation such as I represent. Also, that you'd see the wisdom of acting without delay, before the inevitable occurs.'

Gina's mouth was now so dry she felt she wouldn't be able to speak even if she could find something to say. She desperately wanted to retort that the outcome of the next three weeks was not inevitable. But her resolve was dying. What Scheer had said was, in truth, only a repeat of words she'd already heard in her head a hundred times, whenever she'd recalled Wheldon Hoyt's warnings.

Scheer said, 'Twenty-five million dollars, Mrs Cornell.'

Shock leapt upon Gina. She found her voice. 'Don't be ridiculous,' she flung back. 'West-Rossi was worth at least that twelve months ago. Since then we've added the Monument film studios and the Cornell Hotels.' But even as this last sentence passed her lips she understood its hollow ring.

Scheer didn't laugh, but his features twisted with amused contempt. 'Really,' he remarked, 'you're not so naive. Nor am I. Considering the present state of West-Rossi's public image as well as the company's plunging income, twenty-five million is more than generous.'

Gina inwardly flinched at the harsh truth.

'And in three weeks' time,' said the attorney, 'it will look even more so. However, our offer is not open for three weeks, Mrs Cornell. Only for forty-eight hours.'

Gina began to turn away. 'Goodbye, Mister Scheer.'

'There's something further …' the attorney was opening his document case, 'you should know before …'

'Whatever it is,' Gina swung angrily back toward him, 'I don't want to hear it. Nor do I need forty-eight hours.'

Suddenly all the pent-up fears and frustrations of the past month welled within her. 'I gave Randolph my answer a year ago. It stands. I wouldn't sell my company to that bloated crook for a hundred million.'

Scheer's jaw muscles tightened.

'And make sure you tell him that's what I said,' rasped Gina. 'He and his kind – yes, you, you bootlickers who do his bidding – you're not fit to be in our industry. In any industry. You're a disease. You infect everything you touch.' Her despair flooded forth. 'Now get out of here. Get out before I have you thrown out.'

Scheer had stepped back from the sudden onslaught. All sarcasm had sped from his features. Now his skull looked even more skeletal, a death's head of virulence. When his voice came it was a knife on bone: 'You just made a terrible mistake, Mrs Cornell. You should have listened. We were prepared to negotiate. But that chance has gone. You're finished. You're as good as dead.'

'Get out,' shouted Gina.

'Principessa!' Max Barzini was towering across the room. '*Che cos'e questo*? What is happening here?' He shot a look at the attorney who was zipping shut his document case. 'Whoever you are,' boomed Max, 'you heard the lady. Go.'

Scheer hesitated, on the brink of some retort, but, confronted by Max, backed off. With a parting venomous glare at Gina he turned and strode away.

Gina let out a juddering breath and, briefly dizzied by the blood pressure which had surged with her anger, sank quickly into an armchair.

Max, looking around from the retreating attorney, sat beside her. 'Principessa, what was all that about?'

Seeing her godfather's solicitude, Gina stilled her trembling hands. Max had already been greatly concerned for her these past weeks; she had no wish to give him cause for further worry. 'I'm sorry,' she said with a struggling smile. 'That was foolish of me. A salesman. He was a salesman. Tricked his way in here. Thought he could high-pressure me into doing business with his company. He wouldn't take no for an answer. I'm afraid I rather lost my temper.'

'Who was he?' growled Max. 'Who did he represent? I'll see he never shows his face again.'

'No, please, let's forget it,' said Gina. 'Being buttonholed by characters like that is the name of the game. Besides, I think he got the message loud and clear.' She reached out and squeezed Max's hand. 'Now,' she added, summoning all her reserves to raise a bright face, 'how about joining me for coffee? I was just about to have some when that hustler turned up.'

A frown remained on Max's face for another moment. Then he relaxed. '*Va bene*,' he agreed.

Within a few minutes the coffee had been poured and Gina and Max were chatting generally as Gina glanced through the mail from New York and passed the letters to her godfather for comment. They stayed together for about half an hour until Max left to keep an appointment.

The interlude in Max's company had restored much of the confidence taken out of Gina by her encounter with the man Scheer. When Max had gone she remained sitting, thought again of the attorney, and the Randolph Corporation. Looking back on the incident she wasn't sure why it had so unsettled her. After all, she'd known full well the jackals would soon be gathering. That Randolph, the most brutish jackal of all, was first on the scene should have come as no surprise. And yet just the mention of his name made Gina's flesh crawl.

Stop thinking about him, she commanded herself. The odious creature can't touch you. Forget him.

Determinedly, she returned to the New York mail. She'd purposely not read Irving's financial projections in front of Max lest she was unable to prevent any bad news being reflected in her expression. Now she slid aside Irving's covering memo and picked up the foolscap page of costings.

Gina quickly scanned the figures. Reaching the bottom of the final column she paused, and stared. She re-read the page, more slowly this time, taking in the details. And then she read it a third time, even more carefully, checking the additions and subtractions to be sure there weren't any errors. There weren't. Her pulse began to accelerate.

At last she breathed, 'But that's wonderful news,'

continuing to stare at the projection which concluded that if the latest increase in business was maintained, the break point they'd been aiming for, the return to an income which would ensure West-Rossi's survival, would be reached within six days – at least a fortnight before the bank's deadline.

Gina heaved a great sigh, the tension flowing out of her like a departing sickness. With a final glance over the financial sheet she set it down on the low table. Only then did she remember Irving's memo lying there. She lifted it, and read: Congratulations.

Ten minutes later she was on the phone to West-Rossi headquarters in New York. When Irving eventually came on the line, the first thing Gina said was, 'Thanks.'

There was a smile in the accountant's voice when he returned, 'My pleasure, believe me.'

'I have to admit,' said Gina, 'I was beginning to think we'd never make it.'

'Well, don't let's break out the champagne just yet,' said Irving. 'We have to sustain the cash-flow, remember. Although, from a further check I made this morning with several individual Taverns, it certainly looks as if we're on our way. All the Tavern keepers I spoke with reported a sharp increase in reservations. The anti-West-Rossi brigades seem to have had their day.'

Gina murmured, 'Cassie always said they would.' On that remembrance she added suddenly, 'I must tell her the news.' Then, collecting her thoughts, she asked, 'Or would you rather?' and before he could respond said, 'I think she'd like to hear it from you.' Gina smiled at the sound of Irving's silence.

At last he said, 'Well ... all right, if you think so.'

'I'll have our operator put you through.'

'Fine. There was just one more item.'

'Yes?'

'I was going to phone and let you know.'

'Yes?'

'Detective Sergeant Shaughnessy called.'

Gina held her breath.

Irving said, 'They picked up Gant.'

Chapter Twenty Three

The sun was shining in Manhattan. Gina's favourite city had discarded its grey winter overcoat for its fresh spring outfit of pink and yellow and green. The promise of summer was in the air, reviving the pace of the streets. People bustled enthusiastically along the sidewalks; traffic hummed on warm asphalt. The scent of the city was petrol, May blossom and sea salt. Its heartbeat was the roar of the crowd, the wham of steam-shovels, the yap-yap of river tug boats.

Gina paused on the corner, watching the interchange lights. She absorbed the surrounding sights and sounds and smells. She loved them, drew strength from them, was glad to be back in this place where, so many years ago, her dreams had come true. Only fitting, she thought, that all the traumas of the past six weeks should meet their end here.

The lights changed and Gina crossed the street.

It was early afternoon. She'd flown in from Las Vegas yesterday evening, spent this morning in her office with Irving discussing the updated financial reports which were even better than the previous ones. After a happy reunion lunch with Chang and others at The Lady, ten minutes ago Gina had called Sergeant Shaughnessy to say she was on her way.

She'd already talked with him on the phone from Las Vegas, immediately following Irving's revelation. The detective had said Alfred Gant had been found working at a hamburger café at Coney Island. It had taken so long to trace him because he was registered under three different names, none of them his own, with welfare offices in the city, while his Coney Island job was strictly illegitimate, unknown to the IRS.

Gant had, of course, denied all knowledge of the

Embarcadero Cornell poisoning. Gina had wondered about him now being here, so far from San Francisco, but Sergeant Shaughnessy had said the man had admitted spending the last year with a travelling carnival which was known to have visited the West coast; and, the detective had suggested, Gant, having committed his crime, would have put as much distance as possible between himself and the scene.

Gina had accepted the explanation, was only too relieved the man had been caught; still found it hard to conceive of anyone being so full of hate to poison – risk killing, even – all those people, simply to spite one other.

She halted on the opposite side of the street from the precinct house. The building was four storeys, brownstone, with tall arched windows and stone steps up to the central doors. Gina hesitated. She'd felt a sudden chill. As she stood at the kerb her good spirits began to fade. A shadowy presence was at her shoulder. So tangible was the sensation, she glanced quickly around. And saw – just people passing by.

She turned back to the street and hurried over to the precinct house. No dark premonitions; not this bright, promising day. She went up the stone steps.

There were several noisy men and women petitioning the uniformed sergeant at the high desk. Gina waited for a momentary lull before calling up to the officer, 'Mrs Cornell, to see Detective Sergeant Shaughnessy.'

As the man lifted a phone to relay the message, the racket burst forth anew with a pair of protesting youths being hustled in by a patrolman. Gina backed against the green-painted brick wall. There was an acrid smell of carbolic. Gina wanted to bar it from her nose and mouth with a gloved hand but felt too self-conscious to do so. Her old apprehensions came creeping back; her deep-rooted fears of police-stations and prisons.

'Mrs Cornell,' Detective Sergeant Shaughnessy appeared through a swinging door at the end of the bare corridor, his hand held aloft not so much as a greeting more to attract Gina's attention across the hubbub. He skirted the throng.

Gina offered a smile, felt, as harsh faces glanced toward her, a contrary sense of guilt at being an ally of the policeman, as well as an irrepressible relief at not being one of the common appellants. 'It's good to see you again, Sergeant.' She scanned his lumpy though not unpleasant features beneath the shock of sandy hair, and felt reassured by its friendly familiarity.

'You too,' he said. 'Thank you for coming. Let's get this over and done with. Please, this way.' He part turned, his back to the crowd, one arm extended to form an open space for Gina to pass. As she stepped toward the corridor he followed, fell into step beside her and led her around a corner.

The din fell behind. The loudest noise now was from Gina's high heels, click-click-clicking on the concrete floor. The detective moved without sound on thick soles. Gina wanted to offer some pleasantry but was suddenly lost for words. The qualms she'd begun to feel outside, returned, stronger now.

They reached a grey door. Sergeant Shaughnessy pushed it open, ushered Gina through and requested, 'Please, take a seat at the front.'

The room was about thirty by twenty feet. Ahead was a stage (Gina couldn't think of any other word for it) with side entrances and height markers painted on its scuffed white backdrop. The room's cream walls were naked and windowless. Four rows of six chairs were lined before the stage. A young patrolman stood, removing his cap when Gina entered. She reflexively smiled at him and he smiled back.

Sergeant Shaughnessy explained, 'This officer is here to witness your identification.'

Both men remained standing while Gina sat. The chair was slatted wood and struck chill through her skirt. The lights went out. An instant's blackness and then the stage was scoured by glaring fluorescents. Gina was forced to screw up her eyes for a moment against the abrupt whiteness. Then she blinked, adjusted her vision to normal, and realized there was a vast sheet of glass before her, wall to wall, ceiling to floor, polished very clean. 'Is it one-way glass?' she asked automatically, too late deciding the question was misplaced.

'No,' came Sergeant Shaughnessy's voice from close behind. 'But they'll scarcely be able to see you – light too bright in their eyes. Don't worry.'

Gina decided against further enquiry, concluded the glass was there to prevent prisoners escaping – or leaping out and attacking their accusers.

A man walked hesitantly across the stage carrying a large yellow card stencilled with a black figure 1. He halted and turned to face the glass, squinting in the bright light. Another man followed. And another. Soon there were six men, in a row, holding numbered cards, staring out into the darkness above Gina's head.

She'd recognized him the moment he'd appeared.

He was holding the card lettered 4. There hadn't been the slightest doubt in Gina's mind. As he'd turned toward her she'd seen him in the sunlight of last April, confronting her from beside the swill bins in The Lady's yard. The only difference was, here there was no belligerence in his swarthy features, simply uncertainty as he peered forward, slowly shuffling his feet, clutching with thick fingers his numbered card, like a refugee child holding its identification on an alien railway platform.

A thread of pity spun itself about Gina's conscience. She snapped it, ordering her commonsense into the perspective of reality, pulling her gaze from the man's eyes.

'Mrs Cornell?' Sergeant Shaughnessy's voice prompted.

'Number four,' she said.

'You're sure?'

'Positively.'

For the first time since her arrival here Gina sensed some emotion in the detective as she heard, faintly, his breath exhale, a sigh of satisfaction. Without any audible command the line-up of men trudged from the stage. Gina was escorted out to retrace the corridor route, and then to enter the squadroom.

Several desks and filing cabinets were jammed into the space. Half-a-dozen shirtsleeved men worked and talked into telephones. Two were interviewing an elderly woman with curlers in her hair. Cigarette smoke hung in blue layers beneath the ceiling.

Sergeant Shaughnessy led Gina to the hub of the massed furniture and pulled out a chair for her to sit. When they were beside each other at the desk the detective rolled a pre-printed form into his typewriter, saying, 'A couple of minutes, Mrs Cornell, you can sign your statement.' He began methodically to clatter the keys.

His typing was soon complete. He tugged the statement from his machine and handed it to Gina. 'Will you read it, carefully, please. If you agree it to be accurate, sign on the bottom,' he indicated the line, 'also the carbons.'

There wasn't much to it. Beneath Gina's name and address: 'Having attended an identification line-up at this precinct house, in the presence of the below-named officer, I hereby declare that the man in that line-up known to be Alfred Gant ...' Gina continued down the page, said, 'Yes, that seems all right,' signed and handed the statement back to the detective.

He placed it in a folder. 'Thank you, Mrs Cornell. You won't be needed again unless it goes to trial.'

Surprised, Gina queried, 'Might it not?'

The detective looked somewhat discomfited. 'To be honest, I can't guarantee it. The case might be open and shut on the misdemeanours, and that will be that unless we can get some definite evidence for the poisoning.'

'Misdemeanours?'

'Dumping the garbage in your car and following you in the park. They're what Gant initially confessed to. But since he's been appointed a lawyer from the Public Defender's office he's not said another word.'

'What about chasing me in the apartment?'

'I'm afraid not. From a couple of things he's let slip we know it was him. We know he got a vicious satisfaction from everything he did. But, unfortunately, that's just our intuition, experience, call it what you will. A court wants proof. Which we don't have.'

Gina asked, 'How about the threatening notes?'

'Oh, yes, he did admit to the one you received here in New York, but ...' Sergeant Shaugnessy shook his head, a little wearily, 'that was before he got his lawyer. You see, after we brought Gant in, read him his rights, got him to confess the misdemeanours, we showed him the green crayon scrawl, led him to believe the lab boys could analyse the writing – though, frankly, they couldn't possibly – and so he said, yes, he sent it, early last summer. However, all that got us was some personal satisfaction. We could never have presented it as evidence. And, anyhow, once the lawyer found out what we'd done he had all that part of the confession withdrawn.' The detective sighed. 'I'm sorry.'

Gina returned, 'No need to be.' She gave him a grateful smile. 'I'm only too glad for all your effort. At least it's cleared up who was following me and chased me and everything. I can't tell you what a weight it is off my mind.'

He nodded. 'Nonetheless, I'd like to have nailed Gant. Made certain he was behind bars, out of harm's way. Which is where he belongs.'

Gina didn't immediately respond. Still haunted by the ghosts of her own and her father's persecutions, despite all Gant had put her through, she baulked at wishing him in jail. She said quietly, 'Can you be so sure?'

The detective replied, 'If all he'd done was garbaged your car, I wouldn't be so adamant. Almost everybody lashes out once in a while, in vengeance or anger, to a greater or lesser degree. But, generally speaking, even the ones who commit murder aren't actual psychopaths. Nine times out of ten they regret what they did and never repeat it. Whereas individuals like Gant, who keep after their victims, they're obsessive. To put it bluntly, they're crazy. And therefore dangerous. And I believe characters who are dangerous should be kept off the street.'

Gina murmured, 'Yes.' She understood his concern, and her commonsense agreed with him; yet still she bore a sense of guilt for having identified Gant.

'Anyhow,' Sergeant Shaughnessy interrupted her thoughts, 'we'll do all we can to come up with something to tie Gant to the San Francisco poisoning. I'll call you if we make any progress. In the meantime, thanks again for your help, Mrs Cornell.' He stood. 'I'll walk you to the front door.'

'No, please don't trouble,' returned Gina, rising.

After a few more words with the detective, she parted

from him and retraced her route back to the street. The sun was still shining. Gina remained a while standing on the sidewalk, feeling the warmth on her face. She glanced back up the steps to the closed doors of the precinct house. She thought of Gant, briefly imagined him locked in a cell. She turned from the building, put it, Gant and all that part of her life behind her and walked swiftly away.

The newspaper report said advance bookings for *High As The Sky* would soon set a new Broadway record. Michelle Rooney, it added, was one of the stars whose performance was making the show such a hit. It went on to say that all the Hollywood studios were bidding for the movie rights, and every tinsel town star who could part-way sing and dance (plus several who couldn't) were already clamouring for the major roles.

Gina smiled as she set the paper aside. *High As The Sky* had opened three weeks ago to rave reviews, but Gina, amid the storm of the food poisoning, had been in such a state she'd sent Mickey only the briefest congratulatory cable. Now, she told herself, she'd make the earliest opportunity to take up Mickey's offer of one of her house seats. Gina was so pleased for the young dancer, and so sorry she hadn't yet phoned to say so. She'd remedy that tomorrow.

Also, it was about time she called Filipo. And Cassie, to tell her about this afternoon's identification line-up. And Harry, here in New York, who she hadn't yet seen, to invite him to join her for dinner at The Lady this evening. And Felix, in Los Angeles, to get an update on Monument.

So many people to talk to. So many things to do. And Gina now was eager to get on with it all. Since she'd left Detective Shaughnessy her spirits had been progressively rising. The darkest clouds were rolling away and Gina once more could see her horizons.

As if to set the seal on her hopefulness, the long-distance call came a couple of hours later at seven o'clock. Gina was in the middle of changing into an evening outfit. She pulled the straps of her slip onto her shoulders as the extension beside the bed rang, and hurried to lift the receiver and say, 'Hello?'

'Hello, Gina,' said Fallon.

'Oh!' She almost dropped the phone.

'What? What's wrong?' he called, startled.

Recovering, Gina gave a laugh. 'Nothing,' she returned, sitting on the edge of the bed. 'It's just I wasn't expecting you. Fallon, it's marvellous to hear your voice. Where are you? How are you?'

'I'm fine, thanks. On Key West, at Tante Jeanne's. But what about you? Are you okay?'

'Perfect. Especially now I'm talking to you.'

'I meant are you all right after that food poisoning? I only just read about it in an old *Miami Herald*. I've been holed up at the house these past weeks, no calls, no papers, didn't come up for air till this morning. You're sure you're okay? Were you in hospital?'

Gina could hear his concern. And she could clearly imagine his craggy features as he spoke, his knuckly, sun-burned fist around the phone. Her affection arose and she said, 'Yes, truly. I was one of the lucky ones. I didn't eat the shrimps.'

'And Max? Harry? Everyone?'

'They weren't so fortunate. But they're fully recovered now. So are all the guests, thank goodness.'

'This *Herald* makes it sound like a disaster. Did it have much of an effect on business?'

Gina smiled at the question. And the fact that she was able to do so, strengthened her fresh optimism. 'We survived,' she answered. 'And, though it took a while, trade has now returned almost to normal. In fact, I was thinking only this afternoon, it's time I switched off from restauranting for a while and flew back west to pick up again at Monument. You know, Felix will be announcing a release date for *The Last Summer* pretty soon.'

Fallon said gruffly, 'Which'll mean more publicity interviews, I suppose. And a première. Will I be expected to show up at that in a penguin suit? I think I might arrange to be in Outer Mongolia the latter half of this year.'

'You'll do no such thing. Besides ...' Gina hesitated.

Fallon prompted, 'Yes?'

Gina had been about to tell him he looked very handsome

in a tuxedo. Feelings she hadn't experienced for many weeks were resurfacing. She asked quietly, 'You won't really go to Outer Mongolia, or anywhere else, will you?'

There was a silence until he replied, 'Not if you don't want me to.' He paused again before asking directly, 'Would you prefer me to stay, Gina?'

She answered, 'Yes, Fallon. I would.'

He said, 'I don't mean for publicity or premières.'

Gina took a breath. 'Nor do I,' she said.

Once more there was silence on the fifteen hundred mile line which separated them. In that instant Gina was acutely aware of the huge distance. It was as if Fallon had been beside her one moment and snatched away in the next. So intense was the sudden feeling of loss, Gina experienced a surge of panic, a sense of being utterly alone. She desperately wanted Fallon to be here.

He broke the moment tentatively, 'Remember, when you were down here, before you left, you said you needed some time, to think about what would be for the best. I guess I needed that time too. Frankly, these past weeks, I've spent as many hours staring out of the window as I have writing. Gina, I know what I want. And I know I'm not going to change my mind. So, there's no violent hurry for you to make a decision. On the other hand, I'll be up in New York soon, and I would like to see you, not to pressure you ... just to ... well ...'

'You wouldn't need to pressure me, Fallon.'

'You mean ...'

'Yes. I've made my decision.' She heard him slowly exhale. Smiling, she asked, 'When will you be here?'

He said, 'There are just a few notes I have to type up. I ought to be able to finish them by tomorrow. I will finish them, tomorrow night at the latest. Without fail I'll be in New York forty-eight hours from now.'

'So long as you can get a flight.'

'I'll ride in the cargo hold if necessary.'

'I wouldn't want you to arrive on the doorstep decorated with one of those labels saying, damaged in transit.'

Fallon laughed. Then, more seriously, he said, haltingly, 'You know ... I want you to know ... Gina, I ...'

'Don't,' Gina interrupted softly. 'Don't say it.' Not over the phone. I want to be with you when you say it.' Her voice became even lower. 'I want to be able to see the words on your lips. And for you to see them on mine.'

After a long pause Fallon muttered huskily, 'I think I'd better go and get on with my notes.'

Gina said, 'Yes, perhaps that would be for the best.'

'I'll see you in a couple of days.'

'I'll be waiting.'

'Well, then ...' said Fallon.

'Well, then ...' murmured Gina.

'Put down the phone,' said Fallon.

Gina restrained herself from responding, You first. She said quietly, 'Goodnight, Fallon.'

He said, 'Goodnight, Gina.'

She awoke at nine-fifteen the following morning. So late. She'd slept so well; the first deep, dreamless sleep she'd had in weeks. Gina sat up, stretched, luxuriated in the sense of well-being. Rising, pulling on her robe, she went and opened the window, breathed as appreciatively as a winter-buried animal breaking out to greet a new spring. She leaned out and looked along to the sunlit pigeons on the adjacent sill. 'Hi, fellers,' she called, setting the birds hopping and bobbing and cooing as if in demonstration of a happiness to match Gina's own.

Whistling cheerfully, Gina dressed.

When she arrived downstairs, the restaurant was still busy with late breakfasts. She usually wouldn't eat before lunch but today she wanted to enjoy the privacy of her bliss a while longer. Exchanging brief good humour with staff and regulars she found a table by the wall laid with cutlery for one, decorated with three pink carnations in a slim crystal vase, and ordered hot chocolate, warm rolls and fruit preserves.

After the waiter had retreated Gina leaned back and observed the seemingly effortless efficiency with which guests were seated, served, brought newspapers and packs of cigarettes on silver trays. With a practised eye she identified the businessmen, the celebrities, the tourists, the lovers. She knew intuitively those who were relaxed, those in a hurry, those who were slightly overawed by the stylishness. She loved them all, these friends and strangers who were an intrinsic part of her existence, these men and women who were as essentially The Lady's lifeblood as Gina was its heart.

She smiled to herself, content.

The man who was walking toward her was of medium height, wearing a grey suit and a brown hat. His face, Gina thought casually, was rather expressionless. When he halted in front of her she said, 'Good morning. Can I help you?'

The man asked, 'Mrs Gina Cornell?'

'Yes,' she replied.

He reached inside his jacket pocket, took out a manilla envelope and a small leather wallet. He flipped open the wallet to reveal the shield of a United States Marshal, facing which was his picture and his name. Before Gina could read the name he closed the wallet and handed her the envelope.

'A subpoena,' he said without inflection. 'The subpoena is now duly served and you have accepted service.'

So stunned was Gina she simply stared at the envelope in her hand, and it was several moments before she realized the man was gone. She glanced around. The restaurant continued busily; no one seemed to have registered the marshal's arrival and departure. Gina shook herself back to her senses and tore open the envelope, slid out the single sheet of paper. She read the brief summons.

And felt as if she'd been shot in the stomach.

The pain she experienced was blindingly real. Gina bit back a cry. The sheet of paper slipped from her hand, fell, to lie before her, staring up at her, the blue embossed heading beneath the Government seal shining in the bright morning light: House UnAmerican Activities Committee.

Chapter Twenty Four

The effect was immediate and devastating.

The words on the outside of The Lady's front window, slashed in dripping orange paint, read, FILTHY COMMIES OUT. On the sidewalk, four men and three women took turns in brandishing aloft a scarlet banner on tall stakes declaring, REDS ARE POISONING YOU, while their companions distributed leaflets produced by the United League For The Preservation Of American Life.

It was late-afternoon, six hours after Gina's receipt of the subpoena. Since eleven am when the pickets had arrived, less than thirty people had risked entering the restaurant. All those had been lashed with verbal abuse by the United League members; and one, a man who'd dared to stop to argue his right to eat where he chose, had been spat on by the three women.

At present a newsreel crew was filming the scene.

Gina stood at her office window in the West-Rossi Building, looking obliquely down the street to the distant activity. As the newsreel camera swung around to point in her direction, she returned swiftly to her desk, to drop into her chair. The very sight of the camera made her stomach churn with nausea. Identical cameras had been hugely present on the television news report Gina had watched earlier.

She'd been in a quandary immediately after receiving the summons. Harry had hurried into the restaurant five minutes later and before Gina had had a chance to show him the official letter he'd told her there'd been unconfirmed radio reports that she'd been named as a possible Communist sympathizer.

'But who?' Gina had said desperately. 'Who named me?'

On the television broadcast the reporters had swarmed around the figure climbing from an ivory limousine. 'Is it true?' they'd yawped. 'Did you? Did you name Gina Cornell to the UnAmerican Activities Committee?' The figure had paused, waited for quiet, waited for all the newsreel cameras to focus; then, turning to face the lens directly ahead, 'Yes,' Tony Nevada had replied.

Sickness had erupted through Gina's stomach and she'd fled from the office to the bathroom to retch uncontrollably for several minutes. When she'd finally straightened, her entire body drenched in icy sweat, she'd seen again a mental picture of Tony Nevada's face, the day of their violent encounter last year in the shopping plaza, the singer's cheek livid with the weal of Gina's fingermarks, his eyes burning with hate.

The obscene phone calls had started only moments following the television broadcast. The pickets had arrived soon after. Gina had wanted to stay at The Lady but Harry had said the West-Rossi Building would be safer. He'd accompanied Gina out from the side of the restaurant, around the rear of the adjacent premises, and up the street.

'I'll get you a brandy,' Harry had said when they were in Gina's office, and he'd poured a hefty measure, brought it to where Gina was hunched on the sofa.

She'd swallowed half the liquor in two deep gulps, and its warmth had partially settled her swarming stomach. Within a few more minutes it had flowed into her bloodstream, driven out the worst of her chill. Eventually, as she'd regained some semblance of control, she'd protested, 'But, Harry, it's entirely untrue. I've never been involved in politics in my life.'

Harry had exhaled sadly. 'That isn't the point,' he'd said. 'This whole rotten business of naming names is just a charade. More and more entirely innocent people are being branded, either by characters who are trying to save their own necks, or by so-called friendly witnesses – volunteers – who are simply looking for personal publicity, settling old scores, or currying favour with McCarthy and his gangsters.'

Gina had nodded numbly. 'Fallon once told me something

like that. But, at the time, I suppose I just didn't want to think about it.' She'd suddenly shuddered.

'Take it easy,' Harry had said, his features struggling between disconcertion and reassurance.

Gina had reached out and briefly laid her hand over his. 'Thanks. I'm all right.' She'd taken another swallow of the brandy. When its slow heat had spread, she'd said more firmly, 'Yes, I understand. I'll get my day in front of the Committee. I'll prove my innocence. But by then it will be too late. The damage will have been done. West-Rossi will have been destroyed.' She thought grimly, Which is just what Tony Nevada intended.

As Harry had stared at her she'd seen his eyes begin to well, had known he was unable to speak. Rising quickly she'd said, 'Harry, would you mind if I had some time alone now? Please?' and had hurried to stand at the window, to look out, unseeing, her back to her friend, digging her nails into her palms until she'd heard him say raggedly, 'I'll see you in a while,' and, after a moment, the door opening then closing quietly.

But Gina had not wept.

Through the following nightmare hours she had told herself she would not weep. As reports had poured in from all over the country of an anti-West-Rossi upsurge twenty-times more ferocious than that which had been raised by the food poisoning, Gina had known she must hold her shattered emotions together until the direst decisions had been made, until some hope had been secured for her company and all those within it. She had understood there was only one course to take.

Now, at her desk, she kept her voice from cracking as she called, 'Come in,' to the knock at the door.

Irving entered and came to sit facing her. He said, 'I talked with Wheldon. He offers no alternative.'

Gina nodded. She hadn't expected anything different. During this afternoon, she and Irving had been over the situation again and again. They always came to the same conclusion: West-Rossi would have to be sold.

Irving's face looked tired and drawn. He continued, 'Wheldon offered the bank's apologies, but he said they couldn't possibly support the company until after you've appeared before the Committee. Eight weeks, he said, is out of the question. Gina, our debts are massive, and by the end of this week, maybe even sooner, our cash flow could be virtually non-existent.' He fell silent, swallowed a couple of times, as if having difficulty bringing moisture into his throat, before saying, 'It's all over.'

Gina inwardly flinched. For although this was what she already knew, the words, spoken out loud, held an added, cruel finality. She asked. 'We have to sell everything?'

Irving answered, 'Perhaps not lock, stock and barrel. We might be able to hold on to some part of the company. But,' he cautioned soberly, 'that's just a possibility, a slim chance. If all the prospective buyers want everything ...' he pursed his lips in a gesture of resignation, 'I'm afraid we're hardly in a position to dictate terms.' Then, with more of a determined tone he said, 'Still, I'll see what I can do.'

Gina returned a pale smile of gratitude. 'When will you put out the word we're for sale?'

'First thing tomorrow morning,' Irving replied. 'However, bad news travels fast, Wheldon says the bank has already been discreetly approached by most of the major catering and hotel corporations.'

'So soon?'

'Over a dozen calls since the television report. He told them nothing, of course. But, you know, they can pick up the smell of a financial death as well as ...' He cut off the sentence, his expression faltering self-reproachfully.

Gina said quietly, 'Yes. We've done it ourselves, in the past, haven't we.' She thought bitterly of the times they'd sat at this very desk discussing the gains they might make from some doomed company's imminent demise.

Irving said, 'We'll need to inform everyone – the directors, staff – and put out a press release.'

Gina nodded. Distraught calls had been coming in all afternoon from franchisees, suppliers, employees, friends and relations. But Gina had spoken to no one; not even to Filipo or Cassie or Max when her secretary had announced them on long-distance. It wasn't that she couldn't face talking with them – though she knew how painful this would be – rather that she felt she had to be able to give them some reassurance, tell them something positive when they inevitably asked what the future held. Thus, Gina had remained incommunicado to everyone except Harry and Irving for the past six hours. Now, with the die irretrievably cast, she would gather her last reserves of composure and call her friends.

She said, 'Thanks for all your help, Irving. I don't know what I'd have done without you. I wish ...' She suppressed a shiver of grief. 'It's just that Cornell Hotels ... you, and Cass ... and ...'

'Please,' Irving leaned forward, 'don't worry about the rest of us. We'll survive. Believe me, any company who takes us over won't close any of our operations. On the contrary, West-Rossi is ripe for expansion. I'm sure not a single employee will be made redundant.'

'But, you, personally ...?'

'I told you, don't worry. Gina, I know this has been a terrible day, it's all happened so suddenly, but, in a way, we've gone past the worst just as quickly. Try to switch off for a while now. Take a sleeping tablet if necessary. Get a good night's rest. We'll meet again tomorrow to discuss the practical moves we have to make next. Okay?' He gave her a positive smile.

Gina drew a breath. 'Okay,' she said.

A few minutes later, as Irving closed the door behind him on the way out, she leaned back, tried to rebuild some strength on the foundation of the accountant's reasurrances. She believed what he'd said about the company's future, knew it wasn't in his nature to offer false hopes. What Gina now had to live with was the loss of everything she'd strived for over the years.

Not everything, an inner voice unexpectedly countered. You still have The Lady.

Gina straightened again at this prompting. Throughout the devastation of the afternoon, she hadn't remembered the isolated fact. Yes, The Lady was wholly hers; it was the one item she hadn't pledged to the bank. The thought at once raised her spirits. But within a second she'd tumbled back into guilt. Was it right that she should keep the restaurant when everyone else ...?

She was unable to finish the question, let alone answer it. Her mind had been too mauled to cope with any more interrogations or counter-arguments. Irving had been right; she must try to switch off. She'd go back to The Lady, call Filipo and Cassie and Max, then get some sleep ...

The intercom buzzed.

Gina flicked the switch. 'Yes?'

Her secretary said, 'Mister Cornell is on the line.'

Gina almost said, Who?

'Shall I put him through?' asked the secretary.

Gina pulled her thoughts together. 'Yes, please.' She lifted the telephone and said, 'Hello, Howard.'

'Gina, is that you?'

'Yes,' she returned, trying to keep the weariness out of her voice. She couldn't remember when last she'd spoken with her husband, nor even when she'd given him more than a passing thought. But, then, when had he spared a moment for her? Not one word had come from him following the poisoning. That had been, how long ago? Gina couldn't recall; she was having difficulty following her thoughts.

'No need to be so curt,' said Howard.

'I'm sorry.'

He was silent a moment. Then: 'I saw the news.'

'Yes.'

'Gina, it isn't true, is it, what Tony Nevada said? I know it isn't. Look ... there's something ...' he faltered.

Gina's nerves were tightening.

'The last time we spoke,' said Howard, 'when you said we should discuss ... things.'

Now Gina remembered when last she'd spoken with her husband: their confrontation on the telephone the day after she'd returned from Fallon on Key West. It seemed a lifetime ago. An image of Fallon flashed in her head. She blanked it out and responded levelly to Howard, 'Yes, that's what I said. And you said you'd call me. Why didn't you? Where have you been? You must have heard about ...' She was on the verge of mentioning the food poisoning, but, she decided, there really wasn't any point.

'I went away for a while,' said Howard. 'Out of the country.' There was an uncertain edge in his voice and he seemed about to add something more. Instead, he paused and then asked, 'When can I see you?'

The prospect of discussing the termination of her marriage burned Gina like a fresh wound. But it had to be done, regardless of the present circumstances. She replied, 'Any time you like, Howard,' and added, 'but soon.'

He said flatly, 'Very well.'

Gina said 'Goodbye,' and set down the receiver. It occurred to her she hadn't even asked him where he was calling from. However, prolonging a telephone conversation wasn't a good idea. At least he hadn't had time to become quarrelsome or obstinate again. She thought briefly of how she would cope when they met, but set the speculation aside; too any other bridges to think about before she crossed that one.

It was coming up to five pm. Gina looked around the room, and had a sudden sense of claustrophobia, felt she'd been shut in here for ever. Arising swiftly, she went out to her secretary's office, said she was through here for today and was returning to The Lady. After a few more words, she took the elevator to the lobby. The security guard walked to meet her as she crossed toward the main doors.

'Mrs Cornell, you leaving now?'

'Yes, Ed. I'll see you in the morning.'

He pulled open the glass door, glanced up the street. 'Maybe I should walk with you. Those pickets are still there.' He accompanied Gina onto the sidewalk.

She looked toward where the banner-brandishing United Leaguers were distributing their leaflets outside the restaurant. 'That's okay, thanks all the same, Ed,' she said with a casualness she didn't really feel. 'I'll be all right.'

'Well ...' he said, unsure.

'Really,' assured Gina with a bold smile. 'Goodnight.' As the guard touched the peak of his cap and said, 'Goodnight, Mrs Cornell,' Gina strode across the street and along the opposite sidewalk. When she glanced back over her shoulder, Ed was still standing in the West-Rossi doorway. She was grateful for that.

Two of the female pickets were holding the banner. Their companions were wandering back and forth, pausing to occasionally exchange comments or shout slogans. Gina ignored them, detouring around them to The Lady's entrance.

'Don't go in there,' barked one of the men.

Gina reflexively halted.

Stepping rapidly into her path, the man blocked her route to the restaurant door. He thrust a leaflet toward her. 'Don't want to get poisoned, do you,' he said, as a statement rather than a question. To Gina's fixed stare, he added, 'Hadn't you heard? This is that place owned by Communists.'

Gina said, 'Please step aside.'

'I don't think you understand …'

'I understand you're obstructing the sidewalk.'

'Now look here, lady.' The man's voice was suddenly aggressive. His pals had turned to watch. 'Are you a Commie sympathizer or something? Or don't you realize what's going on in this country. Here, read this.' He waved a leaflet. 'This'll tell you. All about the Reds. You know how many Reds we got, running our businesses, our schools, our banks, our Government even? Millions. Millions is how many. Millions of Stalin's fifth columnists.'

'Saboteurs and subversives,' yelled one of the women.

'Is that what you are?' rasped the man, glaring at Gina. 'Are you one of them?'

Gina said, 'I'm an American.'

The man's face twisted as if he'd been struck. 'Don't get smart with me,' he snarled and threw a glance over her clothes. 'I know, you're one of those rich bitches with more money than sense. Never had to do a day's work in your life. Playing footsie with those bloody Commies and queers and intellectuals. Well let me warn you …'

'Get out of my way,' hissed Gina.

'What?' the man flashed venomously.

'You heard me.'

'I'll give you …' His voice trailed away, his aggression crumpling as he stared into Gina's face.

Her teeth were clenched, her breath sucking into her nostrils. She repeated in a voice that was flat, almost inaudible, 'Get out of my way.' Her features were rigidly expressionless, but the fire in the depths of her eyes was murderous.

The man remained stock still.

Gina stepped around him and went into the restaurant lobby, the door swinging shut in her wake. She halted but didn't look back. Her hands were shaking and her breath was coming in short, hard gasps. As she endeavoured to regain some self-control, Chang hurried out from the restaurant. 'Hi,' Gina said, raising a smile.

'Those thugs,' said Chang, distressed, throwing a look out to the street, 'did they harm you?'

'Not at all,' assured Gina. 'Just tried to sell me some of their religion.' Glancing around, she realized there was no one on duty at the cloakroom counter. Before she could query the situation, however, Chang spread his hands in a gesture of lament, saying:

'No customers all afternoon. All reservations cancelled. A few people try to get in. The thugs, the pickets, warn them off. A fight earlier. One woman knocked down.' He shook his head as if in disbelief at his own words. 'What are we going to do, Gina?'

She faced him in silence. All at once she answered, 'We'll close for tonight.' Recognizing his disappointment, she quickly added, 'Don't worry, I'm not giving in to those louts out there. It's simply that I don't want any would-be customers getting hurt on my account, or having to eat here, afraid what will happen when they leave.'

'When will we open?' Chang asked unhappily.

'I'm not sure,' admitted Gina. 'I'll call you at home tomorrow. But we will open, soon, I promise you. Please, will you inform the staff. Tell them not to worry. They'll all stay on full wages as long as we're closed.' A wave of tiredness swept her. 'Now, if you don't mind, I'm going up to wash and change. When you leave would you turn up the Closed sign on the window. I'll be down in a little while to lock all the doors.'

Chang stood, hesitant.

Though Gina cared dearly for this man to whom she owed much of The Lady's success, she felt she couldn't face any further emotional involvement tonight. She said calmly, 'I'll call you tomorrow,' and walked swiftly away.

In the apartment she sat on the edge of the bed for ten minutes, weighted by the urge to draw up her legs and sink backwards to sleep. But she had yet to call Cassie and the others. Pulling herself to her feet, Gina went out to the bathroom, doused her face in cold water, held her chilled palms to her temples in an effort to pierce some clarity to her brain. Gradually her energy began to seep back, her mind to function.

Changed into a plain beige wool suit, thirty minutes after her arrival here, Gina returned downstairs.

The lights were still on in the restaurant, but it was lifeless and silent. Gina moved slowly amid the white-linened tables, automatically shifting a centrepiece of flowers an inch this way or that, straightening a chair, smoothing the faintest crease from a napkin. She paused, looking across the room and out through the window. The streetlamps were on. Traffic hummed into the approaching night. People hurried by on the sidewalk. There were no pickets.

Gina stared. Hastening to the window, she peered out, left and right. The gang had definitely gone. Gina sighed with a certain relief; at the same time, she determined that if they returned tomorrow she'd somehow be ready for them. The thought gave her a spurt of renewed resolve.

She went to the bar, poured herself a brandy, brought it back to a corner table, sat, her hands around the crystal balloon, staring down into the liquor's glow. Briefly, her mind went back over the day, this terrible day. 'Don't,' she ordered herself, and obliterated the mental images. There was no point in reliving those cruel hours. What was important now was tomorrow, and the day after, and the rest of her life. Gathering the fragments of her determination she began to try to make them whole.

She lifted the glass to drink, raising her head.

And looked directly into Oliver Randolph's eyes.

Chapter Twenty Five

He was standing in the archway from the lobby, his looming bulk seeming to fill the space. Gina was frozen with astonishment. She remained staring at the man as he started toward her between the tables apparently even more gross than when Gina last had seen him.

He halted in front of her table and said, 'Good evening,' his confident mouth curving in a fat smile.

Gina was inwardly shaking; and she damned herself for the reaction, detesting Randolph the more for causing it. But still she was transfixed, unable to utter a word; her mind had been shocked into blackness.

Randolph said unctuously, 'My dear Mrs Cornell, may I?' and pulled out the chair facing Gina and sat, setting a hide briefcase on the floor at his side. 'The security guard at your office told me you'd be here.' He glanced around, surveying the room for several moments before remarking, 'Such a splendid restaurant. Surely the finest in the city.' He nodded with vain acceptance of his own declaration.

Gina was struggling to marshal her wits, the rancour now overriding the race of alarm she'd felt at his initial appearance. At last she found her voice and said curtly, 'I didn't invite you to join me, Mister Randolph. Nor do I intend to. I'd be obliged if you left.'

His smile remained oiled on his face. 'But you haven't yet heard what I have to say.'

As Gina's anger strengthened, her reason recommenced to function. At once she knew why he was here. She said coldly, 'I thought I had made myself fully understood to your man Scheer when he too presented himself unannounced in Las Vegas. I have no intention whatsoever of selling a single part of my company to the Randolph Corporation.'

The gross man gave a coarse laugh. 'So,' he said, 'you have grasped the purpose of this intimate meeting. Good. Excellent. However, I must point out, it is not a single part of your company I intend to purchase, my dear, but all of it.'

Gina contained a snort of derision.

But obviously Randolph could see the emotion in her eyes. A harder edge came into his voice. 'Don't start playing games, Mrs Cornell. I have neither the time nor the inclination. We both know that West-Rossi is for sale. It became so the minute our friend Mister Nevada offered his testimony to Senator McCarthy's investigators. You have no alternative but to sell. Everything. And you will sell it to me.'

Gina burned. But her will was forsaking her. There was something deadly in Randolph's chill confidence.

Lifting his briefcase, he set it on the table, opened it and extracted a slim, grey document. 'A contract,' he said. 'Our bargain will be quite legitimate for all the world to see. Indeed, we will announce it with a press conference. I shall declare how proud I am to be the new owner of the West-Rossi businesses. You will say how delighted you are to have your company taken into the care of America's foremost hospitality corporation.'

Gina automatically had accepted the folded sheaf and was staring numbly at it.

'No need to read it now,' said Randolph. 'Study it later. Show it to your attorneys. They, of course, along with my own advisers, will handle the necessary legalities. All of which, I appreciate, will require time. But not too much. Let us say a week. You have seven days in which to remove all your personal effects before I take possession of this building.'

Gina was feeling physically dizzy, caught in the bizarre spin of events, so that she wasn't sure what she'd heard in Randolph's astonishing speech. 'What?' she said, partly to herself. 'This building? No ...'

'Yes,' rejoined Randolph. 'I thought I made myself clear. All your businesses, Mrs Cornell. I intend to own all of them. Including,' he swept an arm about the scene, 'this splendid establishment.'

'Never,' shot Gina. 'This restaurant ...'

'Will be mine,' rapped Randolph.

'Not in a million years,' Gina retaliated vehemently. 'Sell to you? Allow The Lady to fall into your hands? The suggestion is unthinkable. The very idea is obscene. I would never permit it. It has to do with honour, and self-respect, qualities I doubt you even understand. You and your kind, you racketeers, you're not fit to ...'

'Enough!' Randolph's voice was a whiplash. He moved slightly back, his brow reddening, his cheeks trembling, breathing heavily through his nostrils, so that Gina thought he was about to explode with fury. But after a moment the bestiality retreated and his features petrified to a malignant scowl. Then, slowly, without taking his eyes from Gina, he once more reached into the briefcase, drew out glossy cards, black and white ...

Gina peered.

Photographs. Randolph extended his arm and dropped them on the table before Gina.

She stared down at the scene: a city street in grey rain; a crowd of people fighting; placards; a policeman wielding a baton. Gina frowned, puzzled. And then she saw in the background of the picture, fuzzily out of focus but discernible, the sign above a window – The Kwik Koffee Kup. And she instantly remembered. The AFF demonstration outside the Randolph Corporation snack bar last autumn.

As Gina stared at the photograph, Randolph reached across to slide it aside and reveal an enlargement of a section of it: a hazy close-up of Gina, yelling, apparently battling in the midst of the mob. Again Randolph uncovered the next picture. This showed a group of the demonstrators being bundled into the patrol wagon. Beneath this, the final print, another indistinct enlargement revealing Gina as one of the detainees.

Gina's very mind had become chilled. She was unable to think. The surrounding room seemed to have retreated to a great distance so that the table where she was sitting was marooned in a void. She heard Randolph say:

'Taken by the manager of the cafe where you staged your

rabble-rousing. It's our company policy to obtain graphic evidence whenever possible of disturbances outside our premises so that persistent troublemakers can be, shall we say, dissuaded from further activity.' His mouth twisted maliciously before he went on, 'Unfortunately these pictures were not brought to my attention until quite recently when it occurred to one of my staff that the person being taken into custody bore a marked resemblance …'

'Marked resemblance,' snapped Gina. 'To whom. Me? Is that what you're implying? Is that why you're here with this trash?' She was struggling fiercely to master the situation. 'But this,' she said, flicking a derisive hand at the figure in the hazy prints, 'could be anybody.'

Randolph returned a contemptuous smile.

'Or the pictures could be fakes,' Gina declared, trying to keep the desperation out of her tone. 'Yes, obviously, they are fakes. Stop wasting my time, Mister Randolph,' she clipped with all the scorn she could muster. 'Your cheap trickery won't wash here. Take your tacky photo …'

'Mrs Cornell …' Randolph's gutteral voice interrupted, 'it is you who should stop wasting time. You know perfectly well this evidence is genuine. And surely you don't imagine I haven't had your exploits of that day further investigated.' He stressed the last two words.

Gina flinched, and fear enmeshed her.

'Look,' commanded Randolph and stabbed fat fingers at the photographs. 'How many people are the police herding into that patrol wagon? Ten. But you don't need me to count them, do you? Because you remember. You remember full well there were ten of you taken into detention. Ten held in cells at the precinct house. Ten. But …' He banged his fist down on the pictures with such sudden force, Gina recoiled. 'But,' he repeated, 'how many appeared in court the following morning? Ten? Or one less? How many, Mrs Cornell?'

The question lashed Gina.

Randolph rasped, 'You know how many. And so do I. I also know that your name does not appear on the detainees list. Plus the fact, the investigating officer was a Detective Sergeant Shaughnessy. The same officer you have seen on at least two other occasions.' He glared with aggressive triumph. 'Could it be, my dear Mrs Cornell, that you and the detective have conspired to pervert the course of justice? Can it be that the detective, like you, is a Communist? Ought this matter to be reported to his superiors? Ought his name to be handed to the UnAmerican Activities Committee?'

Gina shrank from the vehemence, her head hammered by the savage assault. Frantically, she tried to grasp some straw of hope amid the whirlpool of her desperation. But before she could even begin to form a response to Randolph, he was snapping shut his briefcase.

'You know as well as I,' he sneered, 'all I have to do now is have your fellow detainees questioned to discover when the detective Shaughnessy contrived your release. And then ...?' He gave a mocking shake of his head. 'But, we don't need to pursue that, do we? Because we aren't going to go that far. You aren't going to allow it. You aren't going to allow the UnAmerican Activities Committee to learn about your part in a violent radical street demonstration and your subsequent corruption of a police officer. You aren't going to allow your beloved family to be smeared by the muck of your own public disgrace. Are you? Are you, my dear Mrs Cornell?'

His eyes were as hard and as cold as black pebbles. Gina looked into them, shaking with the Arctic blizzard of her emotions. She tried to defy his stare; but could not. She dropped her gaze, saw before her the photographs and the slim, grey contract.

Randolph rose to his feet with heavy menace. When he spoke his voice was a bass growl. 'Tomorrow morning, Mrs Cornell, I shall expect your attorneys' confirmation of your sale of all the West-Rossi businesses. All of them.' He held her with his harsh triumph for one long threatening moment before he turned and lumbered across the room. At the distant archway he looked back, his face a brute mask.

And then Gina was alone.

She knew there now was no one to whom she could turn.

The evening had passed. Gina hadn't seen it pass; didn't know what she had done since Randolph's leaving. There had been nothing in her head save his words, all his words, repeating themselves over and over until Gina felt her skull would burst from within. Yet there was no denying them. Their validity was irrefutable. Randolph's trap was inescapable.

Gina stood at the open window of her apartment, stared out at the bright night of her city. She listened to the familiar sounds of the streets, all the intimate activity which had been the background of her life for so many years. She breathed the scent of her room – old wood and leather, lavender, the herbs and wines of the restaurant kitchen far below – the fragrance which was the wellspring of so much of her life's joy.

But, would the future be so bleak without all this? Would her existence be desolate without The Lady? After all, what was this place? Just a building; a restaurant and a nightclub; a small apartment. These were inanimate things. How could parting with them break a heart?

Gina cracked down the window, yanked together the curtains, squeezed shut her eyes.

Her mind travelled back to that day when, after months of chambermaid drudgery and exhausting ten-cents-a-dance nights at the Starlight Room, she'd come with her savings and a mortgage guaranteed by Harry Dix, to a deserted, neglected old villa on Forty-seventh Street. Grime and cobwebs clung everywhere, but rising from the detritus of the years had been the staircase, sweeping upward to the gallery with carved balusters and handrail. And Gina had imagined clearly Manhattan's society ascending and descending there, pausing for a word or joke, the men puffing their majestic Havanas, the women clothed in their latest elegance. She'd foreseen in perfect detail ivory-linened tables, silver and crystal and porcelain and misted buckets of chilled champagne. She'd smelled vases of gardenias, heard romantic music, tasted fine food and wine, felt the grip of her sister and brother's hand as they stood beside her on the opening night. 'But it won't be simply a restaurant,' she'd averred to Max. 'It will be a new beginning for us in our new land. A place to put down roots, where we all can achieve and grow. It will be where we belong. It will be our home.'

Now, Gina opened her eyes. And could not see.

Blinded by tears she fled to her bedroom. She threw herself onto the bed, face buried in the pillow. Then, defeated, her strength and her anger drained, she collapsed under a flood of grief. She wept bitterly. Gina wept for a long time.

She wasn't sure what sound finally pulled her to a sitting position. She didn't really know whether she'd heard anything or if it had been part of a tormented dream; whether she'd been awake on the bed for minutes or, hours ago, had sobbed herself to sleep.

Gina dragged in an anguish-riven breath. Her head ached and her nerves were raw. But her mind was clear now. Tomorrow she would instruct her attorneys to confirm the sale of both the West-Rossi Corporation and The Lady to Oliver Randolph. Her heart shuddered at the thought; but, she knew, the nightmare was a reality, and all her hopes ended here.

The headache was becoming worse. Gina pushed herself to her feet, went out to the bathroom, ran herself a glass of water, opened the medicine cabinet to find some codeine. She rarely took drugs, couldn't remember when last she'd felt the need. The bottle was almost full. Gina hesitated, staring at the mass of white tablets. She recalled someone today had said she should get a good night's rest.

More than a minute passed before she took down the bottle and carried it and the glass of water through the bedroom and out to her desk. She sat behind the desk, the bottle and glass before her. Gina closed her hands around the arms of her chair. This was where she had planned The Lady's first menu, where she had devised the franchising of Rossi Taverns, the expansion into entertainment management, the building of the casino in Las Vegas. This was where Gina had secured her family's future; where she had made every major decision of her life.

She faced the bottle of tablets. A good night's rest. A deep sleep. An end to her pains.

Slowly, she reached forward, took hold of the bottle, twisted off the cap.

Something scraped outside the door.

Gina froze as she saw the door handle begin to turn. Then her thoughts splintered. She leapt to her feet, dropping the bottle, scattering rattling tablets across the desktop, splashing water from the glass.

The door flew open, banged back against the wall. Gant stood silhouetted before the glow of the wall lights.

Gina was too shocked to scream. She recognized the man even though his face was in shadow; his short but powerful body, thick arms flexed at his sides, big hands clenching and unclenching. He was looking directly at Gina, eyes wide in a swarthy face thrust forward from his shoulders. He took a sudden step into the room, a growl issuing from his parted lips.

Gina automatically retreated and the back of her legs bumped into her chair. She halted, feeling desperately trapped, throwing a look across the room to the bedroom door but at once knowing she didn't stand a chance of running there.

Gant took a couple more paces, halted, swaying his shoulders from side to side. His jacket and shirt were open, revealing the glistening corded muscles of his throat. His features gleamed with sweat, their coarse lines and planes accentuated by the yellow glare of the desk lamp.

Gina glanced toward the desk lamp. Could she, the same as before, snatch it and hurl it through the window at her back? Even as the idea occurred, she remembered with despair that she'd pulled the heavy curtains.

As if reading her thoughts, Gant rasped, 'Not this time, lady high and mighty.'

The voice startled Gina as it broke the silence. And its harshness sent fear down her spine. There was nothing sullen in it, not an iota of uncertainty. In that instant Gina knew he wanted to kill her. The realization paralysed her. She was so utterly terrified she couldn't remember how to move or speak.

Gant rasped, 'This time you'll pay, bitch. Pay for treating me like dirt. Pay for your lies.'

'I never lied about you,' blurted Gina.

'You'll scumming pay,' snarled Gant and lunged.

Gina seized the glass of water, flung it into his face,

rammed out from behind the desk, hurled herself toward the bedroom door as Gant roared. Was the key in the other side of the lock? Gina wrenched open the door, almost fell into the room, losing her grip on the handle. She punched at the door, slamming it shut, blindly grabbing for the key, jerking it around even as Gant's body smashed into the opposite side of the timber.

The door held, but the fury of the crash sent Gina tumbling backwards. She tried to turn, arms flailing, but went sprawling on the floor, her brow bashing against the side of the dressing table. Pain cannoned through her head; white light exploded behind her eyes. Another crashing impact detonated against the other side of the door and one of the panels split.

Gina groped for the dressing table edge, dragged herself to her feet, tottered there, realizing there was something liquid streaming into her left eye. She swabbed at it with her hand, brought her fingers into vision and saw them wetly scarlet. The lurid colour shocked her into consciousness. Pushing herself away from the dressing table, she part stumbled, part ran toward the door which gave onto the hall. If she only could get out there she could smash the glass of the fire alarm on the wall before escaping down the stairs.

Gina reached the door. Her breath was sawing in her chest, her hand was shaking uncontrollably as she seized the brass knob, jerked it around. It didn't turn. She frantically tried again. And again. But her fingers just slipped around the metal. Through the whirlwind of panic she understood her hand was slick with blood. Almost out of her wits Gina mopped at the brass with a bunch of her skirt, grabbed with her dry hand, squeezed and twisted. Pulled open the door.

Dashed through.

Into Gant's arms.

Gina screamed.

His hands were on her shoulders, turning her, heaving her off her feet, dragging her backwards, one thick arm across her throat, the other around her waist.

Gina's breath was being forced out. She strove to suck air into her lungs while she writhed and kicked, clawed at Gant's grip. He was panting, rasping obscenities as he hauled her along the corridor. Yet Gina could barely distinguish the words. The roaring of her blood was filling her head. The light seemed to be growing brighter, with crimson darts flashing behind her eyes, needles of pain lancing into her brain.

Gina knew she was choking to death.

They reached the door at the end of the corridor. Gant shouldered his way through, lifting Gina, cracking her knees on the jamb, heaving her into the lobby like a carcass. He was lumbering sideways, grunting, cursing. He halted, shifted his grip.

Gina gulped in a huge breath as his arm slackened on her windpipe. Her throat was on fire. Her entire skull felt as if it was being pounded by fists. She could taste blood in her mouth. In an agony of fear she struggled with the draining dregs of her strength. And then she realized her back was being forcibly arched. Gant's weight was bearing down on her upper body while he strained to change position. The crook of his arm was beneath her buttocks. He heaved. Lifted Gina clear off the floor.

She was being carried.

Scream, her failing reason ordered. But she knew she could not. Her lungs felt crushed. Her limbs were rubber, uselessly flailing. She had no sense of orientation; couldn't tell whether she was vertical or horizontal; didn't know where she was going; was aware only of her lurching, shambling movement, her rising into the air. She was rising, upward, upward and outward.

Again Gant's grasp shifted. Gina turned her head; stared into his contorted, sweating face. His eyes were wide, their whites redly veined, the pupils hugely dilated. Flecks of spittle bubbled at the corners of his mouth as his lips issued hoarse, unintelligible sounds. Gina jerked her gaze away, and saw outward across a void. She looked down. But did not see the floor; saw, at a great distance, the tops of tables and chairs. Momentarily her mind couldn't comprehend the scene. Then it recognized the horrifying reality.

Gina was suspended in mid-air, beyond the balustrade of the stairwell, staring down past this floor and the next to the restaurant far below.

'No!' she screamed.

'Lady High and Mighty,' rasped Gant, leaning outward.

Terror-stricken, Gina grabbed frantically at his shoulders and head as she felt herself being forced further away from his body. Her fingers raked at his face, caught at his hair. She locked her grip in the thick, greasy strands and heard him bellow with rage and pain. He wrenched his head sideways, tearing his hair from Gina's grasp. Her nails ripped down his cheeks and blood burst and poured from the jagged furrows. Gant's arm convulsed.

Gina felt her stomach lurch. She was dropping.

'Gina!'

As her name yelled up the stairwell, she snatched at Gant's shirtfront. He was jerking away, pulling her with him. She held on, dangling momentarily in space, then was swinging into the side of the balustrade. From the corner of her eye she saw the figure dashing up the stairs. Gant had released her. She was clinging to the balustrade, scrambling with arms and legs, scouring the flesh from her elbows and shins. One of her shoes fell. She had an arm over the rail.

Howard reached the landing.

Gant swung to face him.

Gina's legs were turning to lead. The effort to haul her feet up to a ledge was beyond the ability of her battered limbs. She knew she couldn't do it, couldn't possibly save herself. Mental exhaustion too was erasing her ability to think. Her muscles seemed to be melting, her puny hold on the balustrade failing. God help me, she sobbed silently.

A roar of anger ripped into Gina's torpor. As she saw Gant rush upon Howard, with one final surge she shoved her arms further over the rail. And felt the body weight on her muscles decrease. She had some support. A gasp of relief escaped her battered chest.

Gant was locked with Howard. They wrestled and heaved. Gina clung desperately to her handhold. She saw Howard stagger back then recover to throw himself at Gant. The two men stumbled toward Gina. Howard broke away but in the same moment Gant hurled his clublike fist. Gina glimpsed the huge, clenched hand, her husband's head jerking away, his own fist powering forward. She heard the crack of bone on bone. Gant rocked. Howard hit him again, a furious blow.

Gant was slammed backwards.

Gina saw his shoulders rushing toward her, felt the small of his back smash into her arm upon the rail. Then he was arching over her head, flying outward with a terrified animal scream. In a flash of suspended time Gina was looking at her husband. The next instant her shattered arm was flapping into her face and the air shrieked in her ears as she plummetted downward.

Chapter Twenty Six

There was bright, white light and a lot of noise and the smell of blood and antiseptic. Crowds of people seemed to be all around. People touching and stroking and holding. The people's voices were an unintelligible babble. Their faces were stark; their eyes, full of pity and pain. Someone was weeping. Gina couldn't understand why they were weeping. She wished they'd stop because it made her feel sad. She didn't want to feel sad. She wanted to go on being happy. Her only regret was that she couldn't see properly; the scene around her kept fading in and out of a grey mist. She tried to focus, but could not. Still, she thought, no point in worrying. She'd sleep now. She was very tired. She had a sensation of being lifted, of floating along with all those people moving beside. This floating was really rather pleasant. And someone was tenderly holding her hand. It was a man. She couldn't quite remember who the man was, although, she seemed to recall, a short while ago he'd been staring down at her from a great height. Now he was staring down at her and holding her hand. Gina tried to smile at him but was just too tired. She closed her eyes, heard the man saying brokenly, 'Gina, I'm so sorry ... I didn't mean to do it ... I didn't want any of this to happen ...' But then Gina was sinking, deeper and deeper into the grey mist. She didn't mind. She didn't mind about anything any more.

Chapter Twenty Seven

The room was small and painted yellow. It seemed to be full of flowers. The sunlight shining through the single window made the flowers appear very bright. The sunlight fell upon the white-shrouded figure of Gina, upon her hands crossed on her breast, and upon her pale face. It was warm. She felt the warmth and opened her eyes.

Cassie said, 'Hi.'

Gina blinked twice and said, 'Where am I?'

Cassie said, 'They only say that in the movies.'

And Gina gave a small laugh and it ricocheted through her entire body like a fugitive bullet. She gasped.

Cassie was instantly off the bedside chair. 'What?' she said urgently. 'Are you okay? I'll get the doc.'

'No, please don't,' returned Gina. She inhaled deeply, then steadied her breathing. 'It was just a short pain. More of a surprise than anything. Truly.'

Cassie scanned Gina's features. 'Well ...' she murmured, 'if you're sure,' and slowly sat down again. 'But, you know, I'm supposed to call them when you wake.'

'Not yet,' requested Gina. 'They'll stick another needle in my behind, send me straight back to sleep.' She nodded in reply to Cassie's questioning look. 'Yes, I remember, they did it before. Although ...' she frowned, 'I don't know when that was. It's all rather fuzzy.'

'Maybe going back to sleep isn't a bad idea.'

'No. Really. My head is clearing. I realize I'm in a hospital. I'm feeling all right.' Gina smiled, carefully. 'At least I think I am.' She peered downward to where her right arm lay encased in plaster. The plaster ended at her first knuckles. Her protruding fingers were pale blue. She looked at the other arm. It wasn't plastered, but, like its hand, it was almost entirely indigo. Gina stared in alarm.

'It's okay,' Cassie said hastily. 'It's bruising, that's all. Honestly. The doc says it'll look as right as rain in a couple of weeks. The other one's broken, a compound fracture, but they've put some plates and screws in and it's going to be fine. So's the rest of you. Nothing really badly damaged. You're just ... well ... knocked about a bit. Hon, you were so lucky. If it hadn't been for ...' She bit off the sentence, looking vaguely uncomfortable.

'Yes?' prompted Gina.

Cassie cast an uncertain glance toward the door. She nibbled the inside of her lip, then, turning to Gina, she asked tentatively, 'Do you remember what happened?'

Gina's brow furrowed. 'Some of it. Yes ...' She squeezed shut her eyes in concentration. 'I can see ... the top landing at The Lady. And ... two men struggling. I can see ... myself ...' All at once the image flashed vividly in her head. For an instant she was back there, clinging desperately to the balustrade. She was staring into Howard's stricken face. And then she fell. Her stomach lurched and she almost cried out. But she quelled the moment's panic and, opening her eyes, said quietly, 'Yes, I remember, Cass.' She added, 'How long ago was it?'

Cassie said, 'You've been here four days.'

Gina stared. 'Unconscious?'

'Mostly. The doctors tried to explain it to me. A sort of shock, they said. Not just from the physical injuries, but also from the mental strain you'd been under before. But, thank goodness, they say it's passed now. You came out of it early this morning – it's three pm by the way – and talked for a while before they gave you the shot to send you back to sleep. Do you really feel all right, Hon?'

Gina assured, 'I ache a lot, but I'm wide awake.'

'That's good. They said if you did, you'd be fine. I mean, apart from ...' Cassie glanced at Gina's arms.

Gina smiled. Then, wondering, she asked, 'I did fall, didn't I? All the way? Top to bottom?'

'Yes.'

'But ... all I got was a broken arm?'

Cassie nodded.

Gina, troubled, pressed, 'Please, Cass, what happened?'

Her friend drew a breath. 'You were lucky,' she murmured. 'You didn't ... hit the floor. Your fall was ...' She hesitated, her search for the right words written in her face. At last she said softly, 'Gant was underneath you.'

The statement seemed to hang on the air for several moments. Gina understood. She saw again the rushing sides of the stairwell, the high ceiling flying away. But when she tried to recall the final second of her plunge, she could not. Nor, she suddenly decided, did she want to. Nevertheless, she did ask quietly, 'And Gant?'

Cassie said, 'Please, don't worry. It had nothing to do with your fall. The medical examiner was certain. Gant died instantly from a fractured skull when his head struck the edge of a table.' She reached out and gently laid a hand over Gina's.

They sat that way, in silence, for some time.

Presently Gina said, 'I'd like to sit up straighter.'

Cassie said, 'Hon, I don't know. The doc ...'

'Oh, please, Cass. I told you, I feel all right. And after what you just told me, I'd rather not go back to sleep. Is anyone else here with you at the hospital?'

'Well ...'

The door opened and a nurse entered. 'Mrs Cornell, you're awake. The doctor will be pleased. He won't be in until later. I'll give you a shot so you'll sleep till then.'

'You will not,' retaliated Gina in alarm.

'I beg your pardon?'

'I've been asleep for four days.'

'That's as may be.'

'And I don't intend ...'

'Nurse,' Cassie interjected hastily, 'could Mrs Cornell do without the shot if she promised to just lie here quietly? I'm sure she will.' She threw Gina A Look.

The nurse hesitated. After a moment's deliberation she came and leaned forward to peer into Gina's eyes. She made 'Mmming' sounds and stuck a thermometer in the patient's mouth and took her pulse. Having noted the temperature and scribbled on the foot-of-the-bed chart, she declared,

'Very well. But,' she cautioned, 'only very quiet conversation.'

Cassie said, 'There was someone else waiting downstairs to see Mrs Cornell. Might they visit?'

The nurse considered. Then: 'I'll send him up.'

As soon as she was gone, Gina asked, 'Who?'

Cassie said, 'Fallon.'

Gina caught her breath.

'Did I make a mistake?' Cassie asked with concern. 'Hon, I thought …' She frowned apologetically. 'This couple of days, Fallon and I … Well, to be honest, I asked him some questions. I know, I was putting my oar in. But, I was worried for you. About what was going to happen after all this. Fallon was worried too. He told me … nothing personal, you understand, but …' She paused, looking self-conscious. 'Please don't think I was prying, Hon. I wouldn't for the world, only …'

'I know you wouldn't,' Gina said gently. 'I'm glad you talked with Fallon. And I'm sorry I've kept it from you all this time. It was simply that I wanted to be sure about it all before I said anything to anybody. Then I got the subpoena from the Committee and it seemed all my decisions had been shot to pieces. I didn't know what the future was going to hold.'

Cassie nodded. 'Fallon felt the same way. But, Hon, if you'd rather not see him for the time being, I'm sure he'll understand. I can go and stop him …'

'No. Please don't,' said Gina. 'I want to talk to him, very much. I'd rather it was now.'

'Sure?'

'Positive. Will you help me sit up?' Gina saw her friend's hesitation. 'I didn't promise the nurse I'd remain lying down, did I? Please, Cass. I can't talk to Fallon like this. Besides, I have to comb my hair. I must look a sight.'

Cassie faltered another moment before conceding, 'Okay, but don't blame me if they give you an extra sharp shot in the butt tonight.' She moved around the bed, and, very carefully, eased Gina into a semi-sitting position, propped up with pillows. 'That's as far as you're getting,' she declared. 'Now, I'll comb your hair.'

'I can do it,' returned Gina, experimentally raising her unplastered arm. 'Where's a mirror?'

'I don't think there is one.'

'The one in your compact will do.'

'Compact?'

'Come on, Cass. He'll be here in a minute.'

'Gina, I can perfectly well comb your hair.'

'For goodness sake, I'm not an invalid.'

Cassie blew out an acquiescent breath. 'Very well,' she said, opening her purse, producing her tortoiseshell compact, opening it and placing it in Gina's hand.

Gina winced slightly as she closed her fingers around the compact, but she held it and slowly raised it and peered at her reflection and exclaimed:

'Oh my God!'

A large orange plaster was stuck above her right eyebrow; another was on the end of her chin. The left side of her jaw was purple. Her nose was shinily red. Both her eyes were sunken into black sockets which shaded onto her cheekbones in lurid pools of navy and yellow.

Cassie put in reassuringly, 'I told you, it's bruising, that's all. There's no damage apart from the cuts under the plasters. Truly, Hon, a fortnight, you'll look fine.'

Gina, aghast, said, 'But what about ...?'

The door opened and Fallon walked in.

Cassie quickly stepped back from the bed. 'Well,' she said, looking from one to the other, 'I'll leave you both to it. See you later.' And with a smile she ducked out.

Gina was still holding the compact in the air. She stared numbly at Fallon. Then she slowly lowered her arm and said quietly, 'It's very good to see you.'

He said, 'It's good to see you too.'

'I didn't have time to comb my hair.'

He came and sat beside the bed. 'Seems fine to me.'

Gina said, 'I guess I look a bit eccentric.'

He scanned her face. 'Well,' he shrugged, 'you always were a very colourful lady.'

It was the happiest moment Gina had had in she couldn't remember how long. Afterwards, however, she and Fallon talked more seriously. They talked until the nurse came and said Gina really must get some rest. Before the Englishman left, Gina said quietly, 'It's what I have to do, Fallon. You understand?'

Fallon nodded, slowly. 'Yes,' he said, 'I understand.'

Over the next two days there were so many visitors. Cassie came again, with Robbie. Irving followed, and Harry and Max and Chang and Gina's sister Paola and cousins flown all the way from Italy; and they all brought magazines and books and candy and fruit and divers bottles the contents of which were forbidden absolutely said the nurse before joining Gina in sampling ('Purely for medicinal purposes, mind') one of the more golden-hued brews.

Gina felt better with each passing hour. By the afternoon of this day she was out of bed and in an armchair by the window; and in a quiet quarter hour between visitors felt confident enough to close her eyes and relive the events which had brought her here. When she opened her eyes she was trembling a little, but was otherwise unharmed. She could face the past. Now she must build her strength to face the future.

She looked up, and saw Howard.

He stood in the doorway for some moments before advancing slowly into the room. He was wearing a dark grey suit and blue patterned tie; but somehow the clothes looked unfresh, as if they'd been worn for several days, and, as he came closer, Gina saw that his jaw was badly shaved, his hair uncombed.

Gina, disconcerted, said, 'Hello, Howard.'

He looked at her, his jaw muscles working. 'Gina ...' he began, but right away faltered, a painful frown disfiguring his face. He dropped into the chair facing Gina.

She said, concerned, 'Howard, are you ill?'

He stared at her as if he hadn't heard. 'Ill?' He shook his head, glancing around the room. 'No, I'm not ill.' Then he asked abruptly, 'How are you feeling?'

Unsettled by his strange manner, Gina did her best to remain calm. 'Fine, thank you,' she replied. 'Cuts and bruises, apart from the arm. I was lucky. I know what happened, Howard. If you hadn't come up the stairs when you did ... Well, thanks, anyway.' She smiled.

He'd watched her as she spoke, but, she felt, he hadn't really been listening. She thought of what she'd been considering the moment before he'd arrived. The future. She had to talk with Howard about their future, and, despite the present circumstances, it must be soon. But could she do it now? Here under these alien conditions? Would it be better to wait, at least until she was out of the hospital?

He blurted, 'Oh, God, Gina, I never meant any of it to happen. I'm so sorry. But, honestly, I didn't expect it to go so far. I didn't expect ... All those people ... He told me it would be only one or two ... Nothing serious ... Just enough to cause ...' He broke off, his expression tormented.

Gina's thoughts were spinning. She struggled to understand her husband's outburst. 'Howard, what are you talking about? All those people? What people?'

He looked at her. 'In San Francisco.'

Gina couldn't speak. Too much was happening in her head. She stared at her husband's face, and though it remained waxenly inanimate she imagined she saw the lips move and repeat the name. San Francisco. A chill knifed her. She was caught in a blizzard of memories.

Howard said hoarsely, 'At the Embarcardero Cornell. The people who were ... poisoned. Gina, I swear to God, I thought they'd just get a little sick, just a few of them. I never intended ...' He stopped again, wiped his hands across his face as if swabbing away a feverish sweat.

Gina was floundering in a rising tide of alarm. Comprehension of what her husband was saying was breaking over her in frightening waves. With a huge effort of self-control she said levelly, 'Howard, are you telling me you were responsible for what happened at the hotel?'

His answer was a ragged whisper. 'Yes.'

Gina felt suddenly faint.

Howard said, 'Oliver told me it would be all right.'

Blood surged in Gina's head. Her mind rushed toward the point of unconsciousness. She squeezed shut her eyes, teetering on the brink. Then she pulled herself back. She opened her eyes, to see her husband with ice-cold clarity. She said, 'Randolph?'

Howard gave a single nod.

'What did he say would be all right?'

'The shrimp. The contamination. He said there was so little salmonella in the shrimp, only the most susceptible guests would be affected. He said they'd just have stomach pains. I told him I didn't want anyone really harmed. I only wanted ...' Howard looked at Gina. 'I only wanted ... to hurt you.' He released a breath and his shoulders sagged.

Gina was struggling for comprehension. At the same time her brain was being bombarded with the implications of Howard's revelations. The mental turmoil continued for several moments until she realized Howard was speaking again:

'... it was the business. The damn business.' He wasn't looking at his wife, but staring at his hands clenched on his knees. 'At first I thought ... that perhaps ... perhaps I'd just damage the business enough so you'd want to be rid of it. I'd tried to talk about it so often, your giving up the business, but you were always too involved to really listen. That's how it had always been, when mother was alive. All my life there was the damn business.' He fell silent again, still staring at his hands. But presently he looked up, directly at Gina, and when he spoke again his voice was a little steadier:

'It was the note that gave me the idea. Months ago. I saw it in your bedside cabinet, the afternoon when we'd ...' He paused. 'Anyhow, I went back there and copied it. It wasn't so difficult, just a green crayon scrawl. But then I wasn't sure how to use it. It wasn't until ... until I talked to Oliver Randolph, the day after you said we had to discuss our future. That was when all I really wanted to do was hurt you. I told Oliver Randolph – I'd been seeing him on and off, since I'd run in to him months before, one lunchtime at the Plaza. He was sympathetic. And he said he'd help. But, on my life, Gina, I never realized what he was planning.'

Gina's mouth was now so dry she felt she was unable to speak. She strove to put together the pieces of Howard's fragmented discourse. The mass poisoning. West-Rossi's subsequent near-collapse. The Randolph Corporation's offer via the attorney Scheer. Randolph's ruthless empire building.

Howard continued, 'He thought you'd sell. When you

refused, when it began to look as if you – the company – might recover, he had Tony Nevada name you to the UnAmerican Activities Committee.'

Gina whispered, 'My God.'

Howard said flatly, 'Nevada would do anything to further his career. He now has a multi-million dollar contract with the Randolph Corporation's entertainment division.' He quirked his mouth bitterly. 'That's the way Randolph operates. He uses people. If only I'd known before ...'

Gina was still striving to complete the picture. There were so many questions in her head. But, at the moment, she couldn't possibly begin to put them into sequence. She did, however, understand the basic facts. And she believed them. She believed Oliver Randolph to be capable of anything. She believed her husband could have wanted, in his confused way, to hurt her and the company which he had resented all his life. She believed she must bear part of the blame for all that had taken place.

Howard said, 'What will happen, Gina?'

She pulled her attention back to his questioning face. For an instant the light behind his eyes was that of a child before a parent. But the impression passed in a blink and Gina was simply looking at a frightened adult. And that was how it had to be. In spite of all Howard had just revealed – perhaps because of it – Gina knew she must not alter the decisions she'd already made.

She said, 'What's done is done, Howard.'

He faltered, 'But ... all those people?'

'They recovered. They're fine now.'

'The police?'

Gina thought of Detective Sergeant Shaughnessy, something he'd said after he'd secured her release from the jail cell and contrived the disappearance of her name from a detainees list: 'We're both going to tell ourselves we're just like everybody else in this world, trying to get by the best way we know how.'

She said quietly to Howard, 'They assumed the poisoner was Gant. That he was a psychopath. And, it seems, he was. With him dead, I expect the file will be closed. I think it should stay that way.'

Howard sat in silence. Then he passed a hand across his eyes and let out a low shuddering breath. He looked at his wife. 'I'm truly sorry, Gina.'

She returned, 'I know you are.'

'I wish …'

'Please don't.'

Howard hesitated, but then nodded. 'No,' he said, 'there isn't much point now, is there.' He turned to the window, and the late afternoon sunlight softened the drawn lines of his features. He remained staring out for several moments. At last he looked back at Gina. 'When shall we talk?' he asked.

Chapter Twenty Eight

The tan-uniformed security guard in the office block's bustling main lobby didn't question her when she showed him her business card and said she had an appointment. He said, 'Top floor, ma'am. The receptionist will take care of you,' and he smiled, gave a small salute as Gina thanked him and headed for the bank of elevators.

The receptionist, a sharp-faced brunette, looked up abruptly when Gina strode past her desk. 'Who ...? Do you have an appoint ...?' She was on her feet, trying to head Gina off before she reached the door. 'You can't go in ...'

Gina seized the handle, flung open the door, advanced, taking rapid stock of the vast purple-carpeted office, black leather sofas, panelled walls, the huge, curving mahogany desk, the man behind it.

Oliver Randolph jerked back in his baronial chair, shock contorting his gross features.

The receptionist was running in behind Gina, bleating, 'Sir. I'm sorry. I couldn't stop her. She ...'

Gina halted in front of the desk, ignoring the woman completely, dropped her briefcase flat on the desktop, snapped its catches with the hand of her unplastered arm, opened the lid, extracted the black and white photographs and slim, grey contract. 'Some property of yours,' she rapped, tossing the bundle in front of the astonished man. 'I think it would be a good idea if you destroyed them, along with the negatives, and Tony Nevada's contract, and anything linking you to a consignment of contaminated shrimps delivered to ...'

'That's enough,' barked Randolph; words he had thrown at Gina once before, but now they were laced with alarm rather than menace. He shot a look past her to the receptionist. 'Get out,' he ordered the woman. 'I'll take care of this.'

The receptionist hesitated but an instant before retreating and banging shut the door in her wake.

Randolph took the seconds to attempt to gather himself. Gripping the edge of the desk with his sausage fingers, he darted his eyes over Gina's face, which, the bruising's black and blue having turned greener and yellower with healing, was now even more livid than it had been when Gina had first seen it five days ago. Randolph seemed to shudder at the sight. Or it might have been from the savagery he saw in Gina's eyes. His tongue ran rapidly along his fat lower lip.

And Gina knew his mouth was dry. All vestige of the arrogance she had seen on his face when last they met was gone. He had the look of a cornered animal.

Gina didn't give him chance to speak. 'Don't waste time with denials,' she warned harshly. 'You know I wouldn't be here if I didn't have it all. Not the details, of course, like where you obtained the contaminated shrimp, or which of the hoodlums you employ are involved. But the police will soon find out, once they start investigating, once your crooked minions are pulled in for questioning, once Tony Nevada starts squawking to save his own neck.'

Randolph's gross features had become ashen, sweat was standing in beads on his forehead and upper lip. He opened his mouth to speak but was forestalled by Gina again reaching into her briefcase, extracting a folded document, dropping it in front of him and ordering:

'Read it.'

His harrowed gaze travelled from Gina to the document, around the office, back to the document. He lifted it, opened it, slowly scanned the typewritten paragraphs.

Gina grated, 'And sign it.'

Randolph's head jerked up. 'If you think …'

'Yes, I do think,' Gina retaliated viciously. 'It's perfectly legal and above board. And the price is fair. The price is fair for both of us.' She glared at the sweating features before her. 'Sign it,' she hissed, 'or everything I know goes to the police.'

Randolph ventured hoarsely, 'You wouldn't dare.'

Gina said, 'Ten seconds.'

The gross man's mental havoc flickered across his face. All at once a spark lit far behind his eyes. In a voice ravaged by anger and panic he countered, 'If you give anything to the police, your husband ...'

Gina bashed her fist down on the desktop, causing pain to flame up her arm, savaging her battered features into a fearful mask. She thrust her head and shoulders forward. 'My husband,' she rasped, 'is suing me for divorce.'

Chapter Twenty Nine

'How is your arm?' asked Mickey.

'Itches like mad,' replied Gina, smiling, 'but otherwise, thanks, it's fine. How's the show going?'

The young dancer answered enthusiastically, went on to relate all the offers she'd been getting from theatre and movie producers. Gina responded here and there with anecdotes about their mutual showbusiness acquaintances. Filipo cheerfully put in his contribution too.

They were sitting around a coffee table in Gina's office at the West-Rossi Building. It was two days since Gina had faced Oliver Randolph. No one knew that confrontation had taken place. Since then Gina had continued to receive well-wishing visitors from all over the country, but none, not even her closest relatives and friends, had ventured to discuss anything more controversial than the weather. Gina had been grateful for the consideration, but, she had decided this morning, there were realities to face and they couldn't be put off any longer.

She continued to chat pleasurably with Mickey until the young dancer declared she must dash for a photo session with one of the new fan magazines. As Filipo rose to leave with Mickey, Gina said to him, 'I'd like you to stay awhile, if you've time.'

'No problem,' he returned, and after Mickey had said her goodbyes he dropped back into the chair facing Gina. He sat with his feet apart, arms resting loosely on his knees. He was wearing a brown tweed sports jacket and a maroon polo neck sweater. His shiny black hair fell in waves on his brow, and his strong jaw was darkly shadowed.

He was, thought Gina, a very handsome man. She smiled,

'There's something I have to tell you.'

He said, 'Oh? And I you.'

Slightly off her stride, Gina said, 'Okay, you first.'

Filipo looked down at his knuckles before facing his sister and saying, 'It's about Barbara.'

Gina's amiability faltered.

Filipo began, 'These past few weeks, ever since the food poisoning, she's been wanting to talk to you. But, things as they were, the time just wasn't right. And now, what with the UnAmerican Activities hearing and all, she thought you still wouldn't be in the frame of mind to discuss it.' He ran a hand through his hair. 'But,' he went on, 'we have to discuss it sooner or later. It's too important to keep putting off. I know Barbara wanted to be with me when we told you, but, I figured, under the present circumstances it would be better if I talked with you alone.'

Gina's pulse had accelerated.

Filipo searched her face. 'Sis? You look ... Is your arm bothering you?' He frowned. 'Maybe this wasn't such a good idea. I'm sorry. You're tired. We'll talk tomorrow.'

Gina said quickly, 'No. My arm's fine. You have something to say. I'd like to hear it now.' Actually she wasn't too sure about that. Until a few moments ago the memory of the incident in the Embarcadero Cornell ballroom had been far down her list of priorities. However, now that her brother was on the brink of opening up about his relationship with the ex-actress, Gina was not about to let the opportunity pass.

She prompted, 'Well?'

He said, 'Barbara wants to buy into Monument.'

Gina's jaw didn't quite drop to her chest.

Filipo, straightening suddenly, said, 'Sis, I realize you're surprised. I know Barbara's never given you any hint of this. But she has discussed it with me. We've discussed it in detail. You know, she understands a great deal about movies. Sure, she's been out of the industry for a long time, but she's kept in touch with all its developments, technical as well as artistic. And, since she's been back in the States, she's devoted almost all her time to studying the present condition of Hollywood and its product. So, please don't think she's just having a nostalgic whim. Far from it. She has some very dynamic ideas about the route Monument ought to take.' He paused before adding, 'And I absolutely agree with her.' He looked directly into Gina's eyes.

Gina was busy gathering her wits. Her brother's revelation had caught her so off guard she hadn't quite heard all he'd said. But, she thought, she'd heard enough. 'Well,' she said, looking him over as if discovering him for the first time. 'Well.'

Filipo said, 'Well?'

Gina felt rather like a bird with ruffled feathers. Invisibly, she smoothed them, more or less. She said, 'You say you've discussed the matter with her – with Barbara – in detail. Has that included financial detail?'

'Yes.'

'How much does she want to invest?'

'Ten million.'

Gina hoped the astonishment which leapt within her head didn't reach her face. With what she thought was great equanimity, she said, 'I see.' This gave her a few seconds in which to at least partly digest the information.

Filipo said, 'Not necessarily as a lump sum, of course. We've discussed the immediate need for a cash injection of five. Barbara would stand guarantor for the same sum, which would give us a three-fold collateral capacity. We've also studied the real estate potential of part of Monument's acreage. There's another ten to twelve million development value there. But, with long-term rental facility and lease-back arrangements, the figure could be almost treble. Barbara and I have researched the current property market, expansion, and …'

Filipo continued.

And Gina listened. But, again, she didn't hear all of it. She was thinking not so much about what her brother was saying, as how he was saying it. She could see the enthusiasm on his face; she could almost see the excitement in the tension of his muscles as he expounded his financial strategies. And she knew what he was feeling. Because wasn't it exactly how she felt whenever she put her own schemes into words? She watched Filipo, thinking, My brother, the attorney. My brother, the future of the Rossi family.

It was several minutes before Filipo broke off and with an apologetic smile said, 'I guess I'm running on a bit. Beginning to sound like a tycoon. Sorry, Sis. I realize how much you have to cope with right now. But, for the time being, I'd just like to know what you think of the idea in general.' He added, 'So's I can tell Barbara when I see her.'

Gina asked, 'When might that be?'

The sudden question obviously took Filipo by surprise. He gave it a couple of moments' consideration before answering. 'Actually, I might be seeing her this evening. She moved into a new apartment, here in Manhattan, a couple of days ago. I haven't seen it yet. I have an invitation. To be honest, I will be seeing her this evening, for dinner.'

Gina remained quite still. In her head she saw Filipo and Barbara Graham facing each other across a candlelit table. She considered the road she now could go down, and where it might lead. She said, 'I hope you have a pleasant time. Tell Barbara I think her desire to invest in Monument is marvellous news, and very welcome.'

Filipo stared. Then his face lit with pleasure. 'Sis, thanks. Thanks a million. I knew you'd understand.' He moved swiftly forward and kissed her.

As he dropped back, beaming, onto his chair, Gina regarded him with great fondness, and, just for that moment, he was her little brother once more. Then she blinked; and looked at the man. 'Now,' she said with a fresh shot of energy, 'it's my turn to tell what I've been planning.'

Chapter Thirty

The sunlight scattered leafy shadows along the Central Park pathway. On the grass and beneath the trees, youngsters ran and called, old-timers strolled, nannies perambulated their charges, young couples wandered hand-in-hand. It was pleasantly warm. Gina was wearing a pale blue cotton dress, her arm neatly across her middle in a white sling. She was hatless, her blonde hair brushed into a casual halo around her healing face. Sitting on the wooden bench she tossed the last crumbs of the picnic lunch to the sauntering pigeons and continued:

'And they intend turning over four of the sound stages to the production of television programmes. You know how I've always felt about television. Still, Harry says all the major movie studios will soon be following suit. So ...' She shrugged and smiled.

Fallon nodded understanding. He was sitting with his arms along the back of the bench, his legs straight out before him. His plaid shirt was open at the throat. He asked, 'And Filipo and Barbara Graham?'

Gina gave a small sigh. 'I'm really not sure. But, I realize now, it isn't for me to interfere – much as I can't help wanting to. After all, he's twenty-four years old. Can you believe it? Of course, I'd have been over the moon if he'd ended up with Mickey, but, I know, that was never likely, just my wishful thinking.'

Fallon said, 'I can see how it might have been. But, don't worry, Filipo's just taking his first big steps. Maybe he'll trip up a couple of times. But, then, we all have to graze our knees once in a while, don't we?' He looked into Gina's eyes for a moment, then shifted his position, crossed his legs, turned toward her. 'Was Howard okay when he left?'

'Yes,' Gina said quietly. 'It would be wrong to say we parted the best of friends. But we didn't have any cross words. Nor will we in the future. We've agreed on our settlement. The attorneys will take care of the rest.' She paused before adding, 'If you don't mind, Fallon, I'd rather not talk about it just now.'

'Sure.' He turned to watch the sunny scene.

Gina remained looking at his profile: the craggy nose and squarish jaw; his dark hair charged with grey, falling over his shirt collar; eyes that had seen so much. She said, 'We've set up a press conference for the morning. By this time tomorrow it will be public knowledge that I've resigned from West-Rossi.'

Fallon was facing her once more. 'You didn't tell me how they took it at the board meeting.'

'About as I'd expected. Of course they all said I had to stay, that with the investment from Barbara Graham, plus the collateral raised on the proposed Monument land development, the company could ride out the anti-Communist storms which are going to continue until I've appeared before the Committee. But I told them it wasn't what I wanted. They've ridden through enough because of me, and not just Harry and Cass and Irving and all the other directors, but everyone else, from the franchisees to the kitchen hands, from our truck drivers to our ledger clerks. I told them I wanted to end all the storms now; all the anti-West-Rossi publicity, picketing, filthy letters – and worse – being sent to employees' homes. And the surest way to end it was with my resignation, completely and utterly, for all the world to see.' Gina took a breath and concluded, 'So, it's done.'

Fallon studied her, his eyes caring.

'Please, don't worry.' Gina reached out and laid her hand over his knuckles. 'It doesn't hurt. Truly. Well, less, anyway, than I thought it would.'

Fallon gathered her hand into his.

She held onto his grip, tightly. She thought of her coming appearance before the Committee. And the thought frightened her. There would, she knew, be so much to face in the coming weeks. But she'd see it through. She had to see it through. And afterwards? Well, life isn't a fairy tale, you don't just wave a magic wand and make it all come out right in the end. What you do is turn over the page, hope you've learned a little from what went before, start another chapter. It's the learning that's important, thought Gina. Not what you did, but what you learned. Because in the end, the very end, no matter how high the mountain you've climbed, standing on the summit counts for naught if you didn't see anything along the way.

She gave Fallon's hand a squeeze, released it.

'Anyhow,' she said with a sudden bright smile, 'remember I still have The Lady. The only place in town that serves Key lime pie. What more could I want?'

Fallon regarded her from beneath one arched brow.

She leaned forward then and kissed him on the lips. Moving back, she watched his lips.

He said, 'I love you, Gina.'

She said, 'I love you too, Robert.'

The casinos were gigantic jewels – ruby, emerald, sapphire, amethyst, diamond – light blazing from all their facets against the black velvet backdrop of the Nevada night. Automobiles, buses, taxis and limousines streamed back and forth along the glittering ribbon of The Strip. Couples in evening dress wandered the palm-lined walkways. Groups of tourists gesticulated in awe and wonderment. Excitement crackled in the air like summer lightning.

Gina stood beside Max in the paved forecourt, her back to the parade of glass entrance doors, looking out toward the brilliant boulevard. For a moment her mind went back to the first time she and her godfather had come here, to a scantly-used desert highway, a handful of hotels scattered amid the cactus and creosote bushes four miles from the small desert town of Las Vegas. 'It will grow,' Max had said. 'This is where the future lies.' And Gina had seen the hope in his eyes, the wishes she herself had made when first she saw the derelict villa which would become The Lady.

She smiled at him now.

The plaster had come off her arm two days ago, before she

caught the flight from Manhattan. She was holding her silver evening purse in that hand; with the other she extracted a folded sheet of paper and handed it to Max.

The big man, with a puzzled look, took it, unfolded it, and stared. Gina watched his eyes as he exclaimed, 'But, Principessa ... *Che cos'e questo*? What is this?'

She said, 'Something Oliver Randolph signed.'

'But ... *Non capisco* ... Is it ...?'

'All legal and above board.'

Max continued to stare.

Gina looked at his face with all the affection in the world. 'Anyhow,' she said briskly, 'you can read the small print later.' She turned with him toward the entrance doors. 'Right now, how about we look at your new property?' And she slipped her arm through his, moved close beside him, and together they went into the Bikini Beach.